Kätchen's Continued Story

A German Girl
Like Me – Book 2

by
Joseph R. Costa

D1378326

To my wonderful wife Kathy

In memory of my Father and
brothers Bill, Larry and Frank

ISBN-13: 9781520464060

Contents

Chapter 1
Early March 1941

WHEN YOU GET OLDER and think back on your life, there are probably things you wish you had done better or hadn't done. Recently, I have been thinking back on my own life, remembering my years growing up in Nazi Germany, of immigrating to America before the war, and my time here during the early war years. I was worried then about my family still back in Germany and my boyfriend who had been pulled into the war. The times were difficult but memorable ones for me. Even so, I can't help but smile as I remember some things back then, like those two cute little kids, when I worked as a nanny.

* * *

It was late at night as I carefully tiptoed down the carpeted hallway, stopping for a moment outside the kid's bedroom to listen. All was quiet.

"Good," I said to myself. Opening the door slowly, I looked in. From the light of a lamp in the corner of the room, I could see Susan and Jimmy covered up in their beds and hear their deep breathing.

Now six and seven years old, they were running wild when I first came here to work two years ago. Needing a job after being fired from my job at a bakery, I had accepted this job as the live-in cook and nanny. The Gentsch family was one of many affluent families here in Atherton, California. Without much trouble, I was able to shape the two wild little things into those two cute kids sleeping away in their beds.

Closing the door, I continued quietly down the hall to my room. On my Saturday off, I had gone in the morning

1

to help my Aunt Minna in her restaurant in the hills above San Carlos. I spent the entire day there working. So, at ten thirty at night, I was tired and finally back in my room.

After undressing and getting into my night clothes, I sat down at the vanity to brush my hair in the mirror before going to bed. Looking at myself in the mirror, it suddenly occurred to me, that after less than four years here, I now looked like an American, not a German. Maybe it was the California sun, I thought.

My name is Kätchen, which is pronounced "Kay-chen" similar the American word "kitchen." That's as close as Americans could come to pronouncing my German name. It was just another adjustment I made after immigrating to America.

Looking down, I saw the small framed picture sitting on my vanity. As I have done many times before, I picked it up and sadly looked at it up close. Looking back at me were the happy faces of my mother, father, Ruth, and me. It was a picture from happier times in Germany before the Nazis came to power. In 1931 when I was twelve years old, my mother had a street photographer come up one evening to our apartment in Hamburg, Germany to take it. To the best of my knowledge, my mother, father, and Ruth still lived in that apartment. At least, I hoped they did.

Mail service between America and Germany stopped unexpectedly a few months after the war in Europe began in September 1939. Now in early March 1941, I've had no communication with them in the last year and a half, even though America was not even in the war.

In the newspapers, I read how Hamburg has been bombed by the British a number of times. Their apartment was located, fortunately, not near the city center or an industrial area. So I could only hope they were well and still

2

living there in the apartment. Naturally, I thought about them often and worried for their safety.

My sister Ruth looks so pretty in the picture. She was always such a pretty thing. We were as close as sisters could be when I left for America. That's the last time I saw her, when she was fourteen years old. She's eighteen now and must be a pretty girl. I can't imagine she isn't married.

* * *

Back in Hamburg, Ruth stood erect in her bridal dress as the veil was placed on her head. Looking very pretty, she stood still as the woman assisting her made last minute tugs and pulls to smooth out the various lines of the dress and fabric. With the bridal train arranged behind her, the woman stood back admiring her. Ruth smiled at her, and she smiled back. She was ready as she stood waiting for the music to begin.

As the bridal march began playing, the curtain parted and she walked out onto the stage. As she continued out onto the runway, several well-dressed women and a young woman were seated along it admiring the dress as Ruth walked out to the end, turned, and walked back. She stopped in front of them and made several left and right poses as they watched with eager expressions. Next, she continued on to her position on one side of the stage, where she turned again, straightened out her train, and stood smiling

Two models in two other bridal designs next paraded along the runway before taking their places beside her. Ruth exchanged glances and a brief smile with the other models. The customers came nearer to look over the designs more closely. After much discussion, excitement and more turns along the runway, they chose the dress Ruth was modeling and wanted one fitted for their daughter.

Ruth had worked in the dressmaking shop for about six months as an assistant dressmaker. When needed, she was occasionally asked to model dresses since the people there thought she had a nice figure and good looks.

That night, Ruth was setting out plates on the kitchen table as her mother stood at the stove stirring fried potatoes and eggs in a skillet. Her mother's name was Margarete, but to Ruth, she was Mutti (rhymes with "footie"), which is "Mom" in German. Ruth still lived with her parents in the apartment in Hamburg. She had been telling Mutti about the dressmaking shop.

"Is it that bad?" Mutti asked.

"I think so. I'm not sure how much longer their doors will be open. It's not just because of fabric shortages due to the war. The owners are Jewish. Our shop has probably only been allowed to stay in business this long because the wives of Nazi higher-ups think so highly of our dresses."

"I wasn't so lucky," Mutti mused. "The Nazi higher-ups shut down my theater company. The plays weren't German enough or something like that. Most of my sewing work was for them. I miss those times when I was making costumes for them and getting the material from my friend Johanna at her fabric shop. I don't like the woman in the fabric shop on Weide Street.

"But it was good that your friend Johanna was able to get away, to immigrate to Chicago, America. What terrible things they did to her store!"

Mutti replied sadly, "She had to operate those last few months with smashed and boarded up windows. Yes, I'm glad she got away, but I still miss her."

"I wouldn't blame the owners of my shop if they closed and left too, but I think they are hoping the anti-Jewish fervor of the Nazis will pass."

"They would be smart if they did close up and leave. It wouldn't be good for you, Ruth, but they would be smart if they did."

Mutti looked down into the pan of food she was cooking on the stove.

"Ruth, I'm sorry we're having fried potatoes and eggs with mustard gravy again. We have it much too often. I'm not a good cook like Kätchen. The cooking was so much better when she was here. How long has it been?"

"Not quite four years," Ruth said.

"How I wish you were there too. I don't know if your father could do without you, but I'd be happier if you were safe. If only you had been a little older, we would have sent you both back then."

Ruth looked sympathetically at Mutti, who regularly expressed her regrets at not sending Ruth to America with me before the war. Ruth, however, had no intention of going. She wanted to stay and watch out for our parents during the possible hard times. She never had to argue with her parents about it though. When the war started, immigrating to America was no longer an option.

"Of all the bad luck! We can't even send Kätchen a letter now, much less arrange for your immigration," Mutti agonized. "If only we had sent you sooner."

"Don't blame yourself, Mutti. Just be happy that Kätchen is there. Thank goodness Rolf convinced her to go so she would be safe there. He knew a war was coming."

Standing beside Mutti at the stove, Ruth patted her on the shoulder.

"Although I miss Kätchen and her cooking, I like your eggs and potatoes, so don't worry about making them too often."

Mutti smiled at Ruth and turned off the burner.

"The food is ready. Where's your father?"

Right on cue, they heard footsteps out in the hallway, and the apartment door opened. Ruth's father, Gustav, walked briskly in carrying a small paper bag.

"Hello, did I make it on time for a change?" he asked cheerfully.

"Gustav, amazingly you have," Mutti replied as she spooned the eggs and potatoes onto the plates on the table.

"Hello, Vati," Ruth said. "Oh, what have you brought?" She called him Vati (pronounced "faw-tee"), which is "Dad" in German.

After giving Ruth a kiss on the cheek, he opened the bag so she could look.

"A couple Berliners, extras from the restaurant."

Handing the bag to Ruth, he said with a sigh, "These sugar covered doughnuts are the best things coming out of Berlin these days."

"Not too loud, Gustav. Someone will hear you. Hurry and wash up. Dinner is on the table."

"Yes, dear," he said as he gave Mutti a kiss on the cheek and hurried into the bathroom.

Chapter 2
Peril at Sea

STILL AT THE VANITY, I was lost in thought as I gazed at the picture of my family taken years ago back in Germany. With a sigh, I slowly put the picture back on the vanity. I paused, continuing to look at it. Then shifting my eyes to the small framed picture on the other side, I picked up and fondly examined it.

A handsome young man in a Luftwaffe (German air force) uniform sternly looked back at me. The young man in the picture was Rolf, who I planned to marry. Mutti, Ruth, and I had never seen Rolf when he wasn't cheerful and smiling, so we had laughed together when we first saw this picture. Such stern expressions were the required pose for these military pictures.

Rolf and I met back in Germany, fell in love, and would already have been married, if not for his military induction and then the war. As a machine gunner on a German bomber, I had worried terribly about him when the war began. When mail service with Germany ended, he was recovering from wounds received in the initial combat of the war. My fears and worries about him only grew when the war heated up, especially last summer and fall during the great air battles over England.

During all that time, I had no news of him, none at all. Then to my great relief, I received a Red Cross notification saying Rolf was a prisoner of war recovering from his injuries in a hospital in England. Not knowing the extent of his injuries, I could only hope they were not serious. For the last four months, I've been waiting anxiously for further news. In that amount of time, he was probably out of the hospital and in a prisoner of war camp. Still, it was such a relief for me to know Rolf was out of danger, safely recovering somewhere in England.

With that reassuring thought, I smiled at the picture, hugged it, and put it back down on the vanity. After a few more strokes with the hair brush, I set my alarm, climbed into bed, and turned out the light.

* * *

When reveille sounded and Rolf opened his eyes, it took him a moment to remember where he was. His head still hurt sometimes from his injuries and was foggy when he woke up. Looking out at the dense configuration of bunks five high, he remembered he was not in his bunk in the small corrugated metal hut at the prisoner of war camp in England anymore. Instead, he was at sea in the cargo hold of a British merchant ship, part of a merchant ship convoy headed across the Atlantic to Canada.

After his release from the English hospital, he had been held in one of the British prison camps run by the Royal Air Force (RAF) to house downed German airmen. But the camps had become dangerously overcrowded, so the British decided to transport large numbers of the prisoners on merchant ship convoys returning to Canada where they would be held in Canadian prison camps.

The Atlantic crossing was a perilous voyage for the brave men of these merchant ship convoys because packs of German U-boats (submarines) hunted, mercilessly torpedoed, and sank as many of these ships as they could. A total of six British and Canadian destroyers and corvettes were in escort trying to prevent it. The voyage was especially hazardous in the winter when their chances of survival in the freezing waters of the North Atlantic were small. This was true even more so for the German prisoners of war who were locked in their cargo hold, which had been temporarily converted to house and feed them during their trip across the Atlantic. Only the day before, Rolf and his friend Dieter had tried to joke about the frightening threat of being torpedoed by their fellow countrymen. It had possibly eased their tension a little, but they knew the U-boats were a serious threat to their safe passage across the Atlantic.

Later that morning, Rolf and Dieter were getting breakfast when they froze in surprise as the ship's General Quarters alarm suddenly sounded, followed by the announcement.

"General Quarters, General Quarters, all hands man your battle stations!"

Coming during breakfast, this was not one of their drills. Their merchant ship was under attack! With the clamor above of running men and slamming hatches, the threat of being torpedoed, which they had joked about to ease their stress, was no longer a laughing matter.

The ship made several violent maneuvers sending loose gear in their space crashing to the deck. The three inch gun forward began a steady booming fire and smaller caliber gunfire was heard. All indicating some kind of U-boat attack was in progress, which was unnerving for Rolf and the other German prisoners who knew that their chances of survival were very small if torpedoed.

They had already donned extra clothing and lifejackets. With no portholes, they had no means of seeing what was happening. They stood anxiously listening, trying to stay calm as they waited.

Little talk amongst the prisoners could be heard as each considered what might be his own last thoughts. Rolf thought of his family back in Germany and of me. He knew that I was unaware of his current peril. As far as I knew, he was still back in England. Before I left Germany for America, he had told me that if he survived the coming war, he would find me, and we would get married. He had survived several close calls already in the war. Now he needed to get by this one.

As they listened to the ship's big gun up forward booming and the other guns firing, every German prisoner there in the cargo hold was desperately hoping the German Navy would be unsuccessful this time.

Suddenly, a loud deafening explosion rocked the cargo hold, the ship shook violently, and the lights went out. Bunks, storage lockers, and other gear torn loose from foundations crashed down on the men. Many prisoners were knocked down in the dark by the shock of the explosion, and some were hit by and pinned beneath overturned bunks and dislodged gear.

The initial outcry of shock and surprise by many was followed by moments of stunned silence as the ship continued to vibrate. Then the silence was broken by the cries of injured men and sounds of men stirring and groping in the dark to assist each other.

The blast from the explosion had nearly knocked Rolf down. Impacting against someone next to him had kept him from being flung to the deck and injured more than he already was from his bomber crash injuries. Luckily, no structure of bunks had toppled onto him.

Amidst the confusion in the dark, Rolf numbly recognized that the thing they most dreaded had happened. Rolf steadied himself against a bunk and looked around in the darkness.

Several battery-powered battle lanterns came on and dimly lit a few corners of the cargo hold. In the dim light, Rolf could make out the shadowy figures of some of his fellow German prisoners struggling to help those pinned underneath gear. Several cracked water pipes above were spraying cold water, and men were wrapping towels and clothes around them to stop the spraying. Some were steadying themselves on nearby structures and looking about not sure what to do. There was nothing they could do. With their lifejackets already on, they hoped and prayed they would not have to use them.

Rolf noted with some relief that there had been no secondary explosions, and the ship had stopped shuddering. The cargo hold now smelled of smoke as well as its normal acrid smell. The booming of the ship's three-inch gun forward could still be heard as well as other gunfire. Everyone in the cargo hold feared the worst, that their ship had been torpedoed and would be going down. They cursed their own U-boats for attacking these ships despite the fact they knew German prisoners of war might be on them.

Fearing their end might be near, the prisoners grimly awaited the announcement to abandon ship on the ship's loud speaker system. Above on the main deck, they could hear people giving orders, running, yelling, and dragging equipment along. Locked inside the hold, the prisoners looked about nervously as they listened and waited for any sign of what was happening. Injured men were still being removed from beneath fallen bunks and equipment. An excited clamor of noise and talking among the men could be heard but no screaming and panic.

Rolf hoped the crew of this Allied merchant ship would be quick about letting them out of the cargo hold so they could get up to the main deck and to lifeboats. There wouldn't be much time. The torpedo had probably blasted a huge hole in the side of their ship under the waterline. Huge amounts of seawater were probably pouring into the lower decks, and soon the ship would start listing over and sinking.

Having only the single exit hatch and ladder up would be a big problem for the rapid evacuation of several hundred German prisoners from their cargo hold prison. If they did make it outside, the sudden rush of freezing cold air would take their breath away, and then they would likely have to jump into the painfully cold icy water. With luck, no oil and fire would be on the water.

Rolf pictured himself bobbing and swimming in the numbing frigid water, pushing floating debris out of his way. The lifejacket would keep him afloat while he struggled to reach a lifeboat. If he didn't reach it within several minutes, he would die from hypothermia, and his struggle would be over.

Worse yet, he was still recovering from his injuries sustained during their bomber's crash landing in England months earlier. Still stiff and not very mobile, what chance could he possibly have? He shuddered at the thought of his bloated dead body floating on the water. Thinking of his family and me, he knew his death would cause much grief and sadness for which he was sorry.

His friend Dieter had been quick to answer the calls for help by the trapped men after the explosion. Now coming back to check on Rolf, Dieter asked excitedly, "Rolf, are you all right?" Dieter was his friend and crewmate on his bomber. He had pulled Rolf from the wreckage of their downed bomber and saved him that time. Rolf wondered if Dieter would be able to save him again.

In the dim light, Rolf looked at Dieter and nodded that he was okay. But before he could speak, the ship heeled over steeply, and some heavy gear already loose on the deck slid to one side crashing into structures and people. It seemed like an ominous sign that things would soon be getting worse.

"Why aren't they letting us out of here?" someone shouted above the chaos.

Several prisoners were banging with their fists on the closed and locked exit hatch, "Hey! Let us out!"

Another voice yelled to stay calm.

"Dieter, things don't look too good for us," Rolf said shakily. "If you make it and I don't, let my family and Kätchen know that I was thinking of them in the end."

Bracing himself against a nearby bunk, Dieter was hanging onto Rolf and looking about deep in thought.

Rolf was surprised to hear Dieter say, "Rolf, I don't think we're sinking yet. I think we are still maneuvering and moving, not dead in the water. That's a good sign, Rolf. The torpedo must not have heavily damaged us. We haven't heard 'abandon ship' yet and..."

Dieter stopped midsentence at the crackle of the ship's loud speaker system coming on. Dieter hissed, "Listen!" They and everyone else in the cargo hold listened with bated breath, fearing the dreaded announcement to abandon ship.

But instead, something about damage control parties was announced, which they didn't understand. They gave a collective sigh of relief, thankful they did not hear the words "abandon ship." Over the noise in their cargo hold, they could still hear gunfire outside. Rolf braced himself as the ship heeled over to the other side. More heavy loose things slid across the deck to the other side, as well as water from the burst pipes.

By now, an open area in the center of the cargo hold had been cleared. The injured men pulled from the wreckage of overturned bunks were laid in the cleared area.

Others attended to their injuries as the ship heeled back and forth several more times less violently.

When the gunfire outside ceased, the prisoners looked about anxiously, not sure what to make of it. After a minute without any new alarming noises or announcements, Rolf and the others began to feel a glimmer of hope that all might not be lost after all, that the ship might not be going down. Hoping against hope, they waited in the dark.

When the lights suddenly flickered back on, several hundred tense faces began to smile happily and then cheer wildly in celebration! Some cried in their happiness. Dieter grinned and whooped loudly. In his excitement, he hugged Rolf a little too hard. But Rolf didn't really feel the pain in his own excitement.

Rolf, seeing a chair nearby, sat down. After a few stressful moments of shakiness and emotions, he finally was able to breathe a great sigh of relief.

Chapter 3
Little Angels

AWAKENED FROM my sound sleep, I reached groggily for the shutoff switch on the alarm clock. I finally found the switch and stopped the ringing.

Rubbing my eyes, I looked around in my room in the Gentsch's house. Looking again at the alarm clock, I made out that it was seven o'clock. Let's see, that's right. It's a Sunday morning.

I told myself I should get out of bed to wake up my two young charges and get them ready for the day. Too late. Unnoticed by me, the door of my room opened a little and Jimmy peered in. A split second later, both he and Susan burst through the door screaming, "Wake up! Wake up!" They jumped on me in bed and bounced up and down around me.

"Oh, you two monkeys!" I said playfully as I grabbed them and held them to me. Squirming and wriggling to get away, I let them loose. After a few more bounces, they pounced down beside me and cuddled up against me.

"We missed you yesterday," Susan said.

"Yeah, where were you?" Jimmy asked.

"I missed you both too. I was helping my aunt at her restaurant. I got back late and looked in on you. You two were sound asleep like two little angels."

"Were we really like little angels?" Susan asked.

"Yes, wings and all."

Susan looked at me with a big grin, but Jimmy said, "I thought we were monkeys?"

"No, you are my little angels," I said. "But right now we need to get you ready for Sunday school and church, and get you some breakfast."

"Awwww."

I got up and put on my robe and slippers as they tried to hide under my blankets. "Come on. Let's go," I said as I ushered them down from the bed and out the door.

While I was helping them dress in their room, I asked, "Did you have a good time yesterday with your mother?"

"We got to swim in the indoor pool at Mommy's club all afternoon. I got all wrinkly," Susan said excitedly.

"Wow. That sounds like fun."

"Yes, you should have come too. Why did you have to help your aunt?"

"My Aunt Minna helped bring me here from the country where I grew up. You know where that is, right?"

"Germany!" They both shouted.

"Yes, that's right. Well, I appreciate what she did for me, so I try to help her whenever I get a chance."

"Are there lots of germs in Germany?" Susan asked loudly with excitement.

With my hands on my hips in mock exasperation, I said, "Susan, you always ask that silly question!" They both giggled at my mock exasperation. It was a routine we always went through whenever Germany came up.

* * *

On a sidewalk in Hamburg, Mutti stood in line at a bakery. The euphoria in Germany after the initial rapid military victories in France and other countries was over. The people now faced what looked to be another long grinding war. Mutti glanced impatiently at the long line ahead of her and frowned. People walked briskly by her along the sidewalk. They did not look as happy and confident as they had looked not that long ago. A fire engine raced by without a siren. Everyone looked up when they heard a plane zoom by.

The German people had become painfully aware that Hitler was not invincible. He had not defeated the British as he had promised and the British were now starting to wreak their vengeance on German cities. During the month of May, Hamburg was bombed a number of nights. The bombing raids were becoming more frequent and heavier.

Up ahead in the line, Mutti could hear a woman telling those around her, "Compatriots. Hitler is a great man. A military genius! He knows what he's doing. He has a plan and will soon defeat the Englanders. Just like the French!" The other women immediately by her, not wanting to show any disagreement, nodded and said, "Yes, yes."

The woman, thinking they lacked enthusiasm, said, "What? You don't think so? He will. You'll see!"

The other women, fearing their lack of enthusiasm might get reported, said more heartily, "No, compatriot, we agree. It's only a matter of time!"

"Of course!" the Hitler supporter said, "Of course! He's a great man. He wanted peace with them, but now they will pay for their refusal with their blood."

The other women nodded in agreement and looked away. Soon the women in line were quiet again. They all gazed about, some looking impatient, all wondered how much longer they must wait for their loaf of bread.

Chapter 4
Canada

AFTER ARRIVING IN Canada, Rolf and the other newly arrived German prisoners of war were transported by train to a makeshift prison camp on the north shore of Lake Superior. The old wooden unpainted huts for housing the prisoners were built originally for the laborers of the nearby paper mill. A railroad spur from the main line, built originally for the paper mill, brought the prisoners right to the front of the camp.

The German U-boat attack on their ship during their transit across the Atlantic from England had been a harrowing experience for them. Afterward, they heard an account of what actually happened. On their sixth day at sea, the ships of their convoy were attacked in the early morning.

One U-boat had slipped through the escorting warships and appeared out of a fogbank two miles away just off the port bow of their merchant ship. Ten minutes before, the merchant ship had performed a course change as part of their random weaving pattern that by sheer luck put the submarine in the wrong position for a torpedo attack.

When emerging from the fogbank and seeing the situation, the U-boat's captain still thought he could get his kill. He decided to engage the merchant ship with the U-boat's deck gun as they sped across its bow to get away. If he could succeed in disabling the merchant ship before submerging to evade the escort destroyers, they could come back later to finish it off.

The three-inch gun on the bow of the merchant ship put some rounds close to the U-boat without hitting it. When the merchant ship's 20-mm guns had gotten some hits on the U-boat and killed two of their gun crew, the U-boat captain decided to break off the engagement and submerge sooner rather than later.

The U-boat's gun crew had gotten one hit on the merchant ship amidships, a glancing blow, causing a good deal of damage and some casualties. The shell from the U-boat had hit and exploded just aft of the cargo hold where Rolf and the other German prisoners were housed. It had given them quite a scare as they were listening anxiously without being able to see what was happening.

The U-boat managed to submerge and get away. Other U-boats of the pack sank three other merchant ships of the convoy with torpedoes that morning, so Rolf's ship had been very lucky.

A week or two after arriving at their prison camp, Rolf and Dieter emerged after lunch from a wooden building used as the camp dining hall. Before going back to his work at the camp woodshop, he paused with Dieter a few minutes to get some air.

The food served for lunch was filling and tasted good. Wood-burning stoves kept the living quarters warm. The beds were reasonable, and the wash facilities were clean and working. The guards treated them firmly but without abuse or hatred. Rolf expected life in a prisoner of war camp to be much worse.

Much of the work to operate the camp such as cooking, food service, firewood, cleaning, laundry, etc. was done by the prisoners. According to treaties, German officers were not required to work, but this was a camp for enlisted prisoners who were expected to work.

However, the work was something of a relief from the terrible boredom of prison life. Rolf had volunteered to help in the camp woodshop building new chairs, tables, bunks, and other furniture. Having been a cabinetmaker's apprentice in his father's shop before being drafted into the Luftwaffe, he was already experienced at such woodwork, which he enjoyed doing. Dieter was less excited about his assignment to the camp laundry.

So, who were their fellow prisoners? After capture, each German prisoner of war was interrogated and questioned concerning their opinions of Nazis and their conduct of the war. Prisoners evaluated to be Nazi fanatics were considered dangerous, separated from the others and held in high security prison camps. Rolf's camp was for prisoners judged not to be dangerous. They fought for Germany because service in the military was a part of German culture, and because they had no choice in the matter. They were not fanatic types who believed themselves part of an Aryan master race that would rule the world for a thousand years.

Rolf's prison camp still featured a high barbed-wire enclosure fence with guard towers, armed guards, daily musters, and periodic inspections. These seemed prudent precautions and measures to protect the public from the captured men of a ruthless enemy. As a further precaution, the prisoners were issued and wore jackets with a big red circle sewn on the back to identify them as prisoners of war.

Strolling over near the fence, Rolf and Dieter looked out at the nearby houses on the outskirts of the small mill town. Much of the town was hidden from the camp by trees. Several other prisoners were nearby in the yard of the prison camp. On this cool spring afternoon, a thin layer of snow covered the prison yard and its scattered dry tufts of grasses and weeds.

Rolf noticed an increased stir of activity at the prison camp offices outside the fence. Hearing a train whistle, Rolf said to Dieter, "These must be the new arrivals."

"Probably more fellow captives from England, I expect," Dieter said as the locomotive came into sight pulling three passenger cars and a caboose. Other prisoners, hearing the train, began coming out from the dining hall.

Soon, Dorfman, the third crewmember of their ill-fated bomber, was beside them watching too. Surprisingly, after their bomber was shot down and crashed in England, they found themselves still together in captivity. Having been through much together, they were fast friends and knew they could count on one another.

Regrettably, their pilot officer Captain Huber, the fourth member of their bomber crew, was not with them. Being an officer, he had been separated from them back in England and sent to a separate camp for officers. They suspected and hoped Captain Huber was also somewhere here in Canada in an officer's prison camp.

They watched there in the snowy yard for a few minutes with the others as the train came to a stop at the gate. Camp officials and guards were emerging from the buildings outside the gate to receive the new arrivals.

Guards exited from the train cars and took positions on top of and around the cars. An order was given and the prisoners began to file out of the cars carrying the small bags of their worldly possessions. Soon, the guards were forming up the prisoners and taking a muster.

Rolf turned and said, "I should get back to the woodshop. There are still some bunks and furniture to be finished for the new arrivals."

"So long, I'm off to the laundry," Dieter said departing.

It was only about a week after Rolf watched the train come into camp that he found himself on a similar train with Dieter, Dorfman, and others. In a regular passenger railcar, they sat, slept, and ate in the two-person seats on each side of the center aisle. Two armed guards were posted at one end of the car. Although not handcuffed, the prisoners were to remain in their seats during the trip.

Two months before, a prisoner had escaped by jumping out the window of one of these trains. So the guards were being cautious. The prisoner, a fighter pilot named Franz von Werra, made it across the border and turned himself in to authorities in the United States, a neutral country. A year later, he made it back to Germany, the only German prisoner held in Canada to do so during the war. But that's an aside.

Rolf looked up as one prisoner waved to a guard, who motioned for him to come forward. The prisoner stiffly stood up and made his way up the center aisle. After saying something to them, he left the car with one guard. The bathrooms were in the next car. Soon they were back again, and the prisoner returned to his seat.

Turning back to the window, Rolf watched for a while as the endless fields, woods, lakes, and small towns passed by.

"How many days have we been traveling?" he asked Dieter beside him.

"I lost track," Dieter replied stirring from his lethargy.

Dorfman, seated in the seat in front of them, turned around, "Fifty two hours. With an average speed of, say, thirty five kilometers per hour, I estimate we have traveled nearly 1,800 kilometers pretty much due west."

Dieter smiled. "Good old Dorfman. He was tops in dead reckoning in his navigator school, ya know."

"1,800 kilometers and we aren't there yet. How far is it from Rostock in northern Germany to Munich in the south?" Rolf asked.

Dorfman thought for a moment and said, "About 650 kilometers by air. We've already gone almost three times as far. Plus there was the trip from the ship to the first camp.

We passed through Quebec on the way. It took forty six hours from Quebec to the first camp. That adds another 1,600 for a total of 3,400 kilometers with most of it westward."

"Where's my lifejacket?" Dieter quipped. "We may go off a cliff and into the Pacific Ocean at any moment."

"Not likely," said Dorfman. "We haven't even reached their Rocky Mountains yet, and the Pacific Ocean is well beyond them."

"The vast distances here make Germany sound pretty small."

"Oh God, Rolf. Better not say that too loud. You'll be in trouble with some of our fellow inmates," Dieter said.

In a lower tone he added, "Of course, they would probably measure Germany differently, they would include Poland, Czechoslovakia, Austria, the low countries, and France. Oh yes, Denmark and Norway. I wonder why Switzerland isn't on the list too?"

"I don't know," Rolf said.

Dorfman had been listening and, after a few quick calculations in his head, piped up. "That's about 1,900 kilometers across."

Surprised that Dorfman was so engrossed in calculating distances rather than paying attention to his political commentary, Dieter stared at him for a few moments in silence.

He finally said, "1900 kilometers, you say, Dorfman? Yes, that does sound better. Doesn't it? Much better than 650."

Sleepily turning away back toward the window and the passing fields, he added with a yawn, "Better, yes, but probably still not big enough for them."

Chapter 5
Alberta Camp

ROLF EMERGED FROM the back of the covered military truck and paused to look around before climbing down to the ground.

"Come on. Out ya go," a guard said. At this, Rolf rigidly climbed down and followed the others.

"Line up in two ranks. Let's get a head count. See if we lost anyone," another guard commanded.

Only a couple days after their conversation in the train, they were finally at their new camp. The prisoners, stiff after riding several hours, were climbing out of three trucks, parked in front of the main gate of the prison enclosure. Two jeeps escorting the trucks were parked nearby.

Rolf got into the formation and stood as erect as he could. As the head count was being taken, he looked about at their new home. This camp contained the same features as the others: a high barbed wire fence with a gate, guard towers, and drab buildings from some pre-war use. Only this camp was smaller and surrounded by beautiful forests and mountains.

A guard shack stood by the gate and a guard there carrying a rifle was inspecting several prisoners carrying work tools and materials coming back in. One prisoner, after receiving a nod from the gate guard, strode out the gate. He rigidly took up a position next to the guard taking the head count and eyed the new arrivals as he waited.

With the head count completed, the guard announced, "All prisoners accounted for." He looked around and saw the prisoner patiently waiting beside him. Like the others, this prisoner wore no insignias or badges of rank, which were removed after capture.

Even so, to the prisoner at his side, the guard said, "Ah, there you are Master Sergeant. Right on time." Turning back to the new arrivals, he announced, "I'll turn you over now to Master Sergeant Restemeier here. He will take you in to get you a bunk and some lunch."

Restemeier nodded to the guard. He then turned to the new arrivals and snapped to attention. They straightened up too.

"I am Hauptfeldwebel Restemeier! I am in charge of day-to day operations here, and you all will be expected to do your part of the work. Any questions? Good! Dismissed! Follow me!"

He did an about-face and walked toward the gate. The new arrivals relaxed and informally followed him. The guard posted at the camp gate opened the gate and the prisoners filed in behind Restemeier.

In May of 1941, the war in Europe to Rolf seemed far away, which it was. Hitler had postponed indefinitely the invasion of England, but the war still raged in North Africa and the Balkans. No one knew how long the war would last or what the outcome would be.

The camp commandant addressed the new prisoners the day after their arrival. The gist of his speech was as follows. They were in a prison camp in the middle of a vast expanse of Canadian wilderness. It would do them little good to escape from the camp and its immediate enclosure. If they tried, they would either be eaten by the forest wildlife or caught quickly by Canadian Mounties. The camp was run more as a work camp than a prison. Those who became problems trying to escape would be sent to higher security camps, which were like prisons. The war was over for them, and they would probably be here for the duration of the war, however long that would be.

At the last camp, Rolf did some woodworking, which had reminded him of working in his father's cabinetmaking shop at home. He wished the war had never started and he was still back there working in his father's shop. He and I would be together, married, maybe with kids, and living near his parents. The war might appear to be over for him as the camp commandant said. But not really. He was still a prisoner in Canada, not where he would like to be.

Even so, his time in combat seemed to be over, which was a good thing. Earlier in the war, he had been offered the chance to enroll in pilot training and become a pilot, which would represent added status, responsibility and promotions. But he was not in the Luftwaffe because he wanted to be. He had been drafted. He had no ambitions to rise in the ranks and be in charge, so he had respectfully declined the chance to become a pilot.

Now he found himself, through no fault of his own, in the forests of the Canadian Rocky Mountains. Being killed or maimed was the expected fate of a bomber gunner in the war, not working in the woods of Canada. Even more unexpected was how well the Canadians were treating them. He, Dieter, and Dorfman agreed that they had been very lucky to have such good imprisoners. They doubted that Canadians were treated as well by the Germans.

Like the other camps, this work camp was for non-dangerous prisoners, but despite the weeding out process, a number the prisoners in camp were still Nazi supporters loyal to the Führer. They tended to be arrogant and less willing to contribute to camp work. They talked of their duty to escape, but very few escapes had in fact been previously attempted from their camp. Those escapees were quickly captured and returned. Rolf and the other prisoners were loyal Germans who would never inform on other prisoners, but they preferred to stay clear of the Nazi enthusiasts.

Up to this point in his captivity, Rolf had been only temporarily at places and not allowed to send letters to family. Since they appeared to have arrived at their final destination, Rolf learned from Master Sergeant Restemeier that letters to family were permitted. But letters were read, censored and traveled through a lengthy Red Cross transfer process. So he should not expect to say very much in them or to send and receive very many of them. Letters must be submitted unsealed to the camp office. Despite the sergeant's less-than-encouraging description of the mail system, Rolf started right away on letters to his mother and me.

Chapter 6
Decision

I HAD BEEN impatiently awaiting a letter from Rolf. The Red Cross notice had only said he was a prisoner of war in the hospital in England recovering from his injuries. Every day I hoped to hear something more.

In June, I finally received a Red Cross letter, four pages long with about half of the lines blacked out by a censor. Addressed to me at my Aunt's restaurant, Pepe brought it over as soon as they received it.

As I eagerly read through it, I was relieved to learn he was in good health and recovering from his injuries. He was now in a prison camp surrounded by mountains covered with beautiful forests of spruce, fir, and pine. My immediate thought was, "Silly Rolf, being a woodworker, only he would worry about what kind of trees they were."

The name of his camp was blacked out, but the letter seemed to have originated at a military base near Calgary, Alberta in Canada.

"Where was that?" I pondered. "He's not in England anymore. I don't know where Canada is. I'll have to go to the library. That's some country in the north somewhere, I think. Wait a minute. Canada? Does it really say Canada? Yes, it does. That's the country north of the here! He's on the same continent as me! Oh my God, I can't believe it!"

My immediate thought was to go there, see him, hug him, and help him. But I didn't know where or how far away Calgary, Alberta was. And the library was already closed for the day.

The next day, my two charges and I were at the front door of the Atherton library when it opened. I sat at a long wooden table looking at a large atlas.

"There it is. Alberta. Hmm. Canadians call them provinces instead of states. There's Calgary, in the lower part of it, near but not right on the American border."

Hearing Susan giggle, my thoughts were interrupted and I looked over at her. Sitting nearby looking at a children's book named *Ferdinand the Bull*, she was laughing at one of the pictures. Jimmy was bumping against her saying he wanted to see too.

"Shhhh. If you both can look at the pictures quietly for a few minutes, I'll read the book to you. It looks like a good one. Just give me a minute." With my two charges now more quiet, I looked back at the map of Alberta, Canada and then at its border with the US.

"Hmm," I thought as I flipped through the atlas to find U.S. states.

Two weeks later, I met with Magda and Hanni in a small coffee shop to eat lunch on my day off. They were my two girlfriends from the voyage to America. During the month-long trip on the boat, we had been inseparable close friends.

After our arrival here in San Francisco, we found our new homes to be not too far apart, so we periodically got together to reminisce and hear the latest. After meeting in front of the cafe, we came inside, sat down at a table and ordered. I had told them I had big news and they were eager to hear it.

"So, Kätchen, what is the big news you said you had for us? Let see… Mrs. Gentsch gave you a raise?" Hanni guessed.

Magda chimed in, "No Hanni, that's not it. Mr. Gentsch has introduced her to a Hollywood producer, and she's going to be a movie star."

"Good, Magda. I like that one," Hanni said as they both laughed.

"Hanni, Magda, I told you I had big news, and I do. You're not going to believe it."

"Oh, my gosh, Kätchen, did you get a letter from Rolf?" Magda guessed with excitement.

"Yes!"

Both Hanni and Magda looked at me in stunned silence for a moment.

"How is he? Was he badly hurt?" Hanni asked cautiously.

"He says he is in good health and recovering from his injuries. I still don't know the extent of his injuries, but he seems to be recovering from them."

"Oh, that's wonderful, Kätchen," Magda said, as she and Hanni hugged me happily.

"Did he tell you what happened?"

"Some of the letter was blacked out by censors, but it sounds like his plane was shot down over England, and he was hurt in the crash landing."

"But now he's out of the hospital and doing better?"

"Yes, he's now being held in a prison camp and it sounds like they are treating him well."

"Oh, that's wonderful, Kätchen. You've been worried about his injuries and it sounds like they weren't so bad. How wonderful."

Magda and Hanni could hardly contain themselves. They laughed, hugged me repeatedly, and shed tears of happiness. Once they were calmed down at little, I continued.

"But wait, here is the best part. You really aren't going to believe this."

"What? What could be better than what you just told us?"

"Yes, Kätchen, tell us."

"Like I said, you aren't going to believe it."

"Well, tell us then!"

"The prison camp isn't in England where he was captured." Both Hanni and Magda looked puzzled.

"Well, where is he being held?"

"He's in a prison camp in Canada."

"What? Canada, Canada, Canada...Where's that?" asked Magda.

"That's here north of the American states, isn't it?" Hanni said in astonishment.

"Yes, his prison camp is in western Canada, their state called Alberta."

"He's here on this side of the Atlantic? I can't believe it," Hanni said. Both she and Magda stared at me.

"I can't either," I told them. "He's been there a month already and it sounds like they aren't going to be moving him anymore."

"Alberta? Where is that? I can't believe he's here, that close. Is Alberta close enough for you to visit him?" Magda asked.

"I've been to the library. It's still pretty far from here, about a thousand miles."

"A thousand miles? That's still a long distance away."

"On this side of the border is the American state called Montana. There's a small town called Shelby there near the border."

"A small town? Why would you be interested in a small town there?" Hanni asked. Then it suddenly dawned on her, and the expression on her face changed from happiness to shock.

"No! Kätchen! Don't tell me you're thinking of moving there! Shelby? Nobody's ever heard of that place. It can't be anything like here. They might still have cowboys and Indians there, for God's sake."

"I haven't heard of it either," I said, "but yes, I've decided to move there so I can be near Rolf."

"You're doing what?" Magda asked in surprise.

"I'm going to move to that small town in Montana so I can be near Rolf and visit him in his camp."

"What? Are you serious? You don't know anything about that place. How are you going to live in a little town?" Hanni asked with a worried look.

"I'll get a job. My immigration visa allows me to live and work anywhere in the U.S. Leaving the U.S. for a short time is also permitted."

"Did Rolf ask you to move there in his letter?" Magda asked.

"No. I want to see him again, make sure he is well, and help him if I can."

"I guess I can understand you wanting to, but gee, Kätchen," Magda said, still unconvinced.

"Is he being held near the border by that town Shelby, and will they let you visit him in his prison?" Hanni asked.

"I don't know."

"Kätchen, maybe you should think about this some more," Hanni suggested. "Maybe you should just try to visit him first, before deciding to move to this little town you know nothing about." Both she and Magda looked concerned.

"I've already given notice to Mrs. Gentsch and bought a bus ticket. I plan to leave a week from tomorrow."

"Oh, my goodness, Kätchen. I hope you know what you are doing," Hanni said worriedly.

"I feel like I need to do it," I said with a look of determination.

Hanni's and Magda's faces no longer had the look of ecstatic happiness I saw earlier. They continued to question me about my plans and express their concerns, but I was resolved to go.

It would be hard to leave. I would miss my two girlfriends as well as Susan, Jimmy, and Mrs. Gentsch. In my two years, I had grown very fond of the Gentsch family, and I think I was a help to them. I would also miss my Aunt Minna and periodically helping her in her restaurant. It would be hard to leave, but I felt more the need to be with Rolf.

Chapter 7
Shelby

SMOKE CAME FLOATING back from the woman smoking a cigarette in the seat in front of me. Crinkling my nose at the smell of it, I fanned the smoke away with my hand and looked back out the window. A week after telling Magda and Hanni about leaving, I sat with a stoic look on my face, watching the countryside go by.

Looking around at the scattering of people on the bus, I noticed a creepy-looking middle-aged man, seated on the same row on the other side of the bus from me, was giving me the eye. Quickly looking away, I thought to myself, "So this is what bus travel is like." After looking out the window for a while, I could still feel the gaze of the creepy man on me. I turned around, and he was still looking at me with his dopey smile.

"Stop staring at me!" I shouted at him angrily. He was startled by this and quickly looked away. The others in the bus looked around to see what was going on, but I ignored them. I looked back out the window and thought, "God, how much longer till we get there?"

A few days later, I exited from a bus and looked around at the main street of the small town. A sign saying Shelby Hardware was on the front of one store. A hot afternoon in late June of 1941, the bus driver was sweating as he got my bag from the baggage compartment below the bus.

"Here you go, Miss," the bus driver said. "Shelby isn't much of a town." Looking along the street, he added, "You sure this is where you want to get off?"

"Yes, thanks," I said as I took my suitcase from him, smiled, and walked to the sidewalk.

Once on the sidewalk, I put my suitcase down, glad to finally be done with my bus ride. I looked up and down the street. A number of small businesses with storefronts were located along the street. I spotted what looked like a motel sign further down the street. Motels would cost more money than I wanted to pay, but if I couldn't find some kind of boarding house right away, I might have to stay there until I did.

Seeing a sign for Red's Cafe, I remembered my hunger. While getting something to eat there, I could inquire about a place in town to stay. It was a hot day to be trudging around with a suitcase, but thankfully it wasn't far.

When I got to Red's Cafe, I saw it was open and went in. A lunch counter with stools ran along one side, and a row of booths ran along the opposite side wall. A waitress in her mid-thirties wearing a red and white uniform stood behind the lunch counter. Behind her was a counter against a wall with a large opening in it to the kitchen. Through the opening, the cook with red hair looked out at me.

I can't imagine I was a very pretty sight after several days riding on the bus. Two older men with well-worn straw cowboy hats sat at the counter. One couple sat in one of the booths. As soon as I entered with my suitcase, everyone turned to look at me.

They all watched as I walked to an empty booth, put my suitcase on the seat on one side, and sat down on the other. The waitress came over with a pot of coffee and a menu. Her name, Angie, was on her nametag.

"Coffee?" she asked with a polite smile.

"Please." The waitress filled the cup already sitting in front of me and handed me a one-page menu.

"Here's our menu. Tuna Melt is our special today. I'll give you a chance to look it over."

"Thank you." She smiled again as she turned and walked off. After briefly looking over the menu, I decided I didn't want to spend the money for a full meal, even though I was hungry. I put the menu down and, when the waitress came back, ordered just a piece of apple pie.

When the waitress brought the pie, I said, "Thanks. I wonder if you can help me. I'm new in town and looking for a place to stay."

She looked over at my suitcase and then back up at me. "There's a motel a few blocks west of here on Main Street. But if you're gonna be staying a while, which it appears you might be, then you might try Mabel Martin. She rents out rooms in her house."

She led me over to the front window and pointing out the window said, "You go down that street right there. Ya gotta go two blocks, and then it's the third house on the left. A blue house. Can't miss it."

"Thanks." I said.

With a look of concern, the waitress added, "But it's a bit of a walk on a hot day with a suitcase," Glancing around, she said to one of the older men at the counter, "Pete. Maybe you could give her a ride when she's done eating her pie."

"Sure Angie, be glad to," he said giving me a little nod of his hat.

I could only smile and thank them for their helpfulness as I returned to the booth to eat my pie. Of course, everyone in the place was watching and listening. I must have been quite a novelty to them, the stranger with a funny accent.

A little while later, Mrs. Martin showed me into the room. It was roomy enough with a basic set of bedroom furniture as well as a chair and small table in one corner. A couple worn pictures of running horses hung on the wallpapered walls. The bathroom was out in the hallway. As she stood watching, I looked around the room, bounced my seat on the bed and looked out the window. It was clean, and it was cheap, so I told her I would take it.

Mrs. Martin was a middle-aged widow who rented rooms to make ends meet. She seemed nice enough and was not at all distrustful of me because of my accent. We talked some as she stood in the doorway and I brought my suitcase in.

"Kätchen, is that a Norwegian name? We get Norwegians from North Dakota through here every once in a while."

I smiled. "No, I emigrated here from Germany several years ago."

She looked at me earnestly. "Sounds like you got out just in time. Terrible, all that fighting going on over there in Europe. And the last one was supposed to be the war to end all wars. What a joke that is. They can't seem to get along over there. God knows, we'll probably get drawn into it again."

"I hope not, Mrs. Martin. It is a terrible thing. I know firsthand."

"I hope not too," she said with a sigh. Then perking up, "Well, Kätchen, I'll let you get settled. Let me know if you need anything."

"Thank you, Mrs. Martin. I will." At this, Mrs. Martin smiled, turned, and left the room, closing the door behind her.

The next day, I was hoping I might find work at Red's Cafe, but unfortunately, they weren't hiring. I inquired at another cafe, a grocery store, a dry goods store, as well as several others. It didn't take long for me to discover the only jobs in town were for cocktail waitresses at the two clubs on Main Street, which I didn't want to do.

Mrs. Martin knew of people in town who wanted housekeeping help. So the next afternoon, I was on my hands and knees scrubbing a kitchen floor with a scrub brush and bucket of soapy water. The apron I wore was borrowed from Mrs. Martin, but the handkerchief on my hair was my own. Housecleaning would have to do until I could find something better.

Several days after arriving in the little town, I paid a visit to the post office. I had received a letter late last year from the immigration service telling me I must register each month at my local post office. Since then, I religiously reported at the beginning of each month to avoid any problems with my immigration status. I walked into the small post office and up to the window. I didn't see anyone inside, so I said, "Hello, is anyone here?" A woman appeared with an annoyed look.

"Hello, I just moved here. I'm an immigrant and required to register at the post office where I live. Here is my paperwork."

The woman looked at me suspiciously, took the papers, and said, "We never had no aliens register here before, but I remember seeing something about it. Let me look it up. I'll be back in a minute."

"Thank you," I said as the woman disappeared. I stepped back from the teller window and looked around hoping it wasn't going to take long.

About a month after arriving in town, I happily found myself behind the counter at Red's Cafe. Their part time waitress, a local girl named Teri, left to join her boyfriend in Butte, where he had gone to get a job in the copper mines. Teri was apparently not a great employee or well liked, so I found it easy for me to fit right in.

The owner, Red, was a crusty but likeable middle-aged Irishman with a shock of red hair. He seemed to have taken an instant liking to me when I came into town. As soon as Teri left, he got word to Mrs. Martin that an opening was available.

Everyone in this little town seemed to know everything that happened here. I'm sure Red had heard about me doing cleaning work in town, and he probably thought I wasn't afraid of a little work, as they put it.

When I came in to see him about the job, I told him I heard there might be an opening.

He grinned at me and only said, "You're hired." Surprised by his answer, I could only smile and blush with unexpected happiness.

"Now go see Angie about getting a uniform so you can get started," he told me next. Still surprised by it all, I didn't move.

"Go on. You're hired. Go on. Get a uniform," he said, grinning and shooing me off with his hand.

So I rushed off to see Angie. Red got a big kick out of it and soon everyone heard about my "job interview" as he called it.

The waitress job was only part time, providing extra help during the busy times at lunch and dinner. But with the money from the cafe and the housekeeping, I was able to make ends meet and save enough for a trip to Calgary to look for Rolf.

Having done similar work at my aunt's restaurant, I was quickly able to fully perform my waitress duties. Shortly after starting, I carried a coffee pot to check on two regular customers, who wore cowboy hats and sat at our counter sipping coffee and talking for hours on end.

"Would you like more coffee, sir?"

"Sure, I reckon so. Fill 'er up. Only there's no need to be 'sirring' me none. Just call me Earl," he said.

"Will do," I said as I filled his cup.

"Thank ya, Katie."

"You're welcome, Earl," I said smiling at hearing my new name. Red told me the name "Kätchen" sounded too proper and foreign for a little town, so he decided I would be "Katie." I looked down at my nametag and smiled again.

At the end of July, my first monthly rent payment was due. Standing with Mrs. Martin in her living room, I counted out the money and handed it to her. She received it with a warm smile and seemed happy to have me staying with her, giving her some company in the house. Regularly, she would ask me to sit down and have some coffee with her, while she told me about the town and her late husband. Mrs. Martin had been very good to me.

In mid-August of 1941, I set out to visit Rolf. Since arriving in Shelby, I started wondering whether I would be allowed into Canada. I had not thought of that possibility back in California before moving. Back then the main questions were whether I would be allowed to visit him in his prison camp, or even where the prison camp was. Bringing my passport and paperwork with me, and facing this new uncertainty, I climbed on the bus.

The old bus bounced along on the rough road as I sat looking out. The road north to the Canadian border didn't offer much scenery to admire. The dry grass-covered, treeless rolling plains and wheat fields stretched to the horizon with a butte or a mountain in the distance.

Occasionally a farmhouse with grain silos and a few trees around it could be seen.

We lumbered along the old road for over an hour before reaching the little town right on the American side of the border. This town had looked too small on the map back in the Atherton library and after seeing it, I was glad to have picked Shelby.

Unlike America, Canada was at war with Germany, so would they allow me, a German, in the country? If not allowed into Canada, then visiting Rolf would be impossible, and I may as well return to California. Everything hinged on this moment. Would they let me in or not?

As our bus approached the border crossing, I was more than a little worried. The Canadian border guard came on the bus and quickly asked each rider two questions: "Are you visiting or on business?" and, "How long do you plan to stay?" Each person gave a reply and he moved on quickly without checking identifications. I began to think I had worried needlessly and it would be easier than I thought.

When he came to me and I replied, "Visiting", he noticed my German accent, scrutinized me a little more closely, and asked to see my identification. I handed him my passport and, naturally, my German passport with its swastika on the front cover caused his eyes to pop out a bit.

He politely escorted me off the bus to their office where I as well as my passport were photographed. He and another guard examined my papers closely, looked through my possessions briefly, asked a few more questions, and finally seemed satisfied.

It took about fifteen minutes, but I was soon on the bus again, and we were off, to the great relief of the others onboard who had been waiting impatiently. It was no surprise that they would pay more attention to the girl with the German accent, since they were at war with Germany. I was extremely relieved when they finally did allow me to enter the country.

From the border, the bus drove on for another four hours to reach Calgary. I would start asking there at the bus and train stations if anyone knew how I might find a nearby prisoner of war camp, one in the mountains and forests like Rolf had described in his letter.

Chapter 8
First Visitor

THE MILITARY TRUCK pulled up in front of the prisoner of war camp, stopping at the headquarters building outside the gate of the fenced-in area. A middle-aged Canadian soldier climbed out of the driver's side and walked into the building.

He was a member of the Veteran's Guard, which was composed of veterans from World War I who had volunteered for service again in World War II. Considered too old for overseas combat duty, they were being used for military assignments within Canada, one being prison guards at prisoner of war camps. Once inside, he walked up to the duty desk where the duty officer was seated doing paperwork. The soldier came to attention in front of the desk, and the duty officer looked up.

"Yes, Sergeant Evans?"

"Sir, there's a young lady out in the truck. She was in town asking around to find out how to get here to the camp. Someone in town directed her to the barracks there, and they directed her to where we get supplies. She found me there and asked if she could get a ride with me to the camp.

She knows the young prisoner Rolf Hosterman. She's gone through a good bit of trouble and expense to come visit him. She's traveled a long way from across the border. Rolf's a good lad. I was in the last war. So were you. You know how it can be. I felt sorry for the girl, so I gave her a ride."

The duty officer's eyebrows raised, he got a very annoyed look but managed to control his temper.

"Good grief! So you brought her here for a visit. And can you tell me what our visiting policy is?"

"No sir, I can't. We've never had a visitor before, that I know of. I felt sorry for the girl. She seemed like a nice young thing. I suspect that she and Hosterman are planning to get married someday."

The officer strode to the window and saw the young woman sitting in the passenger seat of the truck. Then he returned to Evans.

"I'm just the duty officer," he sputtered. "I'll have to run this by the Colonel."

The Colonel's door on the back wall had been ajar. It now opened and the middle-aged Colonel appeared.

"I heard everything. Bring the young lady in and put her in the meeting room. She has to sit on one side of the table and the prisoner has to sit on the other side. No contact. Have a guard present in the room during the entire visit. She speaks English, doesn't she?"

"Yes, sir, she does, and so does Hosterman," Sergeant Evans replied.

"Good. Let's stipulate they speak only English. Saves the trouble of us having a German speaker monitoring their visit. Okay, let's see... they can have thirty minutes." He paused thinking and then continued, "No, make it one hour. Well, gentlemen, we now have a visitor policy. Write that down if you would, Lieutenant, in case it should come up again."

The duty officer responded, "Very good, sir."

Sergeant Evans came to attention and saluted. "Thank you, sir." He did an about-face and started for the door.

Several minutes later, I sat on one side of a wide table in the meeting room. Sergeant Evans had told me the conditions of the visit, but I was excited at the prospect of

44

seeing Rolf again under any circumstances. I waited impatiently for the closed door of the meeting room to open. After a short time, it opened and Rolf appeared followed by a guard. I noticed he was still stiff from his injuries. His face lit up immediately when he saw me.

"Kätchen, what are you doing here?"

I lit up too and could only say, "Rolf!"

I started to rise to rush to him but then caught myself and sat back down according to the rules of the visit.

He started forward toward me and the guard checked him. "Rolf, remember! Visitation rules are you sit on this side of the table and she on the other. No contact. You only speak English. You have one hour and I'm here the whole time."

Rolf listened and said, "Sorry, Sergeant Brown, I was so excited that I forgot." Rolf excitedly sat down in the chair as the guard took a position near the door.

"Kätchen, I don't know what to say, so I'll have to repeat myself. What are you doing here?"

"I'm here to visit you. I wanted to see you, to be with you."

"I'm happy you did, but it must have been much trouble. It's so good to see you though. You look wonderful."

"You look good too. You're still hurting from your wounds, aren't you?"

"They still hurt some, but they are getting better. They gave me such good care in the hospital back in England. They treated me so well, even when we could hear our bombs falling on London in the distance. I still cannot understand it. And the Canadians have treated us very well ever since we arrived in Canada. They have every reason to treat us badly, but they don't. It's really quite remarkable."

He looked over at the guard who smiled slightly but continued to look straight ahead.

"They have been good to me too. A guard named Sergeant Evans gave me a ride out from town, even though he knew he might get into trouble for doing it."

"It was real nice of Sergeant Evans. I'll be sure to thank him. How long are you here for? Do you still live in California?"

"No, I live across the border now in the American state of Montana in a small town called Shelby. It's not a bad place. My name is Katie, now."

"What?"

"Yes, I work in a ..." And so went our first visit. The sixty minutes flew by, and when our time ran out we said goodbye again across the table.

A little while later, I sat in the passenger seat of the truck, bouncing along the gravel road outside the camp. I think I had been smiling continuously since the visit. I looked over at the soldier driving, and he smiled back. I looked out the window again.

Rolf and I had a wonderful visit. I told him I would be able to visit him again in a month. The camp was nice enough to give me a ride to the train station in a nearby town, so I could catch a train back to Calgary and from there the bus to Shelby. The trip took three days but was worth it. Since I now knew the camp's location and how to get there, I expected the trip next time to take only two days.

Chapter 9
Friends and Enemy

AT THE CAFE, I had become friends with the other waitress Angie, who had been such a big help to me when I first arrived in town. Angie was older than me and had been at Red's for many years. She appreciated my hard work and good rapport with the customers. Being very self-assured, she didn't feel threatened by me. She told me I was a breath of fresh air compared to Teri who she thought was undependable and moody.

America was not at war in August of 1941, but the sentiments I heard about the war in Europe were usually against Germany. Although the townspeople knew I was German, they did not harass or confront me. To the contrary, they tried not to say things in front of me, but I would sometimes by accident overhear them making derogatory statements about Hitler and Krauts. The only positive thing I ever overheard said about Hitler was the favorable opinion of him invading Russia a couple months earlier. Stalin was apparently the only person more despicable than Hitler in the eyes of the townspeople.

A week after I returned from my visit with Rolf, I was working in Red's during the lunch hour. When taking an order for a couple in a booth, I noticed a girl, probably in her early twenties, come in the door. Instead of going to a stool at the counter or to a booth, she stood there at the door looking at me with a sneer.

She stomped over to Angie who was busy nearby. "What's she doing here?" the girl said looking at me.

"She works here, Teri. What are you doing back in town? We thought you were in Butte with Billy," replied Angie with little interest.

"Things didn't work out, so I'm back now. I'd like my old job back. She don't look like she knows what she's doin' anyway. Look at her, she's being too friendly," Teri said with a smirk.

"You quit for good as I recall. We had to find someone else. Katie's been working out just fine. Don't think we need anybody else now. Though I suppose you ought to hear that from Red himself, but I expect he'll tell you the same thing," Angie said as she walked past Teri with some plates of food.

Teri glared in my direction and said, "I reckon I will." She walked past the counter and disappeared into the back. A few minutes later, she came storming back out, walking straight to the front door that she shoved open with a bang. Making a middle finger gesture, she stormed out the door and down the street.

One of the regulars sitting at the counter chuckled and said, "Same to you, Teri." Others chuckled and voiced their agreement. Red came out from the back with a big grin on his face and everyone laughed at him. He had apparently enjoyed telling Teri he couldn't use her.

A few minutes later, Angie was nearby and said, "Don't you worry about that white trash. She's a whole lot of bluster and not much else."

"How long did she work here?" I asked.

"About two years. She was fine for about a month, but then she latched up with that boyfriend of hers. After that, she wasn't worth a shit, excuse my French. They were always having some kind of problem." Then Angie gave me an evil eye and said half-jokingly, "Now don't you be thinkin' you can let up on your work now, just because you've seen how bad the one before you was."

"I won't," I said with a laugh.

"I'm not sure what the gesture she made meant, but I imagine it wasn't good," I added. Angie just rolled her eyes and walked away.

As I was walking down Main Street a few days later, I ran into Teri on the street, and she confronted me. "Thanks a lot for stealing my job, you goddamn foreigner."

"I did nothing wrong. If you…"

"Not just a foreigner but a lousy Nazi to boot," she interrupted.

"I'm not a Nazi, and I did nothing wrong! If you quit your job, then I can't be stealing it. Now get out of my way!" I said as I pushed my way past her.

She was surprised, but as I walked off, she yelled, "Don't think you're gonna get away with it. I'll pay ya back. You'll see."

I ignored her and kept walking. I didn't really see much of her after that confrontation. I heard she got a job as a cocktail waitress in one of the clubs.

In early September, an incident happened at sea in the North Atlantic that almost caused war between Germany and America. Tensions between the countries were high, when a German U-boat fired torpedoes at an American destroyer, the USS Greer, which was tracking it. The USS Greer in return attacked the U-boat with depth charges.

Neither ship was damaged, but it represented open combat between the two countries, which supposedly were not at war. America seemed one step closer to war with Hitler. I knew people in town would be wondering what I thought about it.

Earl and Pete were two weathered old guys with straw cowboy hats who had lived in Shelby and been friends all their lives. They were two of our regulars who liked to kid around with us waitresses, so I got to know and like them over the past several months. They seemed to like me in return.

During lunch one day, Earl and Pete were sitting on their regular stools at the counter observing things and carrying on their normal slow conversation. I noticed them looking at me more than normal and began to suspect they might be talking about me. When Earl waved to me, I grabbed a coffee pot and went over to them.

"More coffee already, Earl?"

"No, Katie, we've got enough coffee. But Pete here and me have got a bet going, and we need you to settle it."

Not having any idea what the bet might be about, I reluctantly said, "Okay, I guess. If I can."

"Fine. Fine. Well, ya see, Katie. Pete and me were just talkin'. That's all we got to do anymore, ya know," he said with a grin. Then he continued, "Well, like I was sayin', Pete and me was just talkin'. We know'd you was from Germany. Heck, everybody in town knows that." He paused and looked around at the other people in the cafe, who were starting to listen in.

I could sense something coming, but still had no idea what. "Yes, I'm from Germany. I have made no secret of it. It would be hard to hide with my accent," I replied with a smile. Several people laughed.

"Heck, Pete here, he don't know one accent from another. But never mind that. Like I was saying, we got to talkin,' and Pete, here, fool that he is, he says that he bets that you've seen Hitler in the flesh."

This created quite a buzz in the cafe.

"Well, I told him that there ain't no way! I mean that there Germany's a big place. I told him he must be plain loco," Earl continued.

"I don't know why, but I just got this hunch you have," interjected Pete.

"Just like that!" Earl said, pointing at Pete. "He kept sayin' that he got this hunch you had! Well, I told Pete that there was no way in hell that Katie has ever seen Hitler in the flesh. I told him I would take his fool bet. We got a six-pack ridin' on it."

General laughter broke out in the cafe at this as people started gathering round to hear.

"So I reckon we need your help to settle our bet. So who's right? Have you ever seen Hitler in the flesh? Now mind ya, that means in person, not on some newsreel."

All eyes turned toward me at this point. Looking around at the people who were eagerly awaiting my answer, I knew that I needed to choose my words carefully when explaining my answer. After a brief pause, I answered.

"Yes, I have."

At this, the whole cafe exploded in a huge uproar of yelling, cheering, and laughter that took a full minute to die down.

"I knew it! I knew it!" Pete shouted as he hopped around slapping his thigh.

Earl alternated between painful looks and laughter. It took Red hollering to "quiet down" for the noise to die down enough for me to continue.

All eyes and ears again turned toward me as they waited to hear more.

"Yes, I did see him in person one time."

Everyone started talking again, but quieted down quickly as I continued.

"I saw him speak at a big Nazi rally in Hamburg, Germany where I lived. I was a little girl in grade school. We school children were forced to participate in that Nazi rally and in many others. If we had refused, our families would have been sent away to prison. Twenty thousand of us school children were there that day when Hitler gave his speech. I remember that he did a lot of screaming and hand waving, but I don't remember anything he said."

"Gosh, you didn't have a choice about going?" Angie asked amid the hush of the listeners.

"No, we were forced to participate in the Nazi rallies. We had no choice. My boyfriend was drafted into the German air force to fight for the Nazis. He had no choice either. He was almost killed in the war about a year ago."

"It sounds to me like you ain't a big fan of Hitler and the war?" Earl said.

"Back in 1936, I had plans of marrying a handsome young man who was a cabinetmaker and of raising our children in the peaceful little town in Germany where his parents lived."

At this point, I got a little emotional, paused, then continued.

"But Hitler and the war changed all that. Instead, I'm now here by myself in America, unable to hear from my family in Germany, and my boyfriend is a prisoner of war in Canada. So, no, I am not a fan of Hitler or the Nazis or the war."

I paused at this point and you could hear a pin drop in the cafe.

"The Nazis were part of the ugly politics back in Germany," I continued, "and I've never liked politics. If I did, I'd still be back in Germany going to Nazi rallies. Wouldn't I? I still don't like politics. I know Roosevelt is the president here, but I don't know who the governor here is."

"Neither do I," Angie inserted and everyone laughed.

Thinking I already had said more than I really wanted to say, I tried to wrap things up.

"So, Earl, I hope that answered your question."

"Yup, only it cost me a six-pack!"

This again created an uproar of laughter and talk. When it died down, Earl, looking a little serious, wanted to say something.

"Ya know, Katie, I'm sorry to hear that your plans didn't work out. You seem all right to me."

"Thank you, Earl. I appreciate that," I replied, genuinely touched.

"I also want to thank you all," I then said to the larger crowd, "for being so nice to me and making me feel welcome here in Shelby. I appreciate that too."

Angie came over, gave me a hug, and everyone started talking all at once.

After that day, I found myself to be quite a celebrity in town. More people than ever were friendly to me. People exchanged smiles and greetings with me wherever I went. I was the only person in town and maybe the entire state of Montana who had ever seen the infamous Hitler in the flesh.

More importantly, I felt I put to rest any incorrect suspicions of me being a fan of Hitler and the Nazis, just because I was German. I expected my notoriety to soon fade and things to return to normal. My life in Shelby seemed to be going well.

Only Teri, who I had to just ignore, still seemed to be a problem. I heard she was always bad mouthing me over at the club where she worked, saying what a shame it was that we got foreigners coming into this country and taking away good paying jobs from Americans.

The morning finally came for my second visit to Rolf. The weather in Montana in mid-September 1941 was starting to get brisk. As I stood by the bus waiting for word to board, I looked up at the sky and felt the nip in the air.

The bus driver came out of the station and motioned for us three passengers to board. Soon the doors closed, and the bus drove off. The same two Canadian border guards from my first visit were again on duty at the Canadian border, and my entry into Canada went smoothly.

I was able to catch a ride to the camp with the supply truck again and had a wonderful visit with Rolf. Like on our first visit, I sat opposite from Rolf at the table. We talked happily as the guard looked on. Rolf looked physically better this time, more healthy and healing, more like his old self.

I told him about Pete and Earl's bet, and how it provided a good opportunity for me to tell them that I was not a fan of Hitler and the Nazis. He listened intently and said, "These Americans sound like an interesting people."

"They are, and they have been good to me even though there is a lot not to like about Germans these days."

I asked him what he did to pass the time in prison. He said he did exercises to help heal his injuries, read books, worked in the camp, but mostly he thought of me.

Chapter 10
Uneasy Feelings

MUTTI WAS KNITTING late at night in the living room of the apartment when she heard the air raid siren go off. She took the warnings seriously because the bombers had come a number of nights this month. Poking her head in Ruth's bedroom, Mutti called to her to get up. She then rushed to wake up her husband in their bedroom. Gustav lay in the bed snoring loudly as Mutti rushed in and began shaking him violently.

"Gustav! Wake up! Gustav! Get Up!"

"What's the matter?" Gustav said groggily looking round.

"What's the matter? Gustav! Are you deaf! The air raid siren is going. Get up! We have to go down to the bomb shelter. Hurry up or you will get us all killed!"

Gustav looked at her sleepily. "You and Ruth go ahead. I'll be there in a few minutes."

"No, come with us now!"

"Go woman! I'll be along in a few minutes!"

Mutti looked at him with a frown. "Okay, Gustav but hurry up."

"I'll be right along. They've been bombing warehouses and wharves along the river to the south. So there's probably no danger, but I'll be along in a few minutes."

Throwing up her arms in disgust, Mutti hurried out the bedroom door. In the living room, she grabbed some knitting, a blanket, and her coat. Ruth came out of her bedroom dressed.

"Ruth! Are you ready? Let's go."

"What about Vati?"

"He's not ready and will come in a few minutes."

"Vati, you're coming, right!" called Ruth grabbing her coat.

"Yes, Ruth. You both go on. I'll be along shortly," they heard from the bedroom.

"Okay but hurry."

"Yes, yes, I will."

Hearing this, they both rushed out the door of the apartment and were soon hurrying along the street on their way to the bomb shelter at the end of their block. Being autumn, the trees along the street looked vaguely colorful in the distant light from the searchlights. The weather was cold and a dusting of snow was on the ground from an early snow. Other families were also hurrying along to the bomb shelter.

They began to hear the drone of the bombers, the engines and guns of fighters, the flak guns firing, and bombs explosions in the distance. The night sky was illuminated by the searchlights and the flashes of explosions. Ruth turned and looked behind them.

"I don't see Vati coming."

"He'll be along."

They reached the stairs in the sidewalk going down to the entrance of the shelter and paused to look for Gustav on the street. Not seeing him, they looked up at the battle in the sky. Hearing only a moderate amount of bomb explosions, it didn't seem to be a bad raid. Other families hurried down past them. Finally, they gave up waiting for Gustav and hurried down inside.

Back at the apartment, Gustav was drowsily and slowly getting dressed sitting on the edge of the bed. He got on his pants and socks. Sitting sleepily erect, he paused to listen to the air battle to the south. After a moment, he sighed and started to stand up.

Suddenly he heard a rapid series of cracks, bangs, pings, and booms as a random pattern of six to eight fist-sized holes appeared in the ceiling and floor.

"God in Heaven!" he cried. Instantly awake now, he jumped up and ran to the door with his arms shielding his head, as if it would protect him. Somehow, Gustav had not been hit by what he suspected was falling shrapnel.

Standing at the bedroom door looking back, he could see several pieces of the shrapnel, in fact, lying on the floor in the light layer of wood splinters and plaster debris. Bang, pow, bang, thump! Another two holes appeared in the ceiling, one in the floor, and a cloud of down feathers exploded on the bed. Behind him in the living room, he heard several more bangs and pows.

"Shit!" he hissed looking around wide-eyed, uncertain what to do. Then with a new determined look, he rushed back to the chair near the bed, grabbed his shirt, coat, and shoes. Pow, pow, ping! More shrapnel sliced through the room just feet away from him. Fumbling with his things and rushing to go, he dropped one of his shoes.

When he frantically bent to pick it up, the other shoe now fell to the floor.

"Shit!" he exclaimed as he scrambled to gather up the shoes. At last, with his clothes and shoes bundled in his arms, he raced out the bedroom door. As he passed out the apartment door headed for the stairwell, he heard another ping, bang, crash in one of the other apartments.

A minute later, on the first floor in the stairwell, he hurriedly put on his things. He looked up as several other residents rushed by him on their way to the basement. The basement of their apartment building seemed like a safe enough place to him, but the shelters would be safer in heavy bombing.

As he opened the outside door to leave, he thought how he wished he had gone earlier with Mutti and Ruth. He was a shelter warden, after all, and was supposed to be there. As he hurried along the front walk to the street, he knew he was going to catch hell from her when he got there.

In the future, Gustav took the air raid sirens more seriously. The flak and anti-aircraft fire from the German defenders were a danger. With more and larger bombing raids, the danger increased. As for the British bombs themselves, the British didn't seem to be targeting their residential section of Hamburg, but stray bombs landed there more and more often. The increased level of enemy bombing raids did not indicate to Gustav that the war was going as well as the Führer had planned.

* * *

At the Phelps' house, I was going room to room with my feather duster in one hand and a rag in the other. She owned a great many knickknacks on her tables so I needed to carefully dust them and around them. As I was dusting on a dresser in front of a window, I looked out and noticed a late-model black sedan drive slowly by the house and down the street.

I immediately thought it was a pretty odd car for this town, too new and an unusual color. But I couldn't let it distract me for very long from my work, so I put it out of my mind and hurried to finish up. I thought of it again later and asked Mrs. Martin about it. She didn't know of anyone with such a car and couldn't explain it either.

Things seemed to settle into a routine in October. My notoriety had died down, which was fine with me. At the cafe, I talked them into letting me do a little cooking too. I told them my meatloaf was pretty good, so they experimented with a meatloaf and mashed potato special on Mondays. It was a big hit, but I resisted doing too much cooking because I didn't want to upset the normal operations of the cafe.

I was waiting on tables one evening and brought orders to Monte and Curtis, two of our regulars, who were sitting in a booth. As I approached, I thought I had overheard them talking about a black sedan.

"Did I hear you say something about a black sedan?" I asked as I put down their food.

"Yeah," Monte replied, "I was just telling Curtis that when I came into the cafe the other day, I saw a black sedan parked down the street from here. I couldn't imagine anyone buying a car that color. When I came out later it was gone."

"That's funny," I said, "I think I saw one pass down the street the other day when I was cleaning at the Phelps' house. What do you think it might be?"

"Don't know. Kind of peculiar though," Curtis said, "but I wouldn't worry about it. Could I get some more coffee, Katie?"

"Sure, Curtis. Everything else okay?" They both nodded and began eating.

"I'll be right back with it," I said as I walked away. Suddenly feeling an urge, I walked out the front door and looked up and down the street. I then returned inside.

Chapter 11
Visiting Rolf

MY THIRD VISIT to Rolf was in mid-October. By now I had the transportation connections worked out pretty well. This time I carried along a bag of cookies I had baked. I wasn't allowed to give them to Rolf, but I wanted to give them to the guards for being so nice to me.

When Rolf walked into the meeting room, he looked nearly back to normal. He had been working to keep busy with the other prisoners clearing trees in an area near the camp that was to become a reservoir. He would mostly work picking up and piling brush, but sometimes he would do the more strenuous ax and saw work. He felt like he was getting stronger.

"Kätchen, I have a surprise for you," he said. "I've heard back from my mother already on how your family is. They're all alive and well, still living in the apartment in Hamburg."

I bolted up in my chair and wanted to jump across the table to hug him, but all I could do was sit back down, put my hands to my face and sob.

"She wrote a letter right away to your mother when I told her you had visited me. She heard back from your mother. I have her letter here. It has more information, but some parts were blacked out by censors. But it is good news. It sounds like they are all doing okay."

After a time, I was finally able to say, "Oh, Rolf. You know how much I've worried about them. Thank you so much for finding out something."

Tears of happiness were flowing from my eyes at hearing they had not been killed or injured in the bombings. I had heard absolutely nothing about them in two years since the mail service was cut off. Rolf was very happy for me and wanted to give me a hug too. He looked over at Sargent Brown who was misty eyed as well. He was getting to know us pretty well in his duty overseeing our visits.

Taking out his mother's letter and looking at it, Rolf said, "Your father still works at the restaurant. Your mother can find very little sewing work. Your sister is grown up and works as a dressmaker's apprentice at a dress shop. She is still single. They are all in good health and still living in the same apartment. They all miss you and send their love." Here he paused and looking up at me, added, "She wrote a few other things too, but they were blacked out by the censors. It isn't much, but at least you know something now. I told my mother you were well, had moved nearby across the border and were visiting me. She passed your news on to them."

"I'm sure they have wondered about me and are relieved to hear something too. Thank you, Rolf, and thank your mother too. Also have her pass on to my family that I miss them and send my love to them too. Gosh, I don't know what to say now. I'm so overwhelmed to find out something so soon, and so glad it is good news."

"Well, Kätchen, I mean Katie, you better think of something. We only have sixty minutes to talk," he said with a laugh. I laughed too, and we did keep talking. Soon the sixty minutes were up, and we needed to say goodbye.

At the end of October, I paid Mrs. Martin another month of rent. She was always good to me and so helpful in getting me settled into town. I was thankful to her and tried to find ways to show it. If a dessert or a dish at the cafe was getting old and might be thrown out, I would ask Red if I could take it home for myself. Mrs. Martin didn't eat out much. So to save her some trouble and expense in cooking, I gave her the food I brought home. She appreciated it.

It made me think of my father bringing home food to us from his restaurant, back when I was growing up in Germany. It seemed I was becoming my father. I wanted to remember to tell Rolf about it the next time I visited, so he could pass it on to my father through his mother's letters.

* * *

Mutti waited impatiently in the line at the train station. No bombings occurred during October in Hamburg, but she wanted to find out about leaving by train for the safety of her sister Rosa's house in the country. It would be nice to know should they all decide to go. She was also considering trying to talk Ruth into going to Rosa's where she would be safer, although she knew Ruth would not want to go without her and Gustav. Well, she could at least find out.

Unfortunately, the noisy throng of people at the train station apparently had the same idea in mind. A line of impatient people waited to see the teller at the lone open ticket window. People there looked to be leaving it without tickets. After a time, she got up toward the front of the line. Disappointed people were leaving the ticket window telling people in line that they weren't selling any train tickets. Soon a policeman came to stand by the window to maintain order.

When Mutti got to the ticket booth herself, she asked the teller about getting three train tickets to central Germany. No, unless you have authorization to leave the city. How about one ticket? No, unless you have authorization. People were not being allowed to leave the city because they were needed in the city's factories and industry to support the war effort.

But asking for such authorization was not something you wanted to do. They might tell you, "No, you can't leave. You are needed for the war effort here. Report for work at such and such factory tomorrow!" And they would then have of course your name, and you would have to do it. Such an inquiry with city officials could probably result in an unwanted outcome.

Without such written authorization to leave, a train ticket couldn't be purchased. So much for Mutti's idea of sending Ruth to safety in the country living with her Aunt Rosa.

* * *

As the weeks in November 1941 passed, it was soon mid-month and time for the monthly visit to Rolf. This time when I boarded the bus, I carried along some fudge for the guards. Last month, they finished off the cookies in no time. It was the least I could do for them.

During our one hour visit, we sat across the table from each other and talked as usual about what had happened since last month.

But then in a more serious tone, Rolf said, "Kätchen, I've been thinking. Maybe you should stop visiting me here."

"What? Why do you say that? Don't you like my visits?"

"Yes, of course I do, Sweetheart. I'm worried for you."

"What do you mean, Rolf?"

"Last month, there was another incident at sea. This time a German U-boat torpedoed and sank an American destroyer killing a hundred American sailors. It's only a matter of time before America joins the war. I'm just worried it might look bad for you then to be associating with a German prisoner of war."

"Rolf, don't be silly. We're doing nothing wrong."

"I know that, but it still might look bad for you. I'll be okay here, and we can still write to each other. You need to think about yourself and staying out of trouble with the Americans."

"Rolf, over here they don't come and arrest you in the night like in Germany. Remember, I know the Americans a lot better than you do, and they wouldn't do that kind of thing. The people in my small town all know me. The county sheriff is one of my regular customers. They know I wouldn't do anything wrong."

"You should think about it, Kätchen. Please tell me you will think about it."

"Okay, Rolf, I'll think about it. We can talk about it again next month."

On the bus ride home, I thought about our visits. It may not seem like much, talking for sixty minutes on opposite sides of a table, not being allowed to touch or hug. Rolf had come so close to being killed that I felt lucky to even have one minute a month. I looked forward to the time when Rolf would not be a prisoner and we could start our lives together. But until then, one hour a month was all I had, and I didn't want to give it up.

Chapter 12
Sudden Change

THE FIRST SUNDAY morning in December, I was working at the cafe. The after-church customers had been coming in all morning. First the Lutherans, then the Catholics, and since it was getting toward noon, soon it would be the Methodists and the Baptists. It was a normal thing here on Sunday mornings, a good outing for families and good for business too. A nice family was just sitting down in a booth and I was asking them what they wanted to drink.

Suddenly, we heard a commotion down the street, and everyone looked up. Curtis's son Jeff came racing up the street into sight. He burst into the front door and shouted, "Have you heard! The Japs attacked our navy base in Hawaii! They sunk a bunch of battleships! It's on the radio!"

Everyone gasped in disbelief. Angie turned on the radio and fiddled with the tuning dial until she heard the special report being announced. "Early this morning, Sunday, December 7th, 1941, Japan launched a surprise attack on our Navy base at Pearl Harbor on the island of Oahu in Hawaii, a U.S. territory. There are initial reports that several battleships have been sunk and a number of other warships have been damaged..." We all gathered around the radio and listened in disbelief as the announcer continued.

America declared war on Japan the next day after the Pearl Harbor attack, but nothing was said about Germany, which apparently had played no role in the attack. America, Britain and the its Commonwealth countries were now in a Pacific war against Japan. Meanwhile, the Soviet Union,

Britain and its commonwealth countries were fighting a second totally separate, unconnected war in Europe against Germany and Italy.

This confusing situation continued for three days until Hitler solved the dilemma by declaring war on America on the eleventh of December. After that, it became a single straightforward, worldwide war with allied countries opposing axis powers. America was at war with Germany.

The following day, I was working in the cafe. With only three days before my December visit to Rolf, I was looking forward to it. The lunch hour rush was over, and I was behind the counter wiping ketchup bottles. I looked at the clock and decided I needed to leave. As I finished and washed my hands, I looked over at Angie who was wiping tables nearby.

"Angie, Are you all right if I go now? I have to do some cleaning for Mrs. Saunders today."

"Sure, but you'll be back later, right?"

"Yes, I'll be back in about three hours," I said as I took off my apron, hung it on a hook in the back and put on my coat.

"Okay, see ya."

"Bye," I said as I walked out the door.

I came out the door and walked briskly down the street in front of the cafe. I was happy. The cleaning at Mrs. Saunders shouldn't be too hard or take too long. Only a few more days until I would see Rolf again. I wondered what I should make for the camp guards this time, maybe some cookies. Mrs. Martin had a recipe for peanut butter cookies, which she said were really good. I still didn't understand why Americans liked peanut butter so much.

My thoughts were interrupted when I noticed the sheriff's car pulled up a short distance in front of me. As I approached, the sheriff got out of the driver's seat and stood looking at me. His wore the expression of someone required to do an unpleasant task.

"Hello, Sheriff."

"Hello, Katie," he said as he continued to look at me.

"Is something wrong, Sheriff?"

"Katie, I'm afraid I have to ask you to come with me to the office. There are some people there who want to talk to you."

"To me? About what?" I asked as he came around to the passenger door and opened it.

"Just climb in, and we'll find out."

"But Sheriff, I'm on my way to Mrs. Saunders to do some cleaning. She's expecting me."

"It'll have to wait," the sheriff said as he motioned me to get in. As I started to get into the car, I looked back and saw the late model black sedan pull up behind the sheriff's car. With a sinking feeling, I got into the sheriff's car, and he closed the door. Looking back at the cafe, I could see people with surprised looks at the windows watching and Angie running out. The sheriff was still getting in the driver's side when she ran up beside the car.

"Sheriff, what's going on?"

"Now, don't get excited, Angie. These men here need to ask Katie some questions," the sheriff said, pointing back at the black sedan.

Angie swung around and looked back. A man in a dark suit and light fedora hat got out of the passenger side of the sedan and stood by the open door giving her an intimidating look.

"Oh, my," Angie said with a startled look on her face.

All I could do was sadly look up at her as the sheriff's car drove off.

There really wasn't any questioning at the sheriff's office. I was there for only a few minutes. They told one of the women who worked there in the office to pat me down for weapons. I think she was more embarrassed about it than I was. I had waited on her and her husband a number of times at the cafe.

The two federal agents in the black sedan had already been to my room at Mrs. Martin's. They searched it, and brought my personal things away with them. I was being taken to a detention center for questioning. They would not tell me about what.

The two federal agents escorted me out of the sheriff's office to their car. The sheriff and one of his deputies followed us out. I knew the sheriff thought well of me. He was a regular at the cafe and a big fan of my meat loaf special. The agents put me into the back seat of their car, climbed in front, and drove off as the sheriff watched, scratching his head and unable to intervene.

Red, Angie, and Earl came to the sheriff's office soon afterward to find out about me, but I was already gone. The sheriff could not tell them anything more than he knew, which was that I was being taken somewhere for questioning by federal agents.

Chapter 13
Detention Camp

I SAT QUIETLY in the back seat of the car. The two men in the front seat said very little during the trip and would tell me nothing. I never thought something like this could happen to me here in America.

On the five hour drive, they stopped for gas once. Not wanting to spend time eating in a restaurant, they bought candy bars and colas at the gas station.

They asked me if I wanted something, and I told them no. When I told them I needed to go to the bathroom, they looked at me suspiciously. They searched the bathroom at the gas station before they let me use it, and they stood outside the door while I was inside. I had no idea why they should take such precautions.

It was getting dark by the time we arrived at what looked like an army base. The car pulled up in front of the large building across from the gate of the large prison enclosure containing rows of wooden barracks surrounded by a high barbed-wire fence with guard towers. Although the setting was different, it possessed all the same features as Rolf's prisoner of war camp in Canada.

The two agents got out and opened my door. As I stepped out, I paused to look at the fenced area. It was still light enough to see a number of men milling about inside and looking at us. They were dressed in what looked like naval uniforms. Looking at them, I wondered if I was going to be held inside there too.

"This way, Miss," said one of the agents as he guided me into the large building, while the other agent followed carrying my suitcase. From my experience at Rolf's camp, the building looked to be the headquarters building for the enclosure or prison camp. They took me through an open entryway to what looked to be the outer office and waiting room for a camp official's office.

After a brief wait, an agent ushered me into the office. Inside, a man seated behind a large desk rose as I walked in.

"Miss Thielke, I'm Mr. Baker, please sit down," he said as he motioned toward the chair in front of his desk. I sat down not knowing what to expect.

"Miss Thielke. You immigrated to this country four and a half years ago…"

"That's correct," I interjected.

Mr. Baker paused for a moment at the interruption, and continued, "As you know, you are classified as an alien while here in the U.S. until such time as you become a naturalized U.S. citizen. You are an alien here from a country with which we are now at war. This, Miss Thielke, is an alien detention facility."

"I don't understand. I've reported on time to the post office every month."

"That will be verified in the course of our investigation."

"Investigation? Why am I being investigated? What have I done wrong."

"As I was saying, Miss Thielke, the United States is now at war with Germany. Any recent immigrants from Germany could be potential security risks, planted here to aid that country. We have to ensure that is not the case. We will soon be interviewing all German immigrants and further investigating ones with activities of a questionable nature. Your activities have already come to our attention, and they must be investigated."

He paused for a moment to gauge my reaction.

"Questionable? I don't know what you mean. I've done nothing wrong."

"If that's true, then our investigation will clear you of any wrongdoing, and you will be allowed to go. Until the investigation is completed, you will have to remain here in this detention facility."

I gasped and said in astonishment, "In custody here? Behind the fence with the men?"

"No, not with the men, Miss Thielke. We do not have a separate detention area for women or children like you saw for the men. You are our first and only woman detainee. You will be housed in our staff area and will be restricted to the base. You will be on your honor not to leave. If you do leave, it would be very bad for you. We would then have to make provisions to confine you or transfer you to a women's detention facility. Do you understand?"

"No, I don't understand why I'm being held here."

"I've already told you all you need to know for now on that point. Do you understand that you will be on your honor not to leave here until the investigation is completed?"

"Yes, but how long will it take?"

"It could be months. We have many cases to investigate and only so many agents."

"Months? But what about my job?" Ignoring my question, he looked past me at a woman who had just entered the room.

"You have to remain here on base until the investigation is completed. Miss Phillips will show you your room and where you get your meals."

He motioned behind me, and I turned to look at the woman who had just entered.

"This way, please," she said.

I sat for a moment, thinking in silence. It appeared that I had no other choice but to obey these people and wait to be cleared. It wouldn't do any good tonight to argue with them or deny any wrongdoing again. It might even hurt rather than help. Dejectedly, I rose up from the chair and followed Miss Phillips out.

Walking with her outside in the dark carrying my suitcase, I did not say anything. Hearing some noise behind me, I turned and looked back. I could make out the two federal agents as they climbed into their car and drove off.

The next day, I stood with my tray at the serving line of their dining hall. The woman serving food put some chicken and peas on a plate as I had asked, and she handed it to me. Still feeling pretty low, I didn't have much of an appetite. Putting the plate on my tray with my glass of milk, I turned to find a table.

Some camp staff sat and ate at several of the tables. I walked dully to an empty table and sat down. The others did not look at me as I passed, but I suspect they were curiously watching me. For them, I was a novelty, the female Nazi detainee. I was not behind fences like the men, but I was isolated.

I expected to soon be called for some kind of interview or questioning. I had nothing to hide and welcomed it. But the days passed, and for some reason, I wasn't called in. I stayed in my room mostly and came out to eat meals in the staff dining hall.

And meanwhile, what was Rolf going to do or think when I suddenly stopped coming to see him? He might think I was in an accident, sick, or dead. He would have no way of finding out. I would ask about writing to him but suspected it wouldn't be allowed.

I learned that my five hour car ride had brought me to the western part of the state of Montana to an army base, part of which they converted into a detention camp. Rolf had been right while I had underestimated the consequences of a war with Germany.

I was probably in detention more because of the Japanese than the Germans. The surprise attack on Pearl Harbor shocked and enraged the Americans, so they were clamping down on any perceived internal security threats with all their energy. I had found some newspapers in the dining hall and read about the hysteria and fear of imminent Japanese invasion on the West Coast of America. I was probably a victim of that initial security hysteria.

At night, I lay in my bed, sadly pondering my situation. I couldn't write to Rolf or my family. I decided not to write to Aunt Minna, Hanni or Magda because I didn't want to cause them trouble by association with me.

I thought of writing to Angie or Mrs. Martin, but who knows what they must think of me now. As a result, I never bothered to ask if I was allowed to write letters there at the detention camp, because I had no one to write to anyway. I felt very alone.

As I lay there in bed thinking about it, I heard a knock at the door. I stood up, opened the door, and saw a camp guard standing there with his clipboard.

"I'm here," I said.

"Thank you, Miss," he said. He made a mark on his clipboard and left. I closed the door and returned to the bed. It was the nightly head count.

Chapter 14
Investigation

I WAS AT the camp for six days before I was called in for my first interrogation. I was hoping things might be cleared up quickly, that they would ask me a few questions and realize a mistake had been made. My hopes were quickly dashed. I sat in a stark room at a table across from two men in suits, Mr. Griffin and Mr. Jenkins.

After introductions, Mr. Griffin started out, "Miss Thielke, you have been accused of being a potential agent of the Nazi government in communication with Nazi prisoners of war in Canada and possibly others. Such communications could represent the passing of information or messages for the purpose of espionage." Both of them stared at me intently to gauge my reaction to their accusation.

"I'm sorry, I don't know what espionage means," I replied, being unfamiliar with the word.

Mr. Griffin appeared to be a little dubious about my question and pointedly said, "Espionage means spying, Miss Thielke." They again scrutinized me for my reaction.

"What? Me? A spy?" I said with a laugh of disbelief. "Is that what this is all about? I've been living in a little town in the middle of nowhere. What is there to spy on there? Shouldn't I be living around an army base or something to be spying? You must be kidding?"

Mr. Griffin was a little put off by my reaction. I think he was hoping I would break down and confess under the pressure of his stern gaze. He looked at me with a stony face and said, "No, Miss Thielke. I assure you, we are not kidding. The United States government must take seriously the possibility that recent immigrants may have been sent

74

here for the express purpose of spying or plotting for Nazi Germany once here. If we get reports of unusual activities, they must be investigated."

"So you deny being an agent of the government of Nazi Germany?"

"Yes, I do!"

"And you have never participated in activity related to the collection of information and passing of information back to Nazi Germany?"

"Never!"

"Very well, let's have a look at some of your letters."

"My letters? From Germany? I haven't exchanged letters with my mother in Germany since mail service was cut off two years ago?"

Ignoring my comment, he dramatically opened a folder in front of him and pulled out some letters. "We've collected these letters from the room where you were boarding. Let's look at this one, for example, from your contact in Germany."

"You mean my mother," I said recognizing the letter from Mutti.

"For now I will refer to the writer as your contact," he said. "This sentence here, when translated, says that Fritzi says to tell you hello and wishes you were back together again at the shooting festival."

"What does that mean?" he asked putting the letter down and looking at me intently

"Fritzi is my cousin. When we were young, we used to go on summer vacations to visit my aunt in the country. The local town there held a shooting festival. Those were carefree days when we were children. He only wishes for those carefree days again."

Mr. Griffin cleared his throat and said, "I see." Meanwhile, Mr. Jenkins jotted down notes.

"And what is this about someone named Rolf saying that the water in their barracks was supposed to be out for a week after a water pipe break, but his pilot captain raised heck and got it fixed in a day?"

"That's about my boyfriend Rolf in the German Air Force, the Luftwaffe. He thought it would look bad to Nazi officials there for a serviceman to be sending letters to someone in America. So he would send letters to my mother with his news and messages for me. She would then include his information in her letters to me. Likewise, she would send him letters passing news from me."

"So you and your boyfriend in the Luftwaffe did not communicate directly?"

"No, because he was afraid of being accused of spying by the Nazi officials on his end."

Mr. Griffin cleared his throat and looked a little uncomfortable on hearing this, since now he was the government official making the same accusation on my end. They took more notes.

When he was finished writing his notes, Mr. Jenkins continued as he held up another letter, "This is another letter from your contact."

I looked at it and said, "It's another letter from my mother."

He looked at me and continued, "This sentence in it says 'Ruth doesn't go to the dances, so she doesn't have pictures of the soldiers like you'. Can you explain to me what that means?"

"Ruth is my sister. I used to go to dances at the army base near our home in Hamburg. The soldiers would give you pictures of themselves to remember them by. I used to bring the pictures home and show them to my mother and sister."

"And here's another something about Rolf. It says he recently was in Nuremburg. He loves the sausages there."

"Yes, that's about my boyfriend Rolf again. Before the war, he flew all over Germany doing whatever they do in the Luftwaffe."

After more note taking, Mr. Griffin brought out a third letter and asked, "This letter says 'You may listen to music there, but it couldn't be as good as the ratcatcher in the park'. What does that mean?"

"The ratcatcher is a touching German song that we saw performed one time at a concert in a park in Hamburg."

This all was starting to seem a little ridiculous to me and I said, "Now really. Are you being serious? What do you think is so bad about those innocent statements?"

"Miss Thielke, some words in those sentences could suggest other meanings. If you haven't done anything wrong, then you have nothing to worry about, do you?"

"That's what I used to think before you brought me here, Mr. Griffin, but apparently I was wrong. I'm not a spy. Those are innocent letters from my mother in Germany over two years ago."

I looked at the letters on the table and thought of Mrs. Martin. "So your agents rummaged through my room and collected my things. Poor Mrs. Martin. Your men probably forced their way into her house and got her all upset. I'm sorry I caused her so much trouble," I said shaking my head.

"The agents reported she was uncooperative and rude to them. She even hit one of them over the head with a broom as they carried boxes out. Knocked his hat off into the mud. The agent wasn't very happy about it," he said dryly.

"Good for her," I said with a smile, picturing it in my mind.

Mr. Griffin was not amused and said, "Let's get back to the questioning, please."

"Miss Thielke, when you lived in Germany, were you a member of Hitler youth or any other political groups?" Mr. Jenkins asked.

The question somehow transported my mind back in time to a previous interview with Nazi officials in Germany when I had applied for my passport. I was momentarily lost in thought when I replied, "No, sir. I'm a young girl who likes cooking and dancing. The job in America seems like a good opportunity for me. That's all."

They both looked at me and then each other curiously. Mr. Griffin demanded, "What? Cooking? Dancing? What are you talking about?"

Coming out of my trance, I told them, "I'm sorry. I was interviewed and questioned by Nazi officials in order to get my passport before leaving Germany. They asked me a question similar to yours and I was just lost in thought remembering what I told them."

The interrogators were a little taken aback by my implication that they reminded me of a previous interview by Nazi interrogators.

"I beg your pardon! Miss Thielke, if you would please stick to answering the questions, we could complete our investigation more quickly."

The truth of his statement struck me. I realized I was being difficult with them. If I cooperated fully and answered their questions without complaint, they would get done sooner. They would find me to be no threat to national security and release me sooner.

"I'm sorry," I said. "I see now that you are right. I'll try to do better. What was the question again?" Afterward I tried to answer their questions quickly, fully, and without comment.

The next day in another session, Mr. Griffin and Mr. Jenkins started asking about my visits to Rolf. "You have been visiting a German POW camp in Canada. Is that true?"

"Yes. I plan to marry one of the prisoners there someday. His name is Rolf Hosterman. He is the same one you read about in the letters from Germany. We met in Germany before I immigrated here. He was on a bomber shot down over England. He became a prisoner of war and was sent to a prisoner of war camp near Calgary, Alberta in Canada. I wanted to see him again to make sure he was okay."

"Did you visit or talk any other prisoners?"

"No."

"Did you ever exchange anything with him, such as a letter, a package, or a note during these visits?"

"No. It wasn't allowed. By the way, is there any way I can get a message to him to let him know I am being detained?"

"I'm sorry, but we are just investigating your case. You will have to take that up with officials when your case is reviewed. Now, Miss Thielke, what did you talk about during these visits?"

I wanted to complain, but I didn't think it would help. I was not being allowed to let Rolf know I was safe. I could only hope the investigation would be completed in a month or two, and then I could see or write him to let him know. Meanwhile I would answer their questions.

As the interrogation sessions continued, they asked their questions in a matter-of-fact, impartial manner, but the tone of the interviews seemed to be less accusatory. I think they were beginning to believe I was wrongfully suspected of spying. They asked about my previous jobs and time in California.

"After you stopped working for your aunt, where did you work?"

"I worked in a bakery in San Carlos, Mr. Steinhauer's bakery."

"Do you remember the street address of the bakery?"

I didn't really hear the question because I was thinking back and remembering Mr. Steinhauer's rage at me after the fight. I thought to myself, "Oh God, he is not going to say anything good about me."

But that reminded me of the fight with Hilda.

"Wait! I just remembered something! I got into a fight at that bakery."

"What? You got into a fight?"

"Yes. There should be a police record of it. I'll bet the San Mateo County Sheriff still remembers me." He can help clear me.

The interrogators looked highly interested, and Mr. Griffin said, "Yes, go on."

"Another German woman named Hilda worked at the bakery. I don't even know her last name. She worked in a different area of the kitchen. I had worked there for months without being around her, but then she was moved to work in my area. I had never been interested in politics and she kept going on and on about how great Hitler was and how powerful Germany was. She kept at it and kept at it, even though I told her I wasn't interested in hearing it. Finally, I couldn't take it anymore and told her, 'If Hitler is so great and powerful, what are you doing here? Why aren't you back there bowing to your Führer and licking his boots!' Well, that set her off, and she attacked me. We got into a big fight and made a terrible mess of the place. The county sheriff was called, and he came himself. He thought it was pretty funny at the time, women wrestling around in a pastry mess and all. He'll remember it and will vouch for me. You should talk to the San Mateo County Sheriff."

"We will get in touch with him. Do you remember the date of this incident?"

I thought hard trying to remember. "Oh yes, it was when Germany marched into part of Czechoslovakia. That's what started it. She was crowing about how scared the English and French were of Hitler. It was something like March or April of 1939."

I couldn't help but feel a little more optimistic after remembering the fight with Hilda. I was sure it would help put to rest any notion I was a Hitler and Nazi supporter. It was documented evidence I was not.

After three days of these interrogation sessions, they seemed to have exhausted their supply of questions, and my interrogations ended. Mr. Griffin and Mr. Jenkins left in their car. Nearly Christmas time, I suspected they were going home to be with their families over Christmas. Afterward, they would be conducting interviews to confirm what I told them. I was hoping to be released by the end of January at the latest.

Chapter 15
Isolation

IT WASN'T MORE than a day or two after the interrogation sessions ended before I was going crazy with boredom. I sought out Miss Phillips and asked her to please find me some kind of work. Shortly thereafter, I was cleaning bathrooms, mopping floors, sweeping, and other house cleaning chores in the buildings. They were happy to have the help, and I was happy to be busy doing something to help the time pass more quickly. As I worked, I worried about Rolf. He would be worried about me after I didn't make my planned visit.

* * *

Deep in thought, Rolf stopped for a moment and leaned on his snow shovel to catch his breath. The camp had received a blanket of two feet of snow overnight, and he had cleared a pretty good section of the path to the gate. Dieter was also shoveling nearby and stopped for a rest too. He came over to his friend who had not been himself since Kätchen had missed her monthly visit.

"So what have you concluded about Kätchen?" Dieter asked.

"Well, even though I told her last month that she should maybe stop seeing me, she seemed adamant that she would come this month. So I think she would have come if she could."

"America entering the war surely has something to do with it," said Dieter.

"Yes," Rolf said, "that's the only thing keeping me from going crazy, worrying if she's been injured or killed in an accident somewhere. America entering the war and her visits stopping at the same time are too big of a coincidence. They have to be related."

"So what do you think it means then?" Dieter asked.

"For some reason she is no longer able to visit me since America entered the war," he pondered.

"Maybe the police there in America have restricted her movements, and she is not allowed to leave the country," Dieter said.

"I hope it's something like that and not something worse because of her visits here," Rolf said with a sigh.

"I don't know much about Americans. They're supposed to be big on rights and justice. They wouldn't just lock her up without good cause," offered Dieter.

"I guess. So let's hope she's still in the little town working in the cafe but not allowed to leave the country. Maybe she'll still be able to write me a letter."

"If she can't visit you any more, Rolf, maybe she'll go back to California."

"That's possible too, but who knows?" Rolf said.

"Well anyway, I wouldn't be too worried about her. You never know, she still might show up again," Dieter said, clapping Rolf on the shoulder and returning to his snow shoveling.

* * *

Lying in bed in my room on Christmas night, I looked over at the window and noticed it was snowing outside. I stood up and walked over to the window. Looking out at the falling snow, I thought about how much I used to enjoy Christmas. This year was different.

I thought of Rolf. He knew I would make the planned visit in December if I could, but I had no way to let him know where I was. With plenty of time on my hands for thinking, I tried to consider my options. In the end, I concluded I only had one option. I should stay and await the results of the investigation, which I hoped would correctly conclude that I was not a spy.

Returning to the bed, I lay down looking up at the ceiling. Thinking of Rolf and my family again, I sadly said aloud with irony, "Merry Christmas."

Several weeks passed without hearing anything. To help pass the time, I decided to try reading books to improve my English. I was allowed to use the library at the camp. Having picked out a book, I was walking with it along the street back to my room. The men's detention area was not far off as I passed by. I was not allowed to go near its fence or talk to any male detainees inside.

A number of Italian and Japanese detainees were held there as well as a few Germans. I learned that most of them were the crews of merchant ships that happened to be in American ports when a decision was made to impound them and detain their crews, even before America entered the war.

I thought they must have been pretty unlucky to be locked up here now. I could only think of one distasteful seafaring person upon whom I would wish such a fate. He was Herr Schneider, who was the second-in-command on the steamship *Vancouver* on which I had come to America. I noticed several of the men wore uniforms similar to those of the *Vancouver* crew. I looked at the men in hopes of seeing Herr Schneider, but regrettably I didn't spot him amongst the detainees.

Although I thought I was being unfairly accused and detained, I also didn't want to complain about my treatment. My greatest fear was that someone would decide I was no longer wanted here in America and should be repatriated back to Germany. I had no desire to participate in Hitler's war effort, even if it meant I would be with my family again. No, repatriation was something I definitely didn't want. With any luck, I would soon be cleared of any suspicions and I could leave this place.

* * *

On a cold wintry morning in late January 1942, Mutti and Ruth stepped carefully along the street on their way to the uniform factory where they both worked. They were bundled up for the cold weather and gazed ahead without enthusiasm.

Ruth had been at the dressmaker's shop for about a year when Nazi officials entered the premises and informed the owners that they were being closed down. They strongly suggested to the now unemployed staff that they were needed at a nearby uniform factory in support of the war effort.

Ruth was not keen on spending all day sewing uniforms, so she looked for work at other dressmakers. Unfortunately, none were hiring, and some were also closing. After a month without success at finding work, she felt she should take the unappealing job sewing uniforms so she could, at least, contribute to the family income. Since the closure of the local theater company, Mutti's income from sewing work had been paltry. Mutti decided that if Ruth was going to do it, then she would too. So together they had gone to the uniform factory and gotten jobs.

Walking carefully on the icy sidewalk, Ruth complained, "I don't know how I can sew army uniforms together very well after such a night of interrupted sleep. We don't have any bombing raids for a month and then are bombed for three nights in a row, as if it's our turn again."

"I didn't get a good night's sleep either," Mutti replied.

They looked up at the long brick building as they approached the gate of the uniform factory. Other workers were also entering the gate. A large canvas covered a gaping hole in the side of the factory building and crude repairs were made to the damaged fence along the outside.

"Well, no new damage from the raid last night. I guess that's good," Mutti observed.

"I suppose so," Ruth said.

"Remember to be careful with that cow of a supervisor. Act as if you are interested in sewing the uniforms, contributing to the war effort. She's a dangerous type," Mutti told Ruth.

"But I don't like sewing uniforms. I wanted to be a seamstress so I could design clothes, not sew uniforms," Ruth protested.

"And you can, after the war. Right now, everything is about the war effort. We need the money from these jobs. You don't want to starve do you? Even your father is spending less at his club."

With a distressed look, Mutti continued, "It's just a shame you had to put all your plans and dreams on hold. But you should count your blessings you aren't a man instead of who you are. You'd be seeing a lot more of the war than we have. Poor Fritzi, that sweet boy. It kills me to think of him on the Russian Front."

"I certainly feel for Cousin Fritzi too, Mutti. I hate this damn war," Ruth muttered.

"Hush, Ruth. Someone will hear you," Mutti said as she glanced around anxiously. Soon they were amid the crowd of women entering the factory gate.

Chapter 16
New Arrivals

THE WEEKS OF waiting for the results of my investigation turned into months. I would check with Miss Phillips regularly to see if she had heard anything, but she always shook her head. I was surprised to find I was getting used to my daily routine of cleaning during the day, meals in the cafeteria, reading in my free time, nightly head count and sleep.

It almost seemed as if I was working at the camp rather than being detained there. I got along well with the staff, who appreciated my hard work and my stoic attitude of waiting without complaining. I sensed that they were sympathetic to my plight, but they could do nothing for me. I must continue to wait. The status of the investigation report was always that it should be here any day.

By the end of March, I still had heard nothing. As I was sweeping the entryway floors of the administration offices one afternoon, a bus arrived outside. I watched out the front windows as the driver, a guard, and a dozen Asian women and children got off the bus. The driver retrieved their baggage, which they then carried into the building.

I felt something ominous about these new arrivals. They might mean my status as a special case would be ending. While I wasn't happy about being detained, I was used to my life here. Being a special case in the camp, I could roam about freely having promised not to try to escape. I didn't know what impact the arrival of other women might have on me. Maybe they were just passing through, and it meant nothing. On the other hand, maybe a women's enclosure would be started here and I would be in it.

The women and children were looking around with curiosity as they entered the building and were halted in the entryway area. They put their baggage down and stood waiting. They were wearing normal American-looking clothes instead of the colorful silk clothes of the Far East I had seen before at Angel Island. The well behaved children stayed close to their mothers. The women spoke their language in low voices between themselves. The secretary from the office came out, and the guard handed her some paperwork. After reading it over quickly, she motioned to me.

"Katie, drop what you are doing there and see if you can find Miss Phillips. She doesn't seem to be in her office. Tell her to come here and then tell the dining hall to prepare a dozen meals for these new arrivals."

"Yes, Ma'am," I said as I put my broom against the wall and hurried off.

"Thank you, Katie," she said as she turned back to the guard. Mr. Baker came out from his office and joined in the discussion.

A week later, I sat in a passenger car of a train staring out the window at the passing barren landscape. A cute little Japanese girl in the seat in front of me thrust a doll into my view. I smiled at the little girl as she kept playing with her doll. I looked around at the Japanese women and children around me, and then back out the window. The guard sat nearby.

The busload of Asian women and children detainees who had arrived at our camp were Japanese detainees on their way to a new women's detention facility in Texas. Since my Montana detention camp was not intended for women, it was decided I should also go with them to the

Texas facility. I had requested to stay since my investigation results might arrive at any time.

But no, my temporary stay at their men's camp was lasting longer than expected, so I should go to a facility for women and children. My case would be turned over to the officials there. Any investigation results received at the Montana facility would be forwarded. It could only mean that getting my investigation results would take longer.

* * *

Rolf sat quietly in the passenger seat of the cab as the supply truck bounced along the rough road leading from the camp. Sergeant Evans was at the wheel on a run to town to get supplies. Rolf was along to help load and unload them. Rolf looked sad and didn't say anything as he looked out the window.

"Rolf, you haven't been yourself lately. I'm guessing it's because of Kätchen?"

"Yes, I know something has happened to her. I don't think she's sick or dead, but something or someone is preventing her from visiting me. At first I was able to not let it bother me, but now it's been eating at me. I don't know how much longer I can take it. I don't want to do something drastic but may be getting to that point. I need to find out if she is all right."

"If I was to tell you something, my boy, would you keep it to yourself and not tell anyone where you heard it?"

"Yes, of course, Sergeant Evans."

"Do you remember the car with the U.S. government plates that was here the other week?"

"Yes, we were speculating that the Americans were here to get lessons on setting up their own camps."

"Not quite. They were here investigating Kätchen's visits to see you. I probably shouldn't say too much more about it."

"Damn!" Rolf groaned. "I tried to warn her she should stop visiting me because it might look bad for her. Unfortunately, I was right."

"They apparently were investigating whether her visits here had anything to do with spying."

"How ridiculous. I can't believe anyone thought that."

"You and I know it's ridiculous, but the Americans had to investigate such a possibility. Pearl Harbor was quite a shock for them. They aren't taking any chances. I can assure you that Sergeant Brown, who monitored your visits, had only good things to say about Kätchen. I did too, of course, as did everyone else including that stick-in-the-mud Lieutenant Boswell. I suspect the Americans will determine she's no security threat and let her go. I wouldn't worry too much about her, but I wouldn't count on her being allowed to visit you anymore."

Evans paused as Rolf sat silently, deep in thought.

"I hope they will at least let her send me letters. I'm her only link to her family back in Germany," Rolf said sadly.

"That would be a shame, Rolf, I agree. But like I said, she'll be okay. She's pretty game. She'll be able to get along once released. With any luck, you'll be together again someday when all this is over. So cheer up, my boy. No need for so much worrying." Saying this Evans slapped Rolf on the shoulder and Rolf perked up a bit.

Evans continued, "I'm sure the purpose of the visit by the Americans will get out eventually, but I thought you should know sooner, so you don't do anything rash."

Rolf stirred again and felt some relief at finally knowing what had happened to Kätchen. He showed some signs of his tensions already easing. She was being investigated for spying and would surely soon be vindicated and freed. He hoped that meant he would hear from her soon.

"Sergeant, I don't know how I can ever repay you for your kindness to me. At least I have an idea now of what happened to her and know that she's not harmed or in danger. Thank you, Sergeant."

"No need for thanks. Thought you deserved to know. Just remember, you didn't hear it from me."

"Right," Rolf said. Sergeant Evans was gratified to see a smile on Rolf's face for the first time in a long while. He began to hum to himself as he drove on down the bumpy road.

Chapter 17
Texas Camp

I PUSHED OPEN one side of the double doors and entered the well-furnished institutional kitchen. At the deep sink along the wall near the doors, I washed my hands. Taking my apron from a peg on the wall, I put it on as I made my way to Mrs. Johnson, the cook.

The camp in Texas was a modern facility only recently built as a low security women's prison, but then converted for use as a detention facility for alien women, children, and couples. With only a small number of detainees having arrived yet, they all were being fed in just one of the dining halls. I was assigned to work in the dining hall's kitchen.

"Hello, Mrs. Johnson."

"Hello, Katie."

"What would you like me to start on?"

Looked at her clipboard, Mrs. Johnson said, "We've got fried chicken, mashed potatoes, rice, and peas on the menu for lunch. Why don't you get eight chickens out and start cutting them up. I'll join you in a few minutes. Then we can start breading and frying them."

"Yes, Ma'am," I said and headed toward the refrigeration units to get the chickens.

About a dozen German women, who had been members of several German American clubs on the West Coast, were already at the camp when I arrived. Older than me and proud of their German heritage, they were indignant at being detained. They were apparently from German upper classes, very different from my working class upbringing.

One particularly arrogant and pushy woman named Frau Strohmeyer seemed to be their leader. She immediately assumed I should be part of her group and began telling me where I was to be at what time so I could participate in such and such of their activities. Seeing that I was of the common German pedigree, she likely invited me to participate just so I could serve them at their events.

I could see through her designs and didn't like her pushiness. So I told her thank you, but I wasn't interested. She was aghast in her disappointment with me and told me I should be more proud of my German heritage. I didn't see what that had to do with it. I told her that I was very proud of my German heritage, but had no interest in being bossed around by her. Her nose went straight into the air, and she huffed off.

After that, I was pretty much shunned by the German women. Whenever one of them did talk to me, they were usually complaining about something. If it wasn't our conditions, the weather or the food, then it was about Frau Strohmeyer. I disliked being around complainers. It was hard enough to endure a bad situation without also having to constantly listen to someone grousing about it. As a result, I was without the companionship of my fellow Germans there in the camp.

A couple dozen Japanese women and children lived at the camp so far, including those detainees with whom I arrived. The German and Japanese detainees kept to themselves and did not intermingle very much. I felt just as isolated and alone as I did back in the Montana camp where I was the only detainee. I wished I could have stayed there.

My room in a large residence building was designed for two, but since few detainees had arrived yet, I occupied it by myself. It was furnished with a basic set of furniture: a bed, dresser, desk, and chair. The large shared bathroom was down the corridor. At night I lay in bed looking at the ceiling, thinking about how many months I have been looking at these detention camp ceilings and wondering how many more months I would be doing the same.

During the day when I wasn't working in the kitchen, I would walk around the perimeter of the facility for exercise. A paved road with a painted centerline went all the way around the inside of the perimeter fence. We were not allowed to cross the centerline of the road and get close to the fence. A guard manned a guard post at the one entrance gate into the fenced camp.

After being at the Texas camp about two months, I was out exercising on my walk around the perimeter road. As I approached the entrance gate, I noticed the arrival of a new group of Japanese women and children, who were outside the gate getting checked in.

I was pleasantly surprised to recognize one of them as the Japanese girl who had blinked hello to me back at Angel Island when I first arrived in America. The poor girl looked very sad and ashamed as she waited. She happened to look up and see me. She brightened at first but then looked away with shame. I was surprised and happy to see her. She and her family had apparently also been taken from their home.

Once they were inside the entrance gate and across the road centerline, I began walking beside her.

"Hello," I said.

"Hello. It seems we meet again," she said without looking up at me.

"Yes."

"You work here?" she asked.

"No, I'm here the same as you."

"Oh, so sorry," she said sympathetically looking up at me for the first time.

"I'd better let you get settled. I'll see you."

"Bye, bye," she said looking back as she walked. I stopped, letting the other Japanese file by. It seemed so improbable we should ever meet again. After a few moments lost in thought, I continued my walk around the perimeter.

I was thinking of the Japanese girl later that day and expecting I would see her at dinner at the dining facility where I worked. I was back in the kitchen when she went through the serving line and we gave each other a little wave. She sat with the other Japanese in the dining hall as she ate. When I went out to wipe tables, I first walked over to her. When she saw me, she brightened up and turned around toward me.

"How are you?" I said.

"I am fine, thank you."

"My name is Katie."

"And I am Miko. Pleased to meet you," she said with a little polite bow.

"Miko. That's a pretty name. Pleased to meet you too," I said as I tried to give her a little bow in return. I began to notice the other Japanese women were watching.

"I don't want to interrupt your dinner, but I could look for you tomorrow if you like."

"Yes, I would like that," she said with a smile. I smiled back and then returned to my work.

The next day, Miko and I were getting better acquainted as we walked along the perimeter road talking.

"How long have you been here?" she asked.

"Two months, and I was at another camp several months before here."

Miko confided, "When I first saw you here, I thought you might be a worker or guard here, and I was now your prisoner. I felt shame. But you are a prisoner here too like me, so I do not feel shame talking with you."

"Do you remember Angel Island where we first met?" she asked and I nodded.

"My mother, brother and I have been in a camp there for several months before coming here."

"What about your father?"

"My father was a lawyer in San Francisco and considered an influential member of our Japanese community. Right after Pearl Harbor, he and the other leaders of our community were arrested and jailed. A few months later, all Japanese, including my family, were put into detention camps. They feared Japan will invade the U.S. mainland and we will aid them."

"And would you?"

"I do not know what Japan might force us to do. I only know we were not spies before the war and we do not desire to be spies now. We were also surprised by the attack on Hawaii and we believe it was very dishonorable."

"The American government thinks I am a spy too. I have to be here while they investigate. I hope to be cleared and released soon."

"No one investigates us. I think the Americans have no plans to release my family or other Japanese."

"I can't believe it. When the danger of invasion passes and they find out you had nothing to do with it, they will release you."

"I do not think so," Miko said, as we walked on.

Chapter 18
My Friend Miko

I KEPT CHECKING with the administrative office at the camp on the status of my investigation. Mrs. Bates, the secretary there, was sympathetic and watching for my investigation to come in, but it never did. She had even telephoned Mrs. Carlson, the secretary at the Montana detention camp. She had not received it yet, but would forward it just as soon as they receive it. Mrs. Bates had worked in government positions for many years and knew the wheels of government turn slowly. She wasn't surprised it was taking a long time, but we hadn't heard anything after six months.

The sweltering heat of summer in Texas was not something to which I was accustomed. In the kitchen where I worked, it was especially hot. I never sweated so much in my life. During heat spells, I tried to cool off after work with a shower but was sweating again even as I tried to dry off with a towel.

The violence of the weather was also surprising to me. During a thunderstorm, the wind howled and the rain pelted the windows so hard I thought they would break. It wasn't a place where I would live if I had a choice.

Miko and I became close friends. Early or late in the day when the temperature wasn't too hot, we'd sit at a picnic table on the grounds and chat. Like my sister Ruth, she also was interested in art. A very talented artist, she showed me some of her drawings of traditional Japanese themes.

"It's beautiful. Such pretty cherry blossoms. How do you do it?" I said admiring one of the drawings.

"It just takes a little practice and a little patience. Here is something I have drawn for you." She reached to the bottom of her pictures and pulled out a small portrait drawing of me.

"It's amazing. I don't know if I look that good, but it is definitely me. You did this from memory?"

"Yes, it didn't take long. It's for you."

"Thank you, Miko. I wish I had something to give you."

"No need. You are my friend. That is enough."

"Can I ask for one more gift then?" I asked.

"Sure, what is it?"

"A drawing of you," I said.

Touched by my request, we hugged, and she said, "Sure." Afterward, I looked again with amazement at the very lifelike portrait she had drawn of me.

More weeks passed without any word on my investigation. Mrs. Bates called the Montana detention camp to check, and it still had not come in. Mrs. Carlson, the secretary there at the Montana camp, couldn't imagine why it was taking so long. She tried to contact the two agents who interviewed me to see what they knew, but they were unavailable due to some special assignment. She suggested Mrs. Bates call Washington, which she did, only to be told that they would get back to her, which they never did.

One day, I sat at the picnic table enjoying the cool fall weather while I waited for Miko to join me. She walked up trying to look normal, but I could tell something was wrong.

"Miko, what's the matter? You look upset."

"I am sorry I am not myself. We have just learned my family is to be sent back to Japan, repatriated." I gasped. I considered being sent back to Germany as the worst possible outcome for my situation. I completely understood her being upset.

"Why? What happened?"

"They tell us we will be exchanged for Americans and others held in Japan. Next summer, they will put us with other Japanese on a ship to meet another ship from Japan. The passengers will be exchanged and we will return to Japan on the other ship."

"Can they do that?" I asked, and she nodded.

"Do you want to go back?"

"My family was very happy with our life here before the war."

"Can you fight it? Can you refuse to go?"

"My family does not want to go back to Japan, but why would we want to stay in a country that does not want us? We will not fight it. If they say we must go, we will go."

"I'm so sorry, Miko. I can't believe they would do it. Maybe they will change their minds."

"No, I do not think so."

"What about your father?"

"He will be sent with us."

"At least you will be together again, but what a terrible thing to do. What will you do back in Japan?"

"My father will probably be required to join the Japanese army."

"How awful!"

"My mother, brother, and I will probably return to our home town of Hiroshima where I grew up. We still have family there to stay with."

"I truly hope you'll be safe there until this terrible war ends. I'm so sorry." I felt terrible for my friend who was innocent of any wrongdoing in this war, just as I was. We sadly hugged and cried.

I lay in bed that night unable to sleep. It had been nine months since I had last seen Rolf and nearly three years since I had been able to communicate with my family in Germany. I still heard nothing about my investigation. When Mrs. Bates had been able to find out nothing about it. I was starting to give up hope.

The only good thing that had happened to me lately was finding my friend Miko, but I couldn't talk to her about my investigation or hopes of being released when all she could look forward to was being sent back to Japan. It was a sad and difficult time for me.

Chapter 19
Bad News

IN SEPTEMBER OF 1942, summer had passed and I had still heard nothing about the status of my investigation. I went to Mrs. Bates one more time to see if she could find out any anything for me. As I stood in front of her desk and the tears began to well up in my eyes. She came around from her seat and tried to comfort me. She was now mad about it herself and she promised to get to the bottom of it. She would call tomorrow and not quit until she got an answer. I thanked her and left.

The next day, I was in the kitchen helping prepare lunch. As I stirred a large pot of gravy, I wondered if Mrs. Bates would finally learn something. She seemed so determined yesterday, I thought this time might be different. After all this time, I didn't want to get my hopes up but felt a little hopeful. When finally finished with the lunch clean up, I took off my apron, washed up, and hurried over to her office.

I entered the office and saw Mrs. Bates sitting at her desk frowning and shaking her head. When she saw me, she waved me in with a deep sigh. I could see that her efforts had been unsuccessful.

"Kätchen, sit down. I am so frustrated! I finally was able to get through to the right office in Washington to find out about your investigation. Naturally, the person there, who I needed to speak to, was out for the day. Arrg! Another person thought he could find the answer but didn't know what he was doing. I know that because what he told me couldn't be right. So I struck out again today but assure you that I will call tomorrow as many times as it takes to get through to the right person and track down the right answer," she said sitting back with a look of exasperation.

"What was it the man told you?"

"No, I don't even want to say. Now I'm sorry I even mentioned it. I know it isn't correct. You should wait until tomorrow when I can give you the right answer."

"I still am curious to hear what he said."

"It doesn't matter what he said. It can't be true. I'll get the right answer for you tomorrow."

"Please, Mrs. Bates, what did he tell you?" I asked again softly.

She looked at me for a moment and then said, "He said they have no record of an investigation being conducted for you."

I sat in the chair calmly without reaction, which surprised Mrs. Bates. She looked at me curiously and continued, "But as I said, it can't be right. You are a case, and there has be an investigation related to your case. It has to be somewhere. I promised I would get to the bottom of this, and I will. I'm going to call them again tomorrow and talk to the right person."

"For some reason, Mrs. Bates," I finally said, "I'm not surprised. So many things have happened lately that nothing surprises me anymore."

"Katie, don't give up. There must be some mistake. I'll try again tomorrow."

"I do appreciate your trying, Mrs. Bates, I really do, but I suspect there's no mistake." I rose up slowly and calmly left the office as she watched sadly.

On the sidewalk outside her office, I walked slowly and miserably along. After a time, a gust of wind blew my hair into my face and brought my attention back to my surroundings. Nearby in front of me was the camp's high barbed wire enclosure fence. I walked trance-like across the centerline of the perimeter road and stood before the fence.

Putting my fingers through the wire of the fence, I gazed out upon the plains and distant hills on the outside. The guard posted at the entrance gate noticed and watched. Seeing a sad pitiful figure, not someone trying to escape, he didn't think alarm was necessary.

I stood at the fence deep in thought. I was now being held in a detention camp being wrongfully suspected of spying. I had just learned that they could find no record of an investigation, which I hoped would clear my name. It meant I would be detained in this camp for quite some time. I was cut off from my family in Germany who probably needed my help and from Rolf in Canada who had no idea what happened to me. Feeling sad, lonely, and miserable, I slowly slumped down onto my knees against the fence.

Reaching into a pocket, I pulled out a worn photograph. It was the family portrait taken back in 1931 when I was twelve years old. I had brought it to America with me and used to have it by my bedside in a frame. The agents took it from my room at Mrs. Martin's house and made copies of it.

While taking a break during my interrogations, I had managed to slip one of the copies under my sweater unseen. I wasn't able to do the same for Rolf's picture. So this worn photograph was a treasured possession, which I would sometimes pull out of hiding to gaze at affectionately.

Deep in thought, I saw myself again as a twelve year old girl running errands for my mother to the sewing shop, walking happily along the tree lined street with my dark hair braided in shoulder-length pigtails. Life was better back then. I looked fondly at the picture, fingering the edges a little as I did so. I studied the faces in the worn photograph.

"Vati, Mutti, Ruth," I said to myself, "I'm so sorry. You thought I might be a help to you, but I can't even help myself."

Aloud, I sadly said, "I miss you all and hope you're safe." I added, "And you too, Rolf." Looking down at the picture clutched in my hands, I wanted to cry, but the tears wouldn't flow.

A few minutes later, a voice behind me said, "Miss? Are you all right? Can I help you up?" As I slipped the photo back into my pocket, I looked up. It was the gate guard who had come over to see if I was okay. He helped me to my feet, and I sadly walked back toward the stark buildings of the detention camp.

Mrs. Johnson was expecting me back at work in the kitchen to help with preparations for dinner. Instead of returning to work, I walked numbly back to my room and collapsed on the bed. I missed the head count that night, so someone came to my room, found me on the bed and checked me off as present.

My sleep was troubled and not very restful, but in the morning I was functional enough to go to work in the kitchen. Mrs. Johnson wasn't happy with me for missing work the day before. But seeing that something had happened, that I wasn't my normal self, she let it pass.

That afternoon, I was sitting at the picnic table, when Miko came up and saw I was feeling down.

"Katie, you are sad. Has something happened?" she asked with concern, as she sat beside me.

"I didn't tell you about it, Miko, but Mrs. Bates at the office has been calling Washington to find out the status of my investigation. Well, she finally got through to someone and found out they have no record of an investigation." Miko looked sadly down without speaking.

"Mrs. Bates is going to call again. She thinks the person was mistaken and didn't know what he was talking about. Maybe he was right. I don't know what to think anymore. After all that has happened to me and you, it wouldn't surprise me."

"Do not give up, perhaps it is a mistake, as she says."

"Thanks, Miko, for being my friend." I put my hand on her arm. She smiled and put her hand on top of mine.

Chapter 20
Hope

THE NEXT DAY, I heard nothing from the office, which seemed to confirm my worst fears. On the afternoon of the second day, I was in the kitchen putting a pan of tamale pie in the oven, when Mrs. Johnson informed me I was wanted at the office when I could take a break.

When I walked into Mrs. Bates' office, she smiled politely and motioned to the chair. "Katie, sit down. I have found something out." I sat down feeling a little bit hopeful.

"Yesterday, I was able to reach the lady at the Immigration office in Washington, the one who was out the other day," Mrs. Bates explained. "I told her how you have been waiting nine months for your investigation. She said she would do some checking and make some phone calls. She called me back this morning."

After a pause, she continued, "The man the other day said he could find no record of your investigation. He apparently checked to see if an active investigation was in progress on you." She took a breath.

"He was correct that there is no active one. But if he had known more, he would have checked further. Then he would have discovered that there is no active investigation in progress because it was... well..." she hesitated, "it was completed five months ago."

* * *

Five months earlier in April 1942, a young girl with bright red lipstick and a tight-fitting blouse sat behind a secretary's desk at the detention camp in Montana. With a bored look she pulled a large envelope from a stack of mail and opened it. Taking a bound report from the envelope, she looked it over casually.

"Hmm," she said. Looking around, she saw no one to ask what to do. Many people were out sick including the secretary for whom she was filling in. Getting up, she straightened out her dress and carried the envelope over to a file cabinet. She opened a drawer labeled *Investigations* and began fingering through the files.

"Let's see, hmm, Accident Investigations, uh-uh. Detainee Investigations, no, probably not. Incident Investigations, nope. Ah, Personnel Investigations, that should do it," she said as she popped the report into the file and closed the file cabinet. She sat back down at the desk, fluffed her hair as she looked in a small mirror. She then picked up another letter from the mail pile and opened it.

Mr. Baker came out of his office and seeing her open the envelope, said, "Ginger, Sweetie, there's no need for you to worry about the mail. It can wait until Mrs. Carlson comes back. I hope she only has a touch of the flu and will be back soon. You just need to answer phones, make coffee and tell me when visitors come in."

"Okay, Uncle Don, no problem. Do you have any magazines here?"

* * *

As I sat listening, Mrs. Bates explained the completed investigation report was sent to the detention camp in Montana only about two weeks after I left. They were supposed to forward it here, but it had been filed by mistake. They think it was probably done by a temp filling in while the regular secretary was sick. I sat dumbfounded in the chair as I listened. I could only think of all the time I had spent waiting.

She continued, "The regular secretary, Mrs. Carlson, has now found the report in their files. She feels terrible about it. They're sending it right away. We should get it here soon. Our attorney will review the investigation report and present its results at a parole hearing here to a judge who will decide whether you should continue to be held or could be paroled."

I gradually recognized that things were not as bad as I imagined in my despair. The investigation had apparently proceeded as they had described to me back in Montana, only maybe a little slower. I might have been paroled five months ago, except for the bad luck of being sent to Texas and the mishandling of the investigation report. At least the report had been found, and I could potentially be paroled if it contained favorable findings. It gave me hope in the remaining process again.

"Thank you so much, Mrs. Bates. I appreciate what you did to find the report," I said as I stood up and shook her hand.

"Try to be patient a little longer, Kätchen. The end may be in sight."

Chapter 21
Release

MY PAROLE HEARING took place in a meeting room at
the camp about one week after the investigation was
received from the Montana camp. An attorney presented
the results of the investigation report to a judge seated
behind a table. I was not invited to attend.

The investigation report documented the agents'
interviews with me as well as their interviews with the
people in the little town in Montana where I had worked in
a cafe, the staff at the prisoner of war camp in Canada and
people back in California where I had initially lived after
coming to America. I hoped the details of the report
presented a favorable opinion of my actions and reassured
the judge I was not a spy. I was curious to know how those
interviews had gone.

* * *

Eight months before, the two agents in dark suits sat
across a table from Earl, the old crusty regular at Red's cafe
in Shelby. Earl was listening to the agents incredulously and
then burst out. "Well, I reckon that is the Goddamn
dumbest thing I ever heard of. Katie ain't no spy, no way.
Why she practically told the whole town that she didn't like
Hitler and the Nazis, and I believe her. I know people and
she ain't no spy. "

Earl looked over at the county sheriff who was seated in
the corner observing. "Sheriff, you don't believe any of this
crap, do you?"

"Nope, I already told 'em," the sheriff said.

Earl pointed his finger at the agents threateningly.
"Now you two yahoos listen here. You go back and turn

her loose. She ain't no more a spy than you or me. Who the hell would tell you that, anyway?" He paused thinking and then said, "I'll bet it was that little tramp Teri, wasn't it? Sure, she wanted Katie's job at the cafe. It was her, wasn't it?"

He looked at the agents without getting an answer. "Well, at least the little tramp didn't get it. She came in right away after you two hauled Katie off to jail. Red told her no way and hired one of the Riley girls instead. That's what started all this, I'll bet.

Dang, I still can't believe how you hauled Katie off like you done. If you'd asked us about her ahead a time, we'd have saved you a whole lot of trouble. We'd have told you she ain't done nothing wrong. She's got a boyfriend in a prisoner camp up in Canada somewhere. She'd go up to visit him once a month. Ain't nothin' wrong in that. She's a good girl. She ain't no spy.

Now seriously, you two take yourselves back there and turn Katie loose. I'm sure there's plenty of spies out there that you need to find and lock up. Katie ain't one of 'em."

The agents interviewed several others from the small town in Montana, and all expressed a similar reaction and favorable opinion of me. They had intended to interview Teri too, but she gave them the slip when she heard they wanted to talk to her.

At the prison camp in Canada, the guards and staff answered the two agents' questions, showed them the table where Rolf and I sat during our visits, and told them of the conditions imposed. They described how Rolf and I never violated any rules and how we always talked in English as stipulated. The agents listened and took notes.

Sergeant Brown, who was the monitor for the visits, thought that the accusations were ridiculous. He had heard every word during our visits, and it had been authentic heartfelt conversation about family and mutual affection, never anything that might even remotely suggest spying or the passing of information.

He and the rest of the guards had only good things to say about me and Rolf. It was their emphatic and unanimous opinion that the accusations of spying were patently untrue.

The agents next conducted a telephone interview with the San Mateo County Sheriff. He remembered me well and the incident at the bakery. He still got a chuckle out of thinking about it. He had raced into the bakery kitchen with his pistol drawn only to find me innocently looking up at him with a pastry-covered face, sitting on the back of a co-worker, holding her down by an arm twisted behind her back.

Our fight caused a terrific pastry mess in the kitchen. The bakery owner, Herr Steinhauer, had been knocked down during the fight. He was raging at us for causing such a mess and he told the sheriff to take us away.

The sheriff conducted interviews afterward and a co-worker Ray, who had witnessed everything, told him that my co-worker had flown into a rage and attacked me as we argued because I was tired of listening to her go on and on about how great Hitler was. The sheriff had documented that in his incident report.

He felt sure that I was not a security risk, definitely wanted to vouch for my character with the agents, and sent them right away a copy of the incident report.

* * *

To my great relief, the hearing concluded I was not a security risk and had done no spying. Soon I would be allowed to leave the detention camp. Afterward, I hugged Mrs. Bates and thanked her for her help.

But my release came with a heavy cost. One condition of my release stipulated that I was forbidden from further visits or communications with Rolf for the duration of the war.

I sat at a table with the paper and pen in front of me. Across the table from me was the lawyer who had been in the parole hearing. I asked him if there was any way we could at least be allowed to write to each other. He only shook his head and said the judge's ruling did not allow it. I sadly signed the paper saying I understood the conditions of my parole. It was a double blow to me because it also meant I would not be able to hear news through Rolf of my family back in Germany.

The day after signing, I stood with my suitcase beside the tan sedan parked outside the camp gate. I sadly waved one more time to Miko who was inside the fence watching. Inside the fence a few minutes before, we hugged and said a final goodbye. Miko had tried to be brave and upbeat, but we couldn't keep from crying many tears at our parting. She would keep her drawing of me as a remembrance and I would keep the drawing of her.

After putting the suitcase in the back seat, I climbed in front. I rolled down the window and waved to Miko a last time as she sadly waved back. It was very hard saying goodbye to Miko. She was genuinely happy for me and I was genuinely miserable for her. We had endured the detention camp life together and were good friends. Neither of us were threats to America, but I was being released while she and her family would remain and be forced to return to Japan.

The driver climbed in, started the car and pulled away as Miko and I waved goodbye. Driving away I started to cry again. They weren't tears of joy at finally being allowed to leave. Instead, they were tears of sadness for my friend who could not leave.

The driver was taking me to the bus station in town. Once released, I planned to go back to Aunt Minna's restaurant in the hills above San Carlos, California. Even if she didn't need my help in the restaurant, she would take me in for a time until I found something else. Mrs. Gentsch surely had another nanny by now.

It didn't make sense for me to return to the little town in Montana since I could no longer visit Rolf. Yet I had grown to like the people there very much and planned to stay in touch with them. I knew now that they still believed in me and had stuck up for me in the investigation.

It had been over four years since I left Aunt Minna's restaurant. Three months ago, I wrote her a letter telling her that I was being detained in Texas and didn't know when I might be released. I told her it was probably better we didn't correspond. I would contact her again when I knew more. It was only yesterday that I knew anything more, so it was pointless to write her again. I would show up at her restaurant in hopes that she would take me back.

Several days later, I walked along the sidewalk carrying my suitcase. Up ahead was the familiar sight of Aunt Minna's restaurant. Although it was lunchtime, I noticed no activity or business as I walked up to the front door. The restaurant did not look to be in very good condition. The exterior trim looked dilapidated and in need of paint.

Entering the front door, I noticed that the interior presented a similar neglected look. A single patron ate a bowl of soup at a table. I didn't see any staff.

"Hello. Where is everyone?" I called.

From the kitchen I heard the familiar voice of Aunt Minna say, "I'll be right with you. Sit down at any table."

I walked back toward the kitchen.

"Aunt Minna. It's me, Kätchen." I heard the crash of a pan hitting the floor and Aunt Minna came rushing out excitedly to hug me.

"Kätchen, you're back. I've missed you so," she said as she hugged me with more affection than she had ever shown before.

"I've missed you too, Aunt Minna," I said sincerely.

"Your letter said you were being detained in Texas. You are here now, so I guess you got things straightened out?" she asked.

"Yes, I guess so, but it took longer than I expected. Do you still have a place for me here?"

"My dear child, you're a Godsend. As you can see, I can't get any help. All the girls are working in factories and shipyards now. I would very much appreciate your help. You have no idea. I'm at my wits end."

Pulling a handkerchief from her pocket, she could contain herself no longer and began to cry into it. I hugged her again to comfort her.

"Kätchen, I'm getting old. I'm so happy you are here again. You can't imagine how much."

"Aunt Minna, I'm happy to be back too. I'll stay here with you and help you get this place running again. Let me put my suitcase in the back, have a bite to eat, and then I'll get started."

Chapter 22
The Homefront

FOR SEVERAL WEEKS since arriving back at Aunt Minna's restaurant, I had been inside scrubbing the dining area, bar, and kitchen from top to bottom and repainting the trim to give the place a little more color. The outside stucco on the restaurant was still in good shape, and I thought its washed-out look gave the place character. I did, however, give a fresh coat of paint to the exterior trim of the doors and windows. The place began to look alive again and open for business.

A few of Aunt Minna's loyal customers had stayed with her the whole time even though the quality of the food and service had suffered. We asked them to pass on to others that we were back in business and would be up to our old standards again. Our old customers as well as new ones soon began to return, and business began to pick up.

When I wasn't scrubbing and painting, I was reconnecting with friends, especially my friends in Shelby. The last time they saw me, I was being arrested and taken away. I did not write to them during detainment. I could only imagine what terrible thoughts and low opinion they had of me after seeing me hauled off that way.

"Well, don't that beat all. She sure had us buffaloed. Here she was a Nazi spy all along!" I imagined them saying.

While I was not allowed to read the investigation report, I gathered that they had not thought such a thing after all, but had stuck up for me and told the agents I was not a spy. So now that I was finally paroled and became aware that I owed them thanks, I wanted to write them.

I wrote to Mrs. Martin and to Red's Cafe to let them know I was finally free and how my release had been delayed so long by the misplaced investigation report. I thanked them for their support in convincing the agents that I had been wrongfully accused.

I told them how fond I still was of them and their little town. I wished that I could go back, but found that my aunt here needed my help badly, so I couldn't. I could only hope that someday I would be able to visit them and thank them in person.

They wrote back to tell me how shocked and disappointed they were to hear that I had been held for so long. They thought that I would be released shortly after their interviews with the agents way back in January of 1942. Mrs. Martin told me that she felt like hitting someone with her broom again.

Angie writing for Red and the others at the Cafe told me how everyone in town knew that it was Teri who had told the FBI that I was a Nazi spy. The whole town was mad at her for it, and either shunned her or made nasty comments to her about it. Even so, she never denied it.

Some people even refused to order drinks from her at the club. She was pretty unpopular in town and one time after work, she found the letters "RLB" painted on both sides of her old pickup. She was furious and asked around what the hell "RLB" meant? Someone told her that they heard it stood for "Rotten Little Bitch," which everyone in town seemed to know. Having had enough, Teri left town in a big huff, and they haven't seen her since.

I suppose I should say that I was sorry to hear that she was tormented, but my present situation of no communications with Rolf and my family back in Germany had been caused by her, which was more than I could easily forgive.

Shortages of some foods and materials existed due to the war. We were able to get enough eggs, potatoes, and vegetables from local farms and markets, but meats were rationed and not very available. Restaurants were issued ration coupons for some foods. Although the restaurant's rations were larger amounts than households, we still could not get as much as we would have liked.

The only meat we were able to get regularly was some god-awful stuff called spam. I didn't care much for it or for the way it was sealed in its can. I grew to hate those little keys that were used to twist around and around each little can to get the top off.

Opening a can of spam one morning, I finally got the darned top off without cutting myself on the sharp metal edges. Stabbing the spam with a fork, I pulled it out of the can. I scraped off the greasy gel stuff, sliced the spam and put the slices on the grill to cook.

"Aunt Minna, this spam is awful stuff, but we go through a lot of it. I don't understand why the customers like it so much," I said to her as she walked past.

"They like it. That's what counts," she replied.

* * *

While I was busy bringing the restaurant back to life, Rolf continued his existence at the prisoner of war camp. Sergeant Evans had confided to him that the American visitors to the camp in January had been investigating the ridiculous spying charges. He expected that I would be released in a month or so.

So Rolf then finally knew that my visits had stopped because I had been detained by the Americans. But that had been ten months ago. He had not heard anything since and did not know why. Having no further knowledge of me was still unsettling to him.

On an early November afternoon, he was out with the others clearing trees from the reservoir, a project on which they had worked for several years. As he carried limbs to piles, he tried to keep his mind off of me for a while. He heard the crackle of the guard's walkie talkie and their guard went to get it. The guard talked briefly on it and then hollered to Rolf.

"Rolf, you have a visitor! Head back to camp!

Rolf turned with a smile to Dieter who was nearby.

"Well, what are you waiting for!" Dieter said with enthusiasm.

Rolf tossed his limb aside, and hurried off at a brisk trot. It would probably take about fifteen minutes to get there and all the while, his mind raced with speculation as to who the visitor might be. He hoped it might be me, but that would be too good to be true. But who else could it be?

When he got to the camp headquarters building, he hurried inside without stopping to catch his breath. Sergeant Evans was there and caught him up, saying, "Whoa, Rolf, take it easy. There's no need for rush. Your visitor is in the conference room. So you are not too disappointed when you go inside, I'll tell you now that it is not Kätchen. She may know something though."

"She?"

"Yes, she, so catch your breath for a second, straighten yourself up a bit and we'll go in. Same rules as with your visits with Kätchen."

"Yes, Sergeant, thank you for letting me know. I suspected that a visit from Kätchen was too good to be true."

I ran my fingers through my hair a couple times, brushed off my shirt and pants, and was ready.

Sergeant Evans then showed me into the conference room and stayed at the monitor of the visit. Across the conference table from me stood a middle-aged thick-set woman with dark hair and pleasant face. She wore a dark print dress and had a purse hanging from one arm.

She looked at me and said, "It's funny. You're just as I pictured you, Rolf. You don't know me, but my name is Mabel Martin. Katie roomed in my house when she lived in Shelby."

"Why don't you both have a chair," Sergeant Evans suggested.

After sitting, Rolf said, "And I have heard much about you too, Mrs. Martin. My Kätchen, Katie as you know her, always had such nice things to say about you. I'm very happy to meet you at last.

"Yes, we got along real well. She got along real well with pretty much the whole town. As a matter of fact, a bunch of the people in town took up a collection to pay for my trip here to see you."

Rolf looked at her expectantly, hoping she had news.

"Me and the people at Red's Cafe just got letters from her. She was just released from her detention and they thought you oughta know."

Rolf choked up with emotion at their kindness in bringing him this news.

"We were damned mad when we heard it took them so long to release her," she continued. "We told them back in January that there was no way she was a spy."

Sergeant Evans inserted, "We told them the same thing here in no uncertain terms when they interviewed us in January. We thought she would surely be released in a month or two."

"So did we!" said Mr. Martin, hotly. "Katie said that it took them over three months to complete it and then it got lost. They didn't find it until a month ago. Don't that beat all. We think she got a pretty raw deal. The least we could do to make up for our government's stupidity was to tell you about her release even though she never asked us to."

"I can't tell you, Mrs. Martin, how much I appreciate what you and your townspeople have done," Rolf told her with emotion. "I haven't heard from her since she visited me last November, about a year ago."

"She said in her letter," Mrs. Martin continued, "that she wasn't allowed to write to you while being detained. Then, for God knows why, the judge said she couldn't write or visit you after she was released either. Well, the judge didn't tell me I couldn't visit you, so I thought I would come visit you myself this one time, without causing too much trouble. Katie misses you a lot and wants to write, but can't until the war is over."

Sergeant Evans stood sadly shaking his head, and Rolf sat back in his chair, speechless."

Finally, he asked, "And where is Katie now?"

"She's with her aunt at the restaurant in California. Her aunt apparently needs her help there in her restaurant real bad. She said she plans to live out the war there. Whenever you are able to write again, that's where she expects to be. She is in good health.

"I'm very happy to hear it."

"She regrets not being able to come back to Shelby, and so do we. We miss her and are glad to do her a favor after the raw deal she got."

"I really appreciate you coming to let me know. I have things to tell her too. When you write back to her, please tell her that my mother still hears periodically from her family in Hamburg. Her family is well and still living in their apartment. Her sister is not married and works as a seamstress in a dress shop. The conditions there in the war are not bad so far."

Dabbing at a tear of happiness, Mrs. Martin said, "Katie will be so happy to hear it. She said in her letter how she worries about them and has no way of hearing how they are. That's wonderful. I'm sure she will be happy to hear it."

"Tell her I will pass her information on to her family."

"Oh, she is really gonna be tickled when we tell her about today. And how about you, Rolf? What should I tell her about how you are doing?"

"Please tell her that I love her and miss her very much. I have been very worried about her, but now thanks to you and her other friends there in Shelby, I am much better. My health is good, and I'm fully recovered from my injuries in the plane crash."

Glancing over at Sergeant Evans, he added, "The Canadians are very good to us. I suspect that I will spend the rest of the war here too. I greatly look forward to the day when Katie and I can get married. Please tell her that."

"I certainly will. I'm glad my visit was a help for you, and I hope, someday, that you and Katie can be together."

Looking about happily and at Sergeant Evans, she said, "Well, I guess that about wraps it up and I should be going now."

"I thank you again from the bottom of my heart, Mrs. Martin. And please thank the others in your town for me too. I wish I could give you a hug of thanks, but contact is not allowed."

As she rose from her chair, Sergeant Evans went to her and said, "Kätchen certainly found very nice friends there in that little town across the border. On Rolf's behalf, I'll give you that hug."

He then gave her a heartfelt hug of admiration and thanks, as Rolf watched smiling.

* * *

I was so happy when I read what Mrs. Martin and the others in Shelby had done. I had to sit down and cry as I continued to read her letter. I had not even considered asking them to do such a thing, not wanting to get them in trouble, and those wonderful people had done it anyway on their own. Now I would rest easier knowing Rolf knew what happened to me, why he has heard nothing from me for a year. And I also had finally heard news of my family. They were okay despite the war and its bombings, and they would hear news of me.

It was all too wonderful. Being able to communicate with them would be better, but this had made things for me much better. Now, it was a matter of waiting until the war was over, when we could communicate again. I finally felt a little better knowing that Rolf was no longer totally in the dark and worried about me. Aunt Minna was happy for me too and could not believe what wonderful friends I had made there in such a short time. I immediately wrote Mrs. Martin back thanking her and the others, telling them how grateful I was.

With my mind now at ease about Rolf, I was able to concentrate better on improving our conditions at the restaurant. No longer was work something to keep my mind from worrying about Rolf. Afterward, I would work hard to make our situation better and make the most of my time waiting for the war to be over. I felt energized.

Butter, for example, was important to our cooking at the restaurant, but it was rationed, and we never seemed to have enough. I wanted to try making my own, so I inquired about getting milk from a local dairy farmer, Mr. Lundgren. I learned he was always in need of help with the early morning milking, so we struck a bargain.

A couple times a week, I woke up early and walked in the dark to the dairy to milk cows. Being still dark outside when we milked, a few overhead light bulbs illuminated the barn as I milked a long row of dairy cows using a surge bucket milker. A few other local people were also there, I think to make extra money.

Mr. Lundgren agreed to pay me in raw milk. He lent me a milk can and a small wagon. With dawn breaking in the eastern sky, I would return home to the restaurant carefully pulling my small wagon with the shiny milk can inside.

We started out small at first in a section of the kitchen set up for our cheese making. Later we would expand the back of the kitchen to provide more room.

The cream in the milk naturally separates and floats to the top of the milk with time, but Mr. Lundgren lent us a hand-cranked cream separator, which saved us time. By whipping the cream in our mixer, we made enough butter for our own use in the restaurant. Sometimes we had extra butter, which we would share with our customers and neighbors or use to trade for other foods.

Since we suspected it might be a violation of rationing, we didn't sell our extra butter. After my previous detainee experience, I did not desire to get into any more trouble. When we had extra cream, I would make sour cream for our use. I think we were the only place in town offering it with baked potatoes.

I knew how to make sour cream from my time on Frau Meyer's dairy farm when I was a sixteen year old girl in Germany. Thanks to that experience, I knew how to make butter and sour cream from cream as well as cheese and a German cottage cheese called quark from milk.

Frau Meyer, back then, made such things once or twice a month for personal use on their dairy. When I told her I was interested in learning how to make them too, we began making cheese and cottage cheese regularly and made a good profit selling them to local markets and restaurants. Frau Meyer had been so pleased with the success of our cheese and cottage cheese making that she considered going into the business for real. My time on that dairy farm in Germany proved valuable to us now.

With our good supply of milk, I was able to make enough cheese and cottage cheese to meet the needs of the restaurant and more. If we still had milk to spare, we would serve big glasses of it for a nickel. We sold our extra cheese and cottage cheese as well to our customers, since they were not a rationed item. They became very popular sellers. Later that year, cheese would also become a rationed item and we stopped selling it, although we still made enough for our own generous use.

One of our main lunch items was the Dutch Lunch. Before the war, it consisted of plates of meat and cheese slices, tomato and onion slices, and bread, as well as cups of mayonnaise and mustard. Using these plates of ingredients, the customers made their own sandwiches.

With meats and cheeses rationed, we offered grilled thin slices of spam and other meats when available, a generous portion of our own cheese, and our own butter for the mayonnaise. Our wartime Dutch Lunch was surprisingly even more popular than it was before the war.

At the time, the war effort was first and foremost in everyone's minds. Since we made our own butter and cheese, we didn't need to buy any with our ration coupons. We were inadvertently helping the war effort, which I didn't mind doing.

Still, it was difficult for me to enthusiastically support a war effort against my own homeland. I wanted the Nazis defeated, but how could it be accomplished without killing many of my own countrymen and maybe my own family? I tried to keep busy and not think about it.

Another war effort in which we participated was the saving of waste grease. Everyone was encouraged to save grease and take it to the local butcher, who paid money for it. He would then sell it to the government for use in making explosives. We kept a big bucket for waste grease in the back of the kitchen.

When full, I put the bucket in my wagon and wheeled it down to the butcher. With the money he gave me, I would buy rennet from him for my cheese making. So it worked out well for both us and the butcher.

Aunt Minna still owned her old 1931 Buick Straight Eight sedan, but we used it very little and therefore used very few of her gasoline ration coupons.

Another war effort, which received much attention was the Victory Garden. With all that I had going, I just didn't have enough time for one.

Chapter 23
Helping Miko

In what little free time I had, I tried to catch up with friends and write letters, which when previously detained, I felt I couldn't do at all.

I got together with my friends Hanni and Magda again and had much to tell them. Relieved to see me again, they had been terribly worried about me when they suddenly heard nothing from me and their letters to me were returned. They might have said "I told you so" about my ill-fated move to Montana, but they didn't.

I made a trip to Atherton to visit the Gentsch family and was warmly received. It was gratifying to see that the foundation of good behavior I drummed into the Gentsch children was still evident. Jimmy and Susan were still good kids who had missed me terribly as I had them. Mrs. Gentsch had been so happy with me, that when I left, she had looked for another German girl as my replacement. After a period of adjustment, Karin had worked out well and was still with them.

In addition to my letter to my friends in Shelby, I also kept in touch with Miko. I told her about milking cows and making cheese, and she sent me several little drawings of people, flowers, and scenes from the camp. Her status had not changed. Next summer, she and her family would be sent back to Japan. I still felt terrible for her and decided I would try to help her. So I paid a visit to my friend, the San Mateo County Sheriff.

When I was shown into his back office, he rose up from behind his desk and laughed. He came around his desk and shook my hand. I was a little embarrassed at the thought of our last meeting, but we were laughing and smiling as we exchanged greetings.

He was happy to see I had been released and still vividly remembered my pastry-covered face looking up at him as I held my co-worker down on the floor of the bakery. He motioned me to a chair in front of his desk, and we both sat down.

I started out, "Sheriff, I came here today because I wanted to thank you again, but I also came to ask a favor."

"Oh, what's that?"

I explained, "When I was in the detention camp in Texas, I was close friends with a Japanese girl named Miko. She and her family were removed from San Francisco where her father had been a community leader. I know them, and they are good people. They had nothing to do with Japan starting the war. And now, not only are they being held, but they are being forced to return to Japan later this year."

"Hmm. Really?" He considered this for a moment, then continued, "The sneak attack on Pearl Harbor was pretty underhanded. It put quite a scare into us here on the West Coast and created some pretty hard feelings toward the Japanese. So, the Japanese nationals here were rounded up and held as a precaution against any further underhandedness like spying and sabotage."

"Miko and her family didn't know about or have anything to do with Pearl Harbor. I'm sure of it."

"That may be true. I don't know. There are lots of innocent victims in war. We're over the fear of an invasion of the West Coast now, but I guess they are still being held." He paused. "I hadn't heard that any Japanese were being forced to return to Japan though. That does sound a little drastic. If you give me their names, I'll call my counterpart in San Francisco. If her father was a community leader there, like you say, he may know them, be able to speak up for them, and keep them from being sent back to Japan."

I beamed with happiness at hearing this. "Thank you, Sheriff. I knew you would know if there was a way to help them. I hope they can be helped. I'm sure they are innocent of wrongdoing." I wrote down their names for him.

"Thank you again, Sheriff. I really do appreciate it." He nodded. I stood up and we shook hands across his desk.

"And please drop in at the restaurant sometime. I promise not to be grappling on the floor with anyone."

He chuckled and said, "Thanks, Katie, I may do that."

I liked him very much. When I came out onto the street from the sheriff's office, I felt a little optimistic that I might be able to help Miko. As I walked along the sidewalk, I pulled the small drawing of her out of my pocket and looked at it fondly. It was the picture of her that she had drawn for me.

Later on, Miko wrote to me from the camp to thank me for thinking of her and her family. The sheriff had been good to his word. His counterpart from San Francisco thought highly of Miko's father and had gone to bat for him to have his case reviewed.

But when Miko's father was notified of it, he declined the help offered! She said her father felt it would be dishonorable to accept special treatment over other Japanese families. I was stunned and bitterly disappointed.

In her last letter to me from Texas, she told me that soon they would be leaving for a nearby port to embark on their ship. She said that many Japanese families being repatriated were actually from South American countries. In July of 1943, Miko and her family were sent via transport ship to the Indian Ocean where they were transferred to another ship on which they were returned to Japan.

They were planning to live with her uncle's family in Hiroshima. I asked her to write to me after the war when mail service between Japan and America was reestablished. It might be several years before I could hear from her again. I would miss her and would worry for her safety.

Later when I read in the papers about the atomic bomb being dropped on Hiroshima, I cried for my friend and hoped that Miko and her family weren't there at the time. Maybe they had changed plans and lived somewhere else. When I didn't hear from her after the war, I feared the worst.

New Year's Eve on December 31, 1942, was not a time of celebration. America was in a desperate war and there had been little good news. German U-Boats had been taking a heavy toll on our merchant ships in the convoys across the Atlantic, as well as along the East Coast and in the Gulf of Mexico. Japanese Forces had advanced across much of Southeast Asia and controlled vast areas of the Pacific, driving Allied forces back nearly to Australia. Naval battles in the Pacific had taken a terrible toll on Allied naval forces.

"I cannot say Merry Christmas" is how President Roosevelt put it in his Christmas Eve address. It was not a time of celebration but of resolve to continue the fight. We stayed open our normal hours on that Thursday night without late night celebrations.

Chapter 24
Ugly Nazi Threats

IN THE HEAVILY damaged cockpit of the Heinkel-111 bomber, Rolf crouched behind the pilot's seat. Too low to bail out, the pilot was trying to crash land in a rapidly approaching field of the picturesque English countryside. The bomber had no engines and the loud rush of wind through the heavily damaged Plexiglas nose of the bomber was the only sound of their rapid descent.

Captain Huber, the pilot, had suffered multiple wounds, but was still flying the plane. Rolf looked at Captain Huber in front of him in the pilot's seat and was alarmed that his head was slumped forward so much that Rolf thought he might have passed out.

"Captain, are you okay? What can I do to help you? Can you fly well enough?"

"Rolf, I'm having trouble holding my head up. Brace yourself behind my seat and hold my head up so I can see."

"Yes, Captain," Rolf said as he quickly wedged himself behind the pilot's seat, put his hands on each side of the pilot's head, and raised his head up from his chest.

"That's enough," the pilot said wincing with pain.

With the ground rapidly approaching, Rolf turned his head and yelled back through the bomb bay to Dieter and Dorfman, "Brace for impact!"

Only then did Rolf notice the noses of the bombs in their racks. He suddenly realized with a sinking heart that their bombs, all eight five-hundred pounders, were still onboard. At that terrible instant, he was sure they would all be killed.

Rolf awoke suddenly and sat up in a panic. He was breathing rapidly and sweating as he looked around frantically. It took him a moment to recognize he was in his bunk in a prisoner of war camp in Canada. It was the middle of the night, and he had been dreaming about the bomber crash in which he was almost killed.

He let out a deep breath, lay back on the pillow and wiped the sweat from his forehead. He lay there for a moment looking up at the springs of the bunk above him trying to clear his mind of the dream. After a time, he managed to fall asleep again.

In the middle of January, it was cold inside their bunkroom early the next morning when a senior German prisoner opened a door, turned on the lights, and announced, "Reveille, everyone up. Muster here inside in fifteen minutes."

He then began walking through the bunkroom repeating the announcement and shaking the bunks of those slow to get up. Most were starting to stir and get up.

"Come on, flyboy, you too," he said as he shook Rolf's bunk. "Muster in fifteen minutes."

"Yes, Sergeant. I'm getting up." He climbed out into the cold and quickly threw his clothes on, as the sergeant continued to rattle other bunks. Rolf's friend Dieter was out of his bunk next to Rolf's and getting dressed.

"Good morning, Dieter."

"Is it? Oh, yes. Morning, Rolf," he replied, not yet his normal smiley self.

"Do you remember today we're going with Sergeant Evans to town to get supplies?"

"Thank you for reminding me, Mother. Yes, Rolf, of course I remember! I look forward to anything that gets me out of here for a while."

With their shaving kits in their hands and a towel over their shoulder, Dieter and Rolf headed for the wash room to wash and shave.

Later that afternoon, the Canadian guard, Sergeant Evans, drove while Rolf and Dieter rode in the cab with him. They were on their way back from town with a load of supplies in the back. Evans' rifle was propped on the seat between him and Rolf, who sat in the middle. They drove along the road through the icy and snowy landscape of hills and evergreen trees.

Both Dieter and Rolf got on well with Sergeant Evans. He knew Rolf and Dieter were not Nazi enthusiasts and needn't be on his guard with them. Having been good to Rolf a number of times in the past, he was more like a father figure to Rolf than a prison guard.

Dieter was sleepily looking out the window of the truck. He suddenly perked up and pointed ahead excitedly. "Look! There's a big buck there beside the road. Venison stew sure would be nice." Evans braked the truck to a stop. He looked around to check where they were and said, "We're outside the game preserve here, so he's fair game." He stopped for a second to think about what he just said and added, "What do you know. That must be where the phrase comes from, but never mind that." He handed the rifle to Dieter.

"Here, Dieter. He's too far away for me. You brag about being a good shot. Here's your chance to prove it. He's about a hundred and twenty yards away. See if you can get him before he runs. The rifle shoots a little low at that range, so aim a little high."

"Okay. I'll give it a try," Dieter said. In rapid succession, Dieter grabbed the rifle, looked it over, chambered a round, quietly opened the passenger door, rested the rifle on the open door, took aim and fired. The deer fell.

"You got him! Lucky shot!" Rolf shouted.

With a surprised look and then a big grin, Dieter said, "What? What do you mean lucky?"

Also a little surprised, Evans said, "Not bad, not bad at all! Jump in and we'll drive over to get him." Still grinning Dieter jumped back in and Evans sped down the road to the deer. The truck pulled to a stop on the road beside the dead deer and Dieter jumped out with the rifle. Dieter, Rolf and Evans stood over the deer and saw it was dead. It was a big buck with a large rack of antlers.

"Wow, look how big he is. He looks dead. Good shot, Dieter," Rolf said giving Dieter a slap on the back.

Evans chimed in, "It's a nice buck. Looks like you hit him right in the heart. You two put him up on the hood and I'll get some rope to tie it down." Dieter, beaming and proud of his shot, handed the rifle to Evans. Evans took the rifle, put it in the cab and walked around to the back of the truck to find some rope. Rolf grabbed the back legs and Dieter grabbed the front legs. Together they began to drag the deer to the front of the truck.

When we arrived back at the camp, several prisoners were outside walking for exercise and saw the deer tied across the hood of the truck. They began cheering and waving, and Dieter waved back out his open window. Venison, when it could be acquired off the game preserve on which they were located, was always a welcome addition to the camp fare.

That evening, Rolf and his two crewmates, Dieter and Dorfman, were standing at Rolf's bunk. They were talking and joking about their recent deer hunting adventure, when two surly arrogant POWs, Heinz and Heinrich, came up.

When Rolf and the others saw them coming, they stopped talking and had their guard up as they faced them.

"Let me see if I got this correct," Heinz began with a sneer as Heinrich smirked. "The enemy gives you his rifle, you use it to shoot a deer and then you give it back to the enemy. Is that what they teach you in the Luftwaffe? In the army, we are taught to use our rifles on the enemy."

"I did, Heinz. I shot the enemy deer," Dieter quipped. Rolf, Dorfman and several others nearby laughed.

"And what would you have done after using the rifle on the enemy, as you say. Escape and make your way back to Germany, I suppose?" Rolf retorted to Heinz.

"These guards are just old men. I would get no satisfaction in killing them. It is too easy to escape from here," Heinz snorted.

"I seem to remember," Dorfman said, "you two up on top of Mount Baldy checking out the surroundings to plan your escape. You were interested enough back then."

Heinz paused as he remembered himself and Heinrich on the summit of the mountain, looking around at endless mountains and forest in all directions.

"The camp commandant let you climb. He wasn't worried about you escaping. He knew what you would see from up there." Rolf added,

"We might have escaped across the American border back then, when America was a neutral country. Back before the Americans made the fatal mistake of angering the Führer and causing him to declare war on them," Heinz said arrogantly.

"But eagle-eyed Heinz couldn't figure out where the American border was, so I guess that's why he's still here," Dieter chimed in.

"There isn't exactly a big white line painted across the landscape. Even you might understand that," Heinrich snarled.

Dieter continued, "But what if you had escaped? Let's say you made it across the American border, then to Mexico and back to Germany on a tramp steamer? I suppose the Führer would have welcomed you with open arms and given you a big fat medal?"

Heinz and Heinrich straightened up and smiled as they imagined receiving a medal from the Führer.

"Yes, we would be receiving medals, and you would still be here," Heinz said disdainfully.

Dieter replied, "Did you ever consider, Heinz, that the Führer expected you to die fighting for his glorious Reich? Instead of medals, he might award you with a firing squad for surrendering and becoming prisoners in the first place."

Heinz and Heinrich looked furious at this. "How dare you say such a thing about the Führer! You may find yourself regretting those words!" Heinz threatened, then he and Heinrich stalked off.

As they left, Dieter said in a low voice, "Assholes."

Dorfman said to Dieter, "They may be assholes, but you better watch yourself, Dieter. No telling what those fanatic types might do." Dieter only grunted in response.

The next day, Rolf, Dieter and several other prisoners worked splitting logs behind one of the camp buildings. Normally they worked during the day clearing trees where a new reservoir was planned, but the snow was too deep lately for the clearing work. So today they were replenishing the firewood stock. For a day's work, the men were paid the grand sum of fifty cents. The work helped the time pass more quickly and the money did allow them to buy necessities in a small store there in the camp.

Chapter 25
Strife at Camp

ONE DAY IN early February 1943, the prisoners at the Canadian camp received some news that affected them all a great deal. The largest battle in the history of human warfare had been raging for months. It was now over and Germany had lost.

Rolf, Dieter, Dorfman and several others were in a lounge area playing checkers when a Canadian guard came in and placed the front page section of the Calgary newspaper on the table by Dorfman.

"Here, fellas, you might be interested in this," the guard said matter-of-factly and left. Dorfman, who could read English well, reached for the paper, unfolded it and started to read. The others gathered around to look and hear.

"Our sixth army that's been trapped in Stalingrad has surrendered to the Russians!" Dorfman declared. The others reacted with gasps and curses.

"They've been holding on for some time there under such terrible conditions," Rolf said.

"Why in the hell didn't they let them try to break out of there!" another complained.

Dorfman continued, "250,000 of our men were trapped there back in November and now only about 100,000 of them are left alive to surrender. The others died of cold, disease, hunger and the fighting." One of the prisoners listening ran out to tell the others.

"God, how awful. What a terrible loss for us. So many killed," Dieter said sadly.

"I pity the poor devils who survived," Rolf said. "The Russians aren't anything like the Canadians." They paused in stunned silence as they considered the miserable treatment those prisoners faced. Dorfman was continuing to read the article when Heinz, Heinrich and several others rushed in. Heinz grabbed the paper from Dorfman, scanned the headlines and became irate.

"Lies! Lies! And if it isn't lies, I blame you for this!" he shouted, pointing at Dieter.

"Me? What do I have to do with Stalingrad?" Dieter said incredulously.

"It's defeatists like you who are responsible!" Heinz said maliciously, glaring at Dieter.

"That's crazy, Heinz!" Dorfman interjected. "What are you talking about? This has nothing to do with Dieter!"

Standing across the table from Heinz, Dieter stared right back at him and calmly said, "You seem to be a little confused, Heinz. I believe our brave soldiers in Stalingrad were defeated by Russians not me."

With a snort of disgust, Heinz ripped the newspaper in several pieces, threw it on the floor and stomped out. Heinrich followed as the others looked on in amazement.

One of the other prisoners, as he was bending over to pick up the pieces of the paper, said, "Hitler not allowing them to fight their way out earlier is to blame for it, I say."

Such a negative statement about Hitler spoken openly was rarely heard, but no one said anything.

Bringing the pieces of the newspaper back to the table, they started putting it together again so they could finish reading it.

Ever since that day a week before, Rolf, Dieter and Dorfman had been on their guard and closely watching Heinz and Heinrich. Having heard what happened, the Canadian guards were also being more careful around them.

It hadn't snowed during the week, so to relieve the boredom in camp, the cutting of trees for the reservoir was begun again. An area with only a dusting of snow on the ground was located. In the cold, the prisoners worked sawing down trees, chopping the limbs from the downed trees, and hauling the limbs to piles for burning. The logs would be hauled off later by a lumber company.

Everyone suspected that Heinz and Heinrich were up to something when they, for no apparent reason, suddenly volunteered to start doing the tree cutting work. Up until that time, they had refused to do it because they said it contributed to what they called the enemy war effort.

The Canadians were also suspicious and added the second armed guard to the tree cutting work detail, which normally would have one.

Heinz and Heinrich were dragging brush to the pile and looking about maliciously. Each time they returned to the brush pile, they seemed to be getting a little closer to one of the guards. Near the pile, they passed Dieter and Rolf.

"Heinz, Heinrich, we don't see you out here much. Decided to get some exercise?" Dieter quipped.

"Yes, we decided to see what all the chopping noise was," Heinz retorted. Heinrich snickered his concurrence as the two kept walking.

"Dieter, why are you egging him on?" Rolf said in a low voice. "He's in a foul enough mood already."

"I'd kind of like to force him to make his move rather than wait for it," Dieter said. Rolf looked alarmed at hearing this.

"Dieter, don't!" Rolf said in a low voice, but Dieter ignored him.

Heinz, Heinrich, Rolf and Dieter were all somewhat together near one of the axe men who was chopping limbs from the tree trunks. A guard armed with a rifle was also nearby. Heinz started to drag a small limb to the pile.

"Heinz, is that the biggest limb you can take?" Dieter commented. "A brave Teutonic knight such as you ought to be able to do better than that!"

At this Heinz snarled, lunged toward Dieter and swung his fist at him. Dieter deflected his swing but was knocked to the ground. Heinz reared around, grabbed the axe from the surprised axe man and rushed at Dieter. Dieter was up again and met him halfway before Heinz could swing the axe.

They locked together and tumbled to the ground rolling over and over fighting for the axe. The nearby guard rushed forward pointing his rifle at the two locked together furiously struggling on the ground.

"Stop! Break it up!" the guard shouted. He was about to fire his rifle into the air when from behind, Heinrich hit the guard on the head with a trimmed branch, which was like a big club. The guard slumped to the ground unconscious and Heinrich bent to grab his rifle.

The second approaching guard, Sergeant Brown, saw what was happening. With his rifle leveled at Heinrich, he yelled for him to freeze. But Heinrich instead jerked up to fire at him and they exchanged nearly simultaneous shots. Heinrich, hit in the chest, slumped to the ground dying. Sergeant Brown was hit in the shoulder and fell sidelong to the ground dropping his rifle.

On hearing the two rapid shots, Heinz lurched quickly up to his feet with the axe in his hand. Dieter also leaped to his feet, looking quickly about him for a weapon.

Heinz craned around wide-eyed, looking to see what had happened. He saw the first Canadian guard collapsed and unconscious on the snowy ground. Next to him was Heinrich slumped on the ground with the rifle lying beside him. Blood was oozing from the front of Heinrich's jacket and from his mouth as he made gurgling sounds. Heinz roared in rage at the sight of his dying friend. He turned in a fury to see who had done it and saw the second guard.

Sergeant Brown was in pain and his arm hung limp. He crawled for the rifle, picked it up and tried unsuccessfully with his one good arm to work the rifle bolt to get another round in the chamber of the rifle. He saw Heinz glaring at him.

"Stay where you are!" shouted Sergeant Brown.

But Heinz was in a rage. He snarled and rushed with his axe raised at Sergeant Brown who was still struggling with the bolt of his rifle. Heinz was close to Sergeant Brown and was about to strike him with the axe, when he was tackled from behind and fell heavily to the ground. He looked around in fury and saw Dieter on top of him.

"What? You!" Heinz shrieked.

"We weren't finished yet, Heinz," Dieter responded.

Snarling savagely, Heinz again grasped the axe and was preparing to swing it when Dieter quickly smashed the surprised Heinz several times in the face with a big rock, knocking him unconscious.

Getting up and looking down, Dieter dropped the rock and said, "Now we're finished, Heinz."

It had all happened so fast. Sergeant Brown rose to his feet and finally got a round in the chamber of his rifle. Rolf and the other prisoners looked on without moving as a jeep raced up and rapidly braked to a stop. Three guards piled out with rifles at the ready.

"Everyone freeze! Drop what you have in your hands and put your hands on your heads!" they commanded as one of the guards rushed over to Brown. He took the rifle from him and looked at his wounded shoulder.

"Get some cuffs on that one," Sergeant Brown said, pointing to Heinz on the ground.

"The one over there on the ground I think is dead. He knocked out Johnston and winged me as I shot him. See how Johnston is doing," he said, pointing.

"Let's get you to the jeep, Sergeant Brown. We'll stop your bleeding and then get you to the doctor," the guard said as he helped the wounded guard over to the jeep.

With his rifle poised, a second guard quickly approached Heinrich who lay crumpled on the ground with the rifle beside him. The guard took the rifle away and looked Heinrich over quickly seeing he was dead.

The guard next knelt down beside the injured guard, Johnston, who was already starting to revive and hold his head in pain. He helped Johnston to his feet and started helping the wobbly injured guard back to the jeep.

The third guard had cuffed Heinz and stood pointing his rifle at the prisoners who stood without talking with their hands on their heads. Soon a second jeep filled with guards arrived.

Of course, an extensive inquiry was conducted into the incident. Heinrich was dead and Heinz was refusing to talk. All present were questioned by a board of investigators.

It was concluded that Heinz and Heinrich were planning an escape, even before Dieter had provoked Heinz. One would create a diversion while the other overpowered a guard to get his rifle. They would escape with the rifle in the nearby truck.

It wasn't known what Heinz and Heinrich planned to do afterward. They probably had no idea either. They possibly just wanted to kill a few people and make some headlines, which might get back to and give their Führer some satisfaction.

The investigation concluded that no other prisoners were involved. Dieter obviously wasn't part of a diversion since he had saved Sergeant Brown from Heinz. Dieter's taunting probably threw off whatever plan they had or at least the timing of it.

Heinz was tried and convicted of attempting to murder a guard and given a lengthy sentence. He was held in solitary confinement for two weeks there at the camp before being transferred to a high security facility where he would finish out the rest of his sentence.

Rolf, Dieter and other prisoners watched from inside the fence as Heinz, in handcuffs and leg irons, was escorted by two guards to a truck. Heinz glared at them saying nothing as the guards loaded him in the back. Soon the truck started up and drove off. That was the last they saw of Heinz.

* * *

A week after Heinz's departure, Rolf was sitting in his bunk writing a letter. Life in the camp after the incident was returning to a more normal and uneventful routine. Work, cleaning assignments, hobbies, and letter writing. He had written a number of letters to his mother back in Germany and received letters back giving news of the family.

Rolf's father had been too young to be in the First World War and was in his mid-thirties when the current war started. He was called up right away, made an army supply clerk and was stationed lately in Italy. Rolf's little sister and brother were thankfully still in grade school.

His mother never talked about the war. She knew the letters were read and censored at both ends. Saying things about the war would get blacked out by censors anyway, and saying something bad about the war would get her arrested and imprisoned.

So she stuck to telling about family and things that Rolf's little brother and sister were doing in school. Rolf relished hearing about them, but at the same time, it saddened him that he wasn't there to be their big brother and see them grow up.

From his writing materials beside him on the bunk, Rolf pulled out a picture postcard of a group of prisoners posing in front of one of the barracks. Recently, a photographer had come into camp and taken pictures of the prisoners in small groups of a dozen or so. The pictures were made into postcards and he was sending this one to his mother. He was the third one from the left. Looking at the others in it, he smiled. After hearing so much about them, his family would finally get to see Dieter and Dorfman.

He wanted to send one to me to let me see he was doing okay, but he couldn't. Thanks to Mrs. Martin, he now knew what had happened to me and where I was. He would have to wait out the war.

* * *

After several months at Aunt Minna's restaurant, the cooking, serving, cleaning, milking, cheese making, and the rest became a day to day, week to week, routine existence for me as I waited for the war to end.

I worried less about Rolf, but thought of him often. The war prevented us from being together, but that seemed hardly a terrible price to pay, considering the suffering and losses of others in the war.

When I read reports of the Allied bombing of German cities, I was naturally very worried about my family in Germany. I was relieved, at least for a while, to learn from

Mrs. Martin that they were still well and their situation not terrible.

I regretted my sister Ruth was too young back in 1937 to immigrate here with me. Unfortunately, she was still there, working in a dress shop, unmarried, and still living in the old apartment with my parents. That was the extent of my knowledge. I had no idea at the time of the hardships and suffering that Ruth would face there with my parents in Germany during and after the war.

It was only afterward that I heard the story. So, at this point, I will let Ruth take over the narration to tell the story of their terrible time back in Germany.

Chapter 26
Ruth's Story Begins

IN EARLY MARCH of 1943, I was nineteen years old and in the flower of youth. I should have been happy and possibly have already found a nice young man to marry. I was pretty enough with a good figure and light brown hair. I might have been playing the field with several suitors trying for my hand. I might have found a young man with money too and lived a long comfortable life.

Instead, I was wrapped in a blanket sitting on a bench in a dimly lit bomb shelter, located just down the street from our apartment in Hamburg, Germany. I huddled next to my mother as I listened to the sounds of the bombing raid outside in the night.

The noise of anti-aircraft batteries could be heard but not a great number of bomb explosions. My father snored nearby on the bench. We sat with the other women, children and older people of the apartments along our street. No young men were to be seen since they were all off at war.

At fifty six years old, my father was the youngest man here. He had fought in the trenches of the First World War and had been considered too old for this war. So he was able to keep his civilian waiter job and was given a smattering of low level civil defense titles, one of which was warden for this bomb shelter.

However, he was more than content to let the other designated warden, Herr Sommer, be in charge. Vati would help people, if they needed it, regardless of being designated as warden. The people in the shelter knew what should or shouldn't be done and caused no unruliness.

Despite being a shelter warden, Vati slept like a log whenever down here. Even if he hadn't been designated a warden, we would still be here. A number of people in our apartment building sheltered down in its basement, but Mutti insisted on us coming to the nearby bomb shelter where she thought it was safer. I thought of my sister Kätchen in America and was glad that she was not here sitting with us in a bomb shelter in the middle of the night.

"It doesn't sound like a very big raid tonight. I don't hear many explosions. You know, Mutti, the bombing raids have been fewer and smaller lately," I said.

Before Mutti had a chance to respond, we heard the whistling of bombs and a series of four nearby bomb explosions shook the ground. The people in the shelter nervously looked at one another as they huddled together even more closely.

"Thank you, Herr Meyer," is what I wanted to say out loud. That was my criticism of those in charge of the war and their inability to stop the Allied bombings. It was a sarcastic comment about Reich Marshal Hermann Goering, the head of the Luftwaffe (Germany's air force).

Several years before in 1940 when the Luftwaffe was the dominant air power in Europe, he had arrogantly boasted that if a bomb ever fell on German soil, you could call him "Meyer" (a German expression implying that something is essentially impossible). Many bombs have fallen on German soil since then. Some Germans in private sarcastically referred to air raid sirens as "Meyer's Trumpets."

Anyway, I knew better than to say, "Thank you, Herr Meyer," aloud there in the shelter. Such complaints or sarcasm about the war were only voiced to family or close friends who you knew could be trusted not to report you to the Gestapo. Even such trivial comments might get you reported and imprisoned.

After those nearby explosions, a few more bombs were heard in the distance and then all was quiet. Ten minutes later, the all-clear siren sounded. We stood up and started to collect our things.

"There's the all-clear siren. Let's go home," Mutti said as she shook Vati.

"Gustav! Wake up. The raid's over. It's time to go back." Vati roused and groggily started to get up. Soon we were all up and working our way to the exit door.

Once outside, we heard the sirens of fire trucks on a nearby street and could see the glow of flames coming from a building hit by one of the bombs. Firefighters augmented by boys from the Hitler Youth would fight the fires and search for survivors. The residents there would also be helping. A call would be put out if more help was needed. On our own street, we were relieved to see no obvious debris and damage. We walked with an old friend and neighbor Ilse Engel. She was a widow and lived in another apartment building along the street. Seeing that no one else was nearby to overhear, we could talk freely.

Mutti said, "It looks like our street has been spared once more, but the people on Beethoven Street weren't so lucky. It frightens me when the earth shakes when the bombs land that close."

"What frightens me is that they are here bombing us in the first place," Vati pondered aloud. "We can't seem to stop them from doing it. That's what frightens me."

"I remember when the Englanders first started bombing our cities. We made fun of their feeble attempts but no more," Ilse said.

"It wasn't a big raid tonight though. Maybe the big raids have become too costly for them?" I said, perhaps being a little too optimistic.

"I don't know. The Englanders seem very determined, even though they lose many bombers in the bigger raids," Mutti responded.

"I think these smaller raids by their faster, less vulnerable bombers are just to torment us," Vati speculated.

"It might just be the bad weather this time of year," Vati added.

"So the bombing may get worse when the weather gets better?" I asked.

"I don't know," Vati replied.

"All I know," Mutti said, "is that if it gets too bad, we'll leave and go south to my sister Rosa's house in the country."

"I have a cousin on the north side of town. That's where I'll go," Ilse said.

"I wish we could go now," I said earnestly.

"I do too, but, we can't without that darned authorization to leave that we can't get," Mutti replied.

"Here's my building. Good night," Ilse said as she waved to us and turned into the entrance of her apartment building.

"Good night," we all replied as we kept walking. While we were walking, Vati had been periodically peering over at the glow of the fire. Shortly after parting with Frau Engel, he said, "You two go on. I had better check to see if they need any help."

"Be careful, Gustav," Mutti said.

"Yes, do," I added.

"I will. Don't worry. I'll probably be back in a few minutes," he said as he turned and headed off into the darkness toward the fire. It was more like a few hours later that he finally returned. Four people were found dead in the debris, but the shaken people trapped in a basement next door had been able to escape.

Mutti waited with other women in a line to buy butter and eggs. The line stretched out the entrance of the store and about twenty feet down the sidewalk. Early on in the war, the availability of food had not been a big problem. While many things were rationed, the ration amounts had been generous enough not to create hardship. The populace like us continued to eat normally and was somehow not impacted by the need to feed our large armies.

But now, things like meat, butter and eggs were in short supply and rationed amounts were much smaller. Our jobs at the uniform factory provided us with enough money to buy food. The food just wasn't as available to buy. We ate mostly eggs, bread, cheese, potatoes and local vegetables. We waited in long lines for some rationed foods.

After what seemed like an hour, Mutti finally arrived at the front of the ration line and handed the clerk her ration cards and money. The clerk ripped off a tab from each ration card. He handed her a small package of butter and eggs as well as her ration cards and change.

As Mutti was leaving, a woman in the line became irritated with the woman behind her. She elbowed the woman behind her and said, "Stop pushing! Pushing on me won't get you your butter any sooner. Give me some room."

The woman behind her shot back, "I wasn't pushing. The nerve of some people!"

As Mutti walked outside along the street, she scrutinized the people coming toward her. They all looked gray and unhappy. None smiled. She thought she probably looked gray and unhappy to them too. These were not happy times or conditions.

Many Germans were apprehensive when we heard the news in mid-1941 that Germany had invaded Russia. It seemed such a huge undertaking to conquer such a vast country and large population. We hoped Hitler knew what he was doing. Now that we had suffered a terrible defeat at Stalingrad, it looked to us to have been a costly gamble and huge mistake by Hitler. It shook our confidence in Hitler's judgement and in the outcome of the war.

People in ration lines might complain about, be short with, and push one another, but people didn't dare complain about Hitler or the war. Such things were reported and imprisonment in a concentration camp was a certainty in such cases.

Although we didn't know the details of what went on in the concentration camps, we suspected the treatment of inmates in these camps was terrible, perhaps even brutal.

One Sunday morning in late May, Mutti and I were seated at the kitchen table. Mutti sipped what looked to be a cup of coffee. The blockade of Germany by the English made some foods like coffee unavailable, so a substitute made from grain had been improvised and sold.

"Let me try a sip of your coffee, Mutti," I asked. She handed me the cup and I tasted it. I gave it back with a little frown.

"Not as good as real coffee, is it?" she said.

"No, it isn't." For some reason, the unsatisfying taste seemed one more affliction for us to bear in this war and made me feel restless and unhappy.

I stood up and went to the window. Looking out, I scanned the skies and brightened a little. I wanted to do something cheerful to get my mind off the war.

"Mutti, it's nice out this morning and not too cold. It's Sunday and we should go for a walk in the park."

"Not me," Vati said as he emerged from the bedroom still dressing. "I don't walk in parks anymore. I didn't know we still have parks."

"Oh, it's a good idea, Gustav, and you're going too." Mutti told him. Vati frowned at Mutti and eyed the food on the table.

"Do I at least get something to eat first?"

A little while later, Vati, Mutti and I walked along a brick walkway that wound through the grass and trees of the park. We passed a bed of brightly colored flowers.

"Look at all the pretty flowers. The park this morning is so nice, I could almost forget there is a war on," I said.

"I wish I could forget a war is on. I miss the beer I used to get. The beer today is watered down, hardly worth drinking," Vati said.

"Gustav, without the beer, you actually act half human. So I don't miss it," Mutti replied.

Gustav grunted and said, "just when you need a good beer to forget about all that is going on, you can't get one. And I can't complain about it either. It's a sad state of affairs."

"Gustav, we're here to forget about things for a while. Look at the fine weather, we have. It's so warm and sunny this morning. After all the rain we've had, it's a nice change," Mutti said.

Gustav looked around and noted, "Yes, I admit it is a nice day. A nice day for hugging my girls." At this, he put one arm around Mutti and one around me, and hugged us close to him for a moment.

"Gustav, are you sure you haven't been drinking?"

"I wish," he said.

As we continued walking, our thoughts could not help but turn back to the war.

"It's nearly the end of May. We've had no bombing raids this whole month and only one or two last month. Do you think the worst might be over?" I asked hopefully.

"We can only hope, Ruth," Mutti said as she put her arm through mine and we walked together.

"It's hard to tell," Vati said thoughtfully, "but we should prepare ourselves for the possibility that it will get worse again."

I would periodically get together with a couple girlfriends from the factory. Sitting in a wooden booth at a small bakery, we'd talk about things as we sipped our colas. They talked mostly about their boyfriends in the service. They always wanted to hook me up with some soldier friend of their boyfriends, but I would always decline.

I, myself, never really had many boyfriends. As a young girl, boys seemed interested enough in me. At the time, I had been more interested in my artwork than in them. When I started to be more interested in them, they all disappeared off to the military and the war.

My good looks did not prove to be an advantage in time of war when every young man was in the service. Early on, I tried dating. I would meet a young man and he would ask me for a date. But the dates proved to be a problem. I couldn't go out on a first date without my date proposing marriage to me. It literally happened every time.

On the one hand, I hated to see the disappointed looks on their faces when I declined. They seemed desperate for a brief moment of happiness before being killed in the war. But how could I chose someone to marry on the first date?

On the other hand, I also feared that one of them might get angry or violent with me when I declined. He might tell me it's my duty to marry him and have children for the future of the Fatherland! He might report me as unpatriotic to the Nazi cause for not wanting to. I had to stop dating and, as a result, I had no boyfriends.

I listened to the other girls' talk about their boyfriends and I worried that one day they'd be sadly telling us that their boyfriends had been killed. Looking at them sometimes, I wondered who would be the first. It was a very real possibility and had nearly happened to Rolf.

We heard about Rolf from his mother who would write to us periodically to let us know how he was doing there in Canada. She said that the Canadians treated him well. Through her letters, we learned Kätchen had moved to a place near the Canadian border and visited him. That was back in the fall of 1941, when we had not heard from Kätchen since mail service to America was cut off nearly two years earlier.

We were so excited to finally get some news of her and learn she was doing well but no longer with her Aunt Minna at the restaurant. We would hear only a few months later through Rolf's mother that when the Americans entered the war, Kätchen stopped visiting him, and he didn't know why.

To our dismay and unhappiness, our brief time of communications with Kätchen abruptly ended, and her whereabouts in America became unknown. Still, Mutti didn't seem worried about Kätchen. She was just so thankful that Kätchen was there instead of here.

Chapter 27
Rain of Bombs

IN THE EVENINGS, Mutti would usually crochet or knit in the apartment to pass the time. Vati usually read the paper. I still enjoyed doing my artwork and worked on various art projects at home. It was one of my few enjoyments these days.

This particular night, I sat in a chair with a cloth in my lap to catch sawdust. I was using a hand jigsaw to cut out pieces from an oval-shaped thin sheet of wood to create a woodcut picture of a German Shepard dog's head. I always wanted a dog. This woodcutting was the closest I could get to having one. Mutti came up and smiled as she admired my work.

In early June, we were devastated to hear from his mother that Cousin Fritzi had been killed on the Russian Front. With the terrible news of Stalingrad and the other setbacks in Russia, we had worried about him a great deal.

At the news of his death, Mutti could only cry and repeat, "Such a sweet boy." It was the saddest thing that ever happened to me. My oma (grandma) passed away about four years before at the age of ninety. I was sad at her death too, but she had at least lived a full life. Unlike Oma, Fritzi was still young with his life ahead of him, and now he wouldn't get to live it.

I cried and cried when I thought of him on that raft back on the Werra River many years ago saying he would someday paddle on the Volga. He had died months before in the awful street fighting in Stalingrad on the banks of the Volga.

One afternoon after finishing work, Mutti and I emerged from the uniform factory entrance with a throng of other workers. I waved goodbye to several other girls. Mutti and I walked along the street past an anti-aircraft gun located outside the factory. Two young soldiers, there doing maintenance on the gun, stopped working and were now happily watching all the young women walking by.

Most of the month of June 1943 passed without a bombing raid. Since we hadn't been down to the shelter in some time, Mutti and I began hoping the worst of the bombing might finally be over.

Not many days afterward, I was sleeping in bed restfully and awoke suddenly at the wailing sound of the air raid sirens. With bitter disappointment, anger and a few choice words under my breath about Herr Meyer, I got up out of bed and started to dress.

In late June and early July, the air raids recommenced with a number of small raids that didn't do much damage. None of the bombs fell near us. But whenever the sirens sounded, we hurried to the shelter for safety. I sat with Mutti and others in the shelter as we listened to the flak guns firing and bombs exploding in the distance. Looking at Vati sleeping nearby, I marveled that he was able to sleep so soundly in that shelter.

The raids ended my brief period of optimism. As I waited in a line outside a market to buy food, I looked up with a gray face at the gray skies. A lull in the bombings occurred in mid-July, but in late July, the bombing raids began again in earnest.

The air raid siren that wailed on the night of the first large raid in late July sounded just like the air raid sirens we had heard many times before. We got up as usual not knowing that this raid would be any different from the others.

Mutti, Vati and I hurried along the street in the dark on the way to the shelter. Sirens were blaring and flak guns firing. We could hear the much louder drone of a much larger than normal number of bombers. Above the skyline, search lights scanned the sky. We could see a cluster of flares high in the sky to the southwest, which we had never seen before.

Many bombs were exploding several kilometers away and occasionally, several landed nearby. Hurrying to the shelter, Vati tripped on some uneven pavement, spraining his ankle and almost falling down. He managed to keep hobbling along with us. When we reached the stairwell in the sidewalk leading down to the shelter, we paused there for a moment to rest and watch the battle above in the sky.

Many bombers and exploding flak were illuminated by the search lights. The bomb explosions were loud and continuous. Several people hurried toward us on the street and down the steps past us. One of the bombers exploded in the sky and its fiery wreckage plummeted to the ground beyond our view.

"Oh, my God!" Mutti exclaimed.

Over the sound of many bomb explosions, Vati said, "This could be a bad one. Let's hope our neighborhood isn't one of their targets. We'd better go inside." Mutti and I helped Vati hobble down the steps and into the shelter.

In the morning, Mutti was looking out the open window of the apartment at the activity in the street below. She could still see and smell smoke from the fires last night. She was nervously clutching a handkerchief. I sat at the table, eating the last of my slice of bread for breakfast and watched her.

Both of us were somewhat in shock after the large bomber raid during the night. Mutti turned with a worried look and said, "The raid last night was just awful. I think it was the worst one yet."

"Luckily, we weren't hit right here. From the fires we could see last night, it looked like the city center and west of here suffered the worst," I said.

"It was just awful."

"Uncle Fritz and Aunt Rachel live in that area. Do you think they are okay?"

"We have no way of finding out. I think they were planning to stay with some friends outside the city. I hope they did. Now that Fritzi has been killed, I'm not sure they really care anymore what happens to them." We paused a moment in sadness thinking of them and Fritzi.

Trying to change the subject, I asked, "Mutti, do you think we should go to work at the factory today?"

"I don't know. I thought we might wait an hour and if things look normal enough outside, I guess they will expect us there, and we should go."

She turned around and looked out again to the street below. Suddenly straining to look down, she said, "Goodness! There's your father! What is he doing coming home from work already? I wonder what that means. I'm going down to find out."

"I'll go too," I said and we both headed out the apartment door.

Mutti and I met Vati on the street below the apartment. He was hobbling along the sidewalk slowly due to his sprained ankle and he saw us as we rushed to meet him.

"Gustav, why are you coming home already? Did your restaurant close? Was it damaged from the bombing last night?" Mutti asked excitedly as we met him.

"No, the restaurant was undamaged and is open. They didn't think I could walk well enough with my sprained ankle to wait properly on our guests, so they told me to go home. We had very few guests anyway. Businesses seem to be open, although people are pretty rattled after last night," he said reflectively.

"How is your ankle, Vati? Do you need help?" I asked.

"No, I'm okay. My ankle is stiff, but I can walk."

Then he suddenly stopped as we walked along together. We stopped too and saw he seemed to be deep in thought.

"What is it, Gustav?" Mutti asked.

"They said at work that the Uhlenhorster Ferry House was totally destroyed in the bombing last night," he finally said.

Mutti and I were surprised and saddened to hear the famous Hamburg establishment was gone.

"It was completely obliterated, flattened, nothing left standing. They've been our rival restaurant and ferry house for many, many years," he said staring vacantly. "I'm sorry to admit it, but I secretly hoped they would get bombed and destroyed. But now that it's actually happened, I feel sad, not happy."

After another moment in thought, he sighed and said, "I guess I am getting old."

"I'm sorry, Vati," I said trying to comfort him. Both Mutti and I patted him on the shoulder and we began walking again.

Shortly after returning with Vati up to the apartment and getting him settled, we reluctantly decided that we should go to work. We wouldn't want to be the only ones who didn't show up that day to do our part for the war effort. It would look bad.

Along the way to work, bomb damage to buildings in a few places caused us to detour from our normal route. Upon arrival at work, we found that we were one of the few who showed up and we were rewarded for our efforts by being reprimanded for being late. Even so, the factory closed in the afternoon earlier than normal due to shortages of materials.

That afternoon, Mutti and I walked home from work at the uniform factory. On this hot clear summer day, we walked along in our light dresses, carrying our purses.

Mutti and I suddenly froze in surprise when air raid sirens began wailing. We looked at each other in disbelief. We had never been bombed before during the day.

"It can't be!" Mutti cried out, hand to her mouth in surprise as she searched the skies.

"What'll we do?" I gasped. Meanwhile, people streamed out of shops and businesses in a panic looking wildly about. The other people in the street were likewise fearfully scanning the skies and hurrying in all directions to find shelter of some kind.

Already starting to hurry, half running, toward home, I asked, "Should we try to make it home or find a shelter here?"

"We can head for home, but we may see one on the way," Mutti said, already half out of breath. We could now hear the drone of bombers and flak guns to the south, but couldn't see them because of the buildings. With people frantically hurrying in all directions, someone bumped into me almost knocking me down.

We paused for a moment against a building to catch our breath. Very little traffic passed on the streets, only an occasional emergency vehicle or fire truck raced by. High above in the sky, we could see and hear the German fighter planes flying about waiting for their chance to attack the bombers.

"Ready?" I asked.

"Yes," Mutti replied. With that we began rushing along the sidewalk again. We reached a large intersection and saw people going into a shelter on the other side of it.

"Look!" I said, pointing. "There's a shelter. We've been past it many times. We should have remembered it. Let's go in there." Mutti nodded out of breath and we started across the street toward it.

As we crossed the wide street, we had an open view to the south and could see the formations of bombers flying through the explosions of the heavy flak fire, dropping long strings of bombs and the explosions of the bombs on the horizon. We had never seen the war as clearly as we now saw it in daylight.

These bombers sounded different from the bombers during the night raids. We learned later that they were the Americans. The British bombed at night and now the Americans were bombing during the day.

Several of the bombers streamed smoke and began to drop out of formation. We stood in the street dazed by the sights and sounds of the air battle as the wailing sirens echoed among the buildings. Some people rushed by and I said, "Mutti, we're standing in the middle of the street, let's go." She looked around at me, regained her senses and we rushed to the other side of the intersection and down into the shelter.

The shelter was a crowded chaotic scene of people, shaken and shocked by this new example of the growing strength of the enemy. After an all-clear siren was sounded, we emerged from the shelter onto the street.

Looking about at the street scene, it seemed different now that we were vulnerable in the daytime too. Like the others in the chaotic shelter, we too had been affected by the raid. As we briskly walked home, we could not help but think and comment that things seemed to be getting worse.

No bombing raid happened that night. The next day, we decided not to go to work, since we thought the factory was probably still short of material and we didn't want to risk being caught in another daytime raid.

It was good thinking, since another bombing raid happened that afternoon to the south again. Another bombing raid, although not a big one, happened that night too. It was all very unnerving.

Chapter 28
Vati and Frau Engel

THE NEXT NIGHT was the night of July 27th, 1943, which I will never forget. Worried about more large night raids, we had begun sleeping in our clothes at night. I was in bed asleep, although not very restfully, when the air raid sirens began sounding a little after midnight. I jumped out of bed and quickly gathered things to take. In the living room, I was gathering light coats for us to take when Mutti came out of the bedroom.

"Ruth, do you have your big kerchief?"

"Yes, I have it with me."

"Wrap some food in it and take it with us. I have a bad feeling about tonight," she said ominously. I quickly put some bread and cheese in the kerchief and put it into our large hand bag. We heard the drone of bombers and the flak guns begin to fire in the distance.

"Where is your father! Gustav!" Mutti called frantically. She rushed back into the bedroom and came back out in a moment with Vati in tow.

"He was still asleep and I had to wake him again," she said with exasperation. Vati was rumpled but dressed. He groggily put on his long coat. His ankle was better and he hobbled only a little. After Mutti and I put on our coats and picked up our purses and the hand bag, we all hurried out the door and down the hallway to the stairwell.

As we hurried along the street to the shelter, a large bombing raid, illuminated by searchlights, could be seen and heard in the nearby sky. Several groups of people and a single woman, who we thought might be our friend Ilse Engel, were ahead of us rushing to the shelter. The noise of the bombers grew louder and we heard the whistle of dropping bombs.

All the people in the street began to run. The bombs exploded on the next block and the ground shook. The woman running ahead of us tripped and fell to the ground. She struggled back up and continued with a limp.

"Look, Gustav, that's Ilse up ahead and she looks hurt. We have to help her." We were about 200 feet from the shelter when we caught up with our struggling friend.

"Mutti, you and Ruth keep running! I'll help Ilse," Vati shouted over the noise of nearby exploding bombs.

"Thank you, Gustav. I fell and hurt my knee," Frau Engel said looking up.

Reluctantly, Mutti and I obeyed and kept running. Vati put Frau Engel's arm around his shoulder and hurried along with her. Several more bombs exploded in the nearby blocks. Mutti and I ran to the intersection and across the street to where the stairwell in the sidewalk led down to the shelter. We got to the shelter stairs and looked back waiting for Vati and Frau Engel. We stood in the stairwell as other people rushed by us down the stairs.

We watched in panic as Vati and Frau Engel reached the corner of the block on the other side of the street from us. They had about sixty feet more to go to the shelter stairs where we waited.

Vati was panting when the loud whistle of dropping bombs was heard. He motioned and yelled to Mutti and me, "Get down!" He flopped to the ground with Frau Engel at the corner. Mutti and I ducked down in the stairwell.

A bomb landed and blew up an apartment building 200 feet down the street behind them. Another exploded in the park across the street behind them and a third bomb hit the one-story pharmacy directly across the intersection from

Vati and Frau Engel. The pharmacy exploded sending debris in all directions and showering burning debris on them.

Some small debris rained down on us, but Mutti and I were unhurt and we popped up our heads again from the stairwell. We saw Vati stirring amid the debris.

"Vati!" I screamed.

I ran to help them and Mutti was right behind me. More bombs exploded in the nearby blocks. Vati and Frau Engel still lay on the ground dazed but not seriously hurt. I kicked and flung away some burning debris around them and helped Vati to his feet. Mutti helped steady Vati as I helped Frau Engel up. Together we hurried across the street to the shelter stairs.

As we were going down the stairs, Vati grabbed his chest and collapsed at the bottom of the stairs.

"Gustav! Are you hurt?" Mutti cried.

"It's my heart, Mutti. I'm not used to so much excitement." He grimaced as someone from inside came out to help and we hauled Vati into the shelter.

We laid him down on the floor and put a rolled up coat under his head. Mutti and I were on each side of him distraught and tearfully holding his hands.

"Oh, Vati."

"Gustav." He looked up at us, first to Mutti's face and then to mine. He gave our hands a weak squeeze, smiled and then closed his eyes and died.

"Oh, Gustav," Mutti said as she slumped down on him crying. I kissed his hand and held it to my cheek as I sobbed, not being able to utter a word in my misery.

Chapter 29
Fiery Hell

MUTTI AND I presented a pathetic scene as we wept beside Vati laying there on the floor. The others around us watched sadly without speaking as more bombs exploded nearby outside and the building shook. With no others apparently coming and so many bombs hitting nearby, the shelter door had been closed behind us.

After a time, Herr Sommer, the shelter warden, came over and put his hand on Mutti's shoulder suggesting that we come sit down. Two of the women gently helped Mutti and I over to a seat as we continued to cry. Several other women carried Vati's body from the center of the room to one side and covered him with a blanket. Frau Engel, who was crying too, limped over to sit by Mutti.

"I'm so sorry, Margarete. I feel terrible. If Gustav hadn't stopped to help me, he would still be alive."

"No, Ilse, it was a heart attack," Mutti reassured her in a weak voice. "It might have happened even if he hadn't stopped. It's not your fault." Frau Engel smiled sadly and continued to sit with Mutti and me.

As we sat, the sound of the bombing outside in the distance became intense. Periodically a few close explosions were heard. The earth shook and dust fell frequently from the ceiling. The people looked around in fear and children cried. The explosions of bombs became nearly continuous. The lights went out and a battery-powered lantern came on.

"Mutti, I'm afraid. I've never heard so many bombs fall at once and they aren't far away."

We hugged to comfort each other and I looked around, fearful the building would soon collapse on us. Mutti did not seem frightened as she numbly looked over at Vati on the floor.

After over a half hour of nearly continuous bomb explosions, the bombing raid finally ended. Mutti and I were leaning against each other, arm in arm. I was so frightened it took me a moment to notice that the sound of exploding bombs had trailed off and stopped. I looked around in disbelief that we were still alive. We were covered with dust. I looked at Mutti who was staring vacantly.

I listened several minutes for the all-clear siren but didn't hear it. The all-clear siren normally sounded a little while after the bombing stopped. But instead of the siren, I heard other ominous sounds outside.

I got up brushing the dust from my hair, face and clothes. I walked over to the front door of the shelter to listen. Everyone was silent, listening fearfully. I could hear winds howling outside and a frightening roaring sound. The others noticed it too and looked around nervously. Herr Sommer came over to listen.

"Herr Sommer, do you hear the roaring wind outside? And no all-clear siren yet. Someone should go out and see what's happening."

"I hear it too," he said with a concerned look.

"We all hear it. What should we do?" another woman shouted.

"I'll go up the stairs and look," he said to calm the others. Herr Sommer, an elderly man, felt the air-tight door with his hand and found it wasn't hot. Cautiously cracking it open, he peered out. Judging it safe to go out, we pushed the door halfway open and he slipped out as I held the door behind him.

The roar of the wind outside was much louder with the door open and everyone could smell the smoke. Some fidgeted and others paced as we nervously waited. In a moment, a frazzled looking warden came back in and the door was shut again.

"There are fires scattered all around us and I think a huge fire to the south in Hamm. I can't see much from the street level. Ruth, come with me out the back door and we'll go up the stairwell to the roof for a better look. It should only take about five minutes."

Awakened from her despair, Mutti asked worriedly, "Does Ruth need to go?"

"I don't mind, Mutti. I want to go." Herr Sommer and I made our way through the crowd of women, children and elderly couples to a back door. On the way, he kissed his wife goodbye.

"Be careful, Manfred," his wife told him.

"I will, dear," he replied and we made our way to the back door. Herr Sommer felt it with his hand, concluded it wasn't hot and opened it part way. More smoke blew in as he looked out and opened it half way. We exited quickly and the door was closed behind us.

The smoky interior stairwell was lit by the light of the fires outside. Every window in the stairwell was shattered and glass covered the floor. The air outside was hot, smoky and filled with embers flying by the empty windows in the strong wind. From the stairwell we could see terrific flames to the south beyond the nearby buildings.

Herr Sommer and I made our way up five flights of glass strewn stairs by the light of the outside fires. When we reached the top of the stairwell and the entry door to the roof, Herr Sommer was panting hard from the climb. He handed a key ring to me as he rested to catch his breath.

I tried several keys and finally found one that unlocked the door. I struggled to control the door as I tried to ease it open in the high winds. The howling wind ripped the door from my hands as soon as I got it a little open and flung it wide open with a crash. I jumped back not knowing if it might slam again on me. We watched the door for a moment and saw that it was held fast against a pipe by the fierce wind.

Herr Sommer carefully edged his way out onto the windblown roof and fought against the wind to a sheltered spot along a wall. I braced myself as I stepped out onto the roof behind him. I thought to shut the door behind me, but the strong wind held it firmly in place as I tugged at it. Giving up, I turned around to look out across the roof.

It was one of those flat apartment house roof areas on the backside of the building where tenants could come up to get sun, read, work on hobbies, or hang out their laundry. Plumbing pipes and chimneys were sticking up in various places. The howling wind was filled with smoke and embers.

With Herr Sommer still braced against the wall near the open door, I made my way along a laundry line out to a chimney pipe to which I clung tightly in the wind. From this vantage point, I could see out in all directions. Herr Sommer joined me there and together we looked around at a scene from hell.

To the south, a huge sea of flames covered a large area of the city. Only a few kilometers away in that direction, the flames were so high they swirled into a funnel of fire reaching thousands of feet in the air. This eerie unnatural thing loomed over us and swayed about as it furiously swirled around. As Herr Sommer and I looked in horror at the sight, we felt intense heat from it. We had to cover our faces with an arm due to the heat.

He said in awe, "God in Heaven."

After a moment, we recovered from our shock and started to look around in all directions. In addition to the fire storm to the south, we saw through the smoke scattered fires in all directions but fewer to the north. I noticed a dark area to the north with no fires and pointed it out to Herr Sommer.

I shouted to him above the noise of the wind, "Look! The dark area! The city park in Winterhude!"

He shouted back, "Yes, I see it!" Turning and pointing to the south, he shouted, "The fire! We have to get away! It's not safe here!" Turning back to the north, he shouted, "We have to get north to the park!"

He and I frantically scanned the streets through the smoke, looking for a safe route northward to the park. After a moment searching, he turned and shouted, "Not so many fires on Barmbeker Street! We can get across the canals on it! We can make it!"

"I agree!" I shouted.

"Back down!" he shouted, pointing to the door. After one last awestruck look around, we carefully made our way in the strong wind along the laundry line back to the door and left the roof.

Chapter 30
Escape to Park

BACK BELOW IN the shelter, Mutti and I said a sad tearful goodbye to Vati. We had to leave him not knowing if he would still be here when or if we returned. We held his hand and looked upon his face one last time. Mutti stroked his hair and kissed him on the forehead. I kissed him one last time too. Finally, we pulled the blanket back up over his face and sadly joined the others.

Herr Sommer would lead the group of about two dozen people from the shelter northward the two kilometer distance to the city park. He asked me to bring up the rear and make sure we didn't lose anyone. A walking stick was found in the first aid supplies for Frau Engel to use. She would be somewhere in the middle of the group being helped by another woman.

Scarfs or handkerchiefs were tied over our noses and mouths for protection against the smoke. Long coats or blankets were worn to help protect us from the heat of the fires and the blowing embers. Everyone was cautioned to keep a tight grip on them or they would be instantly stripped away by the furious wind. Mutti and I watched the others cautiously file out the shelter door and up the stairs to the sidewalk where the smoke-filled wind was howling.

At last, it was our turn. We turned back around to confirm that no one was left behind, took one last look at Vati, gathered our courage and exited out the shelter door.

We needed to brace ourselves against the wind when emerging from the stairs to the street. The trees along the street flailed about wildly in the strong winds, which furiously blew smoke and flying embers everywhere. The street scene and night sky were illuminated by the big fire to the south and other nearby fires.

We could see the line of struggling people ahead of us. Some in our group huddled together, going from object to object to object along the street, getting hand holds where possible, struggling to stay on their feet in the fierce wind. Mothers held their children close and carried small ones. Occasionally, someone would fall and another would help them back up.

The howling wind prevented any talking. Each person could only follow the hunkering figures ahead of them. At times, we could see Herr Sommer in the lead up ahead steadily picking his way through the bomb damage in the streets, but much of the time, he was obscured by the smoke.

It wasn't long before the blanket of one young boy was suddenly ripped from him and flew wildly away. Fortunately, it got trapped in the alcove of an entryway and they were able to retrieve it and put it back on him.

When we came to a burning building, we hurried by on the opposite side of the street in single file holding up our coats and blankets as best we could to shield ourselves from the terrible heat as we worked our way through and over the debris in the street. We were making slow but steady progress, so far without serious mishap. Everyone in our group was still up and moving forward with me bringing up the rear.

The bells of emergency vehicles could sometimes be heard in various directions above the roar of the wind. As we passed one apartment building, a worried looking woman came out from a doorway and shouted to us, "Hello! Where are you going?"

I called back, "There are big fires to the south. We're going north to the city park in Winterhude. It should be safer there. Come with us if you want."

The woman waved and called back, "We're coming with you." She ducked back in and soon a group of women and children emerged and joined us. One mother had too many children to carry herself, so Mutti and I each carried one of her children.

Our route took us past another fire raging in an apartment house. A long fire engine was there with firemen futilely spraying water on the fire. Our group took turns dashing through the heat to the backside of the fire engine. We moved along the length of it using it as a shield from the intense heat. Then we made another dash from it to get far enough away from the heat.

The howling wind and the smoke were lessening as we got further away from the hellish fire storm to the south. Looking back, I saw more and more people were following us as we continued.

At the Osterbek Canal, we were only about a quarter of the way to the park, but we took a short break to let Ilse and the others rest for a moment. She was tired and sore, but the walking stick from the shelter had been a big help for her. As we rested, we looked back and saw the horizon of fires reflecting on the water of the canal. Emergency vehicles raced by southward. Soon we were up again and on our way.

We still encountered areas of scattered damage and fires as we continued. Just when we thought we were seeing less damage, we came upon a building complex on fire. From the metal framework strewn about there, it looked as if one of the large bombers may have crashed there. The intense fire made it too dangerous to get by, so we were forced to backtrack a little and detour around it. Getting back to the main street and continuing north, we found ourselves in a stream of half dazed people plodding northward to escape the fires.

Our group from the shelter managed to stay intact. We were in less danger now. Herr Sommer, less than a hundred feet ahead of me, steadily treaded along with his wife beside him. He looked back regularly, keeping track of the group, and waving to me. I would wave back letting him know things were okay. Although we sometimes got mixed up with the others on the street, our group kept together.

Everyone seemed to be out in the streets, despite the fact that it was the middle of the night. Groups of women with frightened faces watched our procession go by, first looking at us and then at the huge fires in the distance. Some people stopped to rest here and there. Others collapsed from exhaustion in front of buildings and local people offered them water.

Several buildings had been hit here and were burning. A group of teenage boys and girls were working to put the flames out. It was not uncommon to see a woman and her children packing things in a cart, preparing to leave.

We were about two thirds of the way to the park when we crossed the Goldbek Canal and we took another short rest. It was not much farther to the park. This section of the city suffered minimal damage, much different from the hell we had escaped. We were tired but knew we would shortly reach safety.

When we reached the city park, people were being directed to the left toward the old brick drinking hall and the lawn area behind it, the same place where we had enjoyed concerts years before. A medical station there was busy providing first aid to injured and burned people. Many people had come to the park seeking refuge.

Much of the grassy area behind the hall was covered with people, laying or sitting on blankets or coats or on the grass. Some people were crying, some moaned and hugged their children, and others sat silent in shock. The whole scene was partially lit by the eerie glow of the flames to the south, which could be seen through the trees. The wind here was much less in strength and the temperature was warm being late July.

Mutti and I let the children down and they disappeared with their mother in the crowd. We went to Herr Sommer and gave him a hug to thank him for getting us safely through the hellish streets. A couple women in our group went to get something for minor burns to their faces. We looked for Frau Engel to see how she did but were unable to find her in the crowd of wandering dazed people.

Exhausted, sore and in need of rest, we picked out a spot on the grass where we spread out our coats and sat down. As we sat, we could see the glow of the huge fires to the south and watched as occasional flames wafted and swirled thousands of feet in the air. We could only imagine that many had died in the terrible fires in that hellish heavily bombed area.

At the time, the Nazis downplayed the death and devastation on that night, not wanting to admit or reveal to Germans how badly the war effort was going. However, Hitler was said to have been very alarmed by it.

After the war, we learned that forty thousand people had been killed in Hamburg on that one night. Some died when they were sucked into the fires by the strong winds, but most had died from lack of oxygen as they huddled in their basements and shelters. More civilians were killed in that one night in Hamburg than were killed during the entire war in England.

"It could easily have been us in the middle of that inferno. How could anyone survive there?" Mutti asked.

"It might be us tomorrow night," I said.

"No, it's too dangerous in the city. We've had two nights of heavy bombing, there might be more. We have to stay away for a few days until it's over."

"Where will we stay and what will we eat? We don't have much food with us." I asked.

"I don't know. Let's get some sleep now and think about it in the morning." Mutti said laying back.

When I laid down and closed my eyes, I thought of Vati.

"I can't believe that Vati is dead, Mutti. I miss him already."

"I know, dear. I miss him too. Try to get some sleep."

A couple minutes later, we heard vehicles behind us and turned around to see several troop transport trucks pulling to a stop and loading the nearby people in the back.

"Look," I said, pointing. "They're using trucks to take people out of the city. Maybe they're bringing them to an evacuation area with food and shelter."

"Hurry! Let's try to get on one of the trucks," Mutti quickly replied.

We hurriedly picked up our things and hustled over to where soldiers were loading people into the backs of the trucks. People were crowding to get on and soon the trucks were full and drove off. A second set of trucks arrived in a few minutes. Mutti and I managed to get on one.

We stood in numb silence in the crowd of people crammed into the back of the truck as it drove a short way out from the city. Out the open back of the truck, we could see a stream of lost-looking people along the road.

175

Illuminated by the headlights of the passing trucks, they traipsed along moving off the road as the trucks rumbled by. Hundreds of thousands of Hamburg residents were leaving the city to escape the bombing.

The twenty minute truck ride brought us about ten kilometers to open fields at Hummelbüttel, which apparently was an evacuation area. The trucks pulled to a stop along the road beside a grassy field, quickly discharged us from the back and then were off again for another load.

After climbing out of the truck, we followed the others off the road and into a field, where other evacuees were already lying under trees and in the grass. We looked around and saw no facilities for sheltering or feeding the many people as we had hoped. We spread out coats and laid down among the rest. Off in the distance in the dark, we could hear people yelling for evacuees to stay away from their riding club. Their buildings were not for our use.

More trucks soon arrived with more evacuees and were quickly off again. The trucks arrived regularly for hours. Each time, we looked up in hopes that they might be bringing food, water or other kind of assistance for us, but each time they brought only more evacuees. After a time, we gave in to our exhaustion and fell asleep.

Chapter 31
Evacuees

THE NEXT MORNING, the sun was red as it rose through the haze of the smoky sky. The night before, we had used our coats to shield us from the radiant heat of the fires, but now we laid on them there in the grass. We used our purses and bag as pillows. I was already awake when Mutti sat up and rubbed her back.

She sadly said, "I was hoping yesterday was a bad dream and I would wake up in bed. But sadly it wasn't. Poor Gustav is gone. It's just us two now, Ruth."

"I can't believe it either. Poor Vati. I was his little girl. What will we do without him?" I said as I began to cry. I couldn't help it. I had to cry on Mutti's shoulder as she patted me on the back like a little girl.

Mutti may have complained about Vati for years, but I knew she loved him and now would miss him too. As we lay there in the field in the midst of all the other evacuees, our prospects for the future were not very good.

We did not know if our apartment and our possessions in it were destroyed. If not, we would still have a place to sleep until we decided what to do. If our apartment was destroyed, then we had nothing. Either way, we needed to leave Hamburg and somehow travel to Aunt Rosa's.

By late morning, it started getting hot in the open field. We used our scarves to block the sun. Thinking the trucks might return at some point with food and water for the large number of evacuees here, we stayed near to where the trucks had deposited us. But we saw no organized effort to provide food. We asked the people around us if they knew what was going to happen here and none knew.

A farm woman walked by carrying a milk container, ladle and cup. Wherever she found small children, she gave each child a little milk that they drank from her cup. The mothers would thank her and the farm woman moved on to the next group of children.

"I'm getting hungry but don't think we should eat the little food we brought with us. No one is bringing food for all these people here and we may need our food later."

"I agree," Mutti said.

"Mutti, what are we going to do? How many days will we be here?"

"I don't know, Ruth. It depends on how long the bombing lasts."

"And then what? And what about Vati?"

"I suppose the Englanders must have other cities to bomb too. When they move on, we can go back into the city, check the apartment and see what has happened to your poor father. We can decide then."

"If we decide to go to Aunt Rosa's, how will we get there? She lives so far away."

"The trains probably aren't working. If we can't find a ride, then we have to walk," she said. I gave a heavy sigh and laid back using my arm as a pillow.

A little later, it became too hot to lie in the field under the hot sun, so we found a shady spot under nearby trees. We were thirsty and scooped up a drink of water from a nearby stream.

I was asleep in the late afternoon with my scarf over my head when Mutti woke me.

"Ruth! Wake up. Trucks are pulling up along the road. Maybe they are going to pass out food."

I rose up and saw about six trucks. Soldiers climbed out and pulled the covering from the back of the trucks. Soon they were opening boxes and throwing out military field ration boxes to the people crowding around the trucks.

I got to my feet and ran over to the trucks. After a time, I caught a field ration box and returned to Mutti. I handed it to her and sat down as we started to open it, our first food in about twenty four hours.

As we were eating some food, two water trucks pulled up. The drivers were passing out cups and bowls that they were rapidly filling with water from a hose on the truck. People crowded around the trucks urgently waiting their turn to get a cup of water and excited at finally getting one. They would eagerly drink it down and reluctantly give it up to another person before they turned and worked their way back out of the crowd.

We were both thirsty, so while I watched our things, Mutti first went over to the crowd around the truck to get a turn for a drink. When she came back in about a half hour, I then took my turn.

That night as we lay in the field, we could hear the explosions of a small bombing raid on Hamburg, nothing like the two heavy bombing raids. It was maybe a sign that the British had moved on to some other unfortunate city.

To our great disappointment, the city was heavily bombed a third time on our second night in the field. We lay awake in the middle of the night unable to block out the sounds of the intense bombing raid, which probably lasted about an hour. Afterward, large fires could be seen on the horizon.

We could only sadly watch, distressed at the thought of our lovely city being destroyed, as well as perhaps our own apartment and possessions. We cried a little and shook our heads sadly. Some nearby children also cried at the sounds.

After this third night of heavy bombing, the bombers didn't return the next two nights. During these days evacuated, we stayed in the same location and the trucks would arrive once a day to distribute food and water. On the morning after the second night with no bombing, people began leaving the field and returning to the city.

After five nights under rainless summer skies, we joined the steady stream of people walking along the road back into Hamburg to see what was left of their homes and city. We thought our apartment might have survived the terrible bombing raid on the night we left, but we had heard rumors that our section of the city, Barmbek, was heavily damaged in that third big raid, the one we had watched from the evacuation field.

Unfortunately, the rumors proved to be true. We were seeing moderate bomb damage after we passed the city park at Winterhude on our way south. Our hearts began to sink when we saw heavier damage as we neared our street. Tired and hungry, we finally came to our apartment building.

We had hoped that it would still be intact, that we could go back into our apartment and find it not looted in our absence. We hoped to be able to live there temporarily while we sorted through our clothes and belongings, and then take what we could with us when we left for Aunt Rosa's in the country.

But instead, there we stood in the rubble-filled street looking up at the ruins of what had been our home. Some lower floor walls of the building still remained, but the fifth floor, where our apartment had been, was totally gone. Mutti dabbed with her handkerchief at the tears in her eyes as she thought about the apartment where she and Vati had raised their family and lived for over twenty years.

I climbed onto the rubble in front of our destroyed apartment building to get a closer look, but the building was gutted and burned on the inside. I saw no sign of any of our belongings. I turned around and shook my head to Mutti.

We walked all around the building looking at the debris strewn everywhere, peering under rubble, hoping to find any of our things. We found Mutti's sewing machine all bent and broken a distance away. Mutti knelt beside it, put her hand on it, and stroked it gently as if she was trying to comfort an old friend. She sadly stood up and looking around, heaved a great sigh. We had no possessions any more, only what we wore and what was in our bag and purses.

From there, we walked down the street to the bomb shelter to see if Vati's body was still there. A third of the apartment buildings along our street were destroyed and burned, while others were just damaged. The building above the shelter was only partially damaged. The stairwell down to the shelter looked to have been recently cleared of debris, so someone had evidently gone inside since we had left. After several pulls on the door to open it, we went inside and found the shelter still intact.

We returned to the place where Vati's body lay the night we left. It was no longer there. We sadly considered the empty floor and remembered the last time we saw him. He had been removed and buried with the tens of thousands of others who died in the raid. Herr Sommer had put some identification on him before we left, but we suspected that he had been buried in a mass grave.

Before we left the shelter the night of the fire, we removed Vati's personal things from his body such as his rings, watch, money and pocket book. It had seemed like a ghoulish, dreadful thing to do at the time. It proved however to be a wise thing to do since his body was now gone.

We looked to see if any food or water containers were in the supplies stored there and found none. Someone had already been there and taken whatever might be of value.

Later, we left the shelter and walked over to look for Ilse Engel. Her apartment building had been only partially damaged. We climbed the dust covered stairs to her apartment and found her door. Her apartment still looked to be intact.

We knocked on her door. We tried the door knob. We looked for a key. She must have gone to stay with her cousin up north as she had mentioned before. We needed a place to stay, but not wanting to break into her apartment, we left.

Mutti thought of a few other friends, but we soon discovered that their apartments were destroyed like ours.

We decided to see what was left of our old work place, the uniform factory. After a number of detours to avoid damage and smoldering ruins, we found it totally destroyed. We stood on the rubble-strewn street in front of it and looked at the damage. A big bomb crater now existed near where the anti-aircraft battery had been and the tangled remnants of the anti-aircraft gun lay in a heap in the middle of the street fifty feet away.

"I don't think anyone now can say that we can't leave the city because we are needed at our workplace," said Mutti numbly looking at the wreckage of the building.

"Now, there might be no city office standing and city official alive to ask for authorization to leave anyway," she added with a sigh.

"If so," I said vacantly, "that makes me feel only a little better."

Since we had no other place to go, we slept in the bomb shelter that night. The shelter and its benches were covered with a thick layer of dust. With brooms and rags from a closet, we cleared some of the dust away. I'm not sure why we did, since we ourselves and our clothes were not exactly clean after five days and nights of sleeping in fields.

Regardless, we cleaned it up a bit and slept on the benches with our coats covering us. Thank goodness Mutti had put a hairbrush in her purse, so that we could at least brush our hair.

Several other women who we didn't know came in later and also slept there with us. It was a little bit disturbing for me to sleep in the place where Vati had just died. I wondered if I would have nightmares but think I was too mentally exhausted to dream.

Chapter 32
Journey South

WE LEFT FOR Aunt Rosa's house early the next morning, carrying all our worldly possessions in our purses and bag. Fortunately, after the scare of the first bad night of bombing, Mutti had carried all the family's money in her purse as a precaution, so we lost none in the burned apartment.

We first traveled east to avoid the most heavily damaged and still smoldering areas of Hamburg directly to our south. Even so, we passed much damage and destruction. As we walked along debris-littered smoky streets of burned out smoldering buildings, we sometimes needed to climb over great piles of debris in the streets to get by.

We did not see very many people along here, except some who were searching through the debris for possessions. Absorbed in their search, climbing over the shattered beams and collapsed walls, they hardly noticed us as we passed.

Several ravens flew overhead. Not too many days before, deafening explosions were all that could be heard here. Now only the caws of the ravens were heard.

As we walked, Mutti saw the unburned remains of a closet lying in the street. She quickly fingered through the strewn-about clothes, looked around to see if anyone was watching, picked up several sweaters and dresses and rejoined me walking.

Once out of Hamburg, we needed to travel about 400 kilometers (or 250 miles) due south to get to Aunt Rosa's house in Leimbach along the Werra River in the German state of Thuringia.

As we walked along the road in the direction of traffic, I looked back over my shoulder as a truck passed. The truck pulled to a stop along the side of the road in front of us and backed up. I hurried forward to talk to the driver. He rolled down the passenger side window and asked where we were going. I told him south, and he said to get in. I beckoned to Mutti. We climbed in the cab, and the truck pulled away.

Our truck lumbered along on a two-lane highway in open farmland country. Very little traffic was on the road, mostly military staff cars and trucks, civilian trucks, a few horse drawn farm trailers and no personal vehicles.

A scattering of people were walking along the road carrying a suitcase or bag also headed south. They would look back hopefully as we passed and I felt guilty that we were lucky enough to catch a ride, while they were still walking.

Mutti and I sat in the cab of the truck as the cheerful truck driver in his fifties talked away. We had never asked for rides like this before, so we weren't sure what to expect. He seemed nice enough, trying to help us, but I also think he liked having company on his trips, especially a young girl like me with whom he could flirt. I tried to be friendly to him because we did appreciate the ride, but I didn't want him to get too many ideas.

Our driver said he had been strafed (shot at) by Allied planes before when he was part of a truck convoy. He made diving motions with his hands as he talked excitedly about it. He preferred to drive on rural highways instead of the autobahns, where the trucks were easier targets.

But, he said, a single truck like ours wasn't a high value target for the Allied planes, so we have no need to worry. Nevertheless, Mutti and I found ourselves scanning the skies more than normal as we drove.

That evening, our driver pulled to a stop at an intersection to let us out. He was turning here at this little town to head west. Mutti and I, who wanted to continue south, climbed out and waved goodbye to the truck driver as he turned onto a crossroad and drove off.

We were hungry from our daylong ride. Walking south through the little town, we found a market where, not wanting to spend much, we purchased a little bread. We each nibbled on a piece of it as we walked.

After our first experience with a truck driver, Mutti suspected that they probably preferred giving rides to pretty girls. She thought it would pay off to get me looking my best. We found a fountain in the town where we both washed up a bit. With water from the fountain, we cleaned our shoes with our hands.

One of the dresses that Mutti had found was airy, attractively colored, and fairly clean. In an alley, I tried it on and it fit me well enough. After brushing off our clothes and brushing our hair, we were as presentable as possible and began walking south again that evening.

If we could not catch a ride, we would have to sleep by the roadside somewhere and try to catch a ride in the morning. But, luckily we soon caught our second ride with a truck driver on a night run.

That night we mostly slept as the driver drove without stopping all night. At times, I tried to make conversation with him to help him stay awake and to pass the time. But he amazingly seemed wide awake the whole time without need of my conversation.

He told us that he was not supposed to give rides but did anyway. When he saw us, he thought of his wife and daughter back in Hannover and hoped that someone would give them a ride if they should ever be in our situation. Early the next morning, he let us out along the road just before getting to his end destination.

Despite getting some sleep during our night in the truck, we were tired in the morning and decided to get a little rest in a woods by the road. Curled up in the pine needles under a tree, we were able to get a couple hours of sleep. It rained a little, but thanks to the cover of the trees, we didn't get very wet.

Later in the afternoon, we were riding in our third truck, a military-looking one with a canvas covered back. We drove along the two lane highway on a warm partly cloudy day with little traffic. Considering what we had been through, we were feeling only a little sore, exhausted and hungry.

The passing landscape was farmlands, rolling hills and clusters of forest. Along this stretch of road, railroad tracks ran parallel to the road about 200 feet away. We sat in the cab talking with the serious looking truck driver who was in his fifties. We had just described to him the bombing and destruction in Hamburg.

"My god, was it really that bad? Hannover, Bremen and Luebeck have been getting heavily bombed too. It's not good, not good. If the Luftwaffe can't protect our cities and factories from the bombers, I don't see how we can win the war." After saying this, he turned pale, hesitated and gave us a worried look.

"Don't worry," I said to reassure him. "We're not going to report you, but you should be more careful." He looked relieved and relaxed again.

"Thank you. I didn't think you looked the type, but today one never knows. I was saying that I visit many factories in my job and see quite a bit of bomb damage.

Somehow they manage to get much of their capacity back on line quickly, but I don't see how they can keep it up if the bombing continues."

We heard the rumble of a train on the tracks coming up from behind us. We turned in our seats to watch it as it overtook and passed us. The locomotive was pulling a railcar with an anti-aircraft battery, about a dozen box cars, another anti-aircraft battery and finally the caboose. We could see the soldiers in the batteries scanning the skies.

The highway began to diverge a little from the railroad tracks and passed along a cluster of trees. Up ahead we could see the highway converging again with the railroad tracks at a town.

Suddenly, two fighter planes zoomed by close overhead at low altitude with cannons blazing, pouring rounds into the train as it pulled into the town. We could see American markings on them as they passed. These planes weren't sleek looking like our own fighters but were stubby and thick.

The anti-aircraft batteries on the train fired at the fighters as they screamed past the train and continued on at low level. The locomotive was hit multiple times and a large explosion of steam erupted from it. One of the boxcars exploded and a number of buildings in the town were hit and damaged.

Inside the cab of the truck, we had ducked down in surprise as the two planes roared over and the driver had swerved in his surprise. He looked around wildly in the skies for more planes as he floored the accelerator and raced to get under some nearby trees to better conceal the truck.

Before, he had sounded like such an old hand at this kind of thing, so I wondered why he seemed so excited. He braked the truck to a skidding stop by the trees and shoved open his door.

"Quick! Get away from the truck! Hurry! The back is full of explosives!" he shouted excitedly.

Not needing any more encouragement, Mutti and I scrambled wide-eyed out of the cab as fast as we could. As we ran frantically with the driver, we heard the diving sound of planes on the other side of the railroad tracks. Scanning the skies, we spotted a second pair of the stubby fighter planes diving at the train.

"This is far enough," the driver shouted, and we all flopped down in the grass by trees near the road.

The diving planes began firing their guns, and several more boxcars were hit, exploded and caught fire. More buildings and houses in the town suffered collateral damage from the lines of bullets from the planes. The two fighters banked and flew off at low level. One of them looked riddled with bullet holes but continued flying.

With the attack appearing to be over, we stood up and looked in bewilderment at the cloud of smoke rising from the burning train and town.

"How can this be happening? Where are our planes?" the driver exclaimed with exasperation.

As we walked back to the truck, we heard more planes, which looked to be ours, now in pursuit of the Americans.

"There they are but too late," the driver said looking up and pointing at them.

Knowing now that the truck was loaded with explosives, Mutti and I looked at each other when we arrived back at the truck. Did we dare get back in? The driver already inside, looked at us and said, "Well?" I reluctantly climbed in and Mutti followed.

As we rode along, we scanned the skies nervously and were prepared to leap from the cab in an instant. To our great relief, we waved goodbye to the driver many hours later as he pulled away after dropping us off. Soon we were riding again. The dress seemed to be working.

Eventually, Mutti and I caught enough rides to get close enough to walk the final distance to Leimbach. Having been through so much lately, we were exhausted, dirty and unkempt. As we walked up Aunt Rosa's street, it was a great comfort to us to finally see her house up ahead, looking the same as always. While so much had changed for us in Hamburg, so little had changed here. Mutti and I tiredly walked up to the door of Aunt Rosa's house and knocked.

When Aunt Rosa opened the door, her face was a mixture of surprise at seeing us and shock at our exhausted and disheveled appearance.

"Hello, Aunt Rosa," I managed to get out.

"Margarete! Ruth! What's happened? Are you all right?" she asked as she hurried out to us.

After a quick hug, she immediately began ushering us into the house. With tears starting to come, Mutti could only say, "Rosa, dear, you have no idea how good it is to see you."

"My goodness, come inside."

"Rosa, dear, we've much to tell, none of it good. First let us sit down and get off our sore feet."

"Yes, yes, my poor dears, come sit down. I'll get you something to drink and eat too." said Rosa as we made our way into the house.

Rosa helped us off with our coats and things, and with a feeling of great relief, we plopped down on the sofa and a chair.

Chapter 33
Leimbach

AUNT ROSA, my mother's sister, had taken care of their mother in this house for many years before their mother, my oma, died shortly before the start of the war. Aunt Rosa and Mutti corresponded regularly, but we had not seen her for many years.

When we were young, Kätchen, and I would sometimes visit Aunt Rosa and Oma in this house for a month in the summer. Sometimes, Cousin Fritzi would come along too. Back then, we enjoyed such wonderful times here. Now we were here in terrible times. It seemed unfair to me that my older wonderful memories of this house would now be tarnished by these newer bad ones.

We described to Aunt Rosa all that had happened, the terrible bombing, Vati's death, the evacuation and our trip here. Horrified at hearing how bad things actually were, she urged us to be cautious. The residents of this little town had not experienced such bombings and destruction like ours. Our account of what happened was much worse than what was reported on Nazi controlled radio and newspapers.

In effect, we were confirming what many in town had already heard by secretly listening to the German language broadcasts of the British Broadcasting Corporation (BBC). She recommended to us that we not tell people here about the destruction in Hamburg. Our account would sound contrary to Nazi news reports and it might bring unwanted attention to us.

If the local Nazi officials got wind of it, we might be branded as liars, subversives or defeatists. We would surely be arrested. We were bewildered to discover that the truth could be dangerous to us. It was one more example of how terrible these times were.

Aunt Rosa's house had several bedrooms. Not wanting to impose too much on her, Mutti and I shared a large double bed in one of the bedrooms. It was a neat room with doilies on dressers and bed stands. Having shared a bed with Kätchen for so many years, it didn't seem an inconvenience and it might prove beneficial in the cold of winter.

Once recovered from our ordeal and settled in, we needed to find useful work for ourselves. Aunt Rosa told us how the food in town was getting harder to find and more expensive, and how ration quantities were smaller. It was clear that our survival might depend on growing as much of our own food as possible.

We started converting all available space in my Aunt's large walled-in back yard into a garden area. Mutti, Rosa and I used a shovel and pick to dig up the flower beds and bushes. Already August, we would plant fall and winter crops. We struggled mightily with roots, but we managed finally to get the ground worked up and rows of onions and cabbage planted in our new garden area.

In early September, we and other women and children from the town helped in the fields with the local potato harvest. The rows of potato plants were dug up by the farmer who rode on a horse-drawn farm implement that turned over the soil and exposed the potatoes.

Stooping over with our sacks, we picked the potatoes from the turned up soil, brushed off the dirt, and put them in our sacks. It worked out well for us since we received potatoes in payment for our labor.

While bent over picking up potatoes, I looked up and watched as two German soldiers with rifles led a group of several dozen ragged men into the potato field a distance from us. The German soldiers motioned to a pile of potato sacks and then at the turned-up potatoes. The men took the sacks and began filling them with potatoes.

When one of the ragged men didn't move fast enough, the soldier gave him a vicious blow with the butt of his rifle. The man was staggered by the blow but picked himself up right away. Soon all the men were busy picking potatoes. I turned to Mutti in surprise.

"Mutti, look at that. Did you see the soldier hit that poor fellow? Who are they, I wonder? They must be convicts being used for the potato harvest."

Mutti was eyeing the potatoes as she picked, thinking about how tasty they would be with some butter back at home. With her thoughts disrupted by me, she looked up and over at the men.

"No, I wasn't looking and didn't see. Rosa said a foreign labor camp is somewhere nearby. Poles or Czechs, I think, brought in to do labor."

"They look more like prisoners, and not very well fed or clothed ones, either. How thin they look."

"Here are more coming," I said pointing to two more groups of the battered looking laborers coming out into the field, under the stern direction of their guards.

Looking over at them, Mutti said, "Maybe they did something wrong and that's why they are here. I don't know. It's not our worry. We have worries enough of our own."

"Look at all these wonderful potatoes," she added.

With a troubled look, I returned my attention to the potatoes in the turned-up dirt in front of me.

After the potato harvest work was over, I found a part time job in a nearby hotel to help pay for food. Extra help was needed there during busy times when army units were in town or passing through. I had never done maid or housekeeper work before, but we needed the money and I would do whatever work I could get.

The woman hotel owner and manager, Frau Seidel, seemed happy with my work. I was teamed with another regular maid and we would do the normal housekeeping, laundry and cleaning tasks. The manager would sometimes ask if I could help out with dinner at night and I always would say yes. Every opportunity I was offered to work, I took.

As mentioned before, I've loved drawing and artwork all my life. While working in the back yard, I found some old paint supplies in a shed and Aunt Rosa said I could use them. When not busy working, I still found time to dabble with artwork.

While collecting firewood one day, I had stumbled upon a pretty scene of colorful fall trees around a small lake and made a rough sketch of it. Setting up my canvas by the shed in the back yard, I began teaching myself to paint. First I drew the picture on the canvas and thought it looked pretty good.

As I admired it, I wanted to show it off to Vati like I had always done. Suddenly remembering that he was no longer here to praise my drawings, I started to cry. I put the picture of the colorful fall trees aside and began work on a new drawing. My first painting would be a special one.

Soon the days began to pass rapidly and we grew accustomed to our life in the small town. After being there a time and checking with the local officials, we were issued ration coupons like the other local residents for things like butter, cheese and meat.

The ration amounts in this little town were smaller than the ones back in Hamburg, but maybe the rations in Hamburg were now smaller too. At least here, we weren't the target of Allied bombers like in Hamburg and we slept better at night.

After so many terrible things had happened, Christmas was not a time of celebration for us that year. Despite this, Aunt Rosa still placed a few of her traditional decorations about in her living room. There on Christmas Eve, we exchanged some small gifts. Aunt Rosa gave me more painting supplies. I couldn't guess where she was able to get them.

I told Aunt Rosa I was still working on her gift, but my gift for Mutti was wrapped and sitting near me. I gave her the package and when she opened it and saw what was inside, she started to cry. I decided that my first painting should be a picture of Vati, which I had secretly painted from memory. She thought it was wonderful and we all had a good cry over it.

We managed to survive the winter there in the small town in central Germany. We struggled to keep firewood in the stove in the kitchen. Twice a week, weather permitting, we went on wood gathering excursions to the woods southwest of town. With our hatchet, we broke up dead limbs and small branches, filled our cart and pulled it back to the house.

When spring came, the trees blossomed and the birds sang as if they didn't know a war was on. It was a nice reminder of more normal times.

We prepared as much of the back yard for planting of vegetables as we could. Many neighbors were also planting gardens. With the scarcity of food in town, the importance of growing food was readily apparent to everyone. We eventually got everything planted and looked forward to fresh vegetables later that summer from the garden.

One afternoon in early summer of 1944, the war made it even to our small town while I was working at the hotel one afternoon. I was wearing my apron as well as a white kerchief on my head as I swept around the chairs and tables on the outdoor terrace in the back of the hotel.

The terrace was an elevated wooden deck that looked out upon the green valley as well as railroad tracks not far behind the hotel. The terrace was enclosed by a wooden railing and decorated with a number of flower boxes full of pretty flowers.

* * *

That day, two pairs of the American P-47 Thunderbolt fighter planes in the skies above were on their way back to their base in England. They had been escorting B-17 bombers part of the way to their target. Having gone as far as their fuel range would allow, they were now headed back and looking for targets of opportunity on the way.

First Lieutenant Tom "Rhett" Butler scanned the skies from the cockpit of his P-47 fighter plane. He could see his wingman "Lefty" Patterson close by behind and to the left. He didn't see any enemy fighters, which was a good thing. He knew the other pair of P-47 fighters was farther back to his right although he couldn't crane around enough to see them.

Early that morning, his plane had been loaded with two 500-pound bombs for this escort mission in hopes that he could use them now on the way back. He had not gotten into any dogfights with enemy fighters while escorting the bombers and therefore had not needed to jettison them earlier.

They were still flying pretty high up and looking for targets on the ground. Primary targets for them to attack were trains, train stations, military vehicles, trucks, and any other military targets of value that they might spot. They normally strafed these targets with their 50-caliber machine guns, but sometimes would carry bombs and rockets for attacking these ground targets.

They didn't normally risk attacking bridges or factories, which were more heavily defended with anti-aircraft batteries. Anti-aircraft fire (flak) from below and enemy fighter planes (bad guys) from above were their biggest dangers.

Lieutenant Butler and the others were following some railroad tracks in hopes of spotting a train. They could bomb the railway tracks easily enough, but putting bomb craters in the tracks themselves was not worthwhile since they could be quickly repaired.

Tom Butler had grown up in Iowa. Antsy to get into the war as soon as possible, he had volunteered for flight training right after graduating from high school. In flight school, he had done well and, of course, acquired the nickname "Rhett". He now was a wild, brash young fighter pilot, hell-bent on destroying the Nazi war machine, already with a number of combat missions under his belt.

Over the radio, he heard his wingman say, "Rhett, up ahead, looks like a train." Scanning ahead, he too spotted it. In a short time it would be pulling into the train station of a large town. It was a tempting target for them.

"I see it, Lefty. Looks like it will be pulling into that train station soon where the flak will be hotter. It's a little risky." He scanned the skies again.

"Anyone see any bad guys?" After further quick scans of the sky, he got negative replies from the other pilots.

"Rhett, what are you thinkin'?" It was his friend "Brewsky", the leader of the other two P-47s behind him.

"Brewsky, I'm thinking of leaving my two 500-pound calling cards on that kraut train station down there. I'm thinking I can surprise them if I make a treetop level run in on that train as it pulls into the train station. Lefty and I will come in low along the tracks. You and Knute follow in from the right and cover us."

"Roger, will do, but, Rhett, break it off though if it starts looking too risky."

"Will do, Brewsky. Lefty, did you hear that? Low altitude run in along the train tracks. I plan to skip my bombs right into the train station. Are you with me?" Rhett said as he checked his instrument panel.

"Let's do it," Lefty replied.

Seeing no indication of any problems on his instrument panel, his plane looked ready to go, so Rhett said, "Okay guys, here goes. Banking left and down."

"Roger," Lefty replied.

Soon Rhett and his wingman Lefty were screaming along the railroad tracks at below tree top level. Since there happened to be no power lines or poles here along the tracks, Rhett was flying very low. On the right side of the tracks, the buildings and houses of a town streaked by, while on the left side of the tracks were fields and an occasional tree or structure, which they veered around or over.

"Lefty. Try to stay as low you can. Trees coming up on the left."

"Roger."

Any flying mistake or mechanical failure flying so low and fast would be certain death for them. As the tracks and houses whisked by, his senses were on such high alert that everything seemed to go into slow motion. The hairs on the back of Rhett's neck were trying to stand up but were being held down by his leather pilot helmet.

A couple kilometers up ahead, they could see the train pulling into the station. They were not getting any anti-aircraft fire yet. They seemed to have surprised them as they had hoped. He readied his bombs for release and prepared himself to push the bomb release button at the right moment.

Suddenly his eye was caught and drawn to the outdoor terrace of a hotel that was passing close by on the right. There on the terrace was a pretty, young fräulein wearing an apron with a white scarf over her light brown hair.

Such a pretty little thing, innocently sweeping the floor with a broom. Suddenly she looked up in surprise and was knocked or fell to the floor as he roared by so close that he could almost reach out and touch her.

He'd never had the opportunity to see the enemy up close like this. The German girl wasn't the brown-shirted girl in a frenzy, with distorted face and stiff arm, screaming "Sieg Heil!" as he had, for some reason, imagined. Instead, she was a pretty young girl innocently sweeping.

Rhett was struck by the sight of her, such an innocent looking young thing, hardly an evil cog in the Nazi war machine. He was passing by her, and she was in no danger from him. But he was suddenly gripped with the dread of killing her or others like her.

In a split second, he envisioned the train station exploding in two huge balls of fire, carrying over into the town, destroying half of it and killing many of its townspeople, possibly other girls like her. Or worse yet, he might be off a little as he released the bombs, a little high or a little wide, and they would land in the town. The angle and speed of his bombing run into the train station left little room for error.

In that split second, he switched from his bombs to his machine guns. He was probably too distracted by then to drop the bombs accurately anyway. He concentrated the fire of his 50-caliber machine guns on just the train station and the train pulling into it.

He could see the tracer rounds from his wingman Lefty also hitting the targets and saw that their gunfire was doing a lot of damage, causing explosions, without substantial collateral damage to the town.

As he and his wingman pulled up and zoomed over the burning train station and explosions on the train, he heard Brewsky call out, "Rhett! Two FWs on your tail! We're on 'em! Get rid of your bombs!"

"Thanks, buddy! Lefty, banking left!" Rhett called out as he pushed his bomb release button. Without the bombs, he now could maneuver better and had a better chance against the German fighters on his tail.

The bombs arched beyond the town and exploded in a field as the American fighter planes climbed and veered left and right to shake off the German fighters.

* * *

I was nearly finished sweeping around the chairs and tables on the outdoor terrace in the back of the hotel. Because of the warmth of the sun there on the terrace, I was thinking of the nice glass of water I would get for myself when done.

Suddenly with a scream of surprise, I ducked and fell to the floor as a plane roared by at low altitude seemingly just yards away. The dark blur zoomed by in an instant and began firing its machine guns shortly after it passed. It was one of those stubby American fighters again, attacking a train pulling into the railroad station a short distance down the valley.

An instant later, a second one roared by at low altitude about a hundred feet away with its machine guns firing. I picked myself up from the floor and stood in shock looking at the planes as they thundered away along the train tracks.

I could see a train of boxcars just pulling into the railroad station of the nearby town. The bullets from the planes sprayed along the boxcars of the train and across the nearby tracks and buildings. The first two boxcars exploded. The anti-aircraft batteries on the front and back railcars of the train and the ones near the train station building were slow to respond. They must have been surprised by the planes, which were nearly on top of them before they began firing.

As the two American planes passed over the train station and banked away, two German planes appeared from nowhere and were close behind them firing. More tracer rounds of anti-aircraft fire filled the air and more explosions erupted at the train and train station as the two German planes chased the two American fighters up into the air. Fiery clouds from the explosions billowed upward from the train station.

Without being able to tell whose they were, I caught a glimpse of two more planes joining into the melee. Soon a desperate air battle was happening in the sky above.

I stood on the terrace holding my hand over my eyes looking up into the sun trying to see the dogfight above. I could hear the roar of their engines and machine gun fire.

People were now running out onto the terrace from inside the hotel. They looked with astonishment at the explosions at the train station and then up at the battling planes in the sky. We heard a small explosion above and saw one of the planes falling from the sky as the fight broke up and the planes raced off. I cheered excitedly, "They got one! They got one!"

Everyone strained to see the falling plane in the sun. We gasped in disbelief and disappointment when we saw it was a German plane, which soon crashed and exploded a distance off. I could only hold my hand to my mouth in shock.

* * *

Lieutenant Butler and his wingman had been pretty lucky that day. It had taken all their flying skill to escape the bullets from the German FW-190 fighter planes as they climbed up into the air, especially since the German fighters could climb better than their P-47 Thunderbolts.

Even so, their planes were riddled with bullet holes. His buddy Brewsky and his wingman Knute had arrived just in time. The four of them had been able to fight them off in a frantic but brief dogfight and even shot one of them down.

On the flight back to their base in England, the young pilot "Rhett" Butler could not get the image of the pretty fräulein out of his mind. His buddies had asked him why he hadn't dropped his bombs, but all he would tell them is he'd gotten briefly distracted and then thought he would miss.

He would catch a lot of grief from his buddies for bombing a cow pasture instead of the train station. Even so, it still had been a very successful and bravely executed attack for which they all would later receive citations.

Afterward, when on a ground attack mission, Rhett would remember the girl as he started his bombing and strafing raids. He tried harder to keep his ordnance on target after that day. That pretty girl with the scarf on her hair may have saved many lives, and she didn't even know it.

Major Butler survived the war and returned home to Iowa where he became a building contractor, married, and lived a long full life. Yet, he still thought of her that day sweeping on the terrace. Many years later, he could still see her there like it was yesterday. She became a part of his life even though she didn't know it. He hoped earnestly she was able to survive the war but would never know.

His vision of Ruth, who was that innocent young fräulein sweeping on the hotel terrace, stayed with him throughout the war and throughout his life. So he became in effect part of this story too.

Chapter 34
Volunteering

THE NEWS OF the war in mid-summer 1944 was seldom good, with official announcements highlighting the bravery of our fighting men and downplaying the enemy successes on both fronts. Aunt Rosa, Mutti, and I sat listening to news reports on the radio and looked worriedly at one another.

We also started periodically listening to the German broadcasts of the BBC as well as the Nazi broadcasts to get more of the whole story. We, like others in town who listened, needed to be very careful and secretive about it, because it was strictly forbidden and considered treasonous. We learned that Russian armies were advancing from the east, while the Americans and British armies had landed in France and were advancing from the west. We dreaded what was coming.

While our little town itself was not a target of the big American and British heavy bombers, the city of Kassel to the north of us was. Occasionally, the bombers would fly over us on their way to Kassel.

One day on my way to work at the hotel, I heard the bombers high above. I looked up and saw an air battle in progress. A large formation of American bombers and its fighter escort were being attacked by German fighters. I knew they were American because it was daytime.

The drone of the bombers, the engines and dives of the fighters and the machine gun fire could be heard. Other passersby stopped and watched too. Two of the bombers were hit and began spiraling to the ground. We could see parachutes as their crews jumped out. One bomber exploded on impact across the river and the second in a field adjacent to the town.

Later in the fall, I stood in a neat row with the other five housekeeping girls in the lobby area of the hotel. Minutes before, the hotel manager, Frau Seidel, had asked us all to assemble there. It was not normal for the staff to be assembled like this, so we were a little apprehensive and looked about nervously.

We straightened up when an officer in a Nazi SS uniform entered the lobby with the hotel manager, who then addressed us, "I'm sorry to have disrupted your work, girls, but Hauptman Wicker here has asked me to assemble you."

"Hauptman Wicker," she said, turning to him,

He clicked his heels to her and in an unemotional, yet threatening tone, he addressed us.

"I will be brief and to the point. We need local workers for the war effort. Do I have any volunteers?"

We all were stunned including the manager. After our initial shock, all of us in line reluctantly raised our hands. What could we do? We feared what might happen to us if we didn't volunteer.

"Very good," said Hauptman Wicker, without emotion. "Report to the entrance of the salt mine west of town precisely at six tomorrow morning. Frau Manager, get me the names of these six volunteers. Heil Hitler!"

He made a straight arm salute, turned abruptly and left. We girls in line were speechless. We had just been volunteered for work in a salt mine. We reeled in disbelief at our bad luck.

"I'm terribly sorry, girls. God knows I am," Frau Seidel said as tears welled up in her eyes. "He informed me that he would be checking out today but wanted to address the staff first. He didn't say what about, so I thought he was going to thank you for your fine service or something."

One of the girls came forward and comforted her, "It's not your fault, Frau Seidel. What are you going to do now?"

"I don't know," she said. "I really don't know."

As the war situation continued to worsen in Germany, war production efforts had become more desperate. The Allied bombing campaign must have taken a toll on our factories. High priority war efforts like fighter plane production were being moved into hidden below ground facilities. My new job was deep underground in a nearby salt mine.

A large open area several hundred feet long had previously been used to stockpile salt ore before being conveyed to the surface. Now it was converted into a facility for production and assembly of fighter plane components. Several hundred people worked in this area, lit by bulbs suspended overhead. Pallets and boxes of materials were stacked along a wall.

An elevator shaft at our entrance was our only way in and out. If the Allies learned of the aircraft parts production in our mine, they might decide to bomb here too. I didn't want to think about it.

I was assembling sets of bolts and nuts for the landing gear struts of a fighter plane. A cart with landing gear components would be wheeled up to my workstation, where I stood in my smock and cotton gloves. With bags of nuts and bolts beside me and a wooden pattern in front of me showing the required amounts, I prepared a complete set of nuts and bolts for the landing gear.

After inspecting and testing the materials, I would put the set in a wooden box on the cart and then wheel the cart to the next workstation. You didn't want to be the workstation where carts were backing up and holding up production.

As I started on another set, I glanced over at a nearby work station where one of the foreign laborers was putting tubes and tires onto wheel hubs for the landing gear. He looked thin and drawn, and wore shabby clothes.

To my amazement, a majority of the workers here were forced laborers from other countries. We were not allowed to talk with them or they with us.

Our modern war armaments had defeated their countries, and afterward, the common people from those countries were brought here to work as laborers. We didn't know if it was punishment for something, but they looked to be poorly treated here. So now our highest priority war efforts relied on them, slave laborers who resented us bitterly.

It sounded too incredible. I suspected they would be severely punished if they refused to work or were found sabotaging components. While I may have been miserable, my miseries were nothing compared to theirs.

Chapter 35
Losing the War

THE ALLIES HAD been relentlessly pushing back the German forces in the west since early June 1944, while the Russians continued doing the same in the east. It was now late fall, and we had received little good news during that whole time. We began to seriously consider and worry about what would happen when the invading armies would arrive here.

Over time, our rations of basic foods like eggs, meats, butter and bread became smaller and smaller. And many times the rationed items weren't even available for us to buy. Even bread became hard to find.

Thank goodness for the vegetables from our garden that fall. We basically lived on our homegrown turnips, onions, and cabbage, and the potatoes from our potato harvest work. They helped us stave off the hunger, which many felt. We tried to share our extra vegetables with others, especially with those who could not have their own gardens due to sickness or age.

In mid-December 1944, we finally heard some good news from the war front. German forces were counterattacking and driving the Allies back in the west. Aunt Rosa and Mutti sat in the living room intently listening to the radio. They heard the reports of the success of the German offensive in the Ardennes Forest and looked almost giddy in their happiness. We had gotten very little good news lately and the war seemed all but lost.

This news provided a glimmer of hope for us. We secretly hoped it would put Germany in a position for negotiating a peace. We were tired of war and didn't care for Hitler or his dream of world dominance. But one could not say that aloud.

To our great disappointment, Germany's Ardennes offensive was halted by the Allies, who in early January were again pushing the Germans back on the western front. The defeat of this last desperate German offensive was a terrific blow to us. It knocked all the air out of us and could only mean total defeat.

In mid-January, Mutti walked along a street in the cold to share some food with a neighbor. She looked downcast and defeated. She stopped at the doorway of a house and knocked. An elderly woman answered and Mutti pulled a turnip from her bag. She handed it to the old lady who thanked Mutti, patting her on the arm. Mutti smiled weakly, turned, and walked back along the street. She passed two downcast looking women who barely nodded at Mutti and she barely nodded back.

If the news over the radio didn't convince everyone that defeat was imminent, we saw direct evidence of it when some recently formed army units being sent to the front passed through our town. They were recently conscripted teenagers and middle aged men, who showed little spirit and walked in silence.

Only one of them walked proudly with his head up. He was a middle aged man wearing a shooting festival trophy chain around his neck. A veteran from the last war, he had won his local town's annual shooting festival. With annual festivals probably postponed during the war, he had been able to wear his coveted prize for years. He was still wearing his trophy chain with pride as he marched off to the front with little expectation of returning.

The supply wagons and single artillery piece of the newly formed unit were horse drawn. These boys and men may or may not try to do their duty, but we saw little chance of them stemming the tide of the Allied advances.

Standing back from the road, Aunt Rosa and other townspeople watched as they marched through town. At the sight of them, we knew the war would soon end with our defeat and surrender.

In March 1945, the Allied forces in the west had advanced into Germany and our transportation networks came under increasing air attack. One afternoon, three pairs of the stubby American fighters swooped down repeatedly on the railroad yard and station, shooting rockets and strafing anything of value. They totally destroyed a small train, other parked rolling stock and railway buildings, and they blew big holes in the tracks.

The anti-aircraft battery initially fired, but was quickly knocked out. A small fuel storage tank was blown up. Two of the rockets missed and hit houses in the town. Two trucks traveling down a road nearby were strafed and destroyed.

No German fighters appeared. The American fighters swooped away, leaving ruin and flames, as quickly as they had swooped in. Within a matter of minutes, they attacked and totally destroyed our railroad station and yard.

Discussions by groups of excited women became more and more frequent in the streets. The topic and question on everyone's mind was who would capture our town first, the Americans coming from the west or the Russians coming from the east. The Russians had reportedly raped, killed, looted and pillaged ruthlessly and mercilessly in their advance in the east.

The Russians were disgusting, heartless brutes out to wreak havoc on all Germans in revenge for the death and destruction the Nazis had inflicted on their country. The Americans were thought to be the good guys, like in the movies. We hoped, in private, the war would finally be over soon without any further destruction. But we prayed desperately that the Americans would get here first.

As I sat at my work station in the salt mine making electrical harnesses, I glanced up at one of the foreign workers at a nearby work station. He was thin, raggedly dressed with a wild shock of black hair. He looked up and saw me looking at him, and I looked away. Another uneasy worry of the townspeople was the release of all the foreign workers. They had been terribly treated by the German guards. When the Allies came and released them, we worried they would take out their revenge and venom for Germans on us, the local German town.

In late March, the Americans had advanced rapidly through Germany and it was rumored they might capture our town soon. Still, I was surprised one morning when I arrived at the salt mine with other workers at the usual time and found the entrance gate locked. A guard rigidly stood inside the gate. I peered through the fence and saw none of the usual activity inside.

"What's wrong? Why is the gate closed?" I asked the guard.

"Go home. There's no more work here," he said gruffly.

On hearing this, we looked at him stupidly for a moment. None of us were sure what to do. I took one more look inside and could not see any activity. I heard the guard tell another person, "There's no more work here!" I shrugged, turned around, and started walking back home. Others did the same.

As I walked, the realization began to dawn on me that my days of forced labor in the salt mine were over! A smile started to grow on my face, but I still didn't quite believe it. I saw Gerda, one of the "volunteers" from the hotel, coming toward me on her way to work. Looking past me, she could see something was wrong.

Then seeing me, she asked, "Ruth, what's happening? Why is everyone leaving?"

"Gerda, it's closed up! They told us to go home!" I said, starting to laugh happily.

Gerda looked dumbstruck for a moment. Then with a big smile of relief and joy, she said, "Thank God!"

We were both overjoyed. We hugged and laughed, and then joined the others walking back to town.

"I am so glad it's over!" Gerda said.

"Me too. No more work in a salt mine. I feel like I've been liberated!"

"Ruth, you shouldn't say that!"

"You're right, Gerda," I said giddily smiling. "I meant to say, oh, yes, … that I feel like a bird set free!"

With feelings safely described, we hugged again and happily walked arm in arm back home.

In the early days of April, we knew the front was rapidly approaching. Mutti, Aunt Rosa, and I stood outside the front door of the house on the crisp clear night. We were watching and listening to the artillery fire and explosions on the other side of the hills to the north of us.

"The Americans are attacking Eisenach," Aunt Rosa said.

"Are they going to do the same here? Do they ever capture a town without destroying it?" I asked.

"It must depend on whether our troops want to defend a place," she replied.

"The troops we see here seem to be bustling about preparing to leave, not preparing any defenses," I said.

"True. I hope it means we'll be spared. You've seen firsthand what the Americans can do to a railroad yard in a matter of minutes," Mutti said.

"Yes, I have and it's truly frightening," I said.

That night, we decided one of us should be awake at all times to wake the other two should we need to take cover in the cellar. The shifts, four hours long, were started immediately, although it turned out to be quiet in town that night.

The next afternoon, it was my turn again to do the four hour lookout duty. From the chair beside the front window in the living room, I rose up periodically to look down along the street each way. As I did, I suddenly saw something happening down the street. So I opened the window and leaned out to better see what it was.

Chapter 36
The Young Soldier

"SOMETHING'S HAPPENING down the street!" I shouted. Mutti and Aunt Rosa appeared behind me with worried looks. As we watched, a group of about twenty German soldiers ran past the house outside. Soon, one soldier burst into the door with his rifle at the ready and saw us. He was a handsome but tired looking young man.

"Sorry. I need to use your upstairs window. You should go down into the cellar," he said as he looked for and saw the stairs.

He raced to the stairs and up to the second floor. We heard him moving things in the bedroom and opening the window. Mutti and I held our hands to our mouths with a worried look and all three of us climbed down to the cellar.

The cellar was cramped, cluttered and lit by a single bulb at the top of the stairs. The three of us huddled there together in the cold. After a few minutes, we heard only silence. I looked at the others.

"It's cold down here. We need coats or wraps. I'll go up and get some," I said.

"Be careful," said Mutti worriedly.

I cautiously started up the stairs. I emerged from the cellar door, tiptoed to a back room and came back with a bundle of coats. I looked down in the cellar and saw them looking up at me.

"Here," I said as I tossed the bundle down the stairs to them.

Going over to the stairs to the second floor, I looked up toward the bedrooms and listened. Hearing nothing, I walked over to the window in the living room and looked out, seeing nothing. I walked back to the stairs to the second floor and looked up.

"Is it all right to come up?" I called in a low voice.

"If you want," the soldier answered from upstairs. I cautiously climbed the stairs. In an upstairs bedroom, I saw the soldier sitting in front of the open window and watching the street outside with his rifle at the ready.

He turned and looked back at me as I entered. He had moved furniture away from the window. The curtains in the open window fluttered in the breeze. In one corner of the bedroom were some of my paintings and art materials.

"I wondered if you needed anything. We have a little food," I offered.

"Thank you. I could use a little food. We haven't eaten in twenty four hours. Could you fill my canteen with water too?" He unfastened the canteen from his belt and handed it to me. I took the canteen, and he watched me as I left the room.

I returned with his canteen and a small plate holding a couple slices of bread with a thin slice of white cheese on top of each. I handed him the plate, which he took and put on the floor nearby. He took a drink from the full canteen and then attached it back on his belt. I watched him as he took a measured bite from one of the bread and cheese open sandwiches.

"Thank you," he said.

"I'm sorry we don't have more to give you."

"This is fine, thank you."

"Do you mind if I ask you what is happening?" I asked.

"No, it's no big military secret. My unit was in Eisenach last night and slipped out of the town during the shelling. We made our way here on foot. We are on the run trying to stay in front of the Americans and not get captured."

"It doesn't sound like things are going well."

"No, there is little hope of stopping the Americans. They have much equipment, supplies and support, while we have very little. Yet we must try."

"We saw the shelling last night. Is our town going to be shelled too?" I asked. He grunted with disgust.

"The shelling and destruction of Eisenach didn't need to happen. We didn't have enough forces to defend it and were planning to pull back. The military commander and mayor of Eisenach had already agreed with the Americans to surrender the city when an order came from the Führer to hold the city at all costs. The military commander had no choice but to comply, so he informed the Americans that the city would not be surrendering after all."

He paused to take a bite of the sandwich and continued, "The Americans surrounded the city with their artillery and poured tons of shells into it in preparation for an assault. Our forces weren't strong enough to hold the city even before the shells started raining down.

Our unit commander thought it pointless to stay and be captured. So we slipped out during the barrage. The city was being heavily damaged as we left and probably has already surrendered, only a day later. If we had pulled out as planned, we could have saved what little equipment and supplies we still had, but now they are lost."

The soldier must have recognized my concern for our town at hearing this because he tried to reassure me.

"But don't worry. It probably won't happen here. We aren't organized enough anymore to defend a doghouse, much less a town or city. All we can do is slow the Americans up."

"For what purpose?" I asked.

"I don't know. I only know it's our duty to keep fighting as long as we can. We are low on ammunition, so it may not be much longer."

"Ruth! Are you all right?" Mutti called up, getting worried about my absence.

"Yes, Mutti! I'll be down in a minute," I called down the stairs. I turned back to the soldier, "I'd better go down there before they get worried. I'll come back in a while."

"Ruth. That's a pretty name," he said with a smile. I smiled at him and left.

Coming down the stairs into the cellar, I found Aunt Rosa and Mutti bundled up. I picked up one of the coats and put it on too.

"What took you so long?" Mutti asked me.

"I was talking with the soldier and gave him a little of our food. He hasn't eaten in a whole day. He doesn't think there will be a big battle here."

"Thank God," Aunt Rosa said.

"I hope he's right," Mutti added.

That evening, I went back up to the upstairs bedroom with a steaming bowl of soup. The soldier turned and looked happy to see me. He rose and cautiously crouched at one side of the window.

"I brought you some vegetable soup. I found a little bacon and put some in too." He took the bowl and cupped his hands around it.

"Thank you, Ruth. I haven't had hot food in a long time."

"You know my name. What is yours?"

"I am Ulrich Brandt, at your service," he said with a little tilt of his head. "I'm from the Heidelberg area."

"My mother and I are from Hamburg. We were bombed out, and my father was killed, so we came here to stay with Aunt Rosa."

"I'm very sorry."

"Thank you," I said as he tasted the soup and lowered himself to a seated position in front of the window.

"This tastes delicious, Ruth. You're a good cook."

I said smiling, "Now I know you must be hungry, Ulrich."

He smiled back. He ate more spoonfuls of the soup and scanned the street outside again. He looked back at me and nodded toward the paintings.

"Is that your artwork?"

Shyly I replied, "Yes. They aren't very good yet, but I'm learning."

"I disagree. They are very good. The fall trees are very lifelike and beautiful."

"Thank you. I also like to do woodcutting. Here's one I'm proud of. This one I had to remake. The first one was destroyed in Hamburg." I pulled out and showed him the oval woodcutting of the German Shepard dog head.

"Gosh, I like that one very much too. It looks just like my dog back home. It would be a shame to have your artwork destroyed. I've already decided if we haven't already pulled out, I'll move to another house when the shooting starts. Then your house here won't be targeted."

"It would be dangerous for you."

He smiled. "I insist. You've been good to me. I can't put you at risk." He ate more soup and continued to scan out the window.

"If this war ever does end, what will you do afterward?" I asked.

"I can't think that far ahead yet. If I do survive, maybe I could look you up. We could have another bowl of soup together, only I hope under better circumstances."

"I hope so. That would be nice. Try to survive."

"I'll do my best," he replied. We both smiled at this.

Suddenly we heard running footsteps in the street. Both Ulrich and I ducked down. From outside on the street, a soldier called in a shouted whisper. "Ulrich! Ulrich! We're pulling out! Come down."

"I'll be right down," Ulrich called out the window back down to him.

He quickly got to his feet and swallowed one last mouthful of the soup. Putting the half eaten bowl of soup down, he gathered his gear. Then he turned to me and grasped my hand in his hand.

"I have to go, Ruth. I hope to see you again."

"I hope so too, Ulrich." With that, he walked past me and out the door. I followed him down.

Downstairs, Ulrich crossed the living room to the front door. I stood at the bottom of the stairs and watched him as he opened the front door and paused for a moment to look back at me. He then left quickly out the door, closing it behind him. I could hear many footsteps running in the street and walked to the window. Soon all was quiet.

I returned to the cellar where Mutti and Aunt Rosa were still huddled, anxious to know what was happening. I came down the stairs still thinking of the young soldier.

"Ruth! What's going on?" Mutti asked.

"Ulrich left. They are pulling out. There should be no battle here."

"Oh, thank goodness," Aunt Rosa said with relief.

"Ulrich?" Mutti asked.

"Yes, Ulrich Brandt. That was the soldier's name. We can probably go back up to the living room to wait to see what happens. I've heated up some soup. We can have some."

I helped Mutti and Aunt Rosa to their feet, and we started back up the stairs.

Chapter 37
American Capture

WE SLEPT THAT night in our clothes on the living room furniture, with our coats over us. The early light coming in the window woke me the next morning. I stood up, looked out the window down the street, and was surprised at what I saw.

"People have put up white flags on their houses!" I exclaimed.

Mutti and Aunt Rosa awoke with a start. They hurried over to the window and peered down the street.

"White flags. Yes, we should put one out too," Aunt Rosa said. "I'll get something white. Ruth, you find some kind of stick or pole."

"Okay," I said as I headed for the back door. I was already thinking of our hoe or a broom. I would look for some rope or twine too to tie it up with.

A little later outside in front of the house, I looked up at the makeshift white flag sticking out of our second floor window. It fluttered a little in the breeze and would surely convey to Americans that no one in our house would resist.

Hanging up white flags on houses had not been openly discussed in town beforehand. It's no wonder since Nazi officials would arrest and shoot anyone talking of surrender. As the Americans approached, the Nazi officials in the area left in their cars. I looked down the street and saw many white flags hanging from the houses.

I started to go back into the house but then turned around and listened. I could hear the noise of engines in the distance. I called in for Mutti and Aunt Rosa to come out too. Many people were now out in the street looking in the direction of the noise. Within minutes we could clearly hear the rumbling and racing engines of many vehicles.

We looked at one another apprehensively and stepped back into the open doorway of the front door. We weren't certain what to do to ensure they knew we were not hostile. We decided we should stand in our doorway with our hands up.

As we stood there looking down our street, we could see a large number of various kinds of armored vehicles and tanks racing across the fields on the outskirts of our town, soldiers on top with their mounted machine guns at the ready.

"They're coming across the fields and down the main highway! Lots of tanks and trucks!" a woman called out from the second story of a nearby house.

We could hear them on the main highway as they raced along it at full speed, taking positions at intersections and pausing at the town square. No shots were heard.

After their dash across the fields, other armored vehicles had now gained the outer streets of the town and some came toward us on our street. One of the armored vehicles roared past our house at high speed. The gunner on top continuously scanned the houses with his machine gun. Other soldiers were beside him with their hand held machine guns.

The noise and size of these vehicles in our narrow streets was frightening. We pressed back against our house for fear of being crushed. They eyed us three women quickly as the vehicle passed. It stopped beyond our house down the street at an intersection.

Another armored vehicle stopped on our street before getting to our house. Soldiers streamed out of the vehicles and took positions along the street.

The soldiers rushed house to house banging on doors and entering with rifles and machine guns at the ready. Soon they reached our house. We moved out of the door way but continued to keep our hands up. A soldier eyed us warily and entered the house. Soon he was out again, down the street, and into the next house.

After their initial rapid evaluation of us as non-hostile, they paid little attention to us as we stood there with our hands up. They looked to be hard, determined, and battle-tested soldiers with quick unfriendly eyes and a clear readiness to use their weapons at the least provocation. We still had heard no shots fired. The firepower, speed, and capabilities of these men and their equipment were amazing to us.

Down below in the town square, we heard the main force of armored vehicles rev their motors again and race off eastward to the next town.

With the rapid search of our houses completed, the soldiers jumped into their vehicles and were off again to the next blocks down the street. In little time, they had finished their sweep of the entire street and were off.

In the distance, sporadic machine gun and rifle fire were heard, then the noise of a great deal of answering fire and the boom of the guns on the American armored vehicles. Thinking of Ulrich, I looked with concern in the direction of the fighting. But it was quickly over, and the engines of the vehicles were heard roaring off into the distance.

I turned to Mutti with amazement, "Was that it? Have we been captured? My God, how can our men defend against such an assault? They barely had to slow down for our town, and I believe they could have easily destroyed it if they had needed to."

"Thank goodness our defenders left or they might have," Mutti replied.

"Yes, I think we've been captured, Ruth. We've been captured by the Americans!" Rosa said looking at me and breaking into a great smile of happiness.

"Thank God, it wasn't the Russians." she added looking skyward. We all felt very relieved.

"Kätchen's countrymen," I said smiling. "She had good things to say about them years ago in her letters."

Mutti added, "We'll have to see what happens next. Let's hope they are as good as they seem in the movies, Shirley Temple and Fred Astaire, you know."

Again we heard sporadic machine gun and cannon fire in the distance to the east and then silence. Wandering out into the streets, we could see jeeps, trucks, and armored vehicles coming into town from the west. Periodically, pairs of sleek looking American fighter planes would zoom by at low altitude.

We thought we could hear vehicles stopping and a clamor of activity down in the town square. Soon a growing stream of trucks, artillery pieces, and armored vehicles sped along the highway headed eastward.

Mutti, Aunt Rosa, and I walked with our makeshift white flag along the street to the town square where people seemed to be gathering.

One of the women from the town came close to my aunt and said in a low voice, "Rosa, if you have any pictures of Hitler in your house, burn them! If the Americans find them, they will arrest you as a Nazi collaborator."

"They won't find one in my house, since I have none," my aunt replied. The woman shrugged and hurried off to another group.

The town's mayor was there in the square in front of our town hall talking with the Americans. People were crowded in front of and reading a list of rules posted in the square by the Americans.

After his talk with the Americans, the mayor addressed the townspeople gathered there in the square, "People, people, I have talked to the American officer in charge and have surrendered the town to him. He says no one will be hurt as long as we cooperate fully. I have assured him there will be no hostilities from us. He says you should stay calm and go about your normal business. If you have weapons, you must turn them in immediately. The Americans will be searching our houses from time to time looking for weapons and German soldiers. If they find any or if you interfere, you will be arrested."

Pointing to the posted rules, he continued, "Please read their posted rules. One of them imposes a curfew beginning immediately from six at night until eight in the morning. No one is allowed outside your homes during those hours. The Americans are here now, and the town has surrendered. So please, let's stay calm. Let's everyone go back to your houses and stay calm."

After this announcement, a murmur of talk arose from the crowd of townspeople. Some old men remained and examined with interest the men and equipment of the conquering army. A number of people watched in awe as a steady stream of troop trucks, supply trucks, jeeps, and the various armored vehicles drove by without letup.

The American soldiers eyed us Germans with hard eyes and weapons at the ready. There were no smiles, celebration, friendly exchanges, or townspeople saying "thank you for liberating us." There was only our stunned acceptance of defeat.

The only incidence of friendliness was when a soldier smiled at and offered to shake hands with a little girl who had come up close to inspect him. She had smiled, shaken the hand, and scampered back to bury her face in her mother's dress.

To us adults, these were the soldiers who had killed so many of our soldiers. It would have been unseemly and untrue to our own dead to have been too friendly to them, despite the fact that we were very happy and relieved to see them. The Americans had, thankfully, made it to our town before the Russians. There had been no wanton destruction, rape or looting.

Eventually people began drifting away toward their homes. We walked back to Aunt Rosa's home not knowing what to expect in the coming days but thankful that this terrible war may soon be over. Aunt Rosa and Mutti began to weep as we walked, and we tried to comfort one another.

The next morning at eight o'clock, we peered out of our front door and warily stepped outside. We made our way down to the town square to find out any news and to see if the Americans might be distributing food to us Germans.

A number of townspeople were already gathered in the town square, probably with the same hope. Very little food was left in the town, only what people had been able to store in their cellars for themselves.

But, instead of distributing food to us, the Americans seemed to be greatly agitated about something. We wondered if someone had violated the surrender or their rules. They told our mayor to gather up himself, his wife, and a dozen other leading townspeople. They were then loaded into vehicles, which soon departed under military escort.

We and the other townspeople in the square watching were greatly disturbed by this and could not find out where they were being taken. All sorts of rumors circulated in the crowd and no one knew what to expect next. A soldier brandishing his rifle told us to "settle down" and they would be back in a while. We could only mill about and wait anxiously for their return.

Shortly before noon, the vehicles returned and our townspeople spilled out of the vehicles with ghastly expressions on their faces. Some returning women were crying. They staggered away from the vehicles and other townspeople gathered around them to find out what happened.

They told us the Americans had taken them to the foreign laborer camp in the hills behind the town. The camp was also captured and liberated yesterday after the capture of our town. Revolted by the horrific conditions they found and ghastly sights they saw, the Americans insisted the town's people should witness themselves what had gone on there.

Like the Americans, our townspeople were appalled by what they had seen. Several hundred emaciated bodies were still exposed in a shallow partially filled-in mass grave. Other bodies, awaiting burial, were stacked up by buildings. The surviving laborers were starved, barely alive, and grossly mistreated.

The mayor claimed he had never visited the camp and was unaware of the conditions there. I suspected it might not be true, but even if he did know and objected to the harsh treatment, he could have done nothing about it. I knew the foreign laborers were being treated miserably, but I hadn't known how badly. Even if I had known, I could have done nothing about it either.

That afternoon, the occupying Americans conducted a thorough search of the town. No weapons or German soldiers were found. Some townspeople complained that personal items had been taken during the search, but nothing was done about it.

The next day, I walked past one of the American soldiers guarding a street intersection. I smiled at him to try to be friendly. He ignored me and continued his hard look. We eventually learned that the American troops had been ordered not to fraternize or associate with any German men, women or children. They had been instructed that we Germans were not their friends and not to be trusted. We Germans were not sorry we started the war, only that we lost it.

Their discovery of the horrors of the foreign labor camp did not help their opinion of us either. Ghastly pictures of the camp were posted in our town hall. The Americans were convinced the townspeople must have been aware of it and shared in the blame.

While they did not abuse or punish us directly, they did little to help us. Convoys of trucks filled with supplies regularly rolled through town on their way eastward. But none of these supplies were for us. The only thing they brought to us was more Americans who needed to be housed somewhere on their way through. A number of our townspeople were told to give up their houses for them and move in with other families.

The Americans soon dismissed our mayor and appointed a new one. They didn't want Nazis to continue in positions of authority and after reviewing our mayor's Nazi past, they decided he should be replaced. The new mayor was a retired man from our community. He had been a newspaper editor before the war and had not been involved with the Nazis.

Our one remaining policeman was also judged to be a willing Nazi and was fired. Until they could train new volunteer police recruits, the American soldiers would be our police.

The nightly curfew would continue. Any violators of curfew or any other rules would be tried in a military court held in town by the American Commander.

After our capture by the Americans, we had no jobs, no school, no police, no mail, no money, and very little food.

Our situation did not lend itself to nights of peaceful, restful sleep. After three nights of troubled sleep, I should have been tired enough to fall asleep quickly, but I couldn't. I lay beside Mutti awake in my bed wondering what we were going to do, how we were going to survive.

I had just tried closing my eyes again when I heard a low voice say, "Ruth, don't be afraid. It's me, Ulrich. Ruth, are you awake?"

I opened my eyes in surprise, trying not to move and wake up Mutti beside me. I could see his face now peering at me in the open doorway.

"Ruth, are you awake? Don't be afraid," he said.

I pulled off the covers and climbed from bed slowly as Mutti continued to sleep.

Taking my robe from a chair, I went to the door where he stood, and he motioned for us to go downstairs. Down in the kitchen, I put on my robe, turned on a light, and looked at him.

He was wearing civilian clothes now and looked ragged and unkempt.

"Ulrich, I'm glad to see you but surprised. I thought the Americans would have captured you."

"We were on the run from them and I got separated from my unit," he explained. "I've been hiding in the woods above your town."

"How did you get here into town? There is a curfew. They didn't see you?"

"It's not too hard. They don't have many patrols out."

"You must need something to eat. Let me see what we have."

"No, I don't want to eat your food. You have little enough. But maybe you could cook what I brought, and I'll have a little of it," he said pointing to the sink.

I looked with surprise at the skinned rabbit there in it.

"It's ready, Rosa!" Mutti called quietly, as she sat down in front of her bowl of a simple rabbit stew. They had added a bit of onions and parsley from the garden. Rosa came in, sat down, and smelled the aroma from the bowl in front of her. All four of us sat at the table and sampled their stew. Soon they were pulling the meat from the bones and putting the bones aside. Being hungry and not having had more than a morsel of meat for some time, we were busily eating down our stew.

"I never thought I liked rabbit, but this tastes good," said Mutti.

"There are lots of rabbits about in the woods where I've been hiding. I surprised this one with a rock. When the rabbit was cooking, I looked around in your shed and found some tools and materials for trapping them. I'll bring you more."

"Ulrich, you mustn't take such chances coming into town. You should catch them for yourself." I said with a worried look.

"A campfire out there might be too risky. I think I can slip into town at nights without getting caught."

"But if they catch you, Ulrich."

"Then I'll surrender and become their prisoner of war. I don't plan to do any more killing." Looking around for a moment, he said, "I should be going soon while it is still dark."

After finishing our bowls of rabbit stew, Ulrich thanked us for the meal and for the use of our washroom to clean up a bit. He would try to visit us again soon with more rabbits. He apologized to Mutti and Aunt Rosa for disturbing their sleep but hoped the rabbit had made up for it. They, of course, sincerely thanked him for bringing the much needed food.

When Ulrich was outside our backdoor, gathering up his things to take back to the woods, I went out with him to see him off.

"Ulrich, please be careful and don't take such risks."

"I'm going to stay out in the woods as long as I can, so I can help you here."

"Thank you again, Ulrich," I said giving him a hug and putting my head against his chest as he put his arms around me. After a moment, I told him he should be going. He squeezed my hand and left quietly.

Chapter 38
The Polish Laborer

A WEEK AFTER regaining their freedom, some foreign laborers were well enough to travel and wanted to begin their journeys back to their home countries. Late one morning, a number of them did so. One large group passing through our town decided to take out their rage on it.

I was hoeing weeds in the garden. Some plants were already sprouting in the rows. I began to hear a growing level of chaotic noise coming from the highway in town. Alarmed, I dropped my hoe and ran into the house.

Opening the front door, I peered out to see what was happening. An uproar of yelling and crashing glass continued to come from the businesses along the highway. Aunt Rosa joined me at the door with a worried look.

"Where is Mutti?" Aunt Rosa asked anxiously.

"She's out gathering wood."

As one of the neighbors ran in the street past our house, Aunt Rosa called to her frantically, "Gertrud! My God! What's going on?"

"The foreign laborers are looting and burning the town. Lock yourself inside," she called back.

Aunt Rosa and I rushed back inside. We shut and locked the doors and windows. I looked around for some kind of weapon. I thought of the hoe I had just been using, rushed out back to get it, and returned with it.

"What should we do?" Aunt Rosa nervously asked,

"You get a knife and stay in the back room there. Watch the back door."

"It doesn't have a lock," Aunt Rosa said fearfully.

"It'll be all right. I will try to keep them from getting in the front door and window. I have it locked." She went back, while I positioned myself in the middle of the room facing the door with the hoe in my hand. Some wild looking scrawny figures ran by the window.

"Filthy German pigs!" someone outside yelled. There were bangs on the door, and a gaunt face appeared in the window.

"Let me in!" the rioter demanded.

"Go away!" I yelled back at him. The face disappeared and then a brick came crashing through the window, immediately followed by a hand searching for the window's lock. I moved forward and swung the hoe at the hand. I hit it with my second swing and heard a yowl from its owner as it was hastily withdrawn.

After a tense moment of quiet, I was shocked to see the door suddenly get unlocked and swing open.

"You left your key under the mat," he said with a lecherous grin.

I wanted to yell, "Stay away!" But nothing came out.

After a quick glance about, he rushed in and lunged for me. I swung at and hit him with the hoe. He was momentarily stunned. He felt his head where I had hit him and then lunged at me again. This time, he deflected the hoe and grabbed me.

He hit me with his fist, knocking me first against a china cabinet and then to the floor. As I lay stunned in the middle of the floor, he jumped on me and pinned my arms to the floor. Awakening, I struggled but couldn't get loose.

"Dirty stinking German murderers!" he said with a vicious sneer. "Your troops came to my village in Poland. They raped and killed my wife and daughter, as they forced me to watch!"

I could only listen aghast and must have been shaking my head no in disbelief. With a terrible look on his face, he shook his head up and down.

"Yes! Yes!" he screamed. "And then they dragged me off to your slave labor camps. I survived six years in your camps, was forced to do and see unspeakable things, but I survived!"

I listened in horror while Aunt Rosa nervously hid by the door in the other room gathering her courage to use the knife.

The man continued with a wild look, "There were times when I thought I could no longer endure it! But just one thing kept me going! Just one thing!! The thought that someday I would avenge my wife and daughter!"

I struggled and he hit me. Suddenly Aunt Rosa burst into the room with the knife raised high and lunged at him from behind. Hearing her footsteps, he turned and saw her. With a sweep of his arm, he deflected the knife and flung her across the room. Aunt Rosa crashed into and smashed a table and chair. She lay unconscious on the floor against a wall.

The man returned his attention to me. I had tried to get up during this, but he was on top of me again and smashed me across the face as I struggled. I lay back stunned with my arms out. With a terrible laugh, the man grabbed at my dress and underclothes.

Grinning insanely, he glanced over at Aunt Rosa unconscious amid the shattered debris of the furniture and then at me below him still stunned.

As he glanced excitedly from Aunt Rosa to me and back again, the expression on his face was changing from ghastly wide-eyed madness to shocked horror. He stopped fumbling with my dress and slowly got a pained tortured look on his face. I awakened and remained still, seeing that

233

he had stopped and appeared to be in some terrible remorseful agony. The man cupped his hands to his face and began sobbing uncontrolledly.

In wretched agony, he wailed, "My sweet wife. My lovely little girl. They wouldn't want this. Nooo, they wouldn't want this done in their memory."

He slowly rose from me sobbing and staggered out the door in utter and complete misery.

Crying, I slowly picked myself up off the floor. I stumbled to the front door and opened it a bit. I dully fumbled with and got the key on the outside, then pushed to close the door.

But before the door got all the way closed, an arm thrust itself in suddenly. I was surprised but alert enough to push on the door to crush the arm in it. The man on the outside bellowed in pain and shoved hard on the door knocking me backwards. This new laborer looked at me viciously from the open doorway and rushed at me. I didn't have time to grab for the hoe or anything else. He clutched my arms and shoved me backward pinning me against a wall. His face was next to me as he leered at me.

"Well, I was hoping to find some nice fräulein, and I think I hit the jackpot. Let's not waste time," he said shoving me to the floor as I screamed and tried to fight him off. I looked at Aunt Rosa who still lay unconscious on the floor amid the broken furniture. He was now on top of me and staring at my bare neck. He pinned my arm with his leg to free up his hand. But before he could clutch at my blouse, someone whacked him on the head from behind. He stiffened upright, stared vacantly, and started to reach up with his wobbly hand to feel his head. Then he got a second whack. He slumped down on me and I could see Ulrich behind him, holding one of the broken chair legs.

He tossed the man to one side, helped me up, and dragged the man to the still-open front door. Carefully peering outside and seeing no others nearby, he grabbed up the scrawny unconscious man and flung him out the front door almost into the street.

After quickly closing and locking the front door, he came back to me, "Ruth are you all right?"

"Oh, Ulrich," I said crying. Then remembering Aunt Rosa, I stumbled over to her, cleared the broken furniture away and tried unsuccessfully to revive her.

Still crying, I stumbled to the kitchen and came back in a moment with a wet rag. I wetted Aunt Rosa's face, and she began to revive. I lowered myself down on the floor and propped Aunt Rosa up on my lap. I dabbed the wet rag on her head. Aunt Rosa was still very groggy with eyes only half open.

We heard more commotion outside and Ulrich positioned himself beside the broken front window.

Someone pounded on the door and yelled, "Open up, ya rotten krauts. The shoes on the other foot now!"

The window was suddenly unlatched and pushed open. A hairy head appeared as a man started to climb through. Ulrich blindsided him with a fierce whack across the face with the chair leg, knocking the man backwards to the ground outside. He dazedly felt the bloody gash across his forehead, nose, and cheek.

"These are my pickings, find your own!" Ulrich shouted out the window, implying he was a rival looter.

The man slowly picked himself up and stumbled away. The second nearby man was watching as he rifled the pockets of the unconscious man lying near the street. After putting several things in his own pockets, he looked up at the house, and wisely kept walking.

Reviving a bit, Aunt Rosa looked up and asked half dazed, "Ruth, are you hurt?"

"Just bruises, I think. Are you okay, Aunt Rosa?"

"I don't know. I have a terrible headache." I dabbed the wet rag on her head and hugged her.

"Thank you for trying to save me, Aunt Rosa."

"I didn't do very well."

"Did you hear what that man said about his wife and daughter?" she asked.

I nodded numbly.

"And then the slave labor camp. Do we Germans really do such horrible things? That poor man. I'm so ashamed," she said.

Ulrich came over. We helped Rosa up and onto the sofa. Both Rosa and I were crying.

Noticing Ulrich, she said, "Ulrich, you came?"

"I came as fast as I could when I heard the rioting. I'm sorry I didn't get here sooner."

"Ulrich, thank you for coming. You took an awful risk coming here in daylight," I told him gratefully.

"I probably looked like one of the rioters."

We heard someone at the back door and Mutti rushed in. She stopped in astonishment at the scene before her. Then seeing my bruised and swollen face holding a dazed Aunt Rosa, she rushed over.

"Ruth! Rosa! Are you all right? What happened?" she asked, shocked and concerned.

She sat beside Aunt Rosa and they hugged.

"Rosa, dear."

"We were attacked, Mutti. Aunt Rosa was struck and hit her head trying to help me," I said, still stunned.

"I'll be okay," Aunt Rosa said feebly.

"Then Ulrich came and fought off several more rioters."

"Oh, thank you, Ulrich," Mutti said looking up.

We heard more breaking glass and yelling in the distance. Ulrich crept up to the window and looked cautiously out. He ducked down as a looter ran by carrying a handful of necklaces and a loaf of bread.

* * *

Down below along the highway, an American army captain and sergeant were standing by their jeep watching the looters. Three other soldiers were also watching nearby. They had just arrived after receiving the reports of looting. Another jeep filled with soldiers raced by and pulled to a stop farther down the road.

They took in the scene for a moment as the ragged men from the slave labor camp were breaking windows, entering businesses, and smashing things inside. Some fires broke out.

"Captain, I thought we were escorting these guys through town tomorrow?" the sergeant asked.

"Yes, but this group must have decided to leave early on their own. I can see why now."

"Shouldn't we stop them from destroying the town, sir?"

"I guess so," the Captain quietly said. "Those poor devils are just out for a little payback. Can you blame 'em?"

"Nope."

After a moment in thought, "Okay, Sergeant, enough is enough. Tell your men to put an end to it and get the looters on their way out of town."

The sergeant picked up his walkie talkie and said into it, "Okay, Corporal, move in and break it up. Don't kill any of 'em if you don't have to, but stop the looting and get these scarecrows on their way out of town."

The sergeant nodded to the three nearby soldiers. They all pulled out billy clubs and began blowing their whistles as they moved forward toward the looters.

* * *

Mutti and I were still attending to Aunt Rosa when we heard the whistles blowing outside. Ulrich crouched by the window cautiously looking out.

"Something's happening. I think the American soldiers are driving the looters away," he said.

"What about the man in the street, Ulrich? Is he still there?"

"No, he must have come to and wandered off. I want to stay until this is all over. If I see the Americans coming, I'll slip out the back and hide in your shed."

Mutti and Rosa still hugged together on the sofa. They looked up sadly, and Rosa sighed.

We had no more looters that day as we continued to tend to Aunt Rosa. She was still suffering from her bang on the head. Later after it got dark, Ulrich got ready to go. I went out back with him as he was leaving. I hugged him and gave him a kiss of thanks on the cheek. He smiled and then slipped away.

He came back the next night with two rabbits and the night after that with one rabbit. Aunt Rosa had several friends who were suffering from our lack of food, and she covertly took them some of the rabbit meat, which they greatly appreciated.

Chapter 39
Hunger and Suffering

I WAS WALKING deep in thought along the street a few days later. The day before, we had been called down to the town square where we filled out a paper with our information. We were then issued new ration cards and given a ration of a half loaf of bread and a small packet of butter. When asked, they could not say when more food might be distributed.

I still had a few bruises from the attack. As I crossed an intersection, I could see down the street to the main road. There I saw captured German troops being marched along the highway. Of course, I thought of Ulrich and rushed down to the highway to get a better look.

A group of about two hundred German prisoners quietly walked in loose formation westward along the highway. An American soldier carrying a machine gun walked along on each side of them and two more armed soldiers were in a jeep following slowly behind.

Ulrich had just visited last night, so I didn't expect to see him in the group. But I went to the road to watch as they passed, just to make sure. A guard escorting them ordered me to stay back, so I backed up a few steps. The German prisoners looked tired and hungry, and they stared mostly straight ahead as if ashamed of their predicament.

I approached the guard without getting too close and asked, "Where are you taking them, please?"

The guard gave me a hard look and said, "Sorry, Miss, move along."

I wanted to find out where they were being taken, thinking that if Ulrich were to be captured, he would be sent to the same place. I saw what looked to be a senior

American soldier with many stripes on his uniform sleeve, watching nearby with several other onlookers.

I approached him and asked, "Please, Sir, where are the German prisoners being taken?"

"Sorry, Miss. I'm not authorized to say," the soldier replied curtly.

I wasn't very fluent in English and said, "I'm sorry, but I don't understand."

"That means I can't tell you," he replied plainly.

I turned and walked away. I stood watching the group of prisoners continue down the road. I was frustrated that I had not learned where Ulrich might be taken if captured.

Beside me, a voice said, "It's a sad sight indeed. Our once mighty war machine, our invincible army. We were going to conquer the world. Ha! Now look at what has become of it."

I turned around and recognized our new mayor.

"Hello, Mr. Mayor. My father would probably say the same thing if he were alive. Sir, the Americans wouldn't tell me where they are taking them."

"Do you know one of them?" he asked.

"No, but I know a soldier, and he might be wherever they are taking them," I lied.

They're taking them to a temporary holding pen in a field on the other side of Vacha about twenty kilometers from here. I overheard them talking about it earlier."

"Thank you, Mr. Mayor."

With a look of concern, he asked, "Dear, you have some bad bruises on your face. Are you all right?"

"Yes, I think so. We were attacked by the looters."

"Most regrettable," he said with sympathy.

I had never met our new mayor before. He seemed like a nice man, so I thought I could ask him the question that everyone had.

"Mr. Mayor, what is going to happen to us here?"

With a sigh, he answered, "Many people have that question, but unfortunately, I don't have a good answer. We'll have to wait and see, my dear. I'm working with the Americans to get help for our townspeople, but it's been difficult so far. They expect us Germans to provide for ourselves, feed ourselves, and get our own town running again."

With another sigh, he added, "To lie in the bed that we Germans have made for ourselves, so to speak."

Then continuing, "Our most immediate problem is food. The Americans do not provide us food from their supplies, which they said they need for themselves. They are helping us in our efforts to acquire our own food supplies from our local area. But our fields are not being planted, and food supplies are scarce. We will need everyone in town to help in the fields to get them planted, but it takes time for crops to grow. We will have to do our best."

"I see. Well, my aunt, my mother, and I will certainly help all we can. Thank you again, Sir, and goodbye."

"Goodbye, my dear. You're welcome," he replied as I turned to leave.

Ulrich returned that night with another rabbit. After seeing the captured prisoners, I was greatly relieved to see him again, and hugged him close when he arrived. He tried to soothe my concerns, but had some bad news for us.

He told us an old man from town looking for food had stumbled upon him unexpectedly. Ulrich had given the man a rabbit and asked him to keep quiet about him hiding in the woods. But the old man was very talkative, so Ulrich wasn't sure if he was capable of it.

He thought the Americans would hear about him in the woods and come searching. He would move his location and bring us rabbits as long as he could, but he didn't know how much longer it would be before the Americans might capture him.

That night when saying goodbye, I was more emotional than normal and worried that it might be the last time I saw him. We embraced and kissed.

"Ulrich, please be careful. If you have to, move to some distant woods and don't try to bring us food. If they do find you, please surrender. Don't get shot trying to run or fight it out with them. The war is almost over. I don't want you killed in its last days."

"Okay, Ruth. I'll try not to get shot if they find me. I still hope to look you up in better times to have that bowl of soup we talked about."

"I do too, Ulrich," I said with tears and then we kissed again. Slowly and sadly he drew back from me, still holding my hands. Then with a reassuring smile, he slipped away into the night.

It was just the next afternoon that we heard a German soldier had been captured in the woods outside of town. My heart sank at the news. All three of us were stunned and saddened to hear it had happened so quickly.

I rushed down to the town square and found the mayor to see what he might know about it. He told me two dozen troops had gone out that morning to search for the soldier. When they cornered him, he had surrendered without resistance. They had already put him on a truck headed for Vacha, so he probably would be held at the holding pen there west of town where the previous group of prisoners were headed. He did not know the name of the soldier.

Ulrich's visits at night stopped afterward, so I knew it was Ulrich.

The next day, the Americans conducted another search of the town looking for more soldiers in hiding. They found one being hidden in the basement of a house and he too was put on a truck headed toward Vacha. As punishment to the family hiding him, their house was confiscated and they had to move out. The family moved in with friends. One of the previously confiscated houses, used as temporary housing of troops, was then given back to its owner and that family moved back into it. The Americans were governing us with a firm hand.

By the end of April 1945, the people in town were suffering greatly from the lack of food. We had been luckier than others because of the few rabbits brought by Ulrich. Still, we had no way of preserving our meat for very long, plus some of Aunt Rosa's close friends were also in great need of food, so our stock of rabbit meat was soon gone.

The Americans had distributed small portions of food relief to us only a few times. I walked on the street past townspeople who looked thin and hungry. The Americans seemed to have a regular supply of food for themselves. Yet they provided very little to the local people, who were obviously in great need of it.

Their treatment of us might be better than the treatment we would have gotten from the Russians, but that was little consolation for our hungry stomachs. We could only suspect that the Americans were punishing us Germans for the war.

After a bitter costly war with Nazi Germany and the discovery of the horrors of Nazi concentration camps, the

Americans held a very low opinion of us Germans. They seemed to think all Germans knew about and supported what the Nazis were doing. They couldn't appreciate that dissent had been ruthlessly suppressed by the Gestapo. It didn't help that they were not exactly greeted by flag-waving, cheering German crowds thanking them for being liberated either.

The Americans seemed to harbor a deep resentment against Germans for the death, destruction and misery that Nazi Germany had caused in the war. We were hoping for better treatment from them but were disappointed.

In mid-May 1945, the war in Europe was officially over, but nothing changed for us. We sat at the dinner table eating a thin cabbage soup. We wanted to write Kätchen at Aunt Minna's address in America to ask her for help, but with no mail service yet, we couldn't. So we were hungry and suffering.

Several weeks had passed since Ulrich had been captured. I thought about him and wondered how he was being treated. He was a prisoner of war and getting regular meals. He was probably doing much better than us, but I still wanted to visit him if I could.

With the weather looking to be good for several days, I set out early one day to see if I could find the temporary holding pen where Ulrich had been taken. Vacha was about fourteen kilometers away. I hoped to be back within two or three days as I started walking west on the main road. While a supply truck or other vehicle might lumber past occasionally, most of the traffic on the road was foot traffic. A great number of people displaced by the war were on the move in both directions.

In a small town on the other side of Vacha, I found a bakery that was open, although no customers were inside. I approached the man who stood behind a counter, which displayed only a meager supply of bread for sale.

"Excuse me, sir. I'm looking for a temporary holding pen for German prisoners located somewhere around here. I believe a captured soldier I know was taken there."

With a concerned look, he said, "It's about two kilometers south of town. I'm sorry to tell you this, but it is an awful place."

I stood in stunned silence, as the baker continued, "It's a big enclosure in an open field with barbed wire fences and guards surrounding it. There are no shelters or facilities of any kind, just the muddy open field."

* * *

South of town in an open field, a large area had been fenced off to make the temporary holding pen or enclosure for captured German soldiers. One side was near a patch of forest. Guards with machine guns were stationed in jeeps around the perimeter and did not allow the prisoners near the fence. A couple tents were situated on the outside for the guards, but no tents or buildings of any kind were inside.

Inside the muddy enclosure, the prisoners in their filthy uniforms looked hungry. They received no medical attention, and had no sanitary facilities like washrooms or latrines. The prisoners relieved themselves wherever they could, and therefore, the whole camp stunk and filth flowed freely when it rained. The prisoners were not given blankets and had no shelter from sun, rain, cold or heat.

As a result of the awful conditions and lack of medical attention, many German prisoners became sick and a number of them died each day. Two half-naked corpses lay on the ground inside the enclosure gate. The corpses had been stripped by the other prisoners who needed the clothes more than the corpses.

A truck with a water tank was parked outside the fence. A hose from the tank led inside the fence to one spigot where prisoners could cup their hands to drink water. A truck pulled up next to the gate. American soldiers pulled out several large bags from the back of the truck and heaved them over the fence. Several senior prisoners inside came forward and picked up the bags, which contained loaves of hard bread. Loosely organized lines formed as hunks of bread were torn from the loaves and distributed.

Several prisoners carried up a corpse and lay it by the other two corpses. One of these men walked toward the fence. The nearby American guard perked up and pointed his machine gun at the prisoner.

"Stay back from the fence!" he yelled at the prisoner.

"I must protest!" declared the prisoner. "How can you keep us here under such conditions? We're dying in here."

As he spoke, other prisoners nearby turned to watch.

"I thought you Krauts liked barbed wire. A little different being on the inside, ain't it," sneered the guard.

"We need shelter, medicine, more food and water. In accordance with…" continued the prisoner.

"Pipe down!" the guard barked back, interrupting him. "Or I'll give you a little of what you gave our captured boys at the Bulge! That wasn't 'in accordance with' either! Now shut up and back away!"

He fired a line of machine gun bullets in front of the prisoner. The prisoner didn't move.

"I'm not warning you again, buddy. Back away!" the guard threatened, firing a second even closer line of machine gun bullets at the feet of the prisoner.

The prisoner, recognizing the futility of further protest, slowly backed away and rejoined the others.

* * *

At the bakery, the baker behind the counter continued telling me about the holding pen. "They give the prisoners little food and water. Many are dying from disease and hunger. We here in town have tried to take them food and clothes, but the guards won't let us near. They threaten to kill us, and they mean it. I'm sorry to be the one telling you, but your friend is probably not in a very good way."

I had been listening with a stunned look. When I started to faint, the baker grabbed me across the counter. He held me there for a moment until I recovered. Then he came around the counter and helped me to a chair.

After a few minutes of collecting myself, I was ready to leave. He tried to talk me out of seeing the holding pen for myself, but I told him I wanted to see it. After thanking him, I left his bakery shop and made my way south from town.

About a half hour later, I found the awful holding pen in the field but was not allowed near it. I stood along a road sadly looking out at it in the distance. I thought prisoners of war were to be treated in accordance with international treaties. The countries followed these rules because they wanted their own captured soldiers to be treated similarly. I imagined Ulrich would be doing better than us because of these treaties.

However, the war was over. So with no "war," the Allied powers didn't see them as prisoners of "war." They called them something else and didn't feel obligated to treat them according to such treaties. They also had little incentive to do so since Allied prisoners of war were no longer held by Germany.

As I turned and started back along the road to the little town, I wasn't sure what to do, so I returned to the bakery.

From the look on my face when I entered his bakery, the baker said, "So you have seen for yourself?"

"Yes."

"What are you going to do?"

"I don't know. Maybe I could go to the woods on the north side of it and call his name? He might hear or see me, and call to me."

"And you might get shot by the guards!"

"I have to try something."

"Maybe you should go home. There's nothing you can do here," he advised. I looked sadly at him for a moment and left.

Chapter 40
Seeking Ulrich

I WALKED TO the town square of the little town and sat down on a bench trying to decide what to do. I was trying to think of something when a woman sat down beside me. I noticed she was a handsome woman but plainly dressed.

"Are you the girl looking for a soldier in the holding pen?" she asked in a hushed tone.

"Yes," I replied with surprise.

Looking around cautiously, she said, "I might be able to help you find him if he is there. What is his name?"

"Ulrich Brandt."

"It may take several days. Do you have a place to stay?"

"No, I was going to find a corner in an alley somewhere."

"There's a house with green shutters down that street," she said pointing. "The lady there will probably let you sleep in her car shed. I'll come see you there in the morning."

"Thank you," I said as she left. I felt a little glimmer of hope.

I found my way to the house with green shutters and knocked on the door. The lady who answered was very kind and showed me into her car shed. Instead of a car or carriage, various things were being stored there, and a crude mattress with blankets was in the back on the floor. She came in later to bring me a cup of hot tea and half a slice of bread. I felt very fortunate to have anything to eat and thanked her very much. I ate and went right to bed.

The next morning, I was awake and resting on the mattress when the woman from the square came in. She came close and said in a low voice, "I talked to a prisoner in the holding pen last night. He said he would look for

Ulrich today. Meet me by the bakery tonight at nine. You can come with me to the pen tonight. If they find him, you can talk with him at the fence."

"Oh, thank you, thank you. I'll be there," I said gratefully. The woman smiled and left. During the day, I tried to find odd jobs in the town in hopes of earning some food but without success. So I came back to the house with green shutters and helped the lady inside with some cleaning to pay her back a little for her kindness.

At nine that night, I was waiting in the dark by the bakery and saw the lady from the square carrying a large canvas bag. She motioned for me to come with her, and we hurried off into the darkness. After a short while, the woman and I were picking our way quietly through a dense growth of trees. We came to the edge of the trees and crouched down in the underbrush about twenty feet from the enclosure fence.

No floodlights illuminated the perimeter of the enclosure, only a small one off in the distance by the main gate. The only lights nearby were the flashlights carried by the guards as they walked back and forth along their sections of the perimeter.

"You stay here," she whispered to me. "If they have found Ulrich and have him there, I'll wave for you to come up. Try to stay low. You'll only have a minute. Wait for me to wave to you. Understand?"

"Yes," I whispered.

The fence ahead of us was dark but became illuminated by the light of a flashlight carried by an approaching guard. The beam of the flashlight moved along the fence in front of the guard. In its light, I could see the rumpled figures of the men inside the fence sleeping on the ground. I hated to think that Ulrich was one of them. As the guard passed, he cleared his throat.

She touched me and said in a whisper, "That's the signal." After his cough, the guard pointed his flashlight farther ahead leaving the fence in front of us in the dark again.

She crept forward quickly with the shopping bag and lay down next to the fence. A prisoner was lying on the other side. The guard continued walking and ignored them. The woman pulled food silently from her bag and passed it through the fence to the prisoner.

I could barely hear them whispering to each other. I watched intently for the woman's wave telling me to come forward. But the woman crept back without waving, and we left silently.

We quietly exited the woods and were walking through a field back to the road. She hadn't said anything yet, and I asked her what had happened at the fence.

"He said he didn't find your friend Ulrich but would keep looking. We can come back day after tomorrow. If they haven't found your friend by then, you may be too late. Many soldiers have already died. I try to help, but it isn't much."

"How are you able to do it?"

"I can't tell you now, maybe later," she said as we continued walking in the dark.

Over the next two days, I managed to find a few odd jobs on the local farms. After many hours of hoeing, sweeping, or cleaning, the farmer would give me two eggs in payment and maybe a turnip or a potato. I thanked him and carefully put them in my coat pocket. It may not sound like much, but it was a good wage for my work in those times. The eggs and vegetables were valuable to me and to the farmer. When I got back to the house with the green shutters, I gladly shared my earnings with the nice lady there.

Two nights later, the woman and I were back again at the edge of the woods near the holding pen fence. She had her shopping bag with her again as we crouched down in the undergrowth waiting. The guard patrolling along the outside the fence passed and coughed.

"That's it," she whispered. She crept forward quickly and lay down at the fence. She passed food through the fence to the prisoner on the other side. I was nervously dreading that they hadn't found Ulrich. This would be my last chance. If they hadn't found him, then he was likely already dead.

I gasped when I saw the woman look back and wave to me. I tried to control my joy as I crept forward quickly and lay beside the woman by the fence. I saw a filthy sickly Ulrich in front of me on the other side of the fence.

"Ulrich, is that you?"

"Yes, Ruth, it's me. Why have you come here?"

"I wanted you to know I'll be waiting for you and that bowl of soup you promised."

At hearing this, Ulrich managed a weak smile.

"I don't know if I will make it, Ruth. It's best if you forget me."

"No, Ulrich. You have to make it."

"Hurry, we have to go," the woman whispered.

Reaching through the barbed wire fence and squeezing his hand, I said, "Ulrich, if I'm not at my Aunt's, look for me on Mozart Street in Hamburg. I'll be waiting for you. Good bye."

Squeezing my hand in return and then letting it go, he said, "Okay, Ruth. Good bye."

The woman and I silently rose up and crept back quickly into the woods. As we came out of the woods and walked across the field to the road, I was crying quietly but said nothing. The woman patted me on the arm to comfort me.

"I feel so helpless," I said as we walked back to town on the road.

"There isn't anything more you can do for him. You've given him the best thing possible, a little hope, a reason to live."

"Couldn't I stay and help you bring them food."

"No, I'm not going to be able to help much longer. I've heard they will be closing this holding pen in a few days and shipping the prisoners to bigger prison camps along the Rhine around Koblenz. I doubt if those camps are any better."

"Why does the guard allow you to bring food?"

"He just arrived here and wasn't in the fighting. So he's not hardened by the killing and hasn't seen his friends blown to bits by our men. He hasn't learned to hate us Germans like the other guards. I promised him I would only bring food in. No weapons."

"But why does he risk being caught?"

"He's appalled by the conditions here too but can't say anything. It wasn't hard convincing him to help me. It only took a smile. He's just a boy and probably has a crush on me. I've always had a knack for getting my way with men," she said with a smile.

I looked at her and saw she was a very handsome woman without even trying to be.

"And why do you do it and risk being caught?"

After a moment, she said, "I lost a husband and three sons in the war. I do it for them."

I was speechless but finally managed to say, "I'm so sorry."

"Helping soldiers helps me deal with the loss of my soldiers," she said in a gentle voice.

We walked on in silence for a time. Then she said, "As I said before, you have already helped your soldier all that you can. Now you should go back to your Aunt's or Mozart Street. With time, the Americans will get over their rage with us. Then they will send Ulrich and the others home."

"Thank you for everything. I wish I could repay you somehow."

"There's no need. You're quite welcome."

Just outside town, we parted for the last time. After a tearful hug and another grateful 'thank you', she turned and disappeared in the darkness. Early in the morning, I would start back to Aunt Rosa's.

Chapter 41
Becoming Refugees

I HAD MUCH to think about on the walk back to Aunt Rosa's house. If Ulrich did manage to survive, I also must survive. What a cruel trick it would be on him to endure all manner of terrible treatment in hopes of meeting me again, only to find later I had died. Vati as a prisoner of war in the last world war had been released shortly after the German surrender. The current war would be over soon. If Ulrich can survive their mistreatment, he might be released after the surrender and will come looking for me. I had to survive! I would try even harder to get food, maybe plant more in the garden.

At home, I told Mutti and Aunt Rosa about the trip, and under what terrible conditions, Ulrich and the other soldiers were being held. They appeared to be greatly affected by it. They sat together on the sofa hugging each other and crying.

On seeing this, I regretted having told them so much. They explained they were hoping the Americans might begin to sympathize with our plight and start providing more food aid. But after what I had described, it looked like we could expect to continue to suffer with little help from the Americans.

One day, my aunt's friend Inge knocked at our door. When I let her in, she went to Aunt Rosa and Mutti sitting in the living room. They asked Inge to sit down, but she declined.

"In these terrible times," she sadly said, "you have always been good to me, sharing your vegetables and rabbit meat when there is so little to eat. Now I have something for you."

We all watched intently as she pulled a handkerchief from her pocket and unfolded it to reveal a thick square piece of a chocolate about the size of the palm of my hand. We all stared at it in amazement.

"How did you get it, Inge?" Aunt Rosa asked.

"I will tell you, but you have to promise not to tell anyone else. It's very important."

"Of course, we promise," Aunt Rosa assured her as Mutti and I nodded in agreement.

"My niece has made friends with one of the American soldiers, and he sneaks her food, including chocolate bars. If the American higher-ups find out, he'll get in trouble, and she will get no more food. So you have to keep it a secret or you will ruin it for her."

"Yes, Inge, we promise and thank you. Are you sure you can spare it?"

"Yes, this is half of one of the bars, and it's my thanks to you. With God's help we will survive these terrible times," she said. We thanked her again, and she left.

Afterward, we carefully cut it into little pieces. We each took a little piece and put the rest away for later. We were surprised at the taste, not very chocolaty, but, at least, it would provide us with a few extra needed calories. In three days, it was all gone.

I, myself, had noticed a few American soldiers seemed a little friendlier to me too, making eye contact when others weren't looking. At first these soldiers had been like warfighting machines, but it is only natural that they would seek out female companionship in time. However, when one particularly homely and mean looking soldier gave me a lecherous smile and wink, I was totally unnerved by it and hurried away. Afterward I avoided them.

After hearing about Inge's niece, I began thinking that at some point I too might need to seek out an American soldier in hopes of getting food for us. Inge brought us another piece of chocolate a week later. But a few bits of chocolate and a few vegetables were not nearly enough to sustain us.

Aunt Rosa's health began to deteriorate at the beginning of June. We could not tell if it was due to her injury or our minimal diet or a combination of both. She lay in her bed ashen-faced while Mutti sat beside her sister holding and patting her hand. My poor aunt would give Mutti a weak loving smile in return.

I did everything I could to acquire some healthier food for her like meat and butter, but none was available in our little town. Inge gave us a couple small cans of American rations, but it wasn't much. In the bigger town east of us, I traded half of our silverware for a small quantity of sausage, cheese and bread.

Poor Aunt Rosa died soon after taking to bed. She was buried in the local cemetery next to her mother and father. Mutti, Inge, several other of my aunt's friends, and I were there and cried as her wooden coffin was lowered into the open grave.

Then it was just Mutti and me. Not much deliberation was needed for us to decide to stay in Aunt Rosa's house. The house and its contents were all we possessed. It was our only port in a terrible storm. While conditions in the town were not good, we suspected that conditions were not much better elsewhere in Germany. We would have to manage here as best we could.

With the loss of Aunt Rosa and our continuing struggles, it was a terrible, sad time for us. Sitting together on the sofa one night, Mutti and I were eating our meager dinner. Mutti sat staring at the piece of bread she held. It was all we could afford to eat from our limited supplies. I patted her on the arm and she looked up sadly. Seeing me motion toward her bread, she tore off a piece and numbly put it into her mouth.

Not many days after our decision to stay, two women were standing in the street talking when another woman excitedly rushed up and blurted out some news that had only just been posted down at the town hall. Both women gasped at hearing it. One put her hands to her face and turned away crying. The news racing through town that day was about a change in the Allied occupation zones. On the first of next month, July 1945, the Russians would be taking over control of Thuringia, our area of Germany.

The news was devastating to the town. It was well known that the Russians had raped, killed, and plundered with a vengeance and without mercy on their campaign through Germany. Women were raped at the whim of any Russian soldier. Any man trying to protect them was shot. The town had been greatly relieved when captured by the Americans rather than these brutes.

Would they be the same now? Maybe the Russians would be less brutal and marauding now since the town was being peacefully turned over to them without the heat of battle. No one knew, but the townspeople feared the worst. They would be harshly treated, and their possessions pillaged.

It would be especially bad for me as a young pretty girl. The Russian soldiers would always be after me. I might have to become the mistress of an officer or high official to protect me from their frequent rapes. It was a dismal prospect for me. Mutti and I felt we had no choice but to leave instead of staying in Aunt Rosa's house.

In two days, we were packed and ready to go. It was late June of 1945. Others in town were also leaving. We tried to sell what possessions we could, but no one had money to buy things. Before leaving, we traded the rest of our silverware, some personal items and a few pieces of furniture for a meager supply of food. We would take whatever valuables we could with us but were forced to leave everything else behind. We basically gave Aunt Rosa's house and everything in it to Inge for her use until such time as we should return, if ever.

With great sadness, we said goodbye to the house that had been in our family for many years. I stood in front of Aunt Rosa's house with a small cart packed and ready for our journey. Inge was there too to say goodbye.

When growing up, I had such wonderful memories of this house and our summer vacations here. Those fond memories were now just one more thing obliterated by the war.

Mutti came out the front door and closed it one last time. She looked at the house with tears in her eyes for some time. It seemed like she was losing Rosa all over again. I came over and put my hand on Mutti's shoulder. She looked around at me, sadly turned, and gave Inge a goodbye hug.

"Goodbye, Margarete. God be with you," said Inge.

Mutti nodded sadly and started walking up the street. After saying goodbye to Inge, I got between the handles extending in front of the cart, reached down, lifted them up, and pulled. Our food and worldly belongings in the small cart were not heavy, and it began to move without much effort. The first steps of what looked to be a long and arduous journey.

Our small two-wheeled cart with the two pull handles was the same one we had used before for gathering firewood. If we loaded it carefully with the load balanced over the wheels, the cart could be easily pulled. A small tarp held down with ropes would keep our belongings dry. We also took another small tarp for shelter in bad weather. Mutti and I would take turns pulling the cart, although I wanted to do the majority of the pulling.

Without any real means of self-protection, we would be at the mercy of the roads on our trip. The Americans had maintained law and order in our town. We could only hope to find law and order also maintained in other areas. But with so much destruction and so many displaced people, we had no idea what to expect.

We dressed as plainly as we could, so as not to attract the attention of thieves. We had taken all the family jewelry and watches from Aunt Rosa's house and sewn some of them into our clothes as well as hidden some in the cart.

For cooking, we brought a pot, a knife, and a few eating and cooking utensils, as well as a hatchet for chopping firewood, and flint and matches for starting a fire. Inge gave us a wineskin for carrying water.

We each brought along a scarf, shawl, and thick coat for the trip, even though it was summer. We wore the scarves and shawls as protection against the sun as we walked during the day and for warmth at night if needed. We planned to strap the coats on the cart when not needed during the heat of the day. They might be needed at night and definitely would be needed later in winter.

A great many people plodded along on the roads. Some like us were leaving Thuringia because of the Russian takeover, but many were displaced people and foreign laborers. Mutti and I walked with the small cart along the road with the other refugees. As before, few vehicles other than military supply trucks passed by.

Heading west toward Vacha was the most direct way of leaving Thuringia, and also enabled me to see if the holding pen had actually been shut down. Hamburg, our home for so long and the place where I hoped Ulrich might find me, was our destination.

On the other side of Vacha, we came upon the awful holding pen where Ulrich had been held. It was empty now. Mutti and I stood with our cart on the road, looking out at the muddy smelly remnants of it. The field was empty except for the barbed wire enclosure fence and the muddy, trashy mess inside. We spent several minutes there as I described to Mutti how horrible it had been.

At the bakery in the nearby town, we visited the baker who before had been so nice to me. He was behind the counter and recognized me as soon as we walked in. His display shelves were nearly vacant with only a few bread loaves. After our warm hellos and Mutti's introduction, I asked him about the holding pen.

"They closed it about two days after you left and sent them to camps near Koblenz. The Americans supplied me with flour when they ran the holding pen here, so I could bake bread for them. I always managed to put some aside for my own use. Now that the holding pen is gone, it's hard to get any flour, so I'm unable to bake much bread these days."

"We need bread ourselves for our long journey," Mutti told him. "We don't have any money, but I have this amethyst broach I can trade." She handed it to the baker who examined it closely.

He frowned sympathetically, "At other times this would be worth something, but it's only worth about half a loaf in these times."

"That's good of you, we'll take it," she said. The baker put the broach in a drawer and handed Mutti a half loaf.

He said, "It's too bad you don't have cigarettes. They are more valuable than jewelry these days."

"Goodness," Mutti said.

"Thank you again for everything you've done and good bye," I said sincerely shaking his hand.

"Good bye," he said sympathetically. We returned to our cart just outside his door and soon were on our way.

We went to see the lady in the house with the green shutters. She remembered me and greeted us warmly. Someone was already sleeping on the mattress in the car shed. She offered to let us sleep in her living room on a sofa and chair, but we didn't want to leave our cart in the car shed with strangers. So she lent us a blanket, and we slept that night on the ground beside the cart in the car shed.

I asked about the pretty woman who helped me find Ulrich, but she had not been seen in town since the holding pen closed. It was almost like she had been an angel sent to help me find him and then vanished again when her assignment was done.

When we passed Vacha the previous day, we had left Thuringia and entered the German state of Hesse. We no longer had to worry about Russians or so we thought. Today, we would continue walking west. On the other side of Bad Hersfeld, we would run into and take the main road north to Kassel.

We were accustomed to walking every day, but we were not accustomed to walking all day, day after day. So every hour, we would stop and rest. If we took our break alongside woods, Mutti would rest beside the cart, while I would take a few minutes to forage in the woods for wild onions, greens or berries. Unfortunately, chestnuts would not be ripe until late September.

Farmhouses along the road frequently displayed a sign saying "No Food". After passing yet another one of these signs, I commented, "How could a farmer possibly survive sharing food with so many travelers?"

"How will we survive? That's the question, Ruth. We have such a long way to go."

"I'm not sure, Mutti. We have to keep walking north though. The next city is Kassel, then Hannover, then Hamburg. With any luck we can make at least twenty kilometers per day. At that rate, it should take us about three weeks. I don't think we will get any rides this time, so we just have to keep walking."

That afternoon, we reached the city of Bad Hersfeld, which did not get heavily damaged in the war. When Mutti saw the Fulda River there, we decided to have a bite to eat and to soak our feet in it for a few minutes before crossing the bridge. After many hours of walking, it was a nice break for us. Walking through town, we came to their town square and filled our wineskin with water from the fountain there.

Soon we were off again on our way. We would have several more hours of walking to get to the main road north. When we arrived there in the early evening, we looked up and down along the road amazed at the number of people who were on the move. After a brief rest, we joined the flow headed north.

Chapter 42
Young Girls

IT WAS GETTING dark, so Mutti and I followed the other travelers as they left the road to find shelter in the roadside woods for the night. We sat down near two young girls, who looked to be traveling by themselves. Looking over at them, they also didn't appear to have any food. The girls looked back at us but said nothing.

"Are you girls traveling alone?" Mutti finally asked them. The older one nodded her head.

"Do you have any food?" Mutti asked. The older one shook her head.

After seeing my nod of agreement, Mutti reached for our concealed bread and stealthily broke off pieces for her, me and the two girls. She slipped the two pieces to the girls who concealed them as they took bites. Mutti and I did the same.

"Thank you," the older one said.

"You're welcome. Where are you headed?" I asked.

"We're going back home to Münster. We were evacuated from there to Bavaria two years ago because of the bombing. We lived in a youth camp there."

"You were sent to Bavaria without your parents?" I asked.

"Yes, there were lots of us."

I looked at the younger girl who couldn't have been more than nine or ten years old. I was speechless at hearing such a thing.

"What did you girls do there in the youth camp?" I was finally able to ask.

"We worked maintaining the camp, growing food, working on nearby farms. We had ceremonies and parades. The older ones would school the younger ones. We dug trenches to defend against the approaching American army, but they didn't do any good."

"So you were captured and had no way to get home?"

"The camp leader was older than us. She was seventeen. When the Americans got close, she told us that we could go home if we wanted, but she would rather commit suicide than surrender. That's what she did with eleven other girls."

"God in Heaven!" Mutti exclaimed in astonishment.

"Twenty eight of us girls didn't though," continued the older girl. "When the Americans came, they told the nearby town to take care of us. A nice lady took us in. We wanted to go home, but we had no way to get there or tell my parents where we were."

"Your poor parents. I'm sure they must be terribly worried about you," Mutti said sadly.

"I guess so," the older girl said quietly, looking away.

Then she continued, "Another family said they would be traveling north by the roads and offered to take us with them as far as they could. We traveled with them for eleven days, but they had to head west from Fulda, so now we're heading north by ourselves. We ran out of food yesterday."

"I can't believe how terrible, how cruel this war has been. You poor things! We're heading north to get back to Hamburg, and you can travel along with us if you want," I offered.

"Thank you. We'd like that. I'm Marta," the older sister said smiling.

"I'm Helga," the little sister chimed in.

"I'm Ruth, and this is my mother, Frau Thielke," I said smiling. After our introductions, we talked only a little more. Mutti let them have a drink of our water and slipped them each another little piece of bread, which they ate before we all laid down in the grass and fell asleep.

We walked all the next day with the two girls, our cart and the many other travelers on the highway. At times, we passed a military checkpoint where typically two armed American soldiers stood eyeing the passing faces, while two others sat in a nearby jeep. In town after town, we found no relief efforts, only an occasional water fountain in the town square where we would fill our wineskin. Like before, we rested for a few minutes every hour. At noon, we ate a few more bites of our bread.

We passed destroyed tanks, tracked vehicles and artillery pieces along the roadside. These remnants of a battle that happened here only three months earlier were already starting to rust. We looked inside one, but people had long ago picked them over and removed anything of value.

When it started getting dark that evening, the travelers began leaving the road to find a place to sleep in the roadside woods. We pulled the cart off the road and headed toward the woods.

"There have been lots of barns on the way. I wish the farmers would let us sleep in them," little Helga said.

"People would steal from the farmers, Helga," I told her. "We'll be fine in the woods here. It doesn't look like rain. We should be in Kassel the day after tomorrow. Maybe we'll find some kind of relief services there, some soup or bread or a camp. We'll see."

We located a good spot under some trees and began to settle in for the night.

Our travel the next day was uneventful. As we walked, I thought about Marta and Helga, and if we should go with the girls to Münster to get them safely home. It would take us several days out of our way and we might get there and find no parents or relatives. I talked it over with Mutti privately as we walked. She was in favor of taking them.

If we did, we would need to head west from Kassel, instead of continuing north. Having still more time to think about it, we didn't discuss it yet with the girls. We spent the night along the road in the woods again and luckily still without rain.

As we approached Kassel, the steady stream of refugees traveling in both directions increased. The vehicle traffic also increased, mostly in the form of military trucks and jeeps. On its southern outskirts, we started seeing extensive bomb damage to many buildings.

In several places, whole blocks were now rubble with only the road north cleared through. We saw no organized efforts to feed or house the many displaced travelers on the road. We continued along with the girls in the steady stream headed north.

Up ahead, I noticed a woman elevated on a heap of rubble, examining all the northbound people as they walked by. As we approached, the woman saw us, jumped up wide-eyed and screamed, "Marta! Helga!"

The girls froze in their tracks, looked around frantically, then burst with joy when they spotted her and screamed, "Mutti! Mutti!"

The girls and their mother ran wildly to each other, screaming and crying. Soon the mother was down on her knees in the road hugging and crying with the girls.

"I can't believe I found you. I was coming to look for you in Bavaria. I've been watching for you on the way, but I never believed it possible."

"Mutti, oh, Mutti," was all Marta and Helga could say as they sobbed.

All three were locked in a hug and crying as Mutti and I walked up with tears in our eyes too. Others in the crowd looked on smiling at the touching scene.

"How wonderful, girls. We're so happy for you," I said. The girl's mother looked up, reached out her hand to me and I took it.

The girls still could not speak. As we moved them over to the side of the road, the two girls clung tightly to their mother.

After a few minutes, Marta was finally able to say, "Mutti, this is Ruth and Frau Thielke. We've been traveling with them."

"Bless you for watching out for them. Oh, I am so thankful to have my angels back."

"We were with them only for the last several days. They were with another family before they met us."

"I wish I could thank them too. I can't believe I found my two angels. Thank God. Oh, I can't believe it."

After a brief emotional rest beside the noise of people and trucks passing, we all five continued north along the busy road. But soon we had to say goodbye to the girls and their mother when we arrived at the crossroad where they would head toward Münster. We hugged the girls and their mother when we parted, waving a teary goodbye to them as they walked off.

As we continued north, we were disappointed in Kassel or rather what was left of Kassel. It had been heavily bombed in the war and was largely destroyed. The center of the city was a landscape of building skeletons and rubble filled streets. To clear the streets for vehicles and pedestrians to pass, they piled rubble and debris high against the remains of the buildings along it.

A few relief stations were set up to provide food for travelers as well as the local residents. We did manage to get a meal after waiting in a long line with our cart beside us. Traveling north through the city, we asked at an American check point along the road if there were any shelters or camps where we might stay and were told no.

Before it started getting dark, we looked for an empty building along the road to sleep in. We noticed people going in and out of one partially destroyed building. I went inside while Mutti stayed outside with the cart. In the dim light, I could see a number of rooms inside with several families living in each room.

They looked like they had been there for some time and they eyed me suspiciously as I looked around. I probably could have found a back room there somewhere but decided to try another place.

After several more attempts, we found a less crowded building. A woman and her small son were living in one room. I asked her if she minded someone staying in the empty space across the room, and she said no. So Mutti and I brought our small cart through debris outside and into the building with us.

The lady told us their apartment house nearby had been destroyed, so they were living here until housing could be found. We told her in turn that our apartment in Hamburg had also been destroyed.

We spent an uneasy night sleeping in the darkness of the heavily damaged building. It rained for several hours during the night causing small cascades of water inside the building. When water began pooling on the floor, the woman took us over to an elevated pile of rubble where she normally went to stay dry in the rain. It was not a pleasant or comfortable night. We left at first light as soon as we could.

Chapter 43
Traveling With Gerhard

WALKING NORTH from Kassel the next day, Mutti and I noticed more and more rough-looking men, probably released foreign laborers, coming from the other direction. We had seen many foreign laborers before on the roads, ones who looked to be making their way home. These men looked more to be just wandering the roads looking for trouble.

As one nasty looking one walked by, we avoided looking at him, awkwardly staring straight ahead. Once past, I glanced back at him with a worried disgusted look. Ahead of us, we saw an older couple pulling a small wagon traveling with a younger man walking with a noticeable limp.

Mutti and I hurried forward with the cart to get closer to the threesome.

"Excuse me, would you mind if we walk with you. It would make us feel safer. Would you mind?" I asked them.

"We aren't traveling with this young man, but I think you are right. Some people on this road are pretty unsavory looking," the older man said looked around at us and the younger man with the limp.

"I don't mind if you don't think I'll hold you up," the younger man with the limp said.

"No, not at all," I said.

The woman of the older couple said, "I agree. Let's travel together." We introduced ourselves. The older man and woman were Herr and Frau Fischer. The younger man with the limp was Gerhard. So it was agreed, and the five of us walked on together.

"Were you wounded in the war, Gerhard?" asked Mutti.

"Yes, a grenade. I was in a field hospital in Bavaria when I was captured. Our medical staff fled two days before the Americans arrived. Me with my bum leg had to get water for the others and attend to them as best I could. But I could do little for them, and many died. The Americans held me as a prisoner of war for two weeks and then released me. They probably thought I was no longer a threat to them and probably were right. I've been walking, so to speak, for the last two weeks."

"And where are you headed?" I asked.

"Home, a little town south of Bremen."

Herr Fischer said, "We're going north to Trendelberg and then west to a little town where my brother lives. We've lived in Gotha in Thuringia all our lives. It's being taken over by the Russians, so we left."

"We had to leave everything. Everything but what we have in our wagon," Frau Fischer said with regret.

"We also were in Thuringia and left for the same reason. We're headed for Hamburg," Mutti said.

"It seems like everyone is on the move. I don't know if it will help, but traveling together can't hurt," concluded Gerhard, and everyone nodded in agreement.

We walked the rest of the day without incident. Fewer vehicles and foot traffic were on the road now that we were away from Kassel. At noon, we rested for a while and ate a bite of food.

That evening while it was still light, we left the road for the shelter of the trees in the woods. Gerhard and Herr Fischer wanted to use our hatchet to cut two strong straight branches to use as walking sticks, which might be useful as clubs if necessary. They weren't gone long and also brought back some wood for a fire.

Meanwhile, I had gone foraging into the woods and found some wild onions and greens. We made a soup in our pot with them and half a potato and a small piece of sausage.

As we sat around the fire sharing our hot meal, we talked about the old times and enjoyed one another's company. When our soup was gone, we cleaned up and put out the fire so as not to draw attention to us there among the trees.

In the afternoon on the second day, we reached Trendelberg where Herr and Frau Fischer left us to head west. We said our goodbyes at the intersection on the north side of town and watched them as they walked off, Herr Fischer pulling the wagon and Frau Fischer with the walking stick.

We would miss them. They had been good company and their departure left us with only three in our party, less safe in our numbers. Still Mutti and I were glad to have Gerhard walking with us.

"Well, I guess we should keep walking. We still have several hours of daylight," Gerhard said. With that, we turned and started along the road north. The road would take us along the Diemel River to the Weser River, which we would then continue to follow northward.

At some point along the Weser River, we would have to part company with Gerhard as he continued along the river toward Bremen while we headed for Hannover. We might consider traveling further with Gerhard toward Bremen if it seemed safer, but we had many days of travel before we would need to decide.

We were traveling through the Diemel River Valley with its picturesque scenery, but we could not afford to be distracted by landscapes or castles and let our guard down.

We walked near others without seeing a particular party we wanted to join. Some but not all the southbound travelers who we encountered looked menacing. We eventually made it to the Weser River and continued northward along its west bank.

One morning, we were walking with our cart along the highway with the Weser River nearby on the right. A string of dangerous looking foreign men filed by heading south. They eyed the cart as they passed.

While we seemed to be encountering more of these types as we got farther north, we, at least, had been with enough other travelers on the road so that we didn't feel isolated. As we walked, Gerhard made a point of being between us and the travelers we encountered.

Farther up along the road, a single ragged foreign worker headed south approached us. As he neared, he veered his path toward Gerhard who was limping along with his walking stick.

"Do you have the time?" asked the ragged traveler.

"No, sorry," Gerhard replied.

"Oh, come on. You must have the time," the man said as he kept coming.

"I said I don't, so stay away!" Gerhard said firmly, raising his stick as a club.

"No need to get riled. Just asking for the time," the man innocently replied, as he turned and continued past. Gerhard lowered the club and turned to continue on his way. The man suddenly wheeled around and rushed at Gerhard with an ice pick. I screamed.

Gerhard turned, swung, and hit the man in the head with his club. The blow stopped him for a second and gave Gerhard enough time to rear back and hit him again in the head. The man dropped the ice pick and fell to the ground in the middle of the road.

Other people on the road had stopped and turned to look. Gerhard quickly picked up the ice pick from the ground and put it in his pocket.

"Quick! Let's walk fast, and if he wakes up, we'll be long gone."

We hurried along looking back several times. The man continued to lie in the middle of the road. As people walked by him on either side, one passerby rifled through his pockets and found a bunch of watches.

Holding them up and admiring them, he grinned happily at his find, pocketed them, and kept walking. After a minute of hurried walking, we had distanced ourselves from the man lying in the road.

"I think we are okay now," Gerhard said, catching his breath. We slowed down, looked back and saw the attacker was still down.

"Did you see that other man pull the watches out of his pockets?" I asked.

"Yes, I did," said Gerhard. "Anyone who looks down to pull out their watch to give him the time, gets an icepick in the chest for their trouble. Then he takes their watch."

Gerhard pulled the ice pick out of his pocket and examined it.

"This ice pick might be useful as a weapon, but I think I'll stick to using my club, which seemed to have worked well enough. We probably shouldn't throw it away."

He put the ice pick in the cart, and we continued.

When we reached the town of Höxter in the late morning, we wanted to buy some food, at least a loaf of bread if we could find some. After passing several closed bakeries, we stopped a woman passing in front of one and asked where we could get some bread. She told us in a hushed tone of a back street off the highway.

With our cart in tow, we walked to the street that seemed to be an area of black market activity. As we passed one dark man in an alcove, he opened up his coat revealing a number of watches.

Farther on, another man stood holding a couple small cans of meat from military rations. He eyed us to see if we were interested, but we kept walking.

We looked about warily searching for someone selling bread. Down the block more, we came upon a man standing in a doorway. In front of him was a wooden crate turned up on end with two loaves of bread sitting on it. He eyed us suspiciously as we approached. Gerhard told the man we were interested in buying some bread and he nodded down toward the loaves. He also said he had butter.

We showed the man some of our jewelry pieces. The vendor inspected the pieces and told us how much bread and butter they were worth. Gerhard made a counter offer, but the vendor held firm. We decided to accept it.

While Gerhard was concealing our purchase in the cart, I became curious.

"The bakeries in this town are either closed or out of bread. This is the only place with bread. Why is that?" I asked the vendor,

"I don't know. We can get supplies, and they can't." He shrugged.

"Where do you get your supplies?" I innocently asked.

He looked at me suspiciously and said, "That kind of question can get you in trouble here."

"Oh, I'm sorry," I said realizing too late that I was asking prying questions about his illegal activity.

"She didn't mean anything by it," Gerhard said coming to my aid. The suspicious look of the vendor turned into a smile.

"That's okay. I can see the pretty girl means no harm. By the way, we get our supplies from Hannover, but don't tell anyone."

"Oh. Hannover, that's where we're going. So food is plentiful there?" I asked.

"No!" the bread vendor said shaking his head. "The only thing plentiful in Hannover is chaos! Drunken gangs of foreign workers and locals roam the streets there at all hours. They rape, kill, and steal without mercy or punishment."

I gasped in shock at this terrible news.

With a sly look, he added, "The chaos provides us with opportunities to get our supplies."

Concluding, he said, "The Englanders are supposed to be in control, but they aren't. If you are smart, you will avoid the Hannover area. I say this because you seem like a nice girl, and I would hate to see something terrible happen to you."

In my astonishment, I stammered out, "Th-, thank you for the warning. We didn't know."

The vendor nodded, and we walked away. Gerhard looked concerned and thoughtful as we made our way back to the main road.

"What do we do now?" I asked, still in shock.

"It's a lucky thing you asked that man your question," said Mutti, also in shock.

"You certainly can't go that way now," Gerhard said, stopping for a moment to think.

"Well," he said having come to a conclusion, "I think it would be wise for you to give the cities and roads a little time to get less dangerous. The Englanders can't let it go on forever. Come with me to my parent's home and stay a month or two with us until it's safer to travel."

"But your parents?" I said.

"I know them, and they won't mind. You really don't have any other options. The roads are too dangerous right now."

Mutti and I both gave him a hug and told him, "Thank you, Gerhard."

"Good. It's settled," he said as we walked on.

Chapter 44
Perils of the Road

WE WERE NOT very far out of town, before we, unfortunately, experienced the dangers of the road in full. In some sections of the road, we couldn't see very far ahead or behind due to the bends in the road and the patches of woods alongside. Fewer and fewer people traveled on this isolated stretch of road.

When we saw the three men coming toward us, we felt uncomfortably alone along the road. They were obviously drunken freed foreign laborers. A patch of woods was on the left and the Weser River flowed on the right. Looking around, Gerhard could see no other travelers on the road.

"Keep walking, look straight ahead, try to ignore them," Gerhard said in a low voice.

The men wore long coats and had a bottle of wine, which they passed between them. Acting drunken and reckless, they leered at us as they approached.

"What's in the cart?" the first one said.

"Leave us alone. We've done you no harm," Gerhard told him.

The men approached menacingly and Gerhard raised the club in a defensive posture.

The drunk who seemed to be their leader cried out, "Done me no harm. Done me no harm! I was brought here from Russia to work in your mines. I've been beaten, starved, and spit on by you Germans for five long years. Every German has done me harm and every German owes me something!"

The three drunks simultaneously rushed Gerhard, who swung his club and landed a solid blow on one of them. The other two thugs were able to strike Gerhard with their fists during the rush and knock him awkwardly to the ground in the roadway. Gerhard's club was knocked away in the melee. Mutti and I screamed, shying away, not knowing what to do.

Gerhard lay dazed on his back on the ground as two of the drunken thugs hit and kicked him repeatedly while the third thug made for the cart. Still conscious, Gerhard was struggling to protect himself and deflect the blows as best he could.

Seeing the club on the ground, I picked it up and hit one of the thugs over the head. The thug who I hit was only momentarily phased by the blow, but it distracted them enough to interrupt their fury directed at Gerhard. He and the other one paused to turn and look at me standing with the club. They breathed heavily from their drunken exertion, pointed at me, and laughed derisively.

Then returning their attention to Gerhard, they roughly rummaged through his coat and pants pockets looking for valuables as he lay dazed on his back. Frustrated at finding none on him, they kicked him several more times.

The third drunk at the cart had been rifling through its contents and flinging things out. Mad at not finding anything of obvious value, he knocked the cart over violently.

Now all three of these animals turned their attention toward Mutti and me. As we shrank away, me with the club and Mutti behind me, they rushed us knocking the club from my hands. Holding us by an arm, they ripped off our scarfs, shawls and coats, to get a better look at us. They all stared at me, the young pretty one.

The first drunk leering at me said, "I get the fräulein first. You two can fight over the old frau." Mutti and I gasped and moved back in fear.

The second drunk complained loudly, "You got the fräulein first last time, dammit!"

At this, the first drunken thug savagely attacked the second one and knocked him to the ground. The second one lay on the ground with his arms raised to shield his head as the first drunk viciously snarled and loomed over him.

Beating his chest in rage, he screamed, "I get the fräuleins first! I get the fräuleins first! I! Get! The fräuleins! First!"

The third drunk watched, laughed, and rushed to claim Mutti. As she screamed and kicked at him, he shoved her to the ground by the side of the road.

Before he could jump on top of her, the second drunk had recovered from his attack, and was up and grabbing him from behind. They stood over Mutti glaring at and pushing each other.

The first brute now came toward me. I had picked up the club again. I swung it at him as he approached. He dodged my swing and approached again. His two partners momentarily stopped to watch. They laughed and howled with delight when I swung again and the first drunk ducked again.

My grinning attacker was amused too as he circled me and then rushed me knocking me to the ground. I was fighting with him as he pressed his weight on me and kissed at my face and neck. His smell and breath were awful. The other two drunken thugs were now watching and cheering as we struggled.

Suddenly, a click, click was heard, and two shots rang out. The second and third drunks dropped to the ground beside where a startled Mutti lay. The first drunk jumped to his feet in surprise and saw Gerhard sitting on the pavement with an army pistol leveled at him.

"Now, comrade, there's no need to be like that. We were just having a little fun," he said in a soothing voice, smiling maliciously.

Then suddenly sobering up and staring at the pistol, the villain said greedily, "Say. That's a nice pistol. Worth a lot of money. I'd like to buy it. I'll pay you a good price for it. How about it, comrade?"

Gerhard, in pain, responded firmly, "Comrade, you've gotten your last fräulein first."

The drunken villain looked puzzled as he considered the complicated statement. He flinched when he realized the meaning, but Gerhard fired and the ruffian slumped to the ground on top of me. I screamed and pushed him off.

As Gerhard got sorely to his feet, he looked around excitedly and saw no other travelers on the road. With pistol still drawn, he hurried over to the three drunks, checked them out one by one and saw they were all three dead.

"Ruth, Frau Thielke, are you all right? If so, we have to hurry and get away from here," he said putting the pistol in his coat pocket.

Although shaken, Mutti had gotten on her feet quickly saying, "I think I'm okay, Gerhard."

On my feet again, upset, and angry, I said, "Me, too. No thanks to these filthy pigs!"

"Quick! We have to get out of here before someone comes," Gerhard said. "Get your things on and see what they have in their pockets. I'll see if the cart's still usable."

Mutti and I hurried to collect our garments and put them back on. We searched through the pockets of the dead men and put their things in our pockets.

Meanwhile, Gerhard frantically put the cart upright again. He found it was still usable and began throwing things back into it.

When I started to help him, he said, "Ruth, see if you can drag them off the road a little."

I asked Mutti to help, and we soon had them down off the shoulder of the road.

Gerhard was now across the road, going into the woods with the cart. I had picked up the club again, and we ran to catch up with him. Hurrying along a path through the woods, we heard several vehicles on the road coming from the north.

Hiding behind trees, we watched as two American jeeps passed where the dead men laid without stopping. With a sigh of relief, we continued through the woods looking back at times to see if we were being followed. Ten minutes later, we were exhausted and stopped to rest.

"I think we're okay. We should keep working our way through the woods for a while and then go back on the road. Are you both doing okay?" Gerhard asked breathing hard.

"Yes, Gerhard," I said. "Those awful men! What animals!"

"I'm glad they're dead. The pigs! Gerhard, look what I found in their pockets," Mutti said as she pulled out a large wad of American dollars, a bunch of watches and jewelry.

"I found a lot too," I said as I showed them two whole cartons of cigarettes, other valuables and money. It wasn't just packs of the valuable cigarettes but cartons of them. We all looked at the loot in disbelief.

"Wow. We'll have to hide these things somehow. For now, we'll put them in the cart," Gerhard said.

He quickly pulled a sack from the cart, threw the loot in it and stuffed the sack deep into the cart. He then took the pistol from his coat pocket, reloaded it, and stuffed it back under his coat in the small of his back. As Mutti and I watched him doing so, I saw how bruised and cut he was.

"Gerhard, you have cuts on your face that are bleeding," I said as I wetted a handkerchief and wiped at them quickly.

When I was finished, he said, "We have to get…"

He stopped mid-sentence at the sound of a military truck in the distance coming from the south.

As we listened, he continued, "We have to get some distance between us and those bodies before we rest for the night. Okay, are we ready?"

Just as Mutti and I nodded, we heard the truck in the distance behind us screech to a stop.

"They must have found the bodies!" I said.

"Yes, let's go!" Gerhard said, and we started off through the woods again. We all were sore from our encounter but hurried along as fast as we could manage.

Ten minutes later, we heard the truck on the road pass by going to the north. We were too far away from the road to see it. After going another kilometer through the woods on paths and side roads, we saw no indications that we were being pursued.

So we thought it would be safe to return to the main road along the river. As we walked back out onto the main road and headed north, I tried to look normal and not anxious like I felt. We didn't see any sign of the truck.

Soon we were passing through a small town, where we stopped briefly at a water fountain to get a drink and fill our wineskin. We used the chance to clean off Gerhard's cuts again. While there, we overheard some talk about bodies being found, but it did not seem to be creating a stir in the town.

Walking on, we looked about warily, trying to blend in and not be noticed. But Gerhard's appearance stood out. People coming toward us on the road looked at Gerhard and gave us a wide berth as they passed. The cuts and bruises on his face now gave him the look of a ruffian to be avoided.

A half hour later along a rural stretch of road, we paused to rest in the grass beside the road.

"I think we're safe. No one is looking for us, and we can relax," Gerhard said after looking around one more time.

Remembering the incident, Mutti began to weakly cry. I put my arm around her shoulder.

"Thank you again, Gerhard, for saving us from those animals," Mutti said. He turned and nodded.

"Gerhard, thank goodness you had your gun. Where did you get it?" I asked.

"I found it in one of the drawers at the field hospital before the Americans came. It's a standard issue Walther pistol for the German army. I hid it with some ammo in a patch of woods near the hospital. When I was released, I returned to the place and retrieved it. I keep it hidden in the small of my back and extra bullets sewn into the lining of my coat. Today was the first time I needed it."

"I'm tired, Gerhard, and sore from when they threw me down. I know there's still time for walking today, but I don't think I can go any farther today," Mutti said.

"I think we're all tired and sore. We've gone at least five kilometers from where it happened. It should be safe to stop for the night," he replied.

"After what happened, I'm afraid of sleeping at night in the woods," Mutti said.

"Maybe we should try to sleep in a barn tonight," Gerhard thought aloud. "There isn't much foot traffic along here. Maybe a farmer would let us."

He stood up and looked ahead along the road.

"There's a farm up ahead there along the river. We can try there," he said pointing.

Chapter 45
Mayhem

MUTTI AND I stood back from the front door of the farmhouse as Gerhard went forward to knock on it. Noticing the door was slightly ajar, he held the door as he knocked several times.

"Hello, is anyone home?" he called. He pushed the door open and looked inside.

The room was a shamble of broken and overturned furniture with papers, clothes and other debris littering the floor.

"Someone has been here and ransacked the house," he said.

"Oh dear. Be careful, Gerhard," Mutti warned. Gerhard pulled out his pistol, cocked it, and went inside.

With his pistol ready, he cautiously proceeded through the house. He peered into a bedroom and paused sadly at the doorway. A naked woman lay dead on the bed. He quickly searched through the remainder of the ransacked house. Not finding anyone else, he exited the house out the back door.

Outside, he saw me with a shocked look standing over the dead body of a farmer lying on the ground. Mutti came around the corner of the farmhouse and seeing the body, said, "Oh, dear God."

Gerhard cautiously walked forty feet across the yard to the barn. Opening the big door, he stopped suddenly, shaking his head. He sadly stepped inside and after a minute, came out again.

When he returned, he told us, "There are two dead young girls in the barn. I covered them up. The mother is dead in the house." Mutti and I gasped, covering our faces in horror.

"Whoever did this seems to be gone. I suppose we should bury them," Gerhard suggested, and we nodded in agreement.

"We might as well do it now before we sleep here tonight. Look in the barn and that shed to see if you can find some shovels. We can dig a shallow grave over there in the garden," he said, pointing.

"I'll bring the dead woman outside," he said as he put his pistol in his pocket and started for the back door of the house. Mutti and I went to look for shovels.

Gerhard wrapped the dead woman in a blanket, carried her from the house, and laid her on the ground by the garden. Meanwhile I was looking for a shovel amongst the equipment and gear by the shed.

Not finding any outside, I next went to the big double doors in front of the shed. I took off the plank holding the two doors together, opened one door a bit and looked inside.

"Gerhard, look!" I called. He turned around quickly and walked over to where I was at the shed. He was expecting to see something awful when he peered inside. Instead, his eyes lit up when he saw a large rowboat. Pushing the door open more, he stepped inside to inspect it.

Excitedly, he said, "It looks watertight and undamaged. There are the oars. It's perfect. We can float and row down the Weser River, instead of walking and sleeping along these dangerous roads."

Mutti came up and said, "I found shovels in the barn."

"Good. We'll get them buried and then go," he said as he hurried back to get busy.

"I'll get the cart from the front and bring it back," I said.

"Good," Gerhard said, "I know we are tired, but we should get them buried and leave tonight. You can rest and sleep in the boat."

We helped Gerhard carry the other dead bodies over. Wrapped in blankets, they lay near the garden as we hurriedly dug the shallow graves in the soft garden soil. Although we were sore from our incident, we dug as fast as we could.

As we dug, Gerhard told us, "The river flows north, the direction we want to travel. It will take us through Hameln and Minden, well clear of Hannover. We can get off near Nienburg south of Bremen and walk to my home from there. It should be faster too. Maybe two days. It will still be dangerous though. Ruffians will want to steal the boat and our valuables. They may succeed if we aren't careful."

By the time we dug a hole big enough and deep enough for the four people, lowered them in it, and covered them over again; we were exhausted and dirty. As we rested after finishing, we stood looking down at the grave thinking of the poor murdered family we had just buried.

"Farmers are religious folk," I said. "We should, at least, give these poor people a moment of silence." The others agreed, and we stood by the grave for a moment with our heads bowed.

"May God grant them peace," Gerhard said solemnly.

"Amen," said a little voice. We wheeled around and were startled to find a little boy standing beside us.

He looked to be about four years old. I knelt down in front of him.

"Oh you poor little boy. Is this your family?" The boy nodded sadly.

"Are there any others hiding here?" The boy shook his head again.

I hugged the little boy and told him, "Don't worry. We'll protect you now. You can come with us."

Rapidly considering in his mind the situation, Gerhard said, "Yes, yes, we'll take him with us now and look for his relatives later when things have settled down."

"Boy, does your Mutti have a place where she hides food?" he asked.

The boy looked up at Gerhard's bruised face and then back at me. I gave him an encouraging look. Looking back at Gerhard, he nodded.

"Can you show us where?" The boy nodded and started to walk toward the house. An exhausted Mutti sat down on a stump to rest as Gerhard and I followed the little boy.

When we entered the house, he took us to a cabinet in the kitchen with a false bottom. I opened it and pulled out butter, potatoes, cheese, and bread. I quickly bundled it in the table cloth on the table. We hurriedly scanned the ransacked room.

"I doubt if anything of value is left," Gerhard said.

I knelt in front of the little boy and said, "I'm Ruth and this is Gerhard. What's your name?"

"Walter."

"Walter, can you show me where your coat and clothes are?" He nodded and led me into a bedroom.

While Walter and I went to get his clothes, Gerhard looked around in the living room and found a small picture of the family on the floor. He picked it up and looked with sorrow at the unfortunate family.

With the sudden idea that it might help later when he searched for the little boy's relatives, he shoved it in his pocket. He then looked about for a letter, which would have their name and address on it. In the scattered papers on the floor, he found one and stuffed it in his pocket.

Walter and I returned with his coat and some clothes. Gerhard picked up the bundle of food, and we hurried out.

We had to leave the cart behind, but in the barn, we found some sacks to put our things in. Soon we had the boat in the river and everything loaded in it. After filling our wineskin and having a quick bite to eat from our stock of food, we were ready to launch.

As I held the bow of the boat on the grassy bank, Mutti and Walter climbed in and sat down in the stern. Gerhard sat in the middle at the oars. With one foot on the bank and one foot in the bow of the boat, I pushed the boat off, stepped into it, and sat down. The boat swung around, and Gerhard rowed the boat away from the bank.

The river was about 200 feet wide with smooth grassy banks and a good steady current. It flowed northward to the North Sea, so the current was taking us in the direction we wanted to go. Once out in the middle of the river, Gerhard kept rowing and the boat moved swiftly downstream.

It was late at night, but fortunately, the night sky provided enough light for him to navigate the bends in the river and to see any large obstructions we might encounter such as destroyed bridges or other war wreckage.

"We have to be careful," Gerhard told us, "because as Germans were retreating near the end of the war, they would destroy all the bridges behind them to slow the advance of the Allies. Let's hope some bridge spans are still standing and the river is not totally blocked. Otherwise, we have to go up on the bank and carry the boat around the blockage. Those are the times when we will be most vulnerable to attack by thugs."

Chapter 46
Repelling Boarders

THE ROWBOAT WAS moving swiftly along in the river as Gerhard rowed steadily. Mutti and I took shifts as lookouts for Gerhard, helping him to navigate the many bends and to watch for obstructions.

It wasn't long before we started encountering several destroyed bridges. A highway bridge with three spans still had its center span intact and we passed under it. The main span of a railroad bridge was knocked down blocking almost the entire river. Several boats were now mixed in with its tangle as well. Luckily, we had enough room to pass under the sloping span on the left.

Farther down we came upon another highway and railroad bridge. The right span of the highway bridge was still up, and we passed under it. The railroad bridge had only a single span across the river. The left side of the bridge was down in the water. From there, the whole span angled upward to the right support pillars where it was still attached. We had enough room and clearance on the right to pass through underneath.

Hour after hour, Gerhard rowed making good time. Sometime in the middle of the night, Gerhard paused looking about, seeming to get his bearings. I was awake on lookout duty. Downstream, I could see a few scattered lights and what looked to be buildings of a city.

"What is it, Gerhard?"

"We're coming to Hameln," he replied. "Frau Thielke, Walter, everyone wake up."

Mutti jerked up fearing something terrible but was relieved to find the boat still gliding smoothly through the water.

"Gerhard, what is it?" she asked.

He explained to everyone in a low voice, "We're coming to Hameln. There's a lock and dam in the river there. The dam isn't high, only about ten feet, but we don't want to go over it. As I recall, there is a grassy area between a lock on the left and the dam on the right. We can land the boat, carry it down, and launch it again below the dam. We must do it quickly and quietly. Someone may try to steal the boat while we are doing it."

"How far do we have to carry the boat?" I asked with concern.

"It's probably less than a hundred feet. Not far. We'll land by the bow, everyone will get out. I'll carry one side of the boat. You and Frau Thielke will carry the other side. We'll lift it and carry it down the hill as quietly and fast as we can and push it straight in when we get to the river on the bottom side.

If we get in trouble or we can't carry it, we'll push the boat along the ground. I think it's grassy there. Walter, your job is to walk with us alongside the boat and jump back in it when we put it in the water. Does everyone understand?"

"Yes, I think so," Mutti said.

"Yes, me too," I said.

To Walter, Gerhard asked, "Walter, do you understand too? You'll be a good soldier, right? Walk along beside us and jump back in the boat."

To this Walter nodded severely and put a rigid hand to his brow in salute.

"Good boy," Gerhard said with a smile. It was an old style army salute, not a stiff-armed Nazi one. From this, Gerhard guessed that Walter's father had been a soldier.

"Okay, I think we are all set." Gerhard said as he began silently rowing again.

As we got closer, I pointed at dark slanted shapes across the river ahead of us, "Gerhard, it looks like another bridge?"

After scrutinizing the dark shape ahead he said, "That's the railroad bridge south of town. It looks like one side of the center span is still hanging on a pillar. We can go through underneath there. You see what looks like an island on the left beyond the bridge. That's where the lock and dam are."

I tried but couldn't make out any island in the dark. Being a little nervous, I tried to be calm.

A few minutes later, the rowboat glided along silently and smoothly as Gerhard guided it to the landing point. On our right, we could hear the noise of the water spilling over the low dam.

"Everyone ready. Here we go," Gerhard said in a low voice.

The bow of the rowboat landed silently on the grassy bank. I jumped out and pulled the boat up. Although he was trying to be quiet, Gerhard made some noise due to his bad leg as he moved forward to get out of the boat.

Mutti and Walter moved forward, and we helped them out. Together, we pulled the boat farther up onto the grass. We then got on each side, lifted the boat and started walking with it across the grass, with Walter staying close by.

In the darkness, Mutti tripped on something, lost her grip and the boat dropped. While the bottom of the boat only thudded in the grass, the oars and other gear rattled loudly inside.

"Hey! Somebody's got a boat!" someone yelled from the bank.

"Come on! What are we waiting for! Let's get it!" a second voice shouted.

Gerhard could make out five dark figures running along the bank toward us.

"Hurry, let's push the boat," he shouted.

I had already helped Mutti to her feet, and all three of us scrambled to push the boat across the grass, but Gerhard's bad leg made it difficult for him to go fast.

As it skidded along the grass, Gerhard shouted, "Walter! Jump in the boat and climb to the front." Walter running alongside, leaped in as told and scrambled forward in it.

To get to us from the riverbank above the lock, the ruffians needed to get across the water-filled lock, used for raising and lowering boats traveling on the river. The upper gate of the lock was located near where we had landed. So the five dark figures tore along the bank until they reached the upper gate and then ran wildly across the top of it.

The first one fell crossing the gate and held up the others. In a fury, the others kicked the struggling man, knocking him into the water out of their way. Shouting threats for us to stop, the remaining four ruffians streamed across the gate and down the slope to where we had just launched the boat with all of us onboard. Gerhard strained at the oars to pull away from the bank.

All four of the villains splashed into the river and swam furiously toward the boat. As one got near, Gerhard stood with a boat oar and hit him squarely in the head with the blade edge of the oar. After the loud "thunk" and his scream, the stricken thug moaned and sank below the water.

Gerhard was next busy fending off a second one who had deflected several of his blows and continued to approach the boat.

A third desperate ruffian meanwhile was beside the boat near me. Wild-eyed, he reached out and grabbed the side of the boat. I came down hard on his hand with the ice pick.

It went clear through it. He howled but still didn't let loose of the boat, even as I pulled it out and came down a second time, going clear through his hand again.

Cursing, he tried to swing at me with his other hand but missed. When he put that forearm on the side of the boat, I came down a third time on it. Swearing and screaming, he started to reach for me with his first hand, but it didn't work very well anymore.

Losing his grip on the boat with that hand and seeing me start to do another strike on his other arm, he quickly withdrew it. Cursing and groaning, he struggled in the water away from the boat.

By this time, Gerhard had connected with a blow to the second swimmer, who was moaning as he weakly paddled back to the bank.

The last swimmer had also gotten close, but after seeing the welcome his friends had received, he had decided to turn back. But not before delivering a volley of curses at us.

With the oars back in the oar locks, Gerhard strained to row away. Then wheeling about, he remembered the bridge just below the dam.

Only a hundred feet away was the tangle of the bridge in the water. Its framework was blocking most of the river. The left span was down but angled up to the support pillar on the left by the lock. He spotted a narrow clear path underneath the left span, but we would have to pass alongside a high thick stone wall, which formed one side of the entrance to the lock. We might be attacked again as we passed close by the wall, but it was the only way by the tangled remains of the bridge. Although nearly exhausted, Gerhard rowed for the narrow passage.

Our previous assailants, having had enough, did not continue their pursuit of us. Fortunately, no new assailants appeared on the walls above us as we cautiously rowed along the wall underneath the broken bridge. Soon we were safely past the bridge wreckage and out in the middle of the river again.

Finally clear of danger, we breathed a collective sigh of relief. We had been so preoccupied with repelling boarders that we only narrowly avoided a worse disaster of getting tangled in the wreckage of the bridge. Breathing hard, Gerhard stopped to rest.

After catching his breath, he looked up at me smiling. "Good thinking, Ruth. I had forgotten about the ice pick. I guess it came in handy after all."

"Did you hear how he howled?" I said laughing nervously to relieve my tension. We all laughed, and Walter did a few howls imitating him. With the excitement over for the time being, we settled down as Gerhard again began to row.

Looking downstream only a few minutes later, I said, "Gerhard, there's something dark up ahead."

Straining his eyes to make out the dark shape, he finally recognized it. "It's a pontoon bridge. A temporary bridge built by the British or the Americans. With all the bridges blown up by the retreating Germans, they laid pontoon bridges to get across. They probably are still the only river crossings."

He backed water with his oars to slow our speed and give himself more time to think as he continued to look at the approaching structure.

"What do we do?" Mutti asked.

"It looks like there is enough room on the left to go under it, but I think I see guard houses at each end. They might think we're saboteurs and shoot us if we try to slip under without hailing them. We'd better hail them."

He guided the boat toward the left side of the pontoon bridge and shouted to the guards on the river bank there.

"Hello on the bridge. We're traveling downstream and would like to pass."

Immediately, flashlights lit up, searched the river, and found our rowboat.

"Pull over here to the bank," shouted a British soldier.

Gerhard guided the boat to the left bank above the pontoon bridge. A British soldier with a flashlight and another with a rifle came to the boat and inspected it. The soldiers seemed satisfied that we didn't have bad intentions.

"Where are you headed?"

"To Nienburg, then walking."

"That's a nice little boat. Take care not to let some blokes steal it away from you."

"Thanks, We'll do that."

"Going home?"

"Yes."

"On your way then. Here's a chocolate for the boy," he said, tossing a chocolate bar to Walter who caught it.

"Thank you," Walter said smiling. The soldier pushed the boat off. As we all ducked low, Gerhard guided it under the bridge, and then we were off again into the night.

Chapter 47
Destruction and Ruffians

THE REMAINING TWO hours of the night were uneventful. I took over on the oars for a while to give Gerhard some rest and sleep. When morning came, he was still asleep. A week of pulling the cart had helped my upper body strength. I was able to handle the oars to some degree, keeping the boat in the center of the river, headed downstream and maybe adding a little speed to that of the current.

The morning light stirred Gerhard from his sleep. He had a quick bite to eat before returning to the oars. He didn't say anything, but I think he was sore and in pain from our desperate run across the grass last night as well as our other recent adventures.

With Gerhard at the oars, we were soon making good speed again. We were in a rural area, gliding past field after field. When passing small towns, the people on the banks often stopped and pointed at us as we swept by.

We continued to encounter damaged bridges. Now they were single span metal structures blown up so that the broken middle was submerged in the river with both ends usually still hanging from the foundations on each side.

Usually, one of the hanging ends had enough room underneath for us to pass safely, except for the bridge at Ringeln. In late morning, we arrived at it finding it broken in the middle with passage on both ends blocked as well. Under one end was a muddy bank where Gerhard landed the boat. Then he, Mutti and I got out and dragged the boat through the mud under the bridge. We were able to launch the boat again quickly without incident.

The large steel autobahn bridge at Bad Oeynhausen had been one long span across the river. Now blown up, the wreckage of a long section laid in the river on one end, but the other shattered end of the span was shorter and still extended from its foundation in the air above the river. The river underneath was not blocked and provided us enough room to get through.

In the late afternoon, we approached the city of Minden. As a major industrial area, Minden and surrounding cities had been heavily bombed during the war. We saw a great number of heavily damaged factories and bombed out sections of the city.

We were able to pass underneath the ends of a highway bridge and two railroad bridges without trouble at Minden. On the northern side of the city, we came to the canal bridge, which was really a gigantic aqueduct carrying the midland canal over the river.

Or it had been until retreating German soldiers had blown it up. The two main concrete spans of the aqueduct crossing above the river were now lying flat in the river creating a five foot high dam of broken concrete and steel.

It was a crisis for us. The river was completely blocked here by the fallen aqueduct. The river now flowed rapidly across its concrete and steel debris down five feet to the river below the debris dam. On the right side were houses and businesses along a road that was blocked by the aqueduct debris, making it impassable. On the left bank was a series of flood arches, large wide openings under the canal to allow extra water by in times of river flooding.

If we risked going over the debris dam, a piece of rebar or other sharp debris might snag our boat tearing up its bottom or upending the whole boat. If we landed on the left bank and carried the boat through a flood arch to the river below the debris dam, we might encounter ruffians camped under the arches. Those were our only two choices, neither of which was good.

As we approached slowly along the left side of the river, Gerhard stood up in the boat straining to exam the downed massive concrete bridge sections blocking the river.

"Damn! It isn't safe. We can't go over it. We have to carry the boat through the first flood arch there on the left," he finally exclaimed. We all looked anxiously over at the flood arch.

"But what if there are men there?" Mutti asked anxiously.

"I don't like it either, but we have no choice," Gerhard said as he pulled the pistol from behind his back, checked it, and put it in his coat pocket.

"I don't see anyone in there, and this side of the river is pretty remote. Maybe there won't be anyone," I said trying to be optimistic.

"I hope so. We'll carry the boat like we did back at Hameln. Walter walking beside. I may have to use the pistol to keep someone away. Don't panic if I do, just keep carrying. Try to stay calm. Okay, everyone understand?"

Mutti and I nodded, and Walter saluted again.

Gerhard guided the boat over to the left bank by the flood arch. When it landed, I got out and held the boat as the others got out. Gerhard walked up to scout out the arch and returned quickly.

"So far, so good. Let's go," he said.

We pulled the boat out of the water, got on each side and began carrying it. All eyes watched the arches for any sign of villains.

When we were under the cool dark archway, we saw what looked to be two families living against the far wall. As we continued through, two thin haggard women came forward.

"Please, do you have any food? Our children are starving. Please?"

Their pleas were so pathetic that I said to Gerhard, "Gerhard, we can spare some, can't we."

"I guess a little," he said with a frown. Then to the women, he said, "We have to keep moving, but come with us down to the water and we'll give you some."

"Oh, thank you. God bless you," they said as they started to follow us.

When we got down to the water, Gerhard reached in our food supply and gave them each a quarter loaf of bread and a piece of cheese. The women thanked us and hurried back to the archway.

We soon were loaded back in the boat and pushed off. Gerhard looked very relieved to be away.

"I'm surprised they didn't ask to come with us," I said to him as he was putting his pistol again behind his back.

"The poor creatures are so starved, they probably couldn't think of anything beyond food."

"What was that thing we just passed?" I asked.

Looking back at the water rushing over the debris of the downed canal bridge, he said sadly, "It was an aqueduct carrying the Midland Canal over the river. A canal with ships and barges crossing over the river 40 feet above it. It was an amazing engineering accomplishment in its day, but now it's destroyed like everything else."

Gerhard then described to us the remainder of our boat trip. He considered the worst part to be over. For the rest of the evening and through the night, the river would carry us through rural areas and past small towns. He thought we would reach the next city with bridges, Nienburg, in the early morning, then several more hours through rural areas until we landed.

But the worst was not over. Only a mile downriver, we came upon another pontoon bridge with guard posts at each end. Being one of the few bridges across the river, we could see a great deal of walking traffic and some vehicles moving in both directions in the early evening sunlight.

As we approached, a guard on the bank saw us and motioned for us to pull up to them. They again inspected our boat, asked a few questions and authorized us to pass.

Unfortunately, there wasn't enough room to pass under this pontoon bridge. One of the soldiers helped us carry the rowboat across the road so we could relaunch it below the bridge.

We did not like the attention we were getting especially from some unsavory looking onlookers. With Hannover only sixty kilometers to the east, some of these wanderers might be the same villains we had heard about there. We wanted to be away from this crowd as soon as possible.

We made our way with the boat across the road through the throng of people. Everyone was watching us and a number of rough looking types were eyeing the boat and its contents.

"Can we give you some help with that?" One of them said moving toward us.

"No thanks, we have it," Gerhard told them firmly.

The ruffian stopped but watched with an evil look. We set the boat down below the bridge just off the road and pushed the stern out into the water. We thanked the soldier for his help and he started back to his guard post. As we were trying to load back in and relaunch, a woman rushed up to us.

"Please. Can you take me and my husband with you?" Others also approached pleading to be taken along.

"I'm sorry, but we have no more room," Gerhard told them.

"Oh please, we will pay you," the woman said.

"We can pay too," another said.

"No, I'm sorry. We have no more room!"

But they continued to press us for a ride and Gerhard finally had to push and swing at them with an oar to get them to back off. Hearing the melee, the British soldier came back again to break it up.

Several nearby ruffians had started to make a move toward us, but the British soldier and his machine gun had arrived and was hollering for the crowd to move back. One of the nasty looking men motioned to some others, and they began walking rapidly downstream.

The British soldier pushed our boat off, and Gerhard quickly returned to the oars, glad to finally get away from the crowded riverbank.

The boat swung around and Gerhard strained at the oars. He noticed the ruffians hurrying downstream along the road and knew they were up to something. He rowed hard to try to outpace them.

A mile downstream, I saw the half sunken tugboat and barges that formed a tangle of wreckage extending nearly across the river. I pointed it out to Gerhard, and then he knew what they had in mind. They were hoping to get to the wreckage before us and capture us as we tried to pass. He strained at the oars mightily, but the determined thugs ran madly along the bank toward the half sunken wreckage and were getting ahead of us.

Mutti and I anxiously watched them only a short distance off. We yelled at them to go away and leave us alone. They laughed and jeered at us in response.

Worse yet, another group of wild looking men on the other side of the river had seen what was happening and were joining in the chase.

As we approached the wreckage of the tug and barges, the first ruffians were already climbing on and scrambling across it. Only a forty foot gap separated the wreckage on one side from the riverbank on the other.

A jeering pack of wild men now threatened us on both sides of the gap. They armed themselves with metal bars, pipes, bricks and rocks, with which they hoped to stop and capture us. One man was knee deep in the water, readying himself to lunge at us.

We saw them starting to unwrap a mooring line from a fixture on a barge. They probably would try to get it across the gap to catch us. It wasn't looking good for us as Gerhard aimed for the narrow gap.

"Everyone get down. We don't have much choice but to go through. I'll try to scatter them a little before we get there," he said with a determined look. He pulled the pistol from behind his back and cocked it.

About a half dozen of the villains were on each side jumping around threateningly, motioning for us to land or else. The ones on the barge wreckage had hauled the heavy mooring line over to their side of the gap and had already tried one time unsuccessfully to throw it across to the man knee deep in the water on the opposite side.

Gerhard got the boat aimed for the middle of the gap with good speed. As we hunkered down in the boat, only twenty feet would be separating us from the terrible men on both sides.

Just before we reached their throwing range, Gerhard stopped rowing and turned around with his pistol. He fired three times in rapid succession on each side of the gap. Two thugs slumped to the ground, two others were hit but limped away, and the rest ran off or ducked for cover. Gerhard had made a point of shooting the man in the water, who clutched his side, fell, and struggled painfully back toward the bank.

As we passed through the gap, one man emerged from the wreckage of the barge and was about to hurl an iron bar at us, when Gerhard dropped him with one shot.

We were only about fifteen feet from the bank where two thugs came running toward us armed with bricks. As the first one readied to throw, Gerhard shot him, and he fell headlong into the water.

Gerhard aimed the pistol at the second one who stopped, dropped his bricks, put his hands up, and backed away. Gerhard quickly returned to the oars and frantically rowed to get away from the bank. Soon we were through the gap, away from the riverbank, and out of their range.

"It's okay. We made it," he said breathing hard. Mutti, Walter and I rose up, looking back at the wreckage. The enraged would-be thieves were racing about cursing at us and already rifling the pockets of their dead. A couple of them were sitting and grimacing with pain, as they inspected their bloody wounds. None had decided to continue the chase.

We watched them, thankful that we had narrowly escaped their clutches without mishap. I looked down at the icepick in my hand, glad that it hadn't been needed. I had peeked up during the battle several times. It had been a great effort for me not to scream during the shooting and excitement.

I looked at Gerhard who was slumped down at the oars exhausted. Breathing hard, he bent over the railing and reached in the river to splash water on his head and down his back to cool off. Giving him a few minutes to recover, I used the oars to get us back in the middle of the river, meanwhile keeping a lookout in case some new danger arose.

Gerhard, finally recovering, looked up and said, "It's a good thing that last one didn't know I was out of bullets. He could easily have brained me with his bricks."

"Gerhard, you were wonderful! Thank Goodness for your pistol. Again," Mutti said.

Walter must have also peeked, because he was now wheeling around with his imaginary pistol going, "Pow, pow. Pow, pow."

Mutti gestured for him to stop and gave him a hug. They were both grinning happily.

"They didn't leave us much choice for getting through. I didn't see any other way," Gerhard said.

"Do you think the British soldiers at the bridge heard it and will come arrest us?" I asked.

"I'm guessing they are too busy there at the bridge to investigate. If they did hear it, they may report it to some other British unit to investigate. Should they come looking for us, I'll slip the pistol over the side into the river. I would hate to do that. It has come in pretty handy."

"Thank goodness for it," Mutti said.

"We're lucky none of them had guns. We might not have fared so well then," Gerhard added.

After several minutes, Gerhard regained his breath and strength. Soon he had his pistol reloaded, put away, and was again steadily rowing us down the middle of the river. We had two close calls already and weren't sure what else awaited us.

Two hours later, the sun went down, and a partial moon rose. We navigated the river again by the light of the night sky. The rest of the river journey should be relatively uneventful, with no more dams and locks to cross and, we hoped, no more pontoon bridges. We would only have to watch for obstacles in the river, the remnants of the war.

I took over the rowing for several hours to give Gerhard a rest. Mutti helped me navigate the many bends of the river and keep to the middle.

Along the way, we passed a tug boat sunk in the middle of the river with only its smoke stack and mast jutting at an angle out of the water. The barge, behind it, was still attached and slowly swaying back and forth in the current of the river.

We came alongside the barge to see if anything of value might be in it. It suppose it was too much to ask that it be filled with pallets of military food rations. I cautiously stood up and peered over its side. In the dark, I could make out that it was filled with coal, which was of no value to us on our trip, so we cast off and continued on.

At Nienburg, the highway bridge was collapsed into the river with the roadway of the bridge underwater and the upper steel structure of the bridge still above water across the entire width of the river. Fortunately, its steel structure was not totally clogged with other debris, and the stanchions of it were wide enough for our boat to pass through. Once Gerhard could make out the steel structure ahead of us, he guided the boat carefully between two clear stanchions and through the girders of the collapsed bridge.

The nearby railroad bridge was also destroyed, but we were able to pass underneath one end of it as we had already done with many collapsed bridges. Having passed the last of the known obstacles, with only about four more hours before our planned landing south of Hoya, we continued north in high spirits as the sun rose.

At mid-morning, Gerhard was turning around and scanning the countryside happily as we came around every bend. Breaking out into a smile, he pointed to the spot on the west bank of the river and said, "This is it. We're near the town of Bücken. We've made it. We'll land there and walk the rest of the way."

On hearing this, I started to laugh and cry with happiness, and Mutti did too. I reached forward and gave Gerhard a hug from behind as he rowed. Amused by it, he was laughing and smiling too. Mutti and Walter were hugging happily in the stern, as Walter shouted, "Yay!"

The rowboat glided to the bank along a tree lined stretch of the river in open country. The bow of the boat hit the grassy bank, and I jumped out. I pulled the boat up a little onto the bank, and the others got out.

Gerhard climbed out, walked up the bank a bit and immediately stretched out on his back in the grass with an arm over his face to shield it from the sun. I was crying again with happiness as Mutti stiffly climbed out of the boat. We stood together on the bank laughing, hugging and crying in celebration.

Walter scampered out of the boat, and after hugs from us and a little celebration dance, he laid down in the grass imitating Gerhard. We had been through so much. At last, we had successfully reached the end of our river journey.

Chapter 48
Waiting It Out

WE PULLED THE boat from the river bank into the nearby trees and slept there for a couple hours. Gerhard awoke about noon and looked around getting his bearings. He saw a farm house and out-buildings less than a kilometer away and thought that he might talk to the farmer about making arrangements for the rowboat.

With this in mind, he headed off for the farm house. Returning in about a half hour, he said the farmer was happy to keep the boat for them. His boat had been stolen during the night a month before, and he was currently without one.

Later Gerhard would relate to us that he told the farmer how we had acquired the boat. The farmer was greatly affected by the story of the murdered farm family, a family much like his own. He offered to take in Walter until his relatives could be found. Gerhard thanked him for the offer but declined it. Gerhard felt responsible for Walter and wanted to get him back to his relatives himself.

The farmer had given him a small bag of corn. It was food for animals, but he thought that people might be happy to have some in these times. If you boil it in salted water or add some to soup, it wasn't too bad. The farmer would be out in an hour with his boy to load the boat on a farm wagon and bring it back to his shed.

Mutti and I had been gathering all the things together and getting ready for the walk. Gerhard had filled our wineskin when visiting the farmer, so we had water for our walk. We sat down for a few minutes to have a bite and then were ready to leave.

We couldn't leave without saying goodbye to our rowboat. The little boat had served us well and had been a very lucky find. I felt its railing one last time, thankful to it for getting us here. Walter probably remembered it from back on the farm and maybe fishing in it with his father. He told it goodbye and gave its bow an affectionate hug.

With that, we picked up our sacks and started walking. We would be passing through Bücken and traveling westward to Gerhard's home in a little town south of Bremen. He guessed it would take six hours and expected to get there late that evening. We would rest for a few minutes every hour as we had done before.

We encountered little vehicle and foot traffic as we walked steadily along the narrow rural roads passing through the open fields and small towns. Only when we crossed the north-south highway between Bremen and Nienburg did we see a multitude of travelers.

Knowing we were nearing our destination encouraged our progress. Gerhard was smiling and in high spirits as he got closer and closer to home.

Later that evening, Gerhard pointed ahead to a small town just coming into view and happily announced that we were almost there.

Gerhard's little home town appeared unaffected by the war. With no nearby industrial plants or factories, it had not been a target of Allied bombing. Not being a vital crossroad, it had not been destroyed in the battle for Bremen to the north. It survived the war intact.

Gerhard approached the quaint house where he grew up and paused for a moment to take it in. Many times during the war, he had thought of this place and a number of times thought he would never see it again. It was undamaged by the war and changed very little by time. He pushed open the gate and walked into the front yard. Mutti, Walter, and I followed him up to the front door.

He had not heard from his parents in about a year and he hoped they were still in good health. Toward the end of the war, older men and young boys had been thrown into the front lines with little training. He worried that his father might have been one of them and needlessly killed in the last days of the war.

Gerhard knocked on the door of his parent's house. His mother answered and started to cry as she hugged him. To Gerhard's relief, his father soon appeared and hugged him too. We were very happy for Gerhard and stood outside watching.

After many hugs and kisses, his mother finally saw us behind him. After an initial look of surprise, she beckoned us in.

Gerhard's parents were ecstatic to have their son home again and were very welcoming to any friends of his. They quickly made room in their house for all of us to sleep that night.

Gerhard talked with them for hours and then left for a short time to visit a friend. We washed up a bit as his mother fixed us some soup. After eating, she lent us some clean night clothes. By then it was late at night. Tired from our walk, we went to bed and fell fast asleep.

In the late morning, I awoke and felt refreshed for the first time in a long time. After breakfast, Gerhard's mother was washing dishes and I was drying. Mutti and Gerhard sat at the kitchen table watching.

"Where's Walter?" Gerhard asked.

"He's out on a walk with your father. They seem to get along well," his mother replied.

"He's so young and has already been through so much," I said.

"He's been a good little trooper though," Gerhard said.

Putting a dish into the drying rack, his mother turned with a twinkle in her eye.

"You know, Gerhard. You gave me quite a scare last night when I saw everyone with you. I thought, oh my God, he's married with a mother-in-law and little boy already."

We all laughed at this and Gerhard sheepishly said, "Yes, I suppose it might have looked that way."

"I also thought, poor Grete, she's been waiting for Gerhard to come home and now he's married."

"No, she knows me better than that. I paid her a visit last night to let her know I was home.," he replied sheepishly again.

"And were you happy to see her?" His mother inquired.

"Yes, of course," he said with a smile, "she hasn't changed much. Still a pretty girl, maybe a little thinner. And me, I've suffered considerable wear and tear since last seeing her. I thought she might not even recognize me, but she did. She was happy to see me, bum leg and all."

At hearing this, his mother fairly beamed at the thought of them finally getting married and giving her some grandchildren.

We met Gerhard's girl Grete later that day. She was an outgoing pretty girl my age. When she saw me, she looked surprised.

"Gerhard, you didn't tell me she was so pretty!" she scolded him, slugging him in the chest.

At this, we all had a good laugh, even if I was a little embarrassed. Grete was very nice though, and that same night they announced their engagement. From somewhere,

Gerhard's father brought out a little bottle of schnapps, and we toasted them in celebration.

Even though it was crowded in the house after our unexpected arrival, Gerhard's parents made us feel very welcome. Mutti and I tried to impose as little as possible by sharing a bed, while Walter slept on a small makeshift bed in our room too. We also tried to ease the added burden on them of having us in their house, by contributing our part toward work and food.

We now were in the British zone. The Americans before in Leimbach had done little to help us German citizens. The British, at least, recognized our need for some food relief until we Germans could get back on our feet.

Unfortunately, the British suffered food shortages in their own country and did not have a great deal of extra food supplies to spare. Still, they would distribute food periodically, and after long waits in line, we were able to receive some food basics such as flour, powdered milk, powdered eggs, rice, and beans.

The cigarettes, money, and valuables we took from the bodies of our attackers on our trip proved to be valuable in supplementing our food supplies. Mutti and I visited the back streets of the nearby larger town where added food could be bought on the black market.

After much haggling with a shadowy peddler, Mutti and he would agree on a price. Turning around to conceal the contents of her pouch from the vendor, Mutti would get the agreed-to number of cigarettes out and hand them to the peddler. After looking the cigarettes over carefully, he would hand her the agreed-to quantity of bread and butter.

* * *

In the next month, the British finally started getting control of the raping, killing, drunkenness, and looting in the cities. They had been working on the mammoth task of restoring order, government, infrastructure, transportation, housing, and a myriad of other needs in the devastation that they found.

The Allied occupiers had initially anticipated Nazi guerillas, so-called werewolves, fighting on after the war. They envisioned Nazi fanatics forming secret armed resistance cells and doing isolated hit and run attacks on the British occupation forces.

But the Germans were a defeated people. The Nazis brought such pain, fear, suffering, death, destruction, and shame to Germany. It's no wonder the demoralized German populace felt their defeat and had no desire to fight on.

When a Nazi guerilla threat didn't materialize, the roving lawless foreign workers posed the next biggest challenge in re-establishing civil order. Drastic measures were needed, and the British started rounding them up.

British soldiers would seize the dangerous looking wandering laborers at checkpoints or round them up during their normal policing work. They held the collected-up laborers ironically in the same Nazi work camps where they had previously been held and abused as forced laborers.

But their treatment this time was much different. The British deloused, fed, clothed, housed, and used them for local labor projects until they could be processed for return to their native countries.

The British had implemented curfews early on in their occupation and even used the existing air raid sirens, the so-called Meyer's trumpets, to announce the start and end of curfew.

Even so, it took time and resources to reinstitute a civil justice system and overcome all the challenges of policing the chaos and getting control of the violence, drunkenness, and looting in all areas.

* * *

I wanted to get back to Hamburg since I had told Ulrich I would wait for him there. If Gerhard had been released so quickly, then Ulrich might already be released too. But I didn't want to travel there on dangerous roads like we experienced before. So we listened for news of the conditions of the roads and cities.

When we traveled to the black market of the nearby larger town, we would cross a main north-south highway and stop there to watch the passing travelers to get an idea of conditions. Gerhard even offered to walk to Bremen, over thirty kilometers away, to check conditions there, but we told him that was too far.

As the weeks passed, we began to hear reports that the British were making progress restoring order in the cities and on the roads. Despite the destruction and all the shortages of essentials, civil order was getting restored.

After about a month stay with Gerhard's family, we decided it would be safe enough to walk to Hamburg. It was August 1945, three months after the war ended.

Mutti and I would be sad to leave Gerhard's family who had been so good to us. Walter would stay with them until he could be reunited later with his relations. Gerhard guessed that Walter was the only surviving member of his family and therefore owned their family farm. So he thought it was important to get him back to his relatives.

Gerhard discovered that the letter he had picked up at Walter's house was from a relative with their address on it.

It had been a lucky find and should make it easy to connect with Walter's relatives once mail service was restored.

We began preparing for our trip by acquiring another small two-wheeled cart similar to the previous one. Hamburg was about 140 kilometers away and would take us a week to walk at twenty kilometers a day.

It would be more direct to cross the Weser River at the bridge at Achim southeast of Bremen, but we didn't know if we could get across there now. The only sure bridge we knew of was a temporary bridge installed above the blown up Kaiser bridge in Bremen.

We had planned to begin our journey alone, but Gerhard insisted on coming with us at least to Bremen just to make sure the roads were safe. Walter also wanted to go too despite our attempts to talk him out of it. Additionally, Gerhard's father thought it would be a good opportunity for him to check on his sister who lived south of Bremen in Leeste twenty five kilometers away.

It was decided that Gerhard, his father and Walter would accompany us to Leeste where we would spend the night so Gerhard's father could visit his sister. Then the next morning, Gerhard and Walter would accompany us into Bremen, part with us there, and return again to Leeste. We told them it wasn't necessary, but they insisted.

After a grateful goodbye to Gerhard's mother, we set out the next morning. The roads indeed proved to be safer, and we had no problems along the way to Leeste, which we reached in the late afternoon. Gerhard's aunt and her young daughter were so happy to see us. They hadn't seen Gerhard's father in almost a year, and his aunt thanked God tearfully at seeing that Gerhard had survived the war.

We brought extra food with us for her, which she cried with happiness at seeing since she didn't have much. From the talk that night, it sounded like they might be taking his aunt and niece back with them to Gerhard's house. It was nice to see their happy reunion and spend a comfortable night there prior to our days on the road.

Early the next morning, Mutti and I said goodbye to Gerhard's father. After thanking him sincerely for sheltering us in his house for so long, we set out with Gerhard and Walter toward Bremen, just three hours away.

Bremen and its surrounding cities had suffered a great deal of destruction in the war. With a number of high value targets in the area such as submarine pens, shipbuilding, aircraft factories, rail yards, steel mills and oil refineries, Bremen had been a prime target for Allied heavy bombing. In some areas we passed, the destruction was complete.

Following the flow of people, we made our way to the bridge across the Weser River near the heavily damaged downtown area. The temporary bridge was a steel one with a single span crossing the river, unlike the pontoon bridges we had seen before. Despite the destruction, we saw no chaos or roving bands of criminals. Along the way, we passed a number of military checkpoints and soldiers stationed at intersections maintaining order.

After crossing the bridge and walking with us several blocks in the city, Gerhard pulled up.

"Ruth, Frau Thielke, I think this is as far as Walter and I need to go. I've been observing things along the way and it looks to be safe now for you to continue," he said in a sad voice.

When we first heard our names, Mutti and I turned to listen, but as he continued, we began to cry as we slowly approached and hugged him affectionately.

We couldn't speak for some time, but I finally said, "Oh, Gerhard. How can we ever thank you?"

"We've certainly been through a lot together," he said choking up too. "I'm so glad that you hurried up to join us way back on that road."

"Thank you so much for everything, Gerhard. We'll miss you so much," Mutti said.

Walter, by now, had joined in our hug, and I bent down to give him a hug too. "You be a good little soldier, Walter. We're going to miss you too."

"I will. Bye, Bye, Ruth."

There was Mutti's goodbye hug to Walter, a few more tearful goodbyes to Gerhard and our best wishes to him and Grete. Then with a wave, he and Walter turned and started back.

We watched them for a moment and waved back when they turned and waved another time. Sadly returning to the cart, I got between the handles extending in front, lifted them up, and started to pull it along. We waved one more time to them in the distance, and then they were gone.

It was very difficult saying goodbye to Gerhard. We owed him so much. He had been our guide and protector on our perilous trip. We shuddered to think what would have happened to us if we hadn't met him walking along with a noticeable limp near the other older couple.

Chapter 49
Return to Hamburg

MUTTI AND I sought safety in numbers on the trip to Hamburg. Therefore, we traveled main roads where we would be part of a normal stream of travelers. Many people were still on the move, but the roads were safer now that the ruffians had largely been rounded up and detained. Burned out vehicles and other signs of the war still could be seen along the way. We needed to watch out more for the growing amount of truck, jeep, and even car traffic.

As we passed with our cart through a damaged town, we noticed a British soldier and German policeman posted together at an intersection watching the flow of people pass. It was a sign of improving conditions and the reestablishment of German police. I looked around at the destruction in the town and saw women with wheel barrows working to clear rubble from the street. The cleanup of the cities, which would take decades, was starting.

Our trip to Hamburg took seven days. Along the way, we slept where we could as we had done before. While we didn't try to travel with any one group, we always seemed to be in company with others. The trip was much safer and incident free.

Our last night before arriving in Hamburg was spent in Harburg on the south side of the Elbe River across from Hamburg. On the way, we had heard that the bridges across the Elbe River here did not get destroyed like all the others we had seen on the Weser River.

The battle to defend the city from the Allies had started later, only weeks before the end of the war. Seeing the futility of continued fighting, the city leaders had defied their orders to defend the city at all cost and negotiated a surrender with the British. As a result, the bridges had not been detonated as Nazi defenders pulled back across them, which was what normally happened.

From Harburg, we crossed the old bridge across the south Elbe channel and progressed northward across Middle Hamburg, an industrial and port area between the north and south Elbe River channels. A great many large industrial buildings and warehouses here were just steel and brick skeletons.

Two hours later we passed under the old Gothic towers of the New Bridge across the north channel of the Elbe. A famous landmark of Hamburg, bridge was actually an old bridge of unusual design, which was surprisingly undamaged.

Walking northward from this bridge, we came upon a scene of total devastation, blocks and blocks with the burned out empty shells of buildings and rubble piles. In some places crosses stood in the rubble piles marking the places where bodies still were buried under the debris. It was one of the worst hit areas of the city.

Mutti and I were not prepared for the panorama of destruction we saw. As people passed by us in both directions, we paused to look at the shattered remains of what used to be a residential area where thousands of people lived. Mutti put a handkerchief to her face and cried. I put my arm around her shoulder. We wondered what we would find on Mozart Street, less than five kilometers to the north.

Aside from the destruction, we also noticed the city's police force already seemed to be operational. Here, they were maintaining order, controlling traffic, and patrolling the streets. We had gotten accustomed to seeing Allied soldiers maintaining order in other places. Looking to our left toward the old part of the city, the tall tower of the St. Nicholas Church was surprisingly still standing amid all the damage, especially considering that it must have been a prominent landmark and target for the bombers.

Finally arriving back in our old neighborhood of Mozart Street, we noticed and commented that the damage to the neighborhood looked similar to when we had left it. It was still a mixture of intact, damaged, and destroyed buildings. There must have been more bombing raids while we were gone, but they had not caused noticeable added damage in our neighborhood. It was a small consolation.

I pulled the cart to a stop as we arrived at the destroyed remains of our old apartment building. It looked much the same as when we last saw it. We noticed a path cleared to the entrance of the building and saw someone emerging.

"Well, Mutti, we're back at our old apartment building. It's been two years since we left."

"Seems more like twenty," she replied.

"There's not much left, but it looks like people are still living in it. Let's find out," I said. Mutti sighed, and we walked toward the entrance.

We stayed that night in one of the ten intact storage rooms in the basement of our old apartment house. Families occupied four of the other rooms. We were able to get our cart down the stairs and into a middle open area in the basement. We brought our things from the cart into our eight foot by eight foot room. With the other families nearby, it seemed safe enough. We lit a candle for light until we curled up in blankets and went to sleep.

In the morning, we went to look for a better place to stay. Not having a way to lock up our things, we loaded them back in our cart and took it with us. At a city office, we learned no apartments were available in this area. People were being housed in spare rooms and attics of large houses farther out.

People were also being housed in small round metal buildings, called Nissen Huts by the British, in another section of the city. Ordinarily, we might have been interested in the places offered, but I needed to stay in this area of Mozart Street.

We asked about food and rations, and were told that Vati's old restaurant in the ferry house was now a relief kitchen. Going there, we waited in line with our bowls and got a ladle of potato soup and a piece of bread.

As we were eating our meal outside, we sat weighing our options.

"Ilse!" Mutti suddenly said. "With all that has happened, I forgot about my old friend. I wonder if she came back after the bombing."

"I think her building was still there like when we left for Aunt Rosa's. We can see if she is still in her old apartment," I suggested.

"We must have walked past her building today. We would have noticed if it was destroyed. I can't believe I didn't think of her sooner," said Mutti.

We walked back to our neighborhood and saw that her building had survived. I stayed below on the sidewalk with the cart while Mutti went up to Ilse's apartment.

Mutti was just about to knock on the door when from inside the apartment, she heard the voices of boys roughly playing and a woman telling them to behave. Sadly, she let her hand drop. She listened for a moment and continued to hear the boys and their mother. Someone else besides Ilse was now living there.

She came back down and after weighing our options, we decided we would, for now, return to our old apartment building. Later on, with our cart and belongings back down in the basement, we settled into our small new home. We had no water, heat, electricity, bathroom, kitchen or security for our things. From now on, only one of us could leave at a time so that one of us was always there to watch our things.

Soon it would be September, and I imagined how cold it might get down here in the winter. We would need more blankets and heavy clothes. I looked at Mutti curled up in a blanket on the floor and sighed. It was a less than ideal situation.

The next morning, things suddenly got worse. Late in the morning as we sat in our room, a hubbub of activity erupted as five families arrived in the basement and began moving into the other storage rooms. One of the mothers came over and told us that they had just arrived in Hamburg after being uprooted from Silesia in the eastern part of Germany.

The Allied agreements at the end of the war had designated the eastern part of Germany to become part of Poland. The Poles had experienced incredible suffering during the war. They were furious at Germans and wanted none of them on their soil. These families were forcibly gathered up from lands, on which they had lived for generations and shipped here in railroad cars.

Mutti and I looked at the chaos and quickly agreed we could not live here anymore. I would watch our things here while she went to the city offices to get the nearest available attic room, apartment or hut. If I couldn't live nearby, I would visit Mozart Street as often as I could in hopes of running into Ulrich should he come looking for me.

With a determined look, Mutti put on her coat and made her way through chaos to the stairs.

Up on the street, she hurried along the sidewalk toward the city office, worried that the places offered just yesterday might now be unavailable due the influx of people from what had been eastern Germany. As she walked, someone emerged from around a corner and started walking toward her. It was Ilse!

Looking up, Ilse saw Mutti and rushed forward smiling to give her a hug.

"Margarete! Thank God, you survived. And how is Ruth?"

"Ilse, it's so wonderful to see you. Ruth is fine. We made it to my sister's house down south like we planned, but it's been a hard time for us, like many others," she replied, hugging her old friend.

"I went to live with my sister north of here like I said I would. After about a month, I came back though. You just got here? Where are you staying, Margarete?"

"Well, we don't know yet. I went to see you yesterday, but I heard other people inside your apartment and didn't think you lived there anymore."

"Yes, I have another family staying in my spare bedroom. Margarete, you should have knocked."

"I guess I was too disappointed at the thought of you not living there."

"Margarete, you don't know where you are staying?"

"Ruth and I have spent two nights in the basement of our old apartment building. I was just going to the city's housing office," Mutti said.

"Margarete, come live with me. I already have a family living in my second bedroom, but you stay in my bedroom with me."

"Oh, Ilse. You are an angel. Are you sure it wouldn't be too much for you?" Mutti said starting to tear up.

"No, you can stay with me. I still feel terrible about Gustav, you know," Ilse confessed, also getting teary eyed.

"Oh Ilse," Mutti said now crying, "I told you before it wasn't your fault. You shouldn't feel bad."

"Well, even so, you and Ruth should stay with me. No need to go to the housing office. Let's get your things."

"Thank you, Ilse," Mutti said as they turned and walked happily arm in arm back up the street.

We brought our cart and belongings over to her apartment a short time later. When done carrying our belongings up to her apartment, we found a place for the cart in the basement of her building. Without too much difficulty, we got ourselves situated in Ilse's apartment. Mutti would sleep with Frau Engel in her bed while I was to sleep on a feather blanket on the floor.

After her return to Hamburg two years before, Ilse had gone to the housing authorities to offer her extra bedroom to help house the many bombed out people, and a family was assigned. Ilse received a little compensation for it, but she had not done it for the money. The family had lost their apartment in the bombing and consisted of the mother Irene and her two young boys, Max who was 10 years old and Jens who was 8 years old.

Her husband had been reported missing on the Russian front just months before. She stayed in the area in hopes of hearing something about him from a local office. So far, she had heard nothing. She was friendly and thankful to

Ilse for having them there. Food that could be obtained was shared, although Ilse was not obligated to provide them food.

Somehow, the boys seemed like normal young boys despite the terrible times. The Hitler Youth had not affected them greatly, probably due to the influence of their mother who understandably was not happy with the war.

Once settled into Ilse's apartment, the immediate concern was food and finding work to buy more food. Not many ways existed yet to earn money to buy food. We did find work periodically with the city's efforts to clean up the destruction.

One example of such work were the bucket brigades of women formed to whittle away at the endless piles of debris. The front woman scooped or filled buckets by hand, while watching for unexploded bombs, of which there were many. Her filled bucket was passed back via a line of women to be dumped into large bins, and the empty bucket was passed forward again.

Another example was cleaning up bricks pulled from the rubble. We used a hammer or other tool to knock the mortar off and create huge stacks of clean bricks for use in reconstruction.

But still, it didn't do much good to earn money if little food was available to buy in shops or markets. We went to get rations and soup from the relief kitchens whenever they were available. Even so the quantities were not large and seemed to be getting smaller with the influx of thousands of new people from the east. We were always hungry.

We still had a modest stock of cigarettes and valuables when we moved in with Ilse. We tried to avoid using them to buy food on the black market because of the very high prices. But we would use some to buy extra bread when really needed. A black market thrived in the city, despite efforts by the authorities to control it. As the winter progressed, our supply of cigarettes and valuables dwindled.

Mail service to America still had not been restored, so we couldn't write to Kätchen to ask for help.

The only people with food and money in Germany during those days were the Allied soldiers. The unrealistic rules against fraternizing with German girls had been relaxed and largely ignored by the British soldiers by this time. German girls in Hamburg dated them and did whatever they had to do to get some food for their families to survive. Many got married to them.

We were desperate enough for food that winter for me to try to get some food by dating soldiers. I had good looks and should be able to get some dates. Only I wasn't going to become a soldier's mistress or wife. I was still waiting for Ulrich and didn't need to have him finally find me with a baby.

Irene also wanted to contribute to our food efforts, but told us with tears that she couldn't bring herself to dating victorious enemy soldiers after her husband, the father of her boys, had been lost in the war. Instead, she and the boys would try to earn money in whatever city cleanup work she could find.

So I ventured out alone to dances and clubs, where I met and dated a number of soldiers. I let them know I would go out with them so they could have fun and enjoy some female company, but that was it. And I was doing it because my family was in great need of food.

I sought out the bashful types who were thrilled to be with a pretty girl and pleased that I approached them and relieved them of the normal trauma of asking girls for dates. It worked out pretty well for them and for me.

I found they were sympathetic to our plight too. They were interested in what it had been like living in Nazi Germany during the war. I tried to enlighten them but didn't want to dwell on such an unhappy topic. Besides, a big part of our suffering during the war was the death, destruction, and fear caused by their bombs. I don't think they wanted to hear about that.

I tried to talk about happy things and about them, not about my problems. I was able to get some added food for our apartment such as bread, chocolate, tins of meat, and even some tea. These were shared with everyone in the apartment and helped relieve our hunger to some degree.

Another concern for us when it started getting cold was how to stay warm. Ilse had a stove in her apartment, but no coal was available to use in it. Hamburg only had enough coal for use in its power plants and trains. None was available for residents.

We heard how people would steal coal from the coal trains as they arrived in the city. It was a dangerous business climbing up on the slowly moving trains, frantically shoving the coal down to people along the tracks picking it up.

Children were used to climb up in the coal cars to throw coal out, because the guards would shoot adults doing it but not children. Fights would break out among the people scrambling for the coal along the tracks. Everyone then had to run to avoid being caught by the guards. It didn't sound like something we wanted to do. Besides, no power plants were near us.

Another possible fuel, firewood was also hard to find. The parks and woods had been stripped of it during the war. Firewood was a valuable commodity, which needed to be locked up or kept with you in the apartment, or else it would be stolen. Any loose boards on fences or any other structures quickly disappeared.

When it started getting cold, Irene, the boys and I took our hatchet and cart out to look for firewood in destroyed buildings in the heavily damaged areas. Even in those areas, the easy-to-find and easy-to-collect wood had already been taken.

We had to dig through the rubble and seek out the harder-to-find wood debris. Once found, we would chop the boards, planks, and broken furniture into small enough pieces to put in the cart. We also had to watch out for unexploded bombs as we searched, watching where we stepped and sometimes gingerly lifting building fragments and peering below to check for a bomb before lifting the fragments out of the way.

When our cart was filled, we covered it with a tarp to hide its valuable contents. Periodically, we would go on these wood scavenging trips. The firewood was used sparingly in the stove, only during the coldest times of the winter. At these times, we huddled together around it, soaking in its warmth for a time before going to bed and letting the fire die out.

Mostly, we relied on more clothes and blankets to stay warm that winter, which fortunately, was a somewhat mild one.

Chapter 50
Aid and Visitor Arrive

THAT WINTER OF 1945/1946 was a difficult, cold, and hungry one for us and many other Germans. We had been barely surviving on rationed food, black market bread, and the food from dating soldiers.

In April 1946, eleven months after the war ended, Mutti and I learned that mail service to America was finally restored. Mutti immediately sent a letter to Kätchen at her address at Aunt Minna's restaurant, telling her of our situation and asking for her to send us food and cigarettes, which we could use to trade for food.

The last we had heard from Rolf was that she expected to wait out the war there, so we hoped she was there and could help us soon. We were in great need of it. Mutti told her to send smaller packages instead of a big one that might draw more attention and get stolen.

We had run out of cigarettes and jewelry for buying more food. We were at the end of our resources and hope. Ilse was suffering greatly from the lack of food, and Irene had been practically starving herself to give more food to her boys. Then Kätchen's packages started arriving at the post office.

Mutti had been checking there every day. She didn't want to draw attention to them should one arrive, so she had been rehearsing what she would calmly say.

"Oh? A package for me? Oh, how nice. Thank you."

Even so, she could barely contain herself when the teller handed her the first one. She couldn't even get out the lines she had practiced. Instead, she tried to cough and look around awkwardly to keep from jumping up and down with joy. Several packages began arriving per week, and soon our situation improved.

In one of these packages, Kätchen sent us some tins of a meat called spam. It was the first meat we had in many months, and it tasted delicious to us. These tins of meat also proved to be very valuable in trading for other foods. To Kätchen's great surprise, we asked her to send us as much spam as she could.

In our letters back and forth, we told Kätchen a little of the terrible times we had endured here. We didn't want to describe our sufferings in too much detail and make her feel bad about being so safe there during the war. She was greatly saddened to hear about Vati, Aunt Rosa, and Fritzi, but was delighted and thankful to hear Mutti and I had survived.

She and Aunt Minna were successfully running the restaurant, which had prospered during the war. She told us some of the things that happened to her and that she had tried without success to contact Rolf after the war.

She wanted to start right away applying for both of us to immigrate there. But I wrote to her about Ulrich and how I needed to wait for him here, as I had promised.

By the summer of 1946, food was becoming a little more available in the city. The rubble and destruction were slowly being cleared away, and a little bit of normalcy seemed to be returning.

Mutti and I had been through a lot with Ilse, Irene, and her boys. Max and Jens were like my little brothers. We were a close knit group, and now that we had more food we wanted to stay and share it with them.

With the slow return to normalcy in the city, a few shops started opening up here and there. I found a job in a flower shop on Mozart Street. A flower shop may seem to be an unlikely kind of shop to open during the early phases of our recovery, but not when you consider the many new graves with grieving loved ones wanting flowers to put on them.

One day in late summer, I was arranging flowers on a work table facing the back of the store when the front door opened, and Mutti excitedly entered the shop.

"Ruth, wonderful news! We have a visitor!" she announced.

I gasped and excitedly turned around. I could see Mutti and someone in uniform standing near the door waiting expectantly, but a trellis and hanging plants blocked my view of his face. I dropped what I had in my hand, put my hands to my face, and could feel the tears coming as I rushed out. I was so happy. Ulrich had survived his terrible ordeal and now had found us! I had waited so long and could hardly wait to finally hug him at last.

When I cleared the obstruction and saw him, I stopped short in shock and disappointment. I was crushed to find it was Rolf.

Rolf was confused and surprised by my obvious shock and disappointment.

"Ruth, it's me Rolf. I didn't mean to upset you. I'm sorry," he said coming forward and putting his arms around me to comfort me. I just stood there with my head on his chest sniffling and struggling to hold back the tears.

"It's all my fault," Mutti said, feeling terrible. "Ruth has been waiting for someone too and thought it was him. I'm sorry, Ruth. We shouldn't have tried to surprise you. In my excitement at seeing Rolf, I wasn't thinking."

She came forward tearfully and tried to comfort me too.

After a moment collecting myself, I finally was able to dry my eyes and smile.

Drawing back from him, I said, "I'm sorry, Rolf. I really am happy to see you and happy for Kätchen to see you looking so well. Mutti is right. I was hoping to see a soldier named Ulrich. But you are the next best thing. You're finally back from prison in Canada?"

"Yes, I'm back, but I wouldn't call it prison. If I'm looking well, it's probably from all the farm work and good food there. I'm ashamed to say that they were very good to us. We did not suffer like people here."

"Ashamed? It wasn't your fault they put you to work on a farm so far from the war."

"I suppose not, but I still feel badly."

"Well you shouldn't," Mutti interjected.

"That's right, Rolf. The important thing is you are back now. Kätchen will be so happy." I stood back and looked him over.

"And look at you. The last time I saw you, you were a boy. Now you're a man."

"You're the one who has grown up. You were just a little girl then. Now you're a very pretty woman."

"Don't make me sound so ancient."

We heard a door close in the back of the shop, and I turned around to look.

Rolf noticed and said, "We have plenty to talk about, but we'd better let you get back to work before we get you in trouble."

I smiled, hugged him again, and he turned to go. Mutti sadly came up and held my hands. "I'm sorry, Ruth. In my excitement at seeing Rolf, I wasn't thinking."

"It's okay, Mutti. I'm all right," I said, managing to hold back the tears.

Still feeling terrible about what happened, Mutti rejoined Rolf, and they left.

That evening after I got off work, Mutti, Rolf and I sat at a table in a restaurant with coffee and rolls in front of us. Mutti and I listened as Rolf told of his experiences since last seeing us. Mutti and I knew very little of his story. It took some time for him to tell us all that had happened: the war, the plane crash and his recovery, the U-boat scare, life as a prisoner of war, Kätchen's visits and disappearance, friendship with guards, and conflicts with fellow prisoners.

After several hours, we left the restaurant and walked home. On the way, he continued his story of his time in Canada, which is presented in the next chapter as he told it.

Chapter 51
Prisoner in Canada

AFTER THE INCIDENT with Heinz and Heinrich at our prisoner of war camp in Canada, it was decided that our camp was to be downsized. The two large prisoner of war camps, Lethbridge and Medicine Hat, east of us in southern Alberta each had a number of satellite work camps where prisoners were made available to work for local farmers.

Later in the summer of 1943, my friend Dieter and I were among the prisoners being sent to these satellite work camps. A truck to transport us was parked in front of our camp where a dozen of us prisoners, each carrying a small bag of possessions, were getting ready to climb in the back.

For some reason, Dorfman was to stay at the camp. I suspected his help with paperwork in the camp office had become too valuable, and they didn't want to part with him. He was there at the truck with several other prisoners saying goodbye to us. He had given us the address of his parents in Germany so we might someday get together again.

We had already said our goodbyes to our other fellow prisoners, many of whom watched from inside the fenced enclosure as we loaded.

Dieter and I were the last two in line to get onboard. Sergeant Evans shook my hand warmly before I climbed in and then did the same for Dieter. Sergeant Brown, the guard who had monitored my visits with Kätchen, and had been saved by Dieter, was also there, as well as several other guards. They had all come to say goodbye to us. It sounds strange, but the guards had been good to us, and we were sorry to be leaving them. We waved to them, Dorfman, and the other prisoners as the truck rumbled off.

The truck delivered us prisoners to our new work camp just outside a small town east of Calgary. It was one of the satellite camps set up to provide labor to the local farmers. We stayed in a barracks-like building with no fences or guards.

One local policeman was assigned to be in charge of us. He was a no-nonsense kind of guy, who warned us when we arrived, that if anyone gave him the least bit of trouble, he would personally take the offender in handcuffs immediately to the main camp at Lethbridge.

The senior prisoner of our camp, Feldwebel Kraus, was responsible for the operations of the work camp: order and discipline, musters, food, camp work, and assignments to farms. He reported to the local policemen daily. He was fair and efficient in the operation of the camp, although not very congenial or easy to get to know.

He had come to the work camp from Lethbridge three months earlier and gave us such fatherly advice when we reported to him.

"Listen very carefully to what I am about to tell you. I'm telling you this for your own benefit. You maggots would be doing yourselves a great, great disservice if you screw up here and get yourself sent to Lethbridge. So don't screw up!"

Both Dieter and I had no intention or desire to "screw up," even before his thoughtful kind advice. Both the Canadian policeman and our German sergeant seemed to know exactly how to appeal to our better judgment, since none of us desired to see the large prison-like camps farther south about which we had already heard much.

The war naturally produced a great shortage of labor on Canadian farms. The farmers in the area would ask for prisoner help with whatever work was needed on their farms. Usually it was a one day assignment, in which we came back to camp each night after working all day on a farm.

We were in wheat country, but we performed many different kinds of farm labor including bucking hay, which was the strenuous job of getting hay bales from the hayfield to the hay barn.

On one such day in the hayfield under a hot summer sun, one of the farmer's young boys drove the tractor pulling a flatbed trailer past the hay bales lying in the cut hayfield. Dieter, sweating profusely, walked along beside the trailer. As he came to a hay bale lying in the field, he thumped his hay hooks into each end of the bale and heaved it up onto the trailer where I stood sweating profusely.

I likewise thumped my hay hooks into each end of the bale. I would lug and heft it into place in the growing stack of bales on the trailer. Then back I would go to get the next bale which Dieter had just heaved up onto the trailer.

It was tiring, back-breaking work since the hay bales weighed a hundred pounds or more each. When the trailer was stacked full, about five bales high, we headed for the hay barn. Our sore backs got a little rest on the way back to the barn.

Once there, we transferred the bales from the trailer to the big stack of bales in the barn. Then it was out to the fields again to fill the trailer with more bales. So it went for days on end during hay harvesting times.

During wheat harvest time, all attention in the area was on bringing in the wheat crop. It was a time of long dusty hours in the hot sun. Dieter and I rode on the back of a tractor-drawn wheat combine, filling sacks with grain. One poured the newly cut and separated grain from a spout into a sack held by the other.

When full, we quickly tied and sewed up the top of the sacks with twine and a big thick needle, and then eased the sacks over the side to the ground so they could be picked up later that day, by Dieter and I, of course.

Shirtless and tanned, Dieter was there with me filling sacks. The farmer's pretty teenage daughter, Nancy, also worked on the combine doing some other job. She would sometimes look over at Dieter and smile. And, of course, Dieter would grin back at her.

One wheat farmer, Nancy's father, asked for several of us so often that we soon worked only for him and stayed at his farm in a converted bunkroom in an outbuilding. He and his family treated us more like sons than workers.

After a long day in the fields, the sun would be setting as we all sat down to eat dinner together outside by the farmhouse. Dieter, two other older fellow prisoners, and I sat with the farmer, his wife, daughter, and two young sons. Big dishes of food were passed around on the table, and we all were digging in.

At the end of October when less help was needed, the wheat farmer asked to have Dieter and I stay on during the winter, while the other two prisoners returned to the camp. We continued to do farm work, work on equipment, cut firewood for the house, and other tasks to stay busy.

Dieter had always listened with interest when the boys, Kenneth and Steven, talked about Canada's national sport, ice hockey. Kenneth, the older of the two, was on their school's team and would practice after school several nights a week.

One evening after dinner, Dieter and I were sitting in the living room talking with Nancy while the boys were listening nearby to the radio broadcast of 'Hockey Night In Canada'. Dieter was listening too and couldn't help commenting on some missed scoring opportunity in the game. They turned to him in surprise.

"Dieter? Since when did you become interested in ice hockey? They don't play ice hockey in Germany!" Kenneth said laughing. Dieter laughed too.

"You may be surprised to learn, Kenneth, that we do play ice hockey in Germany. I'm from a city called Krefeld, where there is much interest in ice hockey."

"You're just pulling our leg, Dieter. They don't play ice hockey in Germany!"

I was greatly amused by this conversation. I had heard a number of times before from Dieter about his ice hockey playing days and was frankly surprised it never came up before.

"Kenneth, I know you won't believe this, but I have been playing ice hockey since I was a little boy. I used to play for our city's team, and we were pretty good," Dieter said with a big grin.

"You're just joshing us," they said. Then looking at me, "Rolf, he's just joshing us. Isn't he?"

"Well, I haven't seen him do it, but he's told me before that he used to play."

"No way. What position?" Steven asked.

"I played what you call here a wingman, but I could play defenseman too," he said watching for their reaction.

"Wow!" At this Steven jumped up and ran out of the room, shouting, "Dad! Mom! Can you believe it? Dieter played ice hockey!"

They pumped him with question after question, and finally we had to break it up, call it a night, and go back out to the bunkhouse.

The next afternoon, a car pulled up at the shop where Dieter and I were overhauling the transmission of one of the trucks. Both Dieter and I stopped and watched as a man got out and walked up.

"Which one of you is Dieter?" he asked.

Thinking we might be in trouble for some unknown reason, Dieter reluctantly said, "I'm Dieter. Is something the matter?"

"No. My name's Roy Tyson. I'm the coach of our school ice hockey team. Kenneth told me you used to play for Krefeld in Germany. Is that true?"

Relieved to find he wasn't in trouble, Dieter smiled and said, "Yes, yes, it's true."

"I think I've heard of them somewhere. I'm always looking for ways to win more games. See if Ray will let you off this afternoon so you can come down to our team practice."

"I'd like that," Dieter said.

And with that, Dieter became an assistant coach for Kenneth's school ice hockey team. A small school such as theirs had no access to the training and coaching, which Dieter had received in his many years of playing hockey in Germany.

He showed them drills that German players practice over and over to improve their skating, passing, and stick work. He showed them better techniques for defending and scoring, how to work together better, and much more. The players on the team all admired him and rapidly improved their skills.

Their team was soon winning all their games and Dieter was a town hero. He never went to games though, because he and the coach thought his presence would not be appropriate. Canada was at war with Germany and some in the crowd may have lost sons in the fighting.

Two years passed quickly in the wheat fields of Alberta, and then the war was over. It was hard to read about and follow from afar the gradual conquest and defeat of my own homeland. Although I still received censored letters from my mother, I worried about my family there and about Kätchen's. I wished the war had never started.

When I saw the reports and pictures of the mass killing of the Jews and others, I was as shocked as everyone else. I remembered back to the airbase briefing room before the war when I first realized the Nazis actually and truly believed their own propaganda. They really were planning to go to war soon to avenge our defeat in the last war, expand German territory and rule the world for a thousand years.

It wasn't just grandstanding to drum up support for the Nazi party. Unlike my realization then about the upcoming war, it was only now that I realized how much the Nazis meant the anti-Semitic part of their rhetoric too, and how far they would go.

As we rode wheat combines and drove tractors disking up the fields, the war had seemed unreal and far away. The wheat farmer, who we lived with, liked Dieter so well that he wanted to sponsor him for immigration, have him stay in Canada and not be sent back to Germany.

Dieter liked the farmer too, but he was even fonder of the farmer's daughter Nancy. He agreed to be sponsored and hoped to be allowed to stay there in Canada. He didn't have close family any more in Germany. I would sometimes see Nancy and him together after dinner leaning on a wooden corral fence watching the sunset.

This story of my captivity in Canada may sound more like Dieter's story rather than mine. I guess it really was. I was there simply marking time, waiting out the war as best as I could, not trying to make any new connections, and wanting the war to be over. Dieter, on the other hand, had found a new home in Canada.

While the war in Europe ended in early May of 1945, our "captivity" in Canada continued. It wasn't until the early summer of 1946 that I found myself on an eastbound train, sitting in a passenger car filled with other German prisoners. We were on our way to the east coast seaports of Canada. It was the first leg of our trip back to England and then to Germany. At least, we would not have to worry this time about German U-boats sinking our transport ship when crossing the Atlantic.

Looking out the window at the passing fields and towns, I thought of how I was getting farther and farther away from Kätchen. I still had not heard from her. I hoped she was still waiting out the war at her Aunt's restaurant. I would have to find out from her family when I got back to Germany. So I was impatient to get back and be released.

I looked around at my fellow prisoner seated beside me. It was poor Dieter, who was not his normal happy, grinning self. Unfortunately for him, German prisoners of war were not being allowed to become immigrants and stay as Dieter had wanted. So after five years in Canada, we were being sent back to Germany to be released.

Dieter planned to immigrate back to Canada as soon as a quota was available. Before leaving, Nancy had confessed to him that she was the reason her father had kept asking for him. She had a crush on him from the first. She had cleverly coaxed her father into continually requesting him and eventually getting him assigned to their farm full time.

Dieter was beside himself after hearing that! Not only was she the girl of his dreams, but she loved him too. Now he had to leave her to return to Germany! It was hard for him to bear. In private before leaving, she had given him a memorable goodbye kiss so he would remember her. As soon as he could, he planned to return to that pretty blonde girl on that wheat farm in Alberta.

After our arrival back in England, we performed a brief stint of forced labor repairing war damage in England. We got to see firsthand the destruction caused by our bombs, maybe even ones from our own bomber. I couldn't blame the Englanders for wanting to use us to help clean it up. After a month or two of this work, we were finally sent on to Germany.

When we arrived back in Germany, we were shocked by the destruction we saw. Dieter and I exited a train onto the station platform with our group of prisoners. We looked around in amazement at the destruction inside the train station. The fine old metal and glass roof had been destroyed and only segments remained.

Much of the station building and platforms were damaged. Only half of the platforms and tracks had been cleared, repaired, and made usable. The other half of the station was a tangle of metal and concrete, piled there until it could be cleared away.

Our group of prisoners was being escorted by two British guards to a military office here in the city where we would be processed and released. A handful of people looked at us vacantly as we passed through the station.

"I had no idea of the destruction and suffering here in Germany," Dieter said. "Look at these people! They look dazed and half-starved. I feel guilty we haven't suffered even a tiny fraction of what they have."

"I know what you mean, Dieter. Who would have known that being shot down and nearly killed over England was the luckiest thing that possibly could have happened to us."

Dieter was familiar with the city. He and I emerged with our group of prisoners from the battered train station and looked in amazement at the city blocks of damaged and destroyed buildings.

"Look at what's left of that building there," Dieter said, pointing to the burned out hulk of a building. "It used to be the city hall. It had a fine old clock tower with ornate wood and stone carvings on the front. It was 300 years old."

"That destroyed building there, it was the city's cathedral," he said, pointing to another heavily damaged building. "It was 500 years old, with a rich history and beautiful stained glass windows."

Several gaunt-looking expressionless people walked by without saying anything and Dieter looked them over.

"Look at these people. They are hollow walking shells of what we used to be."

We noticed a young boy sifting through a garbage can looking for food. Another bigger boy came up, pushed him away from the can and started sifting through the can himself. The young boy wandered in our direction.

Dieter rummaged through his coat pocket and found a half-eaten bun. He tossed it to the young boy, who greedily caught it and ran off with it quickly.

"Our glorious Führer. Our glorious leader!" Dieter said with disgust. "Look where he has led us. He deserves worse than just burning in hell."

Dieter and I paused for a moment to sadly take in the scene. One of our guards called to us, and we rejoined our group.

"Dieter, where are you going when they release us?"

"I have an aunt and uncle near Dusseldorf. I'll stay with them while I try to get back to Canada."

"You have my mother's address. Write to me there and let me know how you are doing. I'm going to visit her after I try to find out about Kätchen.

If I make it to America, and you have problems getting an immigration quota back to Canada, let me know. I don't know how it works, but maybe we could sponsor you for a while in America until you can get approval to stay in Canada."

Dieter grinned. "Thanks, Rolf. I'll keep it in mind. I'm determined to get back to Canada one way or another, even if I have to swim."

Chapter 52
Two Immigrants

WE HAD BEEN slowly walking home that evening as Rolf was telling us about Canada. We listened in amazement as Rolf came to the end of his story of his years as a prisoner of war. He had been so lucky, while we had not. We expected Kätchen to avoid the danger and suffering we experienced in Europe. But not Rolf who was fighting in Europe.

When we got up to the apartment afterward, we found Ilse had set up a makeshift bed on the sofa for Rolf. We were all tired and went right to bed.

Rolf had successfully found us to learn Kätchen's whereabouts, so he could reconnect with her. Not having seen his family in over ten years, he was naturally antsy to also see them again. In the morning, we lent him a little money so he could take a train early that afternoon to a larger town near his. Once there, he could easily walk the remaining eight kilometers to his house.

Before he left, Mutti and I took Rolf back to the restaurant for coffee and rolls. This time, it was our turn to tell about the war. For several hours, Mutti and I told him of our hardships during and after the war. We finally had to cut it short before noon so we could get back to the apartment and then put him on a train in the early afternoon.

Rolf asked many questions and was astonished to hear the awful things we described, especially of our escape from the horrendous fires that night of the heavy bombing and of our dangerous trek north back to Hamburg. Someday, he hoped he could meet Gerhard and Ulrich. Trying to give me a little encouragement, he told me that he had heard many German soldiers were still being held and used as forced labor by various countries. Maybe Ulrich was still being held too.

Rolf planned to stay with his family while arrangements for immigration to America were made. So it was wonderful to get a chance to see him in person again, even if just briefly. Before his arrival, we only slightly knew him from censored letters and his brief visits before Kätchen's voyage. After his brief stay, we were even happier about him marrying Kätchen.

Rolf's last red cross letter to his family was from Canada. He had not been able to communicate with them during his months of travel from Canada and forced labor in England, so his arrival at home was going to be a surprise. As I waved goodbye to him at the train station, I was thinking of how happy his family shortly would be.

* * *

As Rolf was getting off the train at the station near his house, the man picking up mail thought he looked like a newly returning soldier and asked where he was headed. When Rolf told him, the postman said he could give him a ride. During their ride, Rolf gave him a brief description of his history and the postman earnestly welcomed him home. He said with emotion that his own son did not made it back.

They soon arrived outside the house where Rolf had grown up. It still looked the same. Rolf thanked the driver and waved as he drove off.

With emotions high, he knocked on the front door and stepped inside saying, "Hello. Is anyone home?"

His little sister, a thin 14 year old pixie with reddish blonde hair, appeared in a doorway with a frightened look at seeing a stranger walk into the house.

As she stared at him, Rolf said, "Lotti, don't you know me? My gosh, look at you. How you've grown. Lotti, it's me, Rolf, your big brother. I'm home."

With a sudden look of recognition, Lotti started sobbing and tottering forward to hug him, saying, "Yes, I recognize you now from the pictures you sent."

"It's okay, Lotti. It's been a long time, a very long time," he said as they hugged.

Soon his mother appeared, burst into tears and rushed forward to hug him too. After a minute of greetings, hugs and kisses, his mother said to her daughter who was still crying.

"Lotti, go out to the shop. Tell your father and brother that Rolf is back."

Wiping her eyes, Lotti walked unsteadily out of the room. Out in the shop, her father and brother were staining some cabinets and looked up when they heard her enter. Seeing her tearful emotional face, her father put his brush down and rushed to her, thinking something terrible has happened.

"Lotti, what's the matter? What's happened?" he said with anguish.

After a struggle to stop crying, she said with great emotion, "Rolf is back."

Bursting with joy and emotion, he rushed out, ripping off his apron on the way. Rolf's younger brother Gregor was right behind him.

Rolf had a very happy reunion with his family, which had been fortunate enough to survive the war intact. His mother had missed him greatly and suffered terribly when she was notified in error by the government that he had been killed in the crash of his bomber. What relief she felt when she learned from his Red Cross notification later from the hospital in England that he was alive and a prisoner of war, not dead.

His father survived the war with only minor wounds. As a prisoner of war in Italy when the war ended, he was held there to be used as a laborer to repair war damage. He had worked for a time in a mine, but the Italians experienced so many difficulties getting their prisoner of war labor program off the ground that they gave it up and released all their German prisoners.

About six months after the war ended, his father made it back home. He was again back at work in his cabinetmaking shop and was getting more and more work now with the beginning of reconstruction.

Rolf and his parents were so grateful that Gregor was too young to be drawn into the war. In their rural area, he and Lotti had been less exposed to the intense Hitler youth recruitment and pressures of other places. They had been with their mother during the whole war.

Rolf was angry at having been cheated out of being their big brother while they were growing up. He had much catching up to do with his brother and sister.

* * *

When first agreeing to move in with Ilse, Mutti had hoped to only temporarily impose upon her friend. After living with her nearly a year, Mutti and I thought about getting our own small apartment. When we mentioned it to Ilse, she said she would miss us too much and didn't want us to leave. So we put the thought out of our minds and happily stayed with Ilse, Irene, and the boys.

They had become like family to us. School for the boys had started again, and Irene found a job in their school. Periodically, Irene would hear of a release of German prisoners. She would check lists searching for her missing husband's name. When she didn't find it, she would still go to where the newly released men were brought to ask them if they knew her husband or anything about him. They never did. The releases in our area were German prisoners from the east, so it would have done me no good to go along to ask about Ulrich who had been a prisoner in the west.

Kätchen was thrilled to learn Rolf had found us and started immediately to investigate applying to sponsor Mutti and Rolf. Having become a naturalized U.S. citizen in April 1944, Kätchen could sponsor them herself. She kept in contact with both Rolf and us, and soon the paperwork was being processed.

But then, just when things seemed to be getting a little better, we Germans were struck back down by the terrible cold winter of 1946/1947. In mid-December, it started getting very cold, so cold that schools, cinemas, and theaters closed. My flower shop and other shops that had begun to open, now closed again. Food and fuel were of immediate concern for us. Food was already in short supply, and with the severe winter conditions, it would be even harder for food supplies to reach the city and then reach the people of the city.

The city's coal supply still supported only the city's power generation and train needs. Coal was not available for residential heating. By necessity, we were forced to brave the bitter cold outside to hunt for any kind of wood for our stove. Slogging about in the snow and ice, we would usually manage with difficulty to bring a load home. Even so, when we burned some of our wood in the stove, it did little to warm our freezing apartment.

We started rationing our food supplies since we didn't know when more food might be available or when we might get more from Kätchen in the mail. We also didn't know if the post office would be able to continue operations in such cold weather.

In the newspaper, our city officials thought they were being helpful by telling us that in times of food crisis, we should try to conserve our calories by hibernating like groundhogs do in the winter. Although we weren't trying to hibernate as they had suggested, we did spent much of our time in bed under blankets to keep warm. We wore heavy clothes and many pairs of socks to bed, sometimes our coats too. Irene and her boys all slept together in bed to stay warm. Mutti and Ilse huddled together in bed for warmth while I slept in a fetal position with blankets over my head.

Only a week into what looked to be a long winter, we were already cold and hungry. Sitting in the living room bundled up, we nibbled on our meager piece of bread for dinner.

"Mama, how much longer until Christmas?" Jens asked.

"About a week, dear. Why do you ask that?"

"I was just wondering." After a pause, he asked, "Mama, have I been bad this year?"

"No, Jens. Both you and Max have been good."

"That's too bad. I was hoping you would say I was bad, then Santa would send me a box of coal. That's what we need now. That's what you get when you're bad, right?"

Irene laughed and said, "Yes, Jens, that's right. Come to…"

Mutti interrupted, "Jens! What a smart boy! I wonder if we should ask Kätchen to send us boxes of coal!"

"That's an interesting idea, Margarete," Ilse said, "but I don't know if she could send enough to make it worthwhile."

"It's worth a try, Ilse. It's worth a try. I'll send her a letter," Mutti said, as she got up, draped in a blanket, to get her writing materials.

The next day, I bundled up and took the letter to the post office. I was delighted to find a package from Kätchen already there and brought it back with me. She was, as yet, unaware of our terrible cold and hunger. She had sent us a Christmas package, which she thought would help us celebrate Christmas.

We all watched excitedly as Mutti set it on a table and opened it. Kätchen had included in it several loaves of Stollen, a traditional German Christmas fruit bread. Mutti picked one up and kissed it, not because she hadn't tasted Stollen in many years, but because we needed these loaves badly for our food supply. We also found fudge, divinity, candied walnuts, cookies, and peppermint sticks. It was a Godsend, a treasure to us. Kätchen couldn't know how needed her treats were. We all smiled and happily hugged one another after seeing the contents. So, in effect, it did help our Christmas celebration. We cut a small piece of Stollen for each of us and carefully put the rest away.

On Christmas day, we each got a small piece of each of the treats in the box. It was probably more than we should have eaten, but it was Christmas.

The package also contained a Christmas card, which we saved to open on Christmas day. It turned out to be an even more special present for Mutti and I. Inside Kätchen had included a copy of our old family photograph from 1931. Both Mutti and I burst into tears when we saw it. We looked affectionately at Vati and the other happy faces, and showed the picture to the others. We had not seen it for many years because our copies were destroyed in the bombing. Having treasured it for many years herself, Kätchen knew we would want a copy. I'm so glad Mutti had that street photographer come up to our apartment so many years ago.

In late December, it was announced that electricity would be turned on for only two hours a day for residences due to shortages of coal at the city's power plants. The terrible cold continued into January. The two large lakes in the center of Hamburg, called the Inner and Outer Alster, were frozen solid for months. The frozen conditions of the Elbe River blocked normal barge traffic interrupting the supply of essentials to the city, thereby worsening the food shortage in the city.

Irene and I continued to periodically venture outside into the cold to look for firewood. Now we were ruthlessly attacking the trees in the streets and parks, hacking away at low branches and the bark on the trunk, and finally chopping them down all together until only a little gnawed off stub remained. We and many other people were desperate for firewood. Soon we needed to go far to find trees not already hacked down.

At times, I thought of Ulrich. I had to make it for him. I would have to keep trying, so that the others and I would survive.

Ilse and Mutti never left the apartment and stayed in bed most of the time. Irene and I would regularly walk, slipping on the ice and struggling in the freezing wind, to the relief kitchen to see if rations were being distributed, but rations were seldom available.

We were lucky to have Kätchen's help and were able to survive thanks to the packages from her. We celebrated when we received our first box of coal and carefully placed a few pieces of the coal in the burning wood. The coal helped some while it lasted, but a box didn't last long even though we used it sparingly. We received several food and coal packages in January and February, but none in March. We think others were sent but may have been stolen by postal employees. They must also have been desperate to survive.

That winter, many residents in Hamburg had no fuel to heat their apartments and could not go out in the cold to get food. An untold number, maybe thousands, perished in their apartments, either frozen, starved or from sickness. The cold and lack of food were especially hard on the old and the very young. It saddened me to think that many babies may have died that winter in Hamburg. It was one of the coldest winters in memory that finally ended when the spring thaw came at the end of March.

In April, the weather was less frigid, but food was still hard to find. Thin and pallid, we still were not recovered from our struggle to survive the winter. In the second week of April, we received two food packages from Kätchen packed with cans of spam, loaves of Stollen, nuts, vitamins, and cigarettes. With these food packages and several food distributions, we finally started to get back on our feet and slowly began to look less pallid and our cheeks less sunken.

By late April, Mutti and I were feeling well enough to travel to see Rolf and his family for a few days. Not knowing how they might have fared in the severe winter, we brought some nuts and cans of spam with us. After getting off the train in the nearby town, we looked for a place to buy more food. With cigarettes that we brought, we bartered for two loaves of bread, some butter, and a dozen eggs. Hiding the food away in our big tote bag, we began our eight kilometer walk to their little town.

Without too much trouble, we found Rolf's house. His mother greeted us warmly at the door with a hug. We knew her from letters we exchanged a number of times. Now we were finally meeting her in person. She ushered us in where we met the rest of the family. We greeted Rolf's family and gave Rolf a big hug. They all looked thin, but Rolf looked thinner than the others. They had suffered during the harsh winter too, and I suspected that Rolf had tried to do more than his share to make up for his lack of suffering during the war.

I noticed immediately how nice and warm it was in their house. We had been without a nice warm fire for so long that it felt wonderful. After our initial greetings, I had to excuse myself and stand by their nice warm stove. It was like heaven after our awful winter in the apartment. I called to Mutti, and she joined me. We stood by the stove turning periodically and basking in its warmth as the others watched in amusement.

As they always did, they had laid up a good stock of firewood for winter and had cut more when the winter became severe. They even traded firewood for food successfully several times in the large nearby town. While keeping warm was not a hardship for them that winter, their food supply had been. The summer and fall weather had been drier than normal, and their garden had produced only a small stock of vegetables and potatoes for their pantry. They had a few chickens at the beginning of winter, but with the cold and nothing to feed them, they had eaten them.

Fortunately for them, chestnut trees lined many nearby roads. Although the dry weather reduced the number of chestnuts too, they were still able to gather up a large stock of them, which they practically lived on throughout the winter. For them, it wasn't just roasted chestnuts at Christmas time. It was roasted chestnuts all winter long. But the chestnuts had helped them survive that winter, and they were thankful to have had them.

Seeing how thin they were, we didn't delay showing them the food we brought. They had managed to supplement their chestnuts with bread and butter when they could find it and trade for it. This was the biggest stock of non-chestnut food they had seen in some time. Mutti and I both regretted that we didn't bring more.

We took the food into the kitchen right away and made for each of them a fried egg with a slice of fried spam and a slice of bread. They beamed with happiness as they ate. It was a heavenly delight for them, although only a limited heaven, since they could have used more. Even so, it was our first feelings of high spirits after a very miserable winter.

I asked Rolf why he hadn't written to Kätchen to have her send food. He said their post offices had closed all winter due to the severe cold. He was finally able to send a letter to Kätchen only two weeks ago, but hadn't heard back yet. They could not do cabinetmaking work in their ice cold workshop, so his family had been confined to their house during the whole winter.

"Are you feeling better now that you have experienced some of our suffering firsthand?" I asked Rolf jokingly.

"Not much. I still feel bad about Canada," he said with a slight smile.

The next morning, Rolf showed us the intersection just down the road where he had tackled Kätchen and saved her life. Later on, he had saved her a second time by advising her to go to America where it would be safer when war came. For this, we were doubly indebted to him, firstly because she was safe there in America, and secondly because her packages from America had saved us.

I remembered on the pier when Kätchen was having second thoughts about going to America, Vati told her she should go because we might need her help from there later. This thought had helped convince her to go. Vati had somehow foreseen what came to pass. Mutti and I might not have made it through the terrible winter without her packages.

Not wanting to expend their limited food supply, we left in the afternoon. They offered us some chestnuts and wood to roast them with. We thanked them and took as much as we thought we could reasonably carry.

After saying our goodbyes to Rolf's parents, we started back to the train station. Rolf's brother and sister came along, and took turns carrying our bags of wood and chestnuts. We appreciated their help and enjoyed their company. It was heartwarming to see Rolf, Gregor, and Lotti together. The younger two admired their war hero big brother, and he was trying to make up "big brother time" for all the time he had been gone. They got along so well and were trying to make the most of their time together before he left again for America.

I smiled as they waved goodbye to us from the train platform as the train pulled away. When I hugged Rolf goodbye, I slipped two packs of cigarettes into his coat. It would help them buy food. Lotti had seen me do it, but had only smiled and said nothing.

It had been a short but wonderful visit, and I looked forward to seeing Rolf again that summer in Hamburg where he would need to come for immigration processing.

Conditions in America were so much better than those in Germany that it made sense for Mutti to immigrate to

America too. She had suffered here enough. Kätchen was sponsoring both Mutti and Rolf even though he was not technically a family member yet. In the interest of relief for war ravaged Europe, some rules were being waived and he would become family soon enough anyway after arrival. Rolf visited us several times that summer.

After previously hearing his story of being a prisoner in Canada, I asked Rolf during one of his visits about his friend Dieter. Had he been able to immigrate to Canada as he desperately wanted? Rolf told me no. But the wheat farmer in Canada had a brother-in-law who was a wheat farmer south of Shelby in Montana. The brother-in-law, who lived only about five hours away, had agreed to sponsor Dieter. If things worked out, Dieter would immigrate to the U.S. and live in Montana for a time. He would marry Nancy, spend time both in Canada and Montana, and eventually become a Canadian citizen. His application to immigrate to the U.S. had already been processed and he was waiting impatiently to be assigned an available quota. Poor Dieter, he said, was impatiently biding his time on one side of the Atlantic and waiting to get back to the other, just as I had done during the war. He wasn't ready to start swimming yet but coming close to it.

Mutti and Rolf needed to make a number of trips to a passport office and the American Consulate to complete the processing of their immigration request. Somehow, they were selected to fill two of the limited number of immigration quotas that year. In the fall of 1947, Mutti and Rolf were approved for immigration to America.

While conditions in Germany were not good, they were at least starting to improve again, although an inadequate food supply continued to be a problem. I was able to get my old job back at the flower shop when it reopened. Mutti would be leaving soon, and Ilse asked me to continue staying with her in the apartment. Ilse, Irene, and the boys were like family now. I told Ilse I would stay, and they were all very happy. When Mutti left for America, they would become my new family.

And then the sad day was suddenly here. Rolf and Mutti stood beside me in the crowd of people at a departure gate at Hamburg's airport. They had their tickets and passports in hand as they waited to board the plane. It was an emotional moment for all three of us. I looked at the plane sitting on the tarmac, which they would soon board, and I felt sick. In a matter of minutes, they would be leaving, and I probably would not see Mutti ever again.

A woman attendant opened the gate in the fence and began checking people onto the flight. I hugged Rolf goodbye. He was lucky. Before long, he would see Kätchen again after being separated for so long. But instead of looking happy, he looked miserable on my account. He knew how hard it was for me to say goodbye to Mutti. We had been through so much together, had survived so much.

Mutti looked at me and began crying as we hugged.

"Goodbye, Mutti," I said with difficulty through my tears.

"Goodbye, Ruth dear, I'll write often."

"Me too, Mutti, take care of yourself."

And with a last hug and kiss on the cheek, she turned and walked with Rolf up to the attendant at the gate. They showed the attendant their tickets and passports, walked through the gate and out on the tarmac to the plane. At the top of the stairs, they turned one last time and waved before going in. I watched sadly as the plane closed its doors, started its engines, and taxied to the runway.

With a roar, it accelerated down the runway, soared up into the air, and soon was out of sight. I felt numb and empty as I continued to stand there at the fence. With a deep sigh, I turned to go. It saddened me to think that when I get back to the apartment, Mutti would no longer be there.

I was now by myself, living with my new family, and working in the flower shop on Mozart Street. With Mutti gone to America, so ends the story of our time together in Germany during and after the war. So Kätchen can now continue the telling of the story.

Chapter 53
Arrival in California

I STOOD AT the gate feeling elated as I impatiently waited for them. Ruth saw Mutti and Rolf off in Hamburg and now their plane, after many stops, had just arrived at San Francisco Airport. This flight from Chicago was the last leg of their long trip.

The plane pulled to a stop and cut its engines. Without much delay, the doors opened, stairs were wheeled up to the door, and after a few trying minutes, passengers began to file off. I spotted them as they climbed down the stairs and walked from the plane. We waved excitedly to each other.

When Mutti and Rolf passed through the gate from the tarmac, there seemed to be no appropriate words to say. We just came together and hugged without saying anything. Mutti and I cried while Rolf smiled happily.

Finally Rolf broke the silence, "It's nice to finally be able to hug you again, Kätchen. I suppose we ought to say hello too,"

"Hello, Rolf, yes, it is. Mutti, are you all right? I'm so glad you're here."

Mutti paused from her tears and blew her nose, giving Rolf and I a chance to kiss. Then with my arm around Mutti's shoulder and Rolf's arm around my shoulder, we walked together over to wait for the bags. We were very happy to finally be together again.

Rolf looked much the same as he did when I last saw him over five years ago, only thinner. However, I had not seen Mutti for ten years, which had been hard years for her. She looked much thinner and more than ten years older.

As I drove them in Aunt Minna's car from the airport back to the restaurant, I told them how I had tried to contact Rolf in Canada in 1945 after the war in Europe had ended. I made several attempts to send letters to Rolf not knowing the correct address of his camp. I had even addressed one to Sergeant Evans there. The letters were either unanswered or returned. One returned letter was marked "Camp closed in 1942." If true, then I didn't know what else to do.

I couldn't go in person to look for him. I knew conditions in Germany must be terrible with all the destruction from the bombings. I needed to stay here in case the mail service with Germany resumed and a letter came requesting help. In the end, I had no luck on both counts. I wasn't able to contact Rolf and the mail service didn't start either.

I waited and worried nearly a year before mail service with Germany was restored. I was almost desperate to learn the fate of my family and had been checking with the post office almost daily. As soon as I learned that mail service was restored, I sent a letter to our old apartment address.

Two weeks later, I was flipping through the mail and gasped when I saw the red and blue striped edges of an international mail envelope. I excitedly pulled it from the pile and immediately recognized Mutti's handwriting. I dropped all the other mail and ripped the envelope apart in a fever to find out how everyone was.

Mutti and Ruth were alive! The apartment was destroyed and they were living with Ilse. But they were suffering and in dire need of food. What about Vati? My initial elation was instantly dampened when I read that he, Aunt Rosa and Fritzi were dead. I paused for a moment crying, but remembering they needed my urgent help, I struggled to hold back the tears as I read on.

"They need canned food and cigarettes so they can buy food! Get going!" I said to myself immediately after finishing the letter

"Aunt Minna, Aunt Minna, I got a letter from Germany! Mutti and Ruth are alive but need food!" I shouted, as I rushed into the restaurant.

Aunt Minna appearing in the kitchen doorway, clapped her hands together and looking up said, "Merciful heavens!"

"I have to go to the market and put together a food package for them. Take over for me. Here's the letter. You can read it yourself."

"Yes, Kätchen, by all means, I'll take care of things here. You go."

I grabbed some money from the cash register and hurried out the door to the market. I was able to get the first package into the mail the same day. The postage to send the package cost more than the things inside it, but I was glad to get it into the mail.

Both Mutti and Rolf had been listening intently as I talked and drove. Rolf looked thoughtful for a while

"Good old Sergeant Evans. I haven't thought of him in some time. I hope we can one day see him again," he said.

Mutti became a little emotional and said, "Kätchen, your packages saved us. Ruth and I might not have made it without them."

"I'm so glad I was able to help," I said reaching over and patting Mutti on the arm. She took my hand and held it for a time.

The drive back from the airport took less than an hour. I pulled the sedan up in front of the restaurant, and we all climbed out. They looked around taking in the panoramic scene of the south bay.

"The weather is so nice here. And what a wonderful view," Mutti said.

"Yes, that's the southern part of San Francisco Bay down there. I can remember the first time I saw this view when I arrived ten years ago. There used to be more orchards and open areas down there, not nearly as many houses."

Aunt Minna had been watching for us, saw us pull up, and came bustling out to welcome Mutti and Rolf.

"Margarete, Rolf, you made it. How wonderful. It's so good to finally meet you," she said going first to hug Mutti.

"Minna, dear, it's good to finally meet you too. I don't know how to thank you for all you have done for Kätchen, and us. If it hadn't been for you, Kätchen would have been there in the awful war with us. You don't know how thankful I am to you."

"I'm the one who should be thanking you, Margarete. Kätchen has been a godsend to me, a blessing to me in my old age. Without her, this place would have closed years ago and God knows what would have become of me," Minna said with some emotion.

"I'm so glad," Mutti said as they hugged again.

"Aunt Minna, this is Rolf," I said trying to change the subject.

She stopped hugging Mutti and looked up. She gazed at him affectionately and gave him a hug. Then grasping his hands and drawing back, she looked at him in awe.

"So this is Rolf. Kätchen has been waiting for you for so long, and now you are finally here." She burst into tears and hugged him again.

Rolf could only hug her back as she sobbed with happiness, "It's good to finally be here, Aunt Minna."

Chapter 54
Remembering

MUTTI AND ROLF were tired and hungry after their long trip. Before they got some rest, we sat down at a table and Aunt Minna brought us a Dutch lunch. Rolf eyed the food in front of him hungrily, but paused when he saw the expression on Mutti's face. She had her hands to her face, gaping in awe at the sight of all the food.

"God in heaven, I can't believe all the meat and cheese," Mutti exclaimed. "We saw the abundance of food at the airports here too. Kätchen, you have no idea. We've eaten like mice for so many years."

"I'm sorry, Mutti. I didn't mean to upset you. This is our normal lunch item, our Dutch lunch. I make the cheese myself. It's very good. I'm pretty proud of it. Here, try a piece," I said handing her a slice of cheese.

Mutti hardly believing the big slice of cheese she saw in her hand, took a bite, "It's wonderful. What people back there would give for all this food! Or even just a piece of cheese like this."

"Poor Mutti," said Rolf, "I can appreciate her amazement. I had food like this in Canada not realizing how little they had back in Germany until I experienced it for a while myself. The working classes there could only dream of a plate of cheese like that. Last winter was terrible. My family survived for over three months on chestnuts. I'm not sure if I could ever eat another one."

I put my hand on Mutti's sleeve and said, "Mutti, you used to love coffee, didn't you? Let me get you cup. And how about a big glass of milk, Rolf?" Mutti brightened when she heard "coffee" and Rolf nodded as I got up to get them.

Coming back, I handed the glass of milk to Rolf and put the cup of coffee down in front of Mutti.

Rolf drank it down at once and putting the empty glass down said, "God, I haven't had a glass of milk in probably a year and a half."

Mutti stared at the cup of coffee in front of her. She bent down and smelled the aroma approvingly.

"It's wonderful to have real coffee again. I had some on the plane too. The coffee in the restaurants back in Germany is supposedly real coffee, but I think they still are mixing coffee substitute with it." She slowly brought it up and took a sip.

"It's delicious."

Looking a little sad, she said, "I can't help thinking of Ruth. She has so little to eat and I have all this. Poor Ilse would die to have a cup of coffee like this."

"Dear Ilse, I miss her too. We'll send her some ground coffee."

"No, she has no way to use it."

"There's something now called instant coffee. It's a powder that you mix with hot water. We'll send her some of that."

"I don't think she could use it either. It would probably take too much firewood to boil the water."

"When the fuel situation is better, we'll send her some. This cheese needs refrigeration, so we can't ship it to Ruth, but we'll find some that you can ship. We'll go shopping and you can pick out things for them."

"Oh, that would be wonderful, Kätchen," she said smiling up at me. I gave her a hug and looked over at Rolf. He had made a sandwich and already eaten half of it.

I laughed at him, and he laughed back as he contentedly chewed away and took more big bites. I went to get him another glass of milk and soon returned to have some lunch myself.

While we sat eating, Rolf told how he finally learned what happened to me. He had not tried to contact me in the months after Germany surrendered, because the war apparently was still going. He was still a prisoner in Canada, and no one knew when he might be released. He thought the Americans probably thought the war was still on too, so he wanted to avoid the risk of getting me in trouble again by writing. Hoping to be released in a matter of months, he would wait and then try to write me. He had not expected to be kept in Canada a year after the war in Europe ended.

It was not until his release in Germany that he felt sure that it would be safe to write me. So he first went to find my family in Hamburg to confirm I was okay and still with my Aunt Minna.

He went first to the old apartment building on Mozart Street. Although it was heavily damaged, he saw people at the entrance apparently still living there.

Yes, people were living in the basement, so he went down to ask the people there if they knew Gustav and Margarete Thielke. They were all from what used to be eastern Germany and didn't know them. As he went room to room asking the people, he was shocked by their terrible living conditions.

Having no luck at their old apartment, he next went to find Gustav's drinking club where he had spent time with us during his visit years before. It wasn't far and he was sure he could find it again. Someone there might know where Gustav and his family were living. He might even find her father there drinking with his friends. When he found the place, he saw that it was no longer a tavern, only a pile of rubble. He looked with great disappointment at it for a time, thinking back to what it had looked like before.

After pondering what to do next, he concluded Gustav would have had to find a new one if the old one was destroyed. He remembered seeing one at the end of the block near their old apartment. He would try that one.

The bartender in that tavern was helpful. He knew the family and told him Gustav was killed in the bombings. Ruth and her mother still lived somewhere around here, but he didn't know where. The bartender said he sometimes saw Margarete pass by, so Rolf sat down in one of their booths by the window and waited.

While sitting there, he thought about Kätchen's father. Rolf was sorry to hear he had been killed. He had liked her father very much and had looked forward to knowing him better. Now he wouldn't have the chance. Her father had been so close to his two daughters. It must have been a great loss to them, as well as to her mother. He hadn't seen her mother or Ruth for such a long time. He hoped he could recognize her mother if she walked by.

Four hours later, he was still watching out the window for her when the bartender called out from behind him, "There she is! There in the blue print dress. See her?"

Turning around to see where he was pointing, Rolf saw the woman outside in a blue dress too. It's a good thing the bartender pointed her out because he didn't recognize her.

He scrambled outside and spotted her just reaching the sidewalk on the other side of the intersection. He shouted, "Frau Thielke! Frau Thielke!"

Hearing her name, Mutti turned around and saw a healthy tanned young man in uniform run up and stand in front of her, smiling and happy to see her.

Scrutinizing his face, it slowly began to dawn on her who he was. He could see it and said, "Yes, it's me, Rolf, I'm finally back."

Holding her hands to her face and starting to feel shaky, she struggled to say, "Rolf! Is it really you?"

"Yes, it's me, Frau Thielke," he said and seeing she was shaky, he came forward and held her arms to steady her.

Looking him up and down, she said with emotion, "Rolf, I'm so glad. But is it really you?"

"Yes, Frau Thielke, it's me."

"But you look so good. We thought you might be all scarred and maimed from your plane crash."

"Thanks to the English doctors, I've recovered nicely."

Finally regaining her senses and hugging him tightly, she said, "Rolf, I'm so happy to see you. Kätchen will be so happy too. I'm sure you're wondering about her."

"Yes, of course. Please tell me, is she still okay, working at her Aunt's restaurant."

Moving closer to a building to let people on the sidewalk pass, Rolf listened intently while Mutti told him, "We're in contact with her again, Rolf. She's still with her aunt at the restaurant in California. She's doing well and she'll be so happy to hear from you!"

"So she's okay. What a relief to finally know. Thanks to those wonderful friends of hers in that little town, I know what happened to her. So, she succeeded then. She successfully waited out the war there with her aunt. I'm so glad to hear it. What a relief to know."

"She said she tried to write to you after the war ended but was unable to reach you. I'll let you read her letters."

"And she's not married now or anything like that, is she?"

"Silly boy. She's been waiting for you for years. And what about you, Rolf? You've been a prisoner this whole time?" Mutti asked.

"Yes, I only just arrived back in Germany. After getting released, I came here first to find out what happened to Kätchen."

"And you're not married either?"

"No, of course not."

He started to ask Mutti how her family was, when he remembered what the bartender inside the drinking club had told him.

"They told me inside the club there that your husband was killed in the bombing. I'm very sorry."

Tears welled up in Mutti's eyes.

"Thank you, Rolf. It happened right here, almost where we stand," she said moving slowly away from the building and almost into the intersection.

"I think of it every time I pass. Ruth and I were waiting for him at the stairs down to our bomb shelter over there," she said, pointing at the stairs.

"Gustav was helping a friend, and they had just narrowly escaped being killed by a bomb. We got them up and to the stairs. But it was too much for Gustav. He had a heart attack on the way down and died a few minutes later below in the shelter."

"I'm very sorry. I liked him very much and wish I could have gotten to know him better."

"Yes, it's too bad. I think you two would have gotten on well together."

Mutti dabbed her eyes with her handkerchief and blew her nose. She looked at him and brightened a little.

"Oh it's so good to see you, Rolf. Kätchen will be so happy. We've got to write her right away. First, let's surprise Ruth. You remember her. She was only a little girl when you came to our apartment that day. She works in a flower shop just down the block. Let's hurry. Then we can write Kätchen. She'll be so happy."

And with her arm through his, they walked off cheerfully together.

As Rolf recalled how Mutti had pointed out the circumstances of my father's death, both Mutti and I started to tear up and lean against each other, heads together, one arm around the other. After he finished, we sat around the table for a while without talking, thinking of Vati.

That night, Mutti, Aunt Minna, Rolf and I sat around a table at the restaurant. Being late, only a few customers remained. One customer stood up and walked over to pay at the cash register. Aunt Minna stood up and walked over to take his money. Mutti, Rolf and I looked at one another.

"Together again," I said. "I still can't quite believe it. The last time we were together like this was ten years ago in 1937 at the apartment back in Hamburg, the afternoon before I sailed to California. I was leaving and thought I was never going to see Rolf ever again. Then Rolf unexpectedly showed up in his Luftwaffe uniform at our door."

"He could only stay three hours, so you left right away to be alone before he caught his train back," Mutti mused.

We sat at a table in the restaurant, deep in thought, remembering back.

"So much has happened since then. I feel like we've been cheated out of ten years of our lives by the war," I finally said.

"The damned war. Think how different our lives and the lives of so many others would have been without it," Rolf said.

"The only one who isn't here from that afternoon is Ruth," Mutti said.

"Poor Ruth," I said, "it's been over two years since the war ended, and still she is waiting for her soldier to return."

"I told her," Rolf said, "that Ulrich might still be held as a laborer by one of the countries, but I was just trying to give her a little hope. After so much time, it's getting less and less likely he'll be coming back. He may have died in those terrible prisoner pens she told us about. I'm afraid she's going to be very disappointed."

"Poor Ruth will keep waiting. So young, so pretty, and she waits," Mutti said sadly. We all sat there silent, deep in thought.

Chapter 55
Mozart Street

A YEAR AND a half later, Ruth was in the back of the flower shop trimming roses and humming to herself. She was thinking of Kätchen and Rolf. They were married shortly after Rolf arrived in California and now their baby boy was almost three months old. He was cute and growing fast. They named him Gustav after his grandfather, but they called him Gus. Gus Hosterman, it had a good ring to it.

She thought of the photo they had recently sent. He was such a cute little baby. She would have to draw a birthday card for him for his six month birthday and send it to them. She would make one like the birthday card she sent to Gerhard and Grete for their little girl's second birthday. She was a cutie too.

Ruth still loved to draw and paint. She had some of her paintings here in the shop for sale. People liked and actually bought them. She liked to paint pictures of flowers and street scenes here on Mozart Street.

It was February now, February 1949, the middle of winter after a recent snowfall. So the street wasn't very pretty for painting this time of year.

It was late afternoon, almost closing time. She was in the flower shop by herself and just finishing up in the back. She heard someone come in the door and felt the cold rush of air that came in.

"I'll be right out," she called. She finished trimming a rose, put down the scissors, wiped her hands on her apron, and walked to the front. When she came through the door out into the shop, she stopped suddenly and gasped.

"Ulrich!" she cried in astonishment as she burst into tears and rushed to hug him.

"I made it back, Ruth," he said as they embraced, and she wept.

"I knew you would, Ulrich. I knew you would."

After a number of hugs and kisses, Ulrich drew back and said, "You still look wonderful, Ruth, just as pretty as that last night at the house. And me, I'm much the worse for wear. Are you sure you still want to have some soup with me, Ruth?"

"Yes, Ulrich, I do. I've been waiting like I told you I would."

"For the soup?"

"Yes, for the soup and for you."

"I knew you would wait, Ruth. I came as soon as I could," he said with a little smile.

"I'm so happy you're finally here." They kissed and hugged. Wiping her eyes as they continued to hug, Ruth didn't want to let go of him.

* * *

Ulrich had survived the months in the terrible temporary prison camps after his capture. He might have been released shortly after the war like other German prisoners held by the Americans, but unluckily, he was one of many German prisoners in the American camps around Koblenz who the Americans turned over to the French in May of 1945.

The French thought it was fitting for the German soldiers who had destroyed their cities and towns to be used to clean up their war damage. Their feelings were understandable.

He was first put to work with gangs of prisoners to clear away rubble and war damage. His French captors fed them little and treated them harshly as the Germans had treated the French populace.

After a time, he was assigned to work in a coal mine where he received better treatment and food. Ulrich endured this forced labor in France for three and a half years before being finally released at the end of 1948.

After his release on the southern border of Germany in the French occupation zone, he first visited his mother and father near Heidelberg. Having not been allowed to write any letters during his captivity, it was only when he knocked on their door that they discovered he had not been killed. He needed to catch his mother who fainted at the sight of him.

His parents survived the war, but he had lost his two older brothers in it. It was a very emotional reunion. He stayed there several days to visit, recover, and clean up. He told them about Ruth and of his need to search for her. With money borrowed from his parents, he set out to find Ruth.

Ulrich would first look for her at the house in the town of Leimbach where he had met her. On the way there, he learned Leimbach was now inside the Russian zone. At a road entry point into the zone at Meiningen, near Leimbach, he was hesitant to enter fearing the Russians might not let him back out. First, he would find out about entering the zone. He discovered he had worried needlessly about getting out, since he had none of the paperwork for first getting in. He was turned away by the guards. Having no way of finding out if she was still in Leimbach, he could only hope she was not.

While in the area, Ulrich went back to visit the holding pen west of Vacha where he had been held. Little trace remained of the terrible place. Deep in thought, he strode over to the location near the woods where he had laid in the mud and Ruth had told him she would wait for him. The thought of her waiting for him enabled him to survive all those years of captivity.

Since he could not go into the Russian zone, the only thing to do was look for her next on Mozart Street in Hamburg. The words "Mozart Street in Hamburg" were permanently etched on his brain like words on a stone tablet. He had thought of them many, many times. With the money borrowed from his parents, he bought the cheapest train fare he could to get to Hamburg.

Upon his arrival in Hamburg, Ulrich found an inexpensive room and immediately began his search for Ruth. Soon he was traipsing along Winterhuder Way through the recent snow with a city map in his hand looking for Mozart Street. It should be the next street. There it was. Upon reaching it, he paused looking at the street sign saying "Mozart Street," examining every letter, gratified to finally be on the street that he had thought about so many times.

Looking back at his map, he noted that Mozart Street wasn't very long, only four blocks. He wasn't sure if it was good or bad. He planned first to enter every store and restaurant along the street to ask if they knew a girl named Ruth. He didn't even know Ruth's last name. If that didn't turn her up, then he would go into each apartment building. After that, he would have to expand his search to nearby streets.

With a determined look, he started up Mozart Street. It didn't take long before the next establishment was a flower shop. Looking through the window, he didn't see anyone inside. But the lights were on, and it looked open. He opened the door and stepped inside. He heard a voice in the back say, "I'll be right out."

He instantly recognized it as Ruth's voice, and he choked up with happiness. She had survived too, and he had found her.

* * *

After closing up the flower shop only a short time later, Ruth and Ulrich walked together to a restaurant not far down the street. They sat down at a table. Ulrich couldn't get over how pretty Ruth still was, while Ruth couldn't believe the moment for which she had waited so long was finally here. The waitress came to their table to take their order.

"What do you think, Ruth? Should we have soup?"

"Yes, definitely."

"What kinds of soups do you have tonight?" she asked the waitress.

"Lentil and potato."

"I'll have Lentil."

"Me, too."

After the waitress left to get their order, Ruth reached across the table, and they held hands.

"Ruth, I know why I'm here. It's easy to be attracted to a wholesome young girl as pretty as you are. When you also turned out to be kind, generous, intelligent, and artistic, I knew I was in love."

"Oh, Ulrich," she said squeezing his hand.

"What I don't understand," he continued, "is why you are here, why you waited for me. You could have gotten married a hundred times already."

"It's no great mystery, Ulrich. After our short time together in those desperate times, I knew you were the man for me. I mean you saved me from that brute after all. You were handsome brave, kind, and ready to risk your life to protect me. Both Mutti and Aunt Rosa thought you were wonderful. Poor Aunt Rosa, she died from her injuries about a month or so after we were attacked."

"I'm very sorry to hear it, Ruth. She was a very nice lady. And your mother is now in America with your older sister?"

"Yes, and they will be so happy to hear you found me. You have no idea how happy. They worried that you had died in those terrible pens, and I would be waiting for you all my life. I have to send them a letter right away. It will be a huge relief for them."

"And I'm so happy you did wait for me."

"I knew I couldn't find any better. You were the man for me, and I was in love with you."

Ulrich brought Ruth's hands up and kissed them. "How I could have been so lucky to have entered that particular house on that particular street on that particular day, I'll never know."

"I don't know either, Ulrich, but I'm glad you did."

The waitress returned to the table with their soup and was quickly away again.

"Let's see if this soup was worth the wait," Ulrich said smiling and then tasting it.

Ruth did the same and smiled.

"It's not bad," he said, "but I still like yours better though."

"You were very hungry at the time, remember?"

"Maybe so," he said, then pausing.

"Ruth, I was just thinking," he continued. "They have something called 'wedding soup' where I come from down in Heidelberg. I think you have it up here too. Maybe we can have some soon," Ulrich said with a smile.

With a smile, Ruth said, "I think that was a wedding proposal, Ulrich, a little unusual, but kind of romantic."

"Yes, I suppose it was," he said with a twinkle in his eye.

"I would love to have some 'wedding soup' with you, Ulrich," Ruth said, stretching across the table and kissing him.

When she sat back into her seat, Ulrich said, "I think that was an acceptance of my wedding proposal."

"Yes, I suppose it was," she said with a twinkle in her eye.

The End

And so ends the story of Kätchen and her family, which it has been my pleasure to tell. I hope you have enjoyed reading it and will recommend it to your friends. Thank you very much. JRC

If you haven't already read *Kätchen's Story: A German Girl Like Me, Book 1*, you can also find that book on Amazon and learn the story of Kätchen and her family leading to the circumstances in early March of 1941 at the beginning of this book.

Made in the USA
Monee, IL
29 May 2021

69803589R00225